Amanda Minnie Douglas

Hope Mills; or, Between Friend and Sweetheart

Amanda Minnie Douglas

Hope Mills; or, Between Friend and Sweetheart

ISBN/EAN: 9783337091484

Printed in Europe, USA, Canada, Australia, Japan

Cover: Foto ©Andreas Hilbeck / pixelio.de

More available books at **www.hansebooks.com**

HOPE MILLS;

OR,

BETWEEN FRIEND AND SWEETHEART.

BY

AMANDA M. DOUGLAS,

AUTHOR OF "FROM HAND TO MOUTH," "NELLY KINNARD'S KINGDOM,"
"IN TRUST," &c., &c.

"Abou spake more low,
But cheerly still; and said, ' I pray thee, then,
Write me as one that loves his fellow-men.' "
LEIGH HUNT.

BOSTON:
LEE AND SHEPARD, PUBLISHERS.
NEW YORK:
CHARLES T. DILLINGHAM.

TO

Hon. Marcus L. Ward,

As a Tribute

TO ONE WHO HAS HELD LOYALLY TO GOD AND HIS FELLOW-MEN,
WHO HAS LABORED IN THE NOBLE CAUSE OF HUMANITY,
NOT DISHEARTENED WHEN RESULTS WERE INFRE-
QUENT, BUT CONTENT TO REAP THE REWARD
IN THE GREAT HEREAFTER.

NEWARK, N.J., 1879.

BETWEEN FRIEND AND SWEETHEART.

CHAPTER I.

"There is Fred again with his arm around Jack Darcy's neck. I declare, they are worse than two romantic schoolgirls. I am so thankful Fred goes away to-morrow for a year! and I do hope by that time he will have outgrown that wretched, commonplace youth. Mother, it is very fortunate that Jack is the sole scion of the Darcy line; for, if there were a daughter, you would no doubt be called upon to receive her into the bosom of the family."

"Which I never should do," remarked quiet, aristocratic Mrs. Lawrence, not even raising her eyes from her book.

"Not for the sake of your only son?" continued Agatha, with an irritating laugh.

"Don't be silly, Agatha," returned the mother, with an indifference that took off the point of the query.

Her second sister glanced up from a bit of pencil-drawing, then lowered her eyes to the street where the boy friends stood, one with his arm over the other's shoulder.

"Think of a Harvard graduate arm-in-arm with — well, a mill-hand! No doubt Jack's father will put him in the mill. I cannot see any sense in a boy of *that* class taking two years at the academy."

On the opposite side of the room were two girls, hardly more than children, busily engaged in ornamenting a box with transfer-pictures. One had a rather haughty mien, as became a Lawrence; the other, pretty, piquant little Sylvie Barry, looked toward the elders, knit her brow, with both thought and indignation visible in its lines, and held her picture absently in her hand.

" Why do you listen to that? " asked Irene Lawrence disdainfully. " It is only Jack Darcy, and he's nobody. His father works in the mill."

" I know that ! " was Sylvie's rather sharp retort, answering the latter part of the sentence merely. Child as she was, she experienced a strong desire to do battle, not only for Jack, but for some puzzling cause she could not quite comprehend. With the blood of a French duke in her veins, of soldiers and martyrs as well, she was a sturdy little democrat. It seemed cowardly not to take up arms.

" That butterfly is to go next," remarked Irene, reaching out for it ; and Sylvie held her peace, though she felt the warm blood burning in her cheeks.

Jack Darcy did not need any champion within doors ; for Fred stood up bravely against these three girls, and from them received his first impression that women were small of soul and narrow of mind. As they stood by the gate now, this last hour grudged to them, neither dreamed that this was the final canto in the poem of boyhood. They had been fast friends since the first day pale, puny Fred made his appearance in school, and was both laughed at and bullied by some boys larger in size, but younger in years.

" He will have to get the nonsense rubbed out of him some time," thought Jack ; " and it can never be younger." But, when the contest degenerated into the force of the strong against the weak, one blow of Jack's fist sent Brown reeling and howling.

"Try a fellow of your own size next time," was Jack's pithy advice.

Fred came to him, and cried hysterically in his arms. Jack had experienced the same feeling for some poor rescued kitten. Fred, with his head full of King Arthur and his knights, mythology, and bits of children's histories, wherein figured heroes and soldiers, elected Jack to the highest niche in his regard.

Jack Darcy was a wonderful boy withal, a very prince of boys, who hated study and work, and loved play; who despised Sunday clothes and girls' parties; but who had not his equal for spinning a top, or raising a kite, and when it came to leap-frog, or short stop, he was simply immense. Then he always knew the best places to dig worms, and the little nooks where fish were sure to bite, the best chestnut and walnut trees; and, with years and experience, he excelled in baseball, skating, wrestling, leaping, and rowing. Jack Darcy was no dunce, either. Only one subject extinguished him entirely, and that was composition. Under its malign influence he sank to the level of any other boy. And here Fred shone pre-eminently, kindly casting his mantle over his friend, — further, sometimes, than a conscientious charity would have admitted; but a boy's conscience is quite as susceptible of a bias as that of older and wiser people. On the other hand, Jack wrestled manfully with many a tough problem on which Fred would have been hopelessly stranded. Once rouse the belligerent impulse in Jack, and he would fight his way through.

These two were at different ends of the social plane. Fred's father was the great man of Yerbury, the present owner of Hope Mills; not only rich, but living in luxury. He had married Miss Agatha Hope, and by the death of her two brothers she had become sole heir to the Hope estate; though it was whispered that her brothers had left a heavy legacy of debts behind them. There was family on the Lawrence side as well, but not much money. David Lawrence had prospered beyond his wildest dreams. He had twice been mayor of Yerbury, gone to the State Legislature, and been spoken of as a possible senator; but he did not sigh for political distinction.

Agatha was their first-born; then Frederic De Woolfe, named for some Hope ancestor. Two girls afterward; but Fred remained the only son. He was a delicate boy, and, until he reached the age of ten, studied with his sisters' governess, when he rebelled, and insisted upon his boy's prerogative of going to school. Here he met and loved Jack Darcy.

Jack was a few months the elder, — a stout, hardy, robust boy, full of mischief, falling into scrapes, and slipping out easily. Not vicious or ugly; in fact, he had thrashed Ned Thomas for robbing birds' nests, been known to rescue a miserable kitten from its tormentors, and was always bringing home sore-eyed, mangy curs to be nursed and healed. If he had cared, he could have boasted as good a pedigree as the Hopes and the Lawrences. For his grandmother was of pure old French Jacobin descent, titled too. Many a wild romance and adventure had her family figured in, — now on the top round of prosperity, now in bitter poverty and exile. At the age of eighteen she was living on the western coast of Ireland with her old father, when she fell in love with handsome Jack Darcy, whose persuasive blue eyes were enough to melt the heart of the most obdurate woman; the merriest, wittiest, best-tempered lad for miles around, the owner of a small farm and numberless family traditions that counted back to the time when

> "Malachi wore the collar of gold,
>   He won from the proud invader."

For a while they were prosperous and happy: then came bad seasons, famine, and finally typhus. Two bright, handsome sons and a little daughter were victims, leaving only baby Bernard. They came to the New World, and began life again, managing thriftily, and buying a house and garden in the quaint old town of Yerbury. Mr. Darcy died ; and his son grew to man's estate, settled to the business of carpenter and builder (as he possessed a good deal of mechanical skill), married a pretty, delicate girl, but did not seem to make of life a signal success. Still it is possible that a life of happiness and content may have its use in this world, if it does not serve to point a prosperous moral.

He added a wing to the house, he raised fruit and flowers that were marvels. Grandmother preferred for several years to keep house by herself, raise chickens and geese, and keep putting by a little of her very own. They had a choice garden and a soft-eyed Alderney cow, but Bernard Darcy had surely missed his vocation. He should have been a scientific farmer.

Baby Jack came to them. He certainly had not inherited the beauty of the Darcys nor the Beaumanoirs, not even the delicacy of his mother. The eyes of Irish blue were tinged with gray, his hair inclined to the warmer tints of chestnut, and now he always kept the curls cropped short. However, his magnificently shaped head was not disfigured by the process. He did get terribly freckled and tanned as warm weather came on, and the hair turned almost red by much bathing and sunshine. A striking contrast indeed to the handsome, well-dressed Frederic.

When Fred went to the academy he pleaded for Jack to go, and Grandmother Darcy decided that he should. She had never taken kindly to her son's rather plebeian occupation. After several years of indifferent success, Mr. Darcy had accepted a position at the mill, in which, if there was not so much profit, there were no losses.

Jack was not a student in an intellectual point of view.

He did not care to be a doctor, lawyer, or clergyman, and certainly not a professor. He would have liked to pack a satchel, and start westward, prospect for a railroad, gold or silver mine, and live the rugged, unconventional camp-life. Once he had ventured to suggest this noble ambition; but his timid mother was startled out of her wits, and his grandmother said with a sage shake of the head, —

"A rolling stone gathers no moss,"

"Grandmother," began Jack argumentatively, "of what real value is the moss to the stone, except in the picturesque aspect? Do you know that a great many of these time revered and honored adages are the greatest humbugs in the world?" asked the audacious young iconoclast. "Who wants to be a stone or a clod, or even a bit of velvet moss? They go to make up the world, it is true; but is that narrow, torpid, insensate life any pattern for human souls and active bodies? I think a man's business in this world is to find out new channels, to build up, to broaden and deepen, and somehow to make the world feel that he has been in it. I can't just explain," — and his brows knit into a puzzled frown, — "but it seems to me there is something grander than plodding along and saving a little money."

"No doubt you would be glad enough to have the money, when you have gone off like the prodigal son, and wasted health and substance in foreign lands," said grandmother with some asperity.

Jack had been brought up to reverence the Bible and religion, and to respect his grandmother was the first article in his creed. He relapsed into silence, but the busy brain kept up a vigorous ferment. What was life all about, anyhow? Why did people come into the world, live thirty, sixty, or even eighty years, and then drop out of it. Was it merely to eat, drink, and sleep?

The wider lore at the academy had a peculiar effect

upon Jack, tangled his brain, begat confusing mental processes.   Greek he hated; Latin he barely endured; chemistry and mineralogy interested him, and in mathematics he excelled.   Fred carried every thing before him, graduated with honors, and was to enter Harvard.   The Lawrences went to Newport, and Jack missed his bosom friend sorely.   He rambled through the woods, read every thing that came in his way, and thought a good deal in his crude, undisciplined fashion.

What was he to do with this tough problem of unknown quantities?

He ventured at last to broach the subject to his father.

Bernard Darcy studied his son gravely.   Now, it must be considered that he had never been troubled with this hungry, perplexing view of life that urges one on to dip deep into the secrets of existence.   To have a pretty house and garden, to watch his flowers, vegetables, and chickens grow, to dream over his books in his cosey sitting-room, not to be pinched for money, not to be anxious about employment, but to go on serenely day after day, — this was Mr. Darcy's idea of happiness; and, having this, he was perfectly content.

His mother secretly chafed at his lack of ambition; his neighbors said, "A good, honest fellow, but with no 'push' in him."   Curiously enough, the virtues that are preached from pulpits Sunday after Sunday, that we are always recommending to our friends, are *not* the ones that gain any vast amount of credit in this life.   "Be content! be content!" cries every one, from revelation downward; yet content, pure and simple, is rather despised and flouted by our fellow-men.

"I don't know, Jack," said the elder, gravely shaking his head with slow dubiousness.   "What would you do if you were once away?"

"I'd go on until I found some place into which I just fitted;" and the boy glanced over westward with hungering eyes.

"But, Jack," said his father, after a pause, "I think people oftener fit themselves into a place. There are so few places ready made to one's hand. It's always something. Now, I'll venture to say that David Lawrence, with all his money, doesn't see as much real happiness as I do. His is a slave's life, after all. It's day and night, bills to pay and stock to get, dissatisfied hands, poor hands spoiling work, losses here and there, little leisure, small peace of mind; and all for what? There was a time when I might have envied him: I don't now."

Jack had lost all but the first two sentences.

"That's the thing!" he cried, with boyish enthusiasm, — "fitting yourself; coming to something that takes hold of you like an inspiration; that you could work for, fight for, that rouses soul and body."

Bernard Darcy studied the youthful face, eager, alert, hopeful, and with something else in it that he could not understand.

"I never had any such dreams or desires," he said in an uncertain tone, as if fearful he might lose his way among his son's vagaries. "I wanted a pleasant home, and a loving wife and children. I wish there had been more of them, Jack, for your sake," and his voice took on a tender inflection. "Then, if one wanted to go away, there would have been others left. You see, Jack, mother's heart is bound up in you, and she's getting to be an old woman with but few ties. I might manage to comfort your own mother; but you are so young, Jack. There will be many years before you, doubtless; and if you could give a few to us," with a wistful, loving look. "Now, if you wanted to study"—

"But I don't," in a hasty, husky tone. "I believe I hate quiet. I want life, adventure! I've staid in school this last year just to please Larry."

"Have a little patience, Jack. Old people are not like young ones. They feel the changes keenly. And you are all we have. It would take the sunshine out of our lives. It would seem as if there had been a funeral."

"Yes," said Jack with meek hopelessness that one would hardly look for in a vigorous boy; and winking hard to keep back some tears. No logical argument, no stricture of duty, could have half the weight of this bit of love pleading. Father was right. God had made him a son first of all, given him a son's duties. Jack had never troubled his head much about religion in any theological sense; but his simple creed had some great if old-fashioned truths in it.

"If there's any thing you would like to do, I'd be glad to give you a chance. And there's no need to hurry. You may come to the right thing presently."

Jack swallowed over a great lump in his throat. The two kittens came scampering up the walk, and he caught one, lifting it to his shoulder. Then Sylvie Barry entered the gate with her dainty milk-kettle shining like silver.

They were in a manner neighbors, for Larch Avenue was the next street to Maple Place. Both streets were now given over to what is termed decayed gentility. The larches were old and ragged and brown with clustering cones, and the blue blood of the denizens had grown a little sluggish.

Miss Honoria Barry and her small niece lived together, with a tall and gaunt handmaiden Norman French, and a broad Yorkshire gardener. Miss Barry was the old cream of Yerbury. Here her family had lived since the Huguenot persecution, and dwindled finally to two. Louis Barry was a dissipated spendthrift. He married, and tormented his wife into an early grave, and might have worn out his sister, but Providence kindly removed him. Miss Honoria retrenched, paid off debts and mortgage by degrees, and brought up Sylvie in a quaint, refined, old-world fashion.

Old Mrs. Darcy and Miss Barry exchanged formal calls,

and discussed la belle France. Sylvie took great delight
in listening to grandmother's stories of brave heroes and
handsome women who figured in old legends.

Oddly enough, one of the many points of agreement
between Jack and Fred had been their aversion to girls
in general. Fred judged them from his sisters, who were
always nagging, always exhorting him to be a gentleman,
and always holding up Jack Darcy to ridicule. Jack, on
the other hand, had a bashful fear of girls, and fancied
they were laughing at every little awkwardness ; then they
cried so easily, went off in a huff if they could not have
their own way, were silly, vain, and tattling, ready enough
to beg your assistance if there was a munching cow by the
roadside, a worm swinging from a tree, or a harmless
mouse running across the floor. The great fascination to
the Darcy house was, that the boys could sit in the large,
clean kitchen, trying all sorts of crude experiments, with
Ann to clear away the *débris* and find no fault. Jack
never wanted to go to the great house. In true boy fashion he understood without any explanation. But they
both liked little Sylvie. She was taught at home except
in music and drawing, and she was as much interested in
grandmother's heroes as the two boys.

On the other hand, the Hopes and the Barrys had always
been great friends ; and, from some odd freak of unlike-
ness, Sylvie and Irene Lawrence carried on the intimacy.

She stopped now, and talked about the kitten with Jack ;
and he carried her milk-pail home to the gate.

It was a long, wearisome vacation to poor Jack. Fish-
ing lost its charm, even tramps in the woods became
monotonous. He spent hours in his father's shop, in-
specting machinery, though he seldom asked a question
or ventured upon a remark. Indeed, some of the hands
thought " Darcy's boy wasn't over-bright." Yet here he
laid the foundation of the problem that was to vex and
puzzle his soul in after-years. Here was the great, whir-

ring machinery, belts, bands, spindles, looms, and often-
times a stupid and stolid enough workman at one end,
grinding out luxury and elegance for David Lawrence,
Esq.; that his family might tread on Wilton and Axmin-
ster, dine from silver and crystal, dress in silks and velvets, drive about with high-stepping bays, and scorn all
beneath them. Once as Jack was thinking it over he
laughed aloud.

"You must feel very much amused," said a rather
sour-looking man standing near by, with a peculiar touchi-
ness as if he had been laughed at.

"No, I wasn't amused, I was only thinking" — But
Jack stopped in the middle of his sentence. Could *this*
man take any such position as that of Mr. Lawrence?

Then he came across a volume of self-made men, which
he eagerly devoured. Every one seemed to have com-
menced life without a dollar, and almost without friends.
Were those the important factors in the race, to be light-
weighted? And he had a triple chain.

Fred returned, handsomer than ever, and doubly glad
to get back to Jack. There was just four days grace.
They revisited old haunts, talked endlessly and to little
purpose, like so much of the talk of youth, and now they
were parting at the gate for the last time. Unlike girls
they exchanged no vows or kisses. It is not in boy-
nature to be effusive.

"To think that I shall not be home until Christmas!
If you only *were* going with me, Jack, what jolly times
we would have!"

"I could have gone," answered Jack with some pride,
"that is, if I had been prepared. Father was willing,
and grandmother would have been proud enough;" and
just then Jack wondered why going to seek his fortune
appeared so much more terrible to them.

"Well, why not, Jack?" with impetuous eagerness.
"It isn't too late."

"I don't want the years of study. I should come to hate the sight of a book. No, I'll find out where I belong, some day. Don't worry about me," with an abrupt laugh.

"But I am so sorry!" Then they looked into each other's eyes. All these years had been filled with such good, honest boy-love.

"Good-by, old chap!" cried Jack suddenly; for the wrench must come, and lingering over it was painful. "I shall miss you lots! it seems so queer to be without you! Of course you'll succeed: there's no use wishing about that."

"It's a good wish from you, Jack. Good-by. I hate awfully to say it: I hate to think that our jolly boyish frolics are over."

"But we'll have many a good row on the river, and tramps through the woods. We can't outgrow every thing. And there'll be summers and summers."

"Good-by."

The gate-latch clicked: Jack walked rapidly down the street, whistling "Kathleen Mavourneen" unconsciously. Did he dream the simple faith of boyhood had reached its culmination, and was henceforth to wane?

"Dear old Jack," thought Fred: "I don't know as he is quite Launcelot, though I used to think so at first. But there was Sir Gawain and Sir Bedevere and a host of worthies, and if he only *would* he could come up to the highest. What makes him so obstinate and unambitious, I wonder? Are there any King Arthurs and loyal knights nowadays, or only common men and women?"

His sisters opened upon him with the fatal persistency of narrow feminine natures.

"You may say what you like about Jack Darcy," he flung out angrily, "but you'll never make me give him up, — never, never!"

"Do hush, children," interposed Mrs. Lawrence.

"Fred, I hope you will learn to modulate your voice, and not shriek so."

Sylvie put on her hat to go home. As she passed Fred she said just above her breath, —

"You are right and brave. I wouldn't give up my friend because he was poor; and Jack is so nice!"

"Much she knows about it," thought Fred, with a true boyish disdain. Yet her approval of Jack was a virtue in his eyes.

CHAPTER II.

"FATHER!" exclaimed Jack a few days after this parting from his bosom friend, "I think I will go in the mill for a year or two, if there is any thing for me to do. Meanwhile my inspiration may come along."

"But what would you like best, Jack?"

"That's just the trouble," and the youthful brows knit in perplexity. "All things seem alike to me: I haven't any choice."

Mr. Darcy drew a long breath that was almost a sigh. If Jack only would evince some preference!

However, a place was found as under-bookkeeper. It was desperately tiresome to Jack to sit perched on a high stool all day; and after three months of it he begged to be put at something else.

At this period we had gone through our costly civil war; and, instead of being exhausted as friends and enemies predicted, the machinery of business appeared to have been set in motion with a new and overwhelming impetus. Every thing was wanted; everybody had work or money; and the most useless commodity found a purchaser: as if our anguish had crazed us, and we went into a delirium of mental opium, and dreamed wild, exhilarating dreams which we mistook for reality.

Yerbury had been a slow, solid, conservative town. Property was low, taxes light and easily paid, a balance on hand in the treasury to commence the new year, and very little pauperism in the town. Yerbury officials utilized their inefficient population, and their county jail was not made a palace of luxury. The old-fashioned element in the place held crime as the result of sin instead of occult disease, — a thing to be punished, rather than petted. It had good railroad connections, plenty of water, with one navigable stream, and a variety of industries. Iron, shoes, hats, paper, and clothing were manufactured to a considerable extent, to say nothing of many smaller branches. Hope Mills was the largest, the focus of the town, and had the prestige of being handed down through three generations, though never as extensive as now.

Toward the west there was a succession of pretty hills that lay in the broad sunshine, making you think somehow of Spanish slopes, covered with vineyards, olives, and luxuriant verdure. Over beyond, a wide, diversified country range, farms, woodland, hills and valleys, with a branch of the river winding through, called, rather unromantically, Little Creek.

On these slopes, the new part, dwelt the aristocracy. Streets wound around in picturesque fashion to make easy grades, and many old forest-trees were preserved by that means, giving the place an air of years, rather than yesterday and improvement. There were two pretty parks, — one devoted to Fourth-of-July orations from time immemorial; there were churches of every denomination; a boarding and day school for young ladies, the academy, some excellent district schools; a hall with library and reading-room; a bank; rows of attractive shops and stores; and, coming down in the scale of refinement, beer-saloons and concert-halls, kept generally up to a certain point of morality. There were so many laboring-men, and they must have something by way of entertainment.

It struck Jack with a curious wonder. These stolid faces and plodding steps were part of the human machines out of which wealth was being ground. They went to the beer-shops at night in their dirty clothes, smelling of grease and dye, drank beer, played a few games, and harangued each other, and went home maudlin or stupefied. Perhaps it was more comfortable than the slatternly wives and crying children. Did it need to be so? If you gave the workingman a helping hand, did he turn straightway into an unreasoning demagogue?

He was not likely to be tempted by such doings. His home had always been too clean and pleasant. He still kept up with the boys, and joined the lyceum club; but the intimate companionship of his life was gone.

Fred did not come home for Christmas. College-life was delightful, — would be just perfect if dear old Jack were there. The glowing letters kept alive his own secret dissatisfaction. But how explain it to one who would be sure to say, "Get out of it all, Jack: no one has any right to keep you in such a distasteful round, and thwart your life-plans." To be sure, he had no life-plans.

One raw, cold March day, Mr. Darcy went out to repair a roof that had leaked in the previous storm. He rarely minded wind or weather.

"I declare," he said that evening, dropping into his capacious armchair, "I feel as if I should never get warmed through. I do believe we shall have a tremendous snowstorm to take this chill out of the air. Jack, read the paper aloud, won't you?"

Jack complied. Local items, bits of State news, and the general progress of the country; the starvation of a nation at the antipodes, the discovery of a wonderful silver-mine, plans for new railroads, — how busy the world was! It stirred Jack's youthful blood.

"I'd like to be a railroad-president," said Jack suddenly.

His father stared, then laughed at the absurdity. "Why, you're only a boy, Jack," he replied.

"I know it. But the boy who means to be a railroad-president must begin somewhere. Or if I could own a silver-mine," he went on, with the boundless audacity of youth.

"Could you find use for the silver?" asked his father humorously.

Jack flushed, and lapsed into dreams. Grandmother opposite was nodding in her chair, her knitting still in her fingers. Jack left his vision for a moment, to calculate if the old chest upstairs was not nearly full of stockings. His mother sat sewing some trifle, and just raised her eyes with that longing, beseeching glance mothers so often give to their sons.

"If women only did not care so much for one," thought Jack, "or if there had been a great family of us. And still I can't see the wonderful difference between going to college, and going to seek your fortune. Does two or three hundred miles more matter when you are once away?"

The snow came on through the night. There being nothing urgent on hand, Mr. Darcy remained within; but Jack buffeted the storm gallantly. It would be worse than this out in the new countries where he meant to go some time.

The next day Mr. Darcy was out. There was a dull pain in his breast, going through to his back, and he coughed a little. It went on thus for forty-eight hours, when the pain became intense, and fever set in. Dr. Kendrick was summoned; and, though the case was severe, it had no alarming symptoms at first. Jack went to and fro with his merry whistle; speculative he might be, but he was not introspective or morbid: wife and mother watched at home.

There came one of those sudden and inexplicable turns in the disease. Jack was stunned, incredulous. In his mother's eyes lay a look of helpless terror he was never to forget.

"You'll care for them always, Jack; you'll never leave them," said his father imploringly, in one lucid interval.

"Always," answered the young voice bravely.

"Thank you, my son, my dear boy;" and there was a fervent clasp of the hand.

A few days later Bernard Darcy lay coffined in the pretty parlor, while wife and mother were crushed with grief.

"Dust to dust, ashes to ashes;" and Jack dropped the first handful of earth in his father's open grave. The two women clung to him, — he was their all. Here lay his duty as long as God pleased.

It seemed for weeks after this as if Mrs. Darcy would follow her husband. She looked so white and wan, she was so feeble that some days she could not leave her bed. Grandmother rallied with that invincible determination not to be beaten down if her prop was wrenched away.

Jack was now a few months past eighteen, stout, and growing tall rapidly. There was about him a sturdy persistence and the good common sense that lends an adaptiveness or pliability of disposition, so to speak, that is often mistaken for content. Since he must stay here for some years to come, he would devote himself to learning the business of manufacturing woollen cloth. It entertained him more than keeping books. For the sake of these two bereaved women, he would take an actual interest in the work he had to do.

Looking back in after-years, he was glad he made the resolve, and stood by it manfully. It gave ballast to his character, shaped him to a definite purpose. A narrow life, to be sure; nay, more, a distasteful one: but he did his best, and waited, and that was all that could be asked of him.

Early in June there was a great commotion at the mansion on Hope Terrace. Miss Agatha Lawrence was married to Hamilton Minor, one of the great firm of brokers in Wall Street, 'Morgan, Minor, & Co.' For weeks it had been the talk of the town. The trousseau came from Paris, and was marvellous. The presents were on exhibition, and created a vast amount of envy and admiration, — silver, jewels, pictures, crystal, china, and laces. And last of all a sumptuous wedding, — every delicacy in season and out of season, costly wines, pyramids of cake, and a lavish profusion of flowers. Nothing so grand had ever occurred in Yerbury.

Fred and a stylish Miss Minor were to stand. He reached home just in time; and, as he was to be off again with the bridal party, he sent a note of regret to Jack.

Jack had too much good sense to feel hurt, though he was disappointed. A few weeks later he took his mother and grandmother up to the mountains for change of air, and enjoyed the vacation hugely himself. So it happened he did not see Fred at all.

The second year letters languished, indeed failed, I may as well admit. Jack was being rapidly inducted into the wisdom of the world, Fred into the wisdom of society. They would never meet on the old plane again. The mill-hand would be no companion for the son and heir of David Lawrence, Esq.

It was not in Jack Darcy's nature to be bitter or cynical. He just accepted the fact. Somewhere he and Fred had outgrown each other, and the boyish interests, once such a bond of union. Fred would be an educated and cultivated gentleman.

Why should he be left in the background? His ambition was suddenly roused again, and he more than half wished himself in college. He went back to his books; he joined a debating-society. There was no need of being a mere clod' because he had to work. David Lawrence was a gentleman. And the next spring he took up a little botany and horticulture with his gardening. Old Mr. Rising down the street, who had been gardener to some great lord, — a peculiar, obstinate Englishman, with his head crammed full of odd bits of knowledge, — took a fancy to Jack. They discussed not only fruit and flowers, but trade in its various aspects, as Mr. Rising had relatives at Manchester who had soared to the ambitions of mills and factories.

Time sped on, and they came to the second summer. Miss Gertrude Lawrence was a belle now, and the great house was constantly filled with guests. The Lawrence equipages were seen in every direction. Mrs. Minor was up frequently, in grand state. The lawn was gay with croquet-parties, the evenings were brilliant with lights and music: they had two elegant garden-parties, when the grounds were illuminated with colored lanterns, and the teas were festivals in themselves. Fred had brought home two college chums, and for the first fortnight was deeply engrossed. Then, too, the girls no longer nagged at him. He was developing into an elegant young man, with due regard for the proprieties.

He did go to call on Jack one evening. It was a duty, a rather awkward and embarrassing one, and he took to himself great credit in the point of moral courage. He understood thoroughly now what Agatha had striven so sedulously to explain, the difference in social station. He was not likely in the future to make a blunder on that side, but it would not do to turn the cold shoulder to Jack all at once. "A boy's will's the wind's will," he repeated with much complacency, and it was but natural that it should veer in other directions. Jack was a good enough fellow, but no Sir Galahad or Sir any one now.

He was a little shocked at Mrs. Darcy in her mourning dress and widow's cap. She was pale, and with the extreme delicacy so often pronounced characteristic of American women. Grandmother sat in state and dignity, rather resentful of what she termed in her secret heart Fred's neglect, but a thing she would not have confessed openly if she had been put to torture. And Jack?

Frederic De Woolfe Lawrence studied him with a critical eye. A great, lumbering, inelegant fellow! Jack seemed to have grown out in every direction, without being finished up in any. He was taken somewhat at a disadvantage, too: somehow he fancied, if he had met Fred alone in a stray walk, there would have been less formality.

They talked about college. Fred was doing well, for he was by nature a student. Society's arts and airs would never entirely uproot that love. He meant to distinguish himself, and have one of the prize essays. Jack was rather grave and quiet, hard to get on with, Fred thought; and he was relieved when the duty was ended, and he could go with a good grace.

Jack lingered on the porch, clinching his fingers, and listening to the jaunty retreating footstep. There was something different in Fred's walk even, a buoyancy as if he could override any little difficulties that fate might have in store for him. Jack smiled grimly. Fortune had showered every good gift upon him. He would go proudly, successfully, through life. He would be praised and honored — and for what?

For a moment Jack felt like wrestling with him, shoulder to shoulder, to distance him, to defeat him, to lower his complacent pride. His half-patronizing manner had stung keenly. Then the real nobility of his nature cropped out, and he laughed at his own sudden heat and passion.

"It would be folly," he said softly to himself. " I could not distinguish myself in any line he will be likely to follow. He must work his way: I must work mine. He knows what he means to do; and there he has gone ahead of me, for I really do not know my own mind. No, there's no further basis for a friendship: the boy-love has had its day, and died. After all, isn't that the history of every thing?" and Jack looked up to the stars, still with a little wordless pain at his heart.

He heard during the next week that Fred had gone West with one of his friends, who was nephew to a great railway magnate. It would be only a flying trip, to be sure, but here Jack was tempted to envy him. That boundless West, the land of his own dreams!

Grandmother grew a trifle less energetic, still it could not be said that her health began to fail. Mrs. Darcy remained about the same. Every day Jack realized how much he was to the two women. To leave them would be absolute cruelty.

At Christmas of this year Miss Gertrude Lawrence was married. The wedding was rather quieter, from the fact that it was winter, and the bride was to leave for Europe the next day. Irene was shooting up into a tall girl, and being educated at a fashionable and expensive boarding-school. Nothing happened to impair her friendship with Sylvie Barry, though the two girls were as dissimilar in many respects as Jack and Fred, but they both stood on the same social plane.

Meanwhile matters at Yerbury prospered mightily. The town was quite bright at night with the glow from factory-windows, and people seemed always hurrying to and fro. New shops and stores were started, new streets were laid out, rows of houses built in town, and out on the edge pretty and ugly suburban villas. Property began to increase everywhere.

Gertrude and her husband George Eastman came back to Yerbury in about five months. He had begun his career as clerk in a bank, and joined his brother afterward as an army-contractor. From thence they had branched into general speculating, and were both considered rich men. Mr. Minor owned a Fifth-avenue palace, and Mrs. Minor never came to Yerbury without her maid. Mrs. Eastman could not have the palace in town, so she decided to have a handsome summer residence at Yerbury, and spend her winters at different hotels. Mr. Eastman thought he saw a grand opening just in this pretty spot. Property was ridiculously low. Here were farms and farms that might as well be cut up into building-lots, and turned into cities. Here was the river-front, here were railroads: why not have twice or thrice as many shops? why not call in the people from far and wide, and make Yerbury a place of note? Time had been when our fathers were content to dream and doze, but now it behooved everybody to be up and stirring. In the new race the laggards would fall far behind.

Mr. Eastman set the example by purchasing one large tract, and laying out streets. Then uprose houses as if by magic. Modern improvements, water, gas, bath, butler's pantries, and dumb-waiters; and the houses offered so cheaply that the solid, slow-going, honest business-men wondered how it could be done. The places had a wonderfully seductive look, and were sought after eagerly.

There was a peculiar interest in all this to Jack. When one day somebody said, —

"Downer's property south of the bridge has gone for thirty thousand dollars. Five years ago he'd been glad to have taken ten for it. Crater and Harmon are going to build a big factory," — Jack's heart went up with a bound.

He still wanted to get away from Yerbury. He began to feel that he had made a mistake with his life, and was anxious to rectify it if possible. He did not see how he could do it here. He had gone into the groove, and it was hard getting out. But if some one came along, and offered them a fortune!

The chance drew near. A new street was prospected through Miss Barry's grounds, through the Lanier place farther back, and the southern end would touch the Darcy place, giving it some new fronts and available lots, and placing the house on the corner. There would be sufficient ground for the width of the street. A petition was forthwith circulated.

Alas that there could be people so blind to their own interests and the general welfare of the community! Miss Barry stoutly resisted. She even inspired some of her neighbors to that extent of opposition that they would not sell at any price. Destroy the beauty of Larch Avenue, that had been " Lovers' Walk " in the old days, and held so many tender reminiscences !

" When I am gone I don't care what is done with the place," said Miss Barry. " It will have but little sentiment for the next generation. A change to me now would be like tearing up an old tree by the roots. I could not endure it. They may have their elegant new houses ; but give me my large airy rooms and my old-time flowers, my nectarines and apricots. Let me live my few years in peace and quiet."

" There is certainly enough to improve," returned Grandmother Darcy. " There are miles and miles that people are glad to sell. Let them take that. Let them build up the vacant lots. And where are all the people coming from to fill them ? "

" The factories and mills will bring in the people," said Jack sturdily.

" There is plenty of room elsewhere," returned Miss Barry with some asperity. " There certainly is no need of turning people out of homes they like, and have made comfortable."

" I suppose you cannot look at it in a business light," said Jack. " Women rarely do " —

" There have been just such whirlwinds before, Mr. Darcy," said the shrewd little old lady. " I have lived through two of them myself. And it seems to me it is an epidemic of running in debt, rather than prosperity. If every thing were paid for ; but you see here are improvement-bonds, and our town runs in debt: here is

everybody raising money on mortgages. How is it to be
paid? Do wages and salaries double? History proves
that it is a bad thing for a state when its rich men grow
richer, and its poor poorer."

"I am sure they need not," said Jack valiantly.
"There is a higher scale of wages paid than ever before."

"And no account made of thrift or economy. Entice-
ments at every corner; women flaunting silks and laces
as everyday gear, with no sacredness; old-fashioned
neatness despised, industry ridiculed; men lounging in
beer-shops; girls flirting on the public streets, having no
duties beyond a day's work in a mill. What will the
homes and the wives of the next generation be like?"

"But that was all so irrelevant," said Jack after she
had gone. "Women mix up every thing. Now, here:
you are offered a big price for this property. You two
could live at ease all the rest of your life, and I"—

"You would go away," said his mother sorrowfully.

"Well, perhaps not," trying to make the tone indifferent.

"Jack," began his grandmother, sitting very erect,
and glancing straight before her into vacancy, "I am an
old woman now; and, like Miss Barry, I could not take
a change comfortably. No other place will ever be home
to your mother or me. There is some money,—enough,
I think, to take care of us both. So, if you cannot be
content, if you must have the restless roving of youth out
before your blood can cool, go and try the world. It is
pretty much alike all over,—some one going up while
another goes down; chances here, and chances there.
As for the few years left me"— And there was a slight
tremble in her voice.

"Don't fret. I'm not going away," said Jack crossly,
huskily, too much hurt to study his tone. "If I can't
always see things as you do"—

There were tears in his mother's eyes. Jack rose suddenly, thrust his hands in his pockets, and walked out into the twilight. There was nothing to be done with so obstinate a problem as his life. He would learn the business thoroughly, getting on as fast as possible, and some time make a strike out for himself, become a manufacturer in turn. The thing was settled now. Maybe some one would want him for mayor or congressman. There was a time when David Lawrence, Esq., had been a comparatively poor man; and though Jack felt that he would hardly turn his hand over to have a million of dollars put in it for the mere money's worth, if he could not discover a silver-mine, or build a railroad over the Rocky Mountains, he might become a rich man. Wealth was a mighty lever, after all. He shut his lips grimly, and pushed his hat down over his eyes. In the early summer dusk, fragrant with rose and violet, he went over the old battle-ground. Did some enemy sow it continually with dragon's teeth? To stay here eight or ten years, mayhap, to make all the money he could. Not one year of her life did he mean to grudge grandmother.

It was quite late when he came in, but his mother was watching for him. She put her arms softly about his neck, and kissed him.

"Have a little patience, dear," she said, in tender, motherly tones; but he knew her sympathy was with him.

"Yes, I mean to. I don't care as much as I did an hour ago. I'm going to set myself steadily to business. You'll hear no more moans or groans out of me, mother."

"Jack — you know I would go to the end of the world with you."

"I believe you would — yes, I do. There, goodnight!" for she was crying.

"This is the way we rule circumstances," said Jack dryly, sitting down in his own room, and taking up Carlyle. "What an amount of humbug is talked in this world, — yes, and written too!"

CHAPTER III.

Tʜᴇʀᴇ was an influx of new blood in Yerbury, and it brought in fresh ideas. A new railroad touched it at one edge, and real-estate dealers left off fighting about Larch Avenue. The ancient stages were laid aside for the more modern horse-cars : there was bustle and rivalry on every hand. George Eastman began to be quoted, and his advice asked generally. Mrs. Eastman held her head loftily. Then there came on the arena of action a certain Horace Eastman, cousin to George, who had been abroad as agent for a large firm, and who slipped into the place of general manager of Hope Mills.

Plainly, F. De Woolfe Lawrence was not preparing to follow in his father's steps. He had graduated with honors, and taken a prize essay, and was now a fully-fledged modern young man. He was fond of discoursing on abstruse subjects, he dabbled a little into art, wrote some mystical poems, tied a cravat beyond criticism, and wore faultless gloves and boots. His mother and Mrs. Eastman were extremely proud of him. His father wondered a little what the young man's future would be.

"I have not decided upon a profession," he said, with a just perceptible but extremely stylish drawl. "The next thing is going abroad. I want at least two years of travel, and I should not wonder if I settled myself at some German or Parisian university. We, as a nation, are so sadly deficient in culture. Our country is crude, as I suppose all young countries must be."

David Lawrence nodded slowly, and asked, —

" When did you think of going?"

" I may as well go at once, and have it over," returned the young man, with the princely indifference he affected.

His father did not dissent.   As well in Europe as here, or anywhere.

As for Jack, he was quite as much out of his reach as if the ocean already rolled between.   They used to pass each other quietly, nodding if they came face to face, but often evading any kind of recognition.   Was the old regard dead?

Fred smiled rather pityingly on the boy who had been so blinded in his first love.

" I used to think him such a hero, because he once thrashed a boy in my behalf," mused the young man. " And how I used to fly at the girls, who were always looking at the feet of clay my idol possessed!   How I *did* coax him to go to college!" and Fred gave a little rippling laugh.   " I must admit that he has good common sense, — he has found his place, and keeps it.   There could be nothing between us now, of course.   My lines lie in such different ways."

No moan for a lost ideal under all that self-complacency.

Jack Darcy took the defection in good part.   He did see the utter incongruity of keeping up even the semblance of the old dream.   But, where Fred had made dozens of new friends, Jack had admitted no one to his vacant shrine.   He liked, even now, to recall those old hours, so bright and gay with childish whims and frolics. And he did envy Fred, just a little, that ramble over Europe.   Would it be a ramble?   It was Jack's turn to smile.   Would it not be bits and pictures seen through coach-windows, rather than getting close to Nature's heart?   No, that would not suit *him*.

And so glided by two more years.   De Woolfe Lawrence

—he had dropped the initial now—returned home in a still higher state of cultivation, and quite as undecided as to his future career. A life of leisure and *belles-lettres* looked the most tempting to him. He had read up a little in medicine, but the practice would not please his fastidious inclinations. Law had its objections. In fact, Mr. Lawrence had dropped into that dilettante state into which extreme cultivation, without genius or ambition, is apt to drift its possessor. He was nearing twenty-four now,—handsome, aristocratic, the pride of his family, and the distraction of young women in general. Invitations were showered upon him, and the delicate flattery society loves to use, ministered to his vanity.

Meanwhile what of Jack?

He had improved considerably through these years. The rough angularity of twenty had softened. Tall, but robust and compact, no stooping shoulders or slouching gait. The chestnut hair was no longer faded, but still cropped close ; and the eyes were so deep that they seemed to have a blue-black tint, large, slow-moving, with that unutterable wistfulness which makes one sad. The face was good, strong, and earnest ; and, if his manners were not those of a gentleman of leisure, they bore the impress of something quite as noble, honor, tenderness, and sincerity. The old restlessness had dropped out. Love, being larger than duty, hinted now at no sacrifice. Grandmother Darcy, now grown quite feeble, leaned on this strong arm, always outstretched, forgetting there had ever been any wild dreams of youth.

And, though Yerbury had changed so much, they and the old street remained unchanged. Mrs. Darcy was a little thinner and older, the light hair just touched with silver. The garden was the same : wherever his father's favorite flowers had died out, Jack had replaced them. Only the honeysuckle was like great twisted ropes, and the syringas and lilacs were trees instead of bushes.

Old neighbors had gone, and new ones come, but they were of the quiet, steady kind. Miss Barry seemed smaller and frailer, but she was as active as ever in her refined way. Sylvie no longer came to the gate for milk: indeed, the wide-eyed Alderney had long been given up, and Sylvie was a young woman. Irene Lawrence had been sent to a fashionable boarding-school; but Sylvie had been educated at home, under her aunt's eye, by a French governess who had proved something more than a mere teacher. The coming of Madame Trépier served to cement more closely the intimacy with the Darcy family. Indeed, Jack took a queer, half-shy liking for madame, and began to study French. He had a great fondness for music, and a fine, rich tenor-voice: so he and Sylvie sang duets together, and often walked in the twilight with madame. Indeed, Miss Barry would have kept her for friend and companion all the rest of her life; but there came a very persistent wooer, and madame succumbed a second time to the destiny of women.

Sylvie Barry was piquant rather than pretty: a soft peachy skin neither dark nor fair, with a creamy tint; deep lustrous hazel eyes, that seemed to change with her moods; hair that had barely shaken off the golden tint, and clustered in rings about the low broad forehead; a passable nose of no particular design, but a really beautiful mouth and chin, the latter dimpled, the former with a short curved upper lip, displaying the pearly teeth at the faintest smile; barely medium height, with a figure that was slim yet not thin, rounded, graceful, pliant, with some of the swift dazzling motions of a bird.

While Jack and Fred had drifted so apart, Sylvie and Irene still kept up a curious friendship. On Sylvie's part there was no election: indeed, Irene in her imperious fashion took Sylvie up as the mood seized her. Mrs. Lawrence, now quite an invalid, was fond of Sylvie's bright face and gay inspiriting voice. In Irene's absence she was often sending for her. "Play me a little song before you go," she would say ; or, "Read a chapter in my book for me, will you not? You always make people seem so real." Consequently Sylvie had never left off going to the great house. Mrs. Eastman would fain have patronized her, but in her spirited way she shook off the faintest attempt. But Irene flew to her, and insisted upon a croquet-party or a drive, or a musical soirée.

"I can't do without you, you obstinate little thing," she would exclaim. "I don't know why I take so much trouble about you ; for I don't believe you like me at all, but just tolerate me for the sake of old times. There are twenty girls in Yerbury who would go wild with delight if I were to ask them."

"Why do you not, then?" inquired Sylvie with a tantalizing light in her eyes.

"Because I don't choose to, Miss Impertinence ! Don't be cross now, and torment me to death with your perverse ways."

"You surely need not be tormented."

"Sylvie, you are exasperating."

"Why do you ask me, then, or tease me to do any of these things? I would rather stay at home to-day, and paint."

"But I shall not give you up. I'll stay here, and talk so that your wits will wander ! "

And so at last Sylvie would consent to her friend's demands.

One evening she came over to discuss a costume for a fancy-dress garden-party. Mrs. Eastman had brought some fashion-plates up from New York, but they did not altogether suit her fancy : so the carriage was ordered, and in a few moments it rolled to Sylvie's door.

Sylvie and Jack were at the piano. There was a soft, drizzling, summer-night rain, that made all the air fragrant without any noisy patter. It was just the evening for an old Latin hymn; and Sylvie was playing the strong, rich chords that had in them mysterious hints of heavenly joy, coming up through waves of passionate suffering. Jack's voice seemed toned to these sympathetic vibrations, and the grand old words rolled out simply, with none of the vicious taste of the more modern fashionable school. So engrossed were they, that they did not hear the carriage stop; but Sylvie caught her aunt's voice.

They had reached the end of a verse. "Let me see what auntie wants," said Sylvie, running into the next room; and then it was, "Oh, Irene! oh, Sylvie!"

"Singing to yourself in the twilight!" laughed Irene. "How romantic! I'm going to interrupt you now, and put you in better business. I am just loaded down with the excellent fripperies of this world, and unable to make a choice. And the grand occasion is Mrs. Avery Langton's garden-party. Now, be good-natured, and help me decide."

Uttering this in a rapid breath, she had walked through the sitting-room to the parlor, and tumbled her parcel down on the great antique sofa, whose edges everywhere were studded with brass nails. And there stood Jack, thinking, if he had been quicker, he could have stepped out of the window into Miss Sylvie's pretty flower-bed, now purple with odorous heliotrope. But, as he had not, there was nothing to do but to stand his ground manfully.

He had often seen Irene Lawrence in the carriage and on horseback; but as she stepped into the room now, and stood there rather surprised, she might have been a daughter of Juno. Tall, slender, arrowy straight, but lithe and faultlessly rounded, her fleecy white shawl like a gossamer web falling off her shoulders, her haughty carriage, her wealth of purple-black hair coiled about her shapely head, a hundred times handsomer than any artifice of dressing, her brilliant complexion, her large eyes with their long sweeping lashes that veiled their depth, but seemed to add a certain imperiousness, her coral-red lips that shaped differently with every breath, her straight nose, with the nostrils thin as a bit of shell, and the softly rounded chin, made her a picture that Jack Darcy never forgot.

"Oh!" in a tone of surprise, "I thought you were alone: pardon me."

Sylvie was bringing in another lamp, and placed it on the great clawfoot centre-table. Then it occurred to her that Irene might not know Jack. She should recognize him here socially, anyhow.

"My friend Miss Lawrence," she said with a world of dignity, "Mr. Darcy."

Jack bowed, in no wise abashed by this proud and handsome Miss Lawrence, though as a child she had snubbed him many a time. And she glanced him over with a sudden interest. It was a manly face and a manly figure; and she wondered from what remote corner of the earth Sylvie Barry had summoned this fair, stout giant, who made her think of the Norse gods of her childish romances. She always liked strength: Sylvie was for tenderness, pathos, and beauty.

"Good-evening," inclining her proud head. "Did I interrupt? You were singing?"

"That is finished," returned Sylvie, with her peculiar manner, as if, being hostess here, she should have proper respect paid to her position; and each guest should be as deferent to the other as if she were a little queen, and this her court.

She picked up a stray piece of music that had fallen to the floor, seated Irene, and half turned to Jack. Any other woman might have been awkward.

"I will leave you two ladies to yourselves," began Jack; but Irene interrupted, —

"No, Mr. Darcy: I shall think I have driven you away;" with a beguiling smile. "If you understand music, you may have a taste in the fine arts of dress as well. At all events, look over these elegant women in their party-gowns, and tell me which is fairest and rarest.''

The honesty of the glance, although it was coquettish, told Jack that Miss Irene did not remember him. For, of all the haughty Lawrence women, she had the name of being the haughtiest. She gathered up her skirts in other people's houses when the plebeian element came too near. Now she waved him to a chair, and gently sank into another, her trailing robe of thin filmy black with golden flecks falling about her like clouds in a gusty sky.

He took the seat indicated. Some strange feeling moved him, an enchantment that he had never before experienced. The very air about her was filled with a subtle, indescribable perfume that he should always associate with a tall, dark-eyed woman, — a glimpse of the Orient and its sweetness, he fancied.

Sylvie took her place, and began to tumble over the colored plates.

"I'm so tired of those Watteau things!" began Miss Lawrence disdainfully. "They all savor of bread-and-butter girls, — a shepherdess with her crook, — bah! And I've been Marie Stuart so many times. If it were a masquerade ; but garden-parties are beginning to prove bores, after all. There is nothing new about them, only to outshine every other woman. A high ambition, is it not, Mr. Darcy?"

"A temptation perhaps."

The tone had in it a bit of delicate homage. Irene understood. She knew at once that this man was a little dazed by her beauty, just as many other men had been. Puny, delicate, namby-pamby men she despised, and always gave them a cut with her sharp tongue. Where had Sylvie picked up this Saul among his peers?

They were all interested in the pictures, and soon fell to making merry comments on them. Sylvie had a quick eye and a bright wit, and something made Jack Darcy brilliant. They selected bits of fine taste here, they made an elegant costume of no partic.lar style, and Irene was struck with what she knew would be its becomingness.

"Mr. Darcy, are you an artist?" She remembered just then what an odd way the Barrys had of picking up people with some gift or grace.

"No," and Jack flushed boyishly.

"Then you must have a houseful of sisters."

"No, I never had a sister."

"When all things else fail with you, you can set up opposition to Worth. I shall come to you for designs. Now, this will be a peculiar source of gratification to me, because no one can possibly have the same combination. And you never can depend upon a modiste. Mr. Darcy, what makes women so faithless to one another?"

"Are they?" he asked with a man's simplicity.

She laughed gayly, and met Jack's fun-loving, shady blue eyes. How handsome they were!

Miss Barry entered the room, and joined in the pleasant chat: then a rumble of carriage-wheels was heard.

"It has stopped raining," said Sylvie, going to the window. "A few soft, melancholy stars have come out."

"You have been very obliging, Sylvie," said Miss Lawrence. "Miss Barry, I shall send the carriage over to-morrow. Good-night."

Jack Darcy handed her out, pushing aside a trailing rose that it might not catch her shawl. Then she half turned, and said "Good-night" in a softer tone.

Sylvie was standing on the porch. "It has been as good as a play, Jack," she said with her gay-humored laugh. "I don't believe she ever thought" —

"That I worked in her father's mill!" and Jack laughed; but it was a rather pained, jarring sound.

"Jack — why do you? You are a puzzle to me!" and Siylvie's voice sharpened unconsciously. "You do not like it. Why did you not go on at the academy, or" —

“Raise myself in the social scale? That’s what you mean, Sylvie ; although we pass just as pleasant hours as if I were a prince, and you the lady of high degree. Well, we have gone over the ground a good many times, and it is always the same thing. I have no fancy for a profession ; I have no genius for art, though Miss Lawrence suggests that I might become a man-milliner — is that what you call it? You know, I am staying here because mother and grandmother will not go anywhere else. And I dare say I make as much money as young Dr. Romer or Ned Remington. And somehow, now that I’m in it, I go on with a stubborn, plucky feeling. Some day I’ll be a great manufacturer.”

This time his laugh was cheerful and ringing.

“You see, Sylvie, your good-nature places you on the debatable ground. You and your aunt could be hand-in-glove with all these great people, and yet you open your generous heart to take in everybody.”

“No, not everybody, Jack. And what a little coward I am just this minute! No, it is not that either. Jack, you *do* know that I should never be a bit ashamed of you before any one. I feel vexed when I think that you could take the high places, and yet you let people put you down, — people not half as worthy or half as good as you. There’s Horace Eastman. He came here a comparatively poor man ; and now he owns half Yerbury, and talks of the mill-hands as if they were — well, a flock of sheep.”

“An apt comparison, Sylvie. To my mind, they are shorn pretty close to make broadcloth for their masters.”

“And there is Fred — have you seen him since his return?”

“Not to speak to him, of course.” And then Jack flushed deeply, with a little hurt feeling.

“And what friends you were! Is it the way of the world? Then it is a mean, hateful world!”

“Sylvie, you are talking wildly. Don’t you see there

is no point of union in our lives? Now, I do not feel
so badly over an outgrown friendship. When I was a
little boy, I remember having a wonderful fancy for Tom
Deane. We traded jack-knives; we told each other of
the best nut-trees; we hunted squirrels; we coasted together; and, I dare say, he was as much of a hero in my
childish eyes as I used to be in Fred's. But think of
any friendship between us now! There isn't a greater
loafer in all Yerbury than Tom Deane. Why, we have
not a feeling in common.''

"Still I think it is rather different," and a shade of
annoyance passed over her face. If Jack only would not
call up these people below him, if he would not identify
himself so strongly with that common brotherhood! He
had so many nice tastes, such a clean, pure, honest soul.
And, young as Sylvie was, she knew this was not always
the result of culture or wealth or ambition.

Jack guessed what was passing in her mind. From his
father he had inherited a kind of womanish intuition. A
pleasant-tempered man Bernard Darcy had always been
called, but it was that delicate tact, the intuitive knowledge of what would be pleasant to others.

"What else can I do here, Sylvie?" Jack cried with
sudden heat. "If the chance ever comes, I shall be
fitted for a good business man. You may think there is
no worthy ambition in that, but wait. Do not judge me
too hastily."

"I am impatient at times, I know; but it is because I
see your capabilities, and I can't bear to think of your
going through the world unappreciated."

"Do not worry about that. Good-night!" rather abruptly. "Miss Barry, I have forgotten myself. Pleasant
dreams!"

"And we did not have our old hymn, after all," said
Sylvie regretfully.

Jack took the short cut across the garden. There was

a dim light in the sitting-room ; and his mother lay in the
hammock on the latticed porch, her favorite evening
resort. She came in now, and Jack bolted the doors.
Then, with a good-night kiss, he went to his room, and
in ten minutes was asleep. Sylvie, on the other hand,
girl-like, tossed and tumbled. Why was the world so
queer and awry and obstinate? After all, you could do
so little with it. Your plans came to nought so easily.
Lizzie Wise, in her Sunday-school class, preferred going
in the mill, and buying herself cheap finery, because the
other girls did it. And so all through. You tried to
train some one, and he or she followed the *ignis fatuus*
more readily than any high, ennobling truth. It was hard
lifting people out of their old grooves.

How bright and entertaining Jack had been this evening! Of course Irene had not remembered him. Would
she be vexed, Sylvie wondered, — she who held herself up
so high, and believed in a separate world as it were?

CHAPTER IV.

THE garden-party was a success, and Miss Lawrence
the acknowledged belle of the evening. No one else
could have carried off the peculiar style of dress. She
knew that she was radiant; and triumphs were a necessary sweet incense, that she always kept alive on her
shrine. There was no need of making a hurried election:
indeed, her chief aim now was pleasure and conquest.

They were sitting over their dainty lunch, Mrs. Eastman having dropped in; and, after the party had been
pretty thoroughly discussed, a little lull ensued. Fred
toyed with some luscious cherries, in his usual indolent
manner. Nothing in this world was worth a hurry or a
worry, according to this young man's creed. He had
dawdled through the party, waltzing with a languid grace
that most girls considered the essence of high-breeding.
It was all one to him. His "set" affected to think life
something of a bore. Intense emotion of any kind was
vulgar.

"By the by, Rene," said Mrs. Eastman, "do you
suppose Sylvie Barry is engaged to that Darcy fellow?
It was odd that she should go off on a picnic with him,
instead of the party. She has the queerest, mixed-up
tastes."

"What Darcy fellow?" asked Irene in surprise.

"Sylvie Barry! Jack Darcy!" exclaimed Fred, in
as much amazement as his superfine breeding would
allow.

Mrs. Eastman gave a mellifluous laugh.

"Don't you remember? but you were such a child!
Fred does.   The Damon to his Pythias."

"Oh!"

A vivid scarlet ran up to the edge of Irene's white
brow. So that was Jack Darcy. What a blind fool she
had been, *not* to think! She had laughed and chatted with
him, smiled on him, worn the costume of his designing, —
a common workingman! For a moment she could have
torn her hair, or beaten her slender white hands against
the table.   What had possessed her?

"I do recall some green and salad days," rejoined Fred
with a laugh.

"How Agatha and I used to badger you! We were
little fools to think such a thing ever went on when one
came to years of discretion. Only I believe we were
afraid the elder and idiotic Darcy might foist his son on
some college. I must say Yerbury has become quite endurable now that party lines have been set up;" and
Mrs. Eastman crumbed her cake, watching her diamond
sparkle.

"How do you know Sylvie went on a picnic?" asked
Rene, with an angry glitter in her eyes.

"Didn't the dear confess? Rene, you do not keep
your penitent in very good order."

Mrs. Eastman had a faculty of putting something extremely irritating in her voice. It was honey smooth, and
yet it rasped.

"Really," answered Irene indifferently, "I do not see
that Miss Barry's selection of friends need affect me much,
so long as she keeps the distasteful ones out of my way.
I may wonder at her choice of pleasures, but I suppose
she suits herself."

"My nursery-girl belongs to the mission-school. It
was very good of Lissette to let her off for a whole day,
I thought. I left her to settle it. What Sylvie sees in
such people, I cannot imagine. I own I was a trifle sur-

prised when I found this remarkable Mr. Darcy was our old *béte noir*, Jack. Is he still in the mill, I wonder?"

"Apply to papa," laughed Irene.

"I don't believe papa could tell you the names of five workmen. As if he troubled his head about that!"

"Sylvie is a nice little thing," remarked Fred patronizingly.

"I have no patience with her!" declared Mrs. Eastman. "As if it was not necessary to have a line drawn somewhere! These people are all well enough in their way: they are a necessary factor,"—picking the words slowly to give them weight,—"and society establishes schools and homes for them, trains teachers, provides employment: what more do they want? A holiday now and then, of course; but why not go off by themselves as a class, as the French do? This maudlin, morbid sympathy we Americans give, spoils them. There is no keeping a servant in her place here. Before you know it she studies and graduates at some school, teaches for a while, goes abroad, and paints a picture, likely as not."

"Do not excite yourself, Gerty," and Fred pulled the ends of his silky moustache.

"Well, it does annoy me to see a young girl like Sylvie Barry with no better sense. Some day we shall have all these people rising up against us, as they did in the French Revolution. I hate socialism and all that; and I took good care to say to Mrs. Langton that Miss Barry had been casting in her lot that day with a parcel of charity-children, and would no doubt be too tired to enjoy the exquisite pleasure of her fête."

"I do not think Sylvie cares a penny!" said Irene with a touch of scorn, anxious to return her sister's little stab. "I suppose she comforts herself with the remembrance of her old blue blood, while Mr. Langton made his fortune as an army-contractor."

"The Wylies were a very good family, Irene."

"If you are through eating, I will have a cigar," said the young man, sauntering over to the bay-window.

What was there in this simple announcement of Sylvie having gone on a charity-school picnic with Jack Darcy that should so rouse the art-cultured pulses of Fred Lawrence? He had always liked Sylvie: her freshness and piquancy stirred him like a whiff of mountain air, — a sure sign that all healthy tone had not been cultivated out of him. It would be very foolish for Sylvie to commit a *mésalliance* with this young man, who was no doubt good enough in his way, — a rather rough, awkward, clownish fellow, with a coarsely generous heart. Sylvie so delicate and refined, with her pretty ways, her genius, — yes, she really did have a genius! In Paris or Rome she might make herself quite a name. He must see a little more of her: he must — well, did he want to marry any one?

Irene and Gertrude retired to the room of the former, and discussed Newport and Saratoga.

"I do hope we shall have a cottage at Newport another summer," said Mrs. Eastman.

"It gives you tone, of course," was Irene's response; "but honest, now, Gerty, don't you think it a little poky? I do not want to go anywhere for a whole summer: I like the fun of all. Agatha is to spend a month at Long Branch, and I am going down just for a little dazzle and to give my gowns an airing."

Their siesta was passed in this kind of small talk. Late in the afternoon she drove Mrs. Eastman home, and then went for Sylvie in her pretty pony-phaeton. As Sylvie was about nothing more important than a pale-blue zephyr "fascinator," she accepted the invitation.

What a delicious drive it was! A dappled under-roof of cloud with the sun just behind it, a golden-gray haze filming the air, and fragrant breezes suggestive of roses and honeysuckle. All the way was starred with daisies. Sylvie drew in long breaths of delight, for she never wearied of nature.

They turned homeward early. The bells were ringing for six, and the mills and factories began to empty out their swarm of human beings.

" Why do you go through here? " asked Sylvie in surprise. " I thought you hated all this."

" So I do," briefly.

She let the pony walk now. These shrill sounds jarred on the summer air. Groups of girls in procession in faded gear or tawdry finery; brawny men with an old-country, heavy cast of feature, in blue flannel, with arms bared to the elbow, and throats exposed; pale stripling youths of the American type, boys with the rough fun not yet knocked out of them by hard work or the harder blows of fate, — a motley crowd indeed.

It thinned a little just here. Two or three men came along leisurely, — one tall and compact, with a slow, firm step, the face grave, the eyes glancing over beyond the hills. Irene Lawrence shut her lips with a touch of displeasure. Was she to miss the satisfaction that had been brooding in her mind for the last hour, for the accomplishment of which she had driven through this dusty, ill-smelling street?

The pedestrian raised his head. A sudden warm, smiling glow overspread the face, no longer grave, but brightening like an April sky. The outlook of the eyes was so frank and clear; the half-smile playing about the parted lips had the honesty of a child. He touched his hat, and bowed with an almost stately deference.

Sylvie nodded and smiled, leaning forward a bit. What sent the glad light so quickly out of his countenance? The girl glanced at Irene.

Miss Lawrence had stared coolly, haughtily, decisively. This man might look at her hundreds of times in the days to come, but he would never again expect a social recognition from her. And, oh, perfection of cruelty! Sylvie, his fellow-sinner in these social laws, had witnessed his pain and discomfiture.

She turned with her face at white heat, one of those inward flashes of indignation that transcend any scarlet blaze of anger. Her eyes glowed with a fiery ray, and the curves of mouth and chin seemed as if frozen.

"It was a deliberate insult, Irene! How dared you"—

"How dared I pass one of my father's workmen? Well, Miss Barry, I happen not to be hand-in-glove with them. I can relegate them to their proper place when an ill-judged vanity brings them unduly forward."

"You met him at *my* house: he is *my* friend, and the friend of my aunt. His birth is as good as yours, or mine."

"Oh, I dare say!" with a satirical laugh. "Are you really going to marry him, Sylvie? Have you the courage to throw yourself quite away?"

"Stop!" and she caught at the reins. The next moment she was on the sidewalk. "Good-evening," she exclaimed with the dignity of a queen.

"The little spitfire!" laughed Miss Lawrence.

Sylvie's displeasure mattered very little to her. A few days later she was on her way to Long Branch, and the episode was soon danced out of mind.

As for Sylvie Barry, she made up her mind never to go to Hope Terrace again. The friendship was not of her seeking, and now it should end. Friendship, indeed! It disgraced the word to use it in connection with Irene Lawrence.

That very evening she went around to the Darcys. Neither she nor Jack mentioned the rencontre, but there was an indescribable something in her manner that told Jack the insult had been as much to her as to him.

Hardly a fortnight later the Lawrence carriage stood at the gate of the pretty court-yard, and the liveried driver brought a note to the door.

DEAR SYLVIE, — [in a tremulous, uncertain hand] I am wretched and lonely. Fred and Irene are away, and Mr. Lawrence

has gone West on business. Will you not, out of the generosity
of your heart, come and cheer me up a bit? I was in bed all day
yesterday with a frightful headache, and can just crawl to-day.
Do not disappoint me. I have set my heart on hearing you read,
and have some nice new books.

Ever your obliged friend,   A. L.

"You must go," was her aunt's comment in a sympa-
thizing tone. "I have promised all the afternoon to the
School Club, you know, and you would only be home
alone. Poor Mrs. Lawrence! What an invalid she has
become! And think of me," — with a cheery laugh, —
"able to get about anywhere!"

So Sylvie went up to Hope Terrace in the luxurious
carriage she thought she had tabooed forever.

Mrs. Lawrence did look very poorly. She kept to her
room a great deal nowadays; or rather there were two
of them, — one off the bedchamber, with a pretty oriel
window, and exquisitely fitted up with every luxury wealth
and taste could devise.

Mrs. Lawrence had already lost her interest in life.
Her two daughters were well married. Irene would be,
of course; but marriages were an old story for her. She
had loved to shine at watering-places, but the gayety no
longer lured her. She had dazzled in diamonds, silks, and
velvets, been admired on the right hand and on the left,
until it was an old, trite story. Servants managed her
house admirably. Mr. Lawrence never wearied her with
any business details. Her clothes were ordered, and
made, and hung in the closets. The carriage was always
at hand. Not a want of any kind, hardly a desire, that
could not be instantly satisfied. She had sunk into a kind
of graceful semi-invalidism, and enjoyed the coming and
going of her children, but her own time was over.

"How good you are, Sylvie dear!" and, drawing the
young girl to her, she kissed her fondly. "I don't know
what I should do without you. Irene would stay at home

if I wanted her; but she is so full of life and excitement, that it wears me out.   You are not always in such a whirl of society, and then you *are* different.   You have such a sweet, sympathetic nature, child!   I can always feel it in your hand, and your voice is so soothing.   What a difference there is in voices!"

Her own was finely modulated: indeed, Sylvie used to think sometimes that these Lawrences had more than their share of the good things of this world.   No physical gift or grace had been denied them.

So Sylvie read and talked, and sang two or three songs before she went home.   Then she came again and again, sometimes with her aunt, oftener alone.   Miss Barry took duty calls with her neighbors as one of the demands of society, to be fulfilled with the fine grace of thorough good-breeding.   Beyond the little formalities that always surrounded her like a delicate hoar-frost, there was a large heart for the weal and woe of all who could in any way be benefited.

"It is a pity to see such a waste of life," she said of Mrs. Lawrence.   "Some people, after they have served their own turn, and had their good time, set about doing something for God and their neighbors at the eleventh hour; but she still clings to self, even when all the pleasure has dropped out.   If she only would exert herself a little, her health and interest would improve, and she has so much in her hands."

One day Sylvie had turned the last leaf of her book, when Fred Lawrence crossed the hall, having come home unexpectedly half an hour before.   "Miss Sylvie is with your mother," the housekeeper had said; and he had begged that they should not be disturbed.   He stood now listening to the cool, soft voice, and an odd thought entered his mind.

Sylvie should really be a daughter of the house.   How his mother liked her, depended upon her!   She was not always going to watering-places and parties and theatres, she did not talk continually of dress and conquests. He did not despise cultivated elegance : in fact, it was a strong point with all the Lawrences; but he knew that a great deal of this much-praised culture ran into artificiality, while Sylvie's elegance had the comprehensiveness of nature. It would be quite impossible for her to do an awkward or ungraceful act; for her innate sense of beauty, harmony, and right guided her. Something higher than worldly maxims toned her soul. And though he, a man with his hands full of gold that he had never earned, could content himself with indolent dilettanteism, he wanted an earnest, honest, truthful woman, if he ever took a wife. He had flirted in a lazy fashion, common with young men who find themselves an object to women, and who have only to raise their hand, sultan-like, to bring a host of houris. That he had kept out of many grosser pleasures was perhaps a credit to him, although that was not the weak side of his character.

He did not fall in love with the picture before him, sweet as it was, — the young girl in a soft flowing white dress (she was too true an artist to have starchy outlines), the shimmering hair, the delicate wavering color, the proud poise of the head, the plump white arm and slender fingers with their pale-pink nails, and, above all, the exquisite voice that seemed so to enter into the culmination of the story, the last few sentences of pathos, joy, and complete fruition.

She closed her book. Neither of the ladies spoke. Mrs. Lawrence had been deeply touched. She lived almost exclusively in this world of fictitious sentiment, I was going to say; but I remember that it is often a transcript of human lives. Still she liked sentiment in books, out of them she scarcely recognized it.

There was a step and a low tap at the door; then, before Mrs. Lawrence could answer, Fred marched in, kissed his mother dutifully, and shook hands with Sylvie.

He had always liked Sylvie better as a little girl than any one else who ever came to the house, and he liked her now. How happy his mother would be! for of course they would go on living here. Irene would be away presently, and his parents would need some one. His summer work was mapped out before him; and really it was a pleasure to think he should escape the bore of society as one found it at summer-resorts, and entertain himself with this piquant brown-eyed girl with a heart fresh as a rose. He did not want a woman who had been wooed by every Tom, Dick, and Harry.

Yet another and more heroic thought entered his mind after chatting with her a few moments. He would save *her* as well. She might have a slight fancy for Jack Darcy: his sisters had spoken of it, and these great, fair, muscular giants were often attractive to women, through the very strength and rude force with which they pushed their suit. But such a lumbering, vulgar fellow in Miss Barry's dainty, womanish parlor! and he smiled at the thought. Yes, he would be doing a good deed to snatch Sylvie from any such possibility.

Fred Lawrence suddenly assumed a new importance in his own eyes. He made himself very agreeable to both ladies. Sylvie remained to dinner; and, when Mrs. Lawrence would have sent her home in the carriage, he proposed to escort her, — he wished to pay his respects to Miss Barry.

They did not take the most direct course, but, leaving the streets with their noise of children and possibly vulgar contact, strolled through "Lovers' Lane." The old trees met overhead; there were dooryards full of sweet, old-fashioned flowers, and now and then the sound of a weak piano or a plaintive voice.

"I am glad these streets have been kept free from the vice of modern improvement," said he. "It always brings back a touch of my boyhood when I walk through them.   Your aunt made a good fight, Miss Sylvie, when she refused to listen to the golden tongues of speculators, though of course you would have been much richer.   But it can be turned into money any time.''

"Money is not every thing,'' answered the young girl, with a touch of sharpness.   "Are one's own desires and old associations to count for nothing?   This place was very dear to my aunt and to many others.   I am sure there is quite enough of Yerbury laid waste now.   The town looks as if it were a sort of general house-cleaning, and every thing was thrust out of doors and windows. And it was so pretty !'' with a curious heat and passion. "It was like a dream, with its winding river and green. fields, and men at their hay, and cows grazing in knee-deep pastures.   Now all the milkmaids are herded in mills and factories; and the children, — well, there are no children any more !''

"No children !'' lifting his pencilled brows in languid surprise.   "Why, I think you can find swarms of them. The poorer the man, the larger the family.''

"There are babies and babies; then little prigs and drudges.   I am not sure I am in love with the so-called civilization.   For the great majority it only means harder work.''

"Did we not learn in some school-book — I am quite sure I did — that

'Satan finds some mischief still,
For idle hands to do'?''

"Are you not afraid?''   She turned with a bright, tormenting smile to the handsome young fellow, who flushed under her clear glance.

"For those who have brains, manual labor may not be the only chance of salvation,'' he returned with a somewhat haughty flippancy.

"I wonder they do not turn their brains to some account.''

They reached the gate, and Miss Barry was sitting on the porch. Sylvie was too pretty and too womanly to be quarrelled with for the sake of a subject that did not in the least interest him. Beside, he meant to come in; so he opened the gate for her, and followed in a well-bred, gentlemanly way, that had nothing obtrusive in it. Miss Barry welcomed him with the quaint formality, the subtile air of education, refinement, and morality, so much a part of herself. It pleased him extremely, and settled him in his determination.

"Sylvie has a touch of radicalism," he mused to himself; "but it is a disease of youth, and thrives by association. Take her quite away, and she will soon recover her normal tone."

He found his mother still up on his return, and rather restless. She lay on her sofa, and dozed so much through the day, that night had but little slumber to bring her.

"I am so glad you did not go to Long Branch," she remarked, as she toyed with her son's silken, perfumed hair. "I get so lonesome when your father is away; and he seems to think of nothing but business"— in a complaining tone. "I do not know what I should do but for Sylvie. She is such a charming little body! Fred, do you think there is any truth in Gertrude's gossip about her and that — one of your father's mill-hands, is it not? How can Miss Barry allow it?"

"There is no truth in it," with a light, scornful laugh. "The families are neighbors, you know; and I suppose the boor takes a look for encouragement. I shall not go away this summer. I can find pleasanter employment."

She pressed his hand, and smiled, as their eyes met. Sons-in-law were very little to one, except in the way of respectability, but a daughter like Sylvie would be such a comfort! Fred had no need to marry a fortune, but Sylvie would not be poor.

CHAPTER V.

Now that Fred Lawrence had come home, there was no
need of going so often to Hope Terrace, Sylvie thought.
Time never hung heavy on her hands; for she was not
indolent, and there were friends and pleasures. Miss
Barry had a conscientious misgiving that Sylvie ought to
be taken about like other young ladies; but she shrank
from fashionable life herself, and could not resolve to
trust her darling with any other person. Beside, Sylvie
always seemed contented.

She was content indeed; at least, with her home and
her aunt. Up-stairs, just out of her sleeping-chamber,
she had a studio, chosen because this room, of all in the
house, had the finest view in summer, when the tall old
trees shut out so much. From here there were two
exquisite perspectives. The trees and houses were so
arranged that a long, arrowy ray of light penetrated
through a narrow space over to a small rise of ground
called Berry Hill on account of its harvest of blue-
berries. Two old, scraggy, immense oak-trees still remained; and she used to watch them from their first faint
green to the blood-red and copper tints of autumn, when
the sun shone through them. Down behind he dropped
when the day was done; sometimes a ball of fire, at
others bathed in roseate hues, tinged with all the wondrous
grades of color, and making fleecy islands in a far-off,
weird world, dream-haunted. She used to study the
grand effects of shifting light, that made the hill bold and
strong, or fused it into dreamy harmonies that seemed to

have the subtile essence of music; then contrasts that
were abrupt and apparently dissonant, quite against well-
known edicts of human taste. Who was right, — the
great Author of all? She smiled to herself when she
heard people talk so glibly of nature, as if the one little
rose-leaf were the whole world.

The other picture held in its soft, still, light, an old-fashioned; low-gabled house with wide eaves ; a broad door-
way, with the upper half always open in summer ; a well
with curb and sweep and bucket where farm-hands came
to drink ; a pond with a shady side, where cows herded
in their peaceful fashion, wading knee-deep on hot days,
chewing their cud contentedly at others, browsing through
golden hours ; fields of glowing grain, then tawny stubble,
a bit of corn with nodding tassels, and not infrequently
a group of children, picturesque in this far light. It all
stood out with the clearness of a stereoscope.

She had her ambitions too, this bright little girl. They
were tinctured with the crudeness of youth, and its boundless vision, it is true ; and sometimes the passion of
despair seized her soul in a cold grasp, when she felt
hemmed in on every side, and longed for some opening,
some step in the great world higher than fashionable
frivolity.

Miss Barry had no taste for famous women. They
were well enough in the world : she paid a proper and
polite deference to Mrs. Somerville, Mrs. Browning, and
Rosa Bonheur, — that kind of intellectual deference that
sets them out of the sphere of ordinary women. Wives
and mothers were better for the every-day life of the
world ; since pictures and poetry were luxuries, accesso-
ries, but not home or food or clothes. Though she had
missed her woman's destiny, she had not lost faith in it ;
though she had held out her hand to the woman who had
made shipwreck of her own life for the wild, graceless
brother's sake, she still looked on clear seas and smooth

sailing as possible for lovers' barks. In her plans for Sylvie there was a fine, manly, generous husband; a love so sweet and entire that the girl should forget her restless yearnings; baby hands to cling to her, baby lips to press, young lives to mould, and a future to plan for others.

Miss Barry believed in work devoutly, but gentlewomen had a firm place in her creed. The paintings and music were well enough as accomplishments, and she was proud of them; but she delicately repressed the other dreams and desires until Sylvie ceased to speak of them except to her friend Jack.

Miss Barry had experienced some anxiety on this point, it must be confessed. You would never have perceived it from the wise little woman's face or any tone of her voice. She went more frequently to the Darcys of an evening with Sylvie: she rolled her easy-chair and work-table to the opposite side of the sitting-room, where it commanded a view of the piano and the sofa in the parlor, the door being always open. She could hear and see, she could make pleasant, trenchant remarks: indeed, she was one of themselves, as young in heart, if the hair did glisten silvery under the bit of exquisite thread-lace that did duty as an apology for a cap.

Jack and Sylvie were not lovers. A rare good friendship it was, more perfect than brotherly and sisterly regard, in that it held no duty-element, and was spontaneous. Sylvie never laughed at Jack in his awkward boyish days: he had never tormented her small belongings as brothers are wont to do.

Miss Barry feared the flame might be easily fanned. A little opposition or warning would bring Sylvie's innocent wandering thoughts to a focus, and kindle the fire. She was very wary. She trusted Sylvie to Jack with an air that said, "You are too honorable to betray the confidence I repose in you."

The old class prejudice spoke out in this covert objection to Jack as a suitor. She honored him sincerely for giving up the dreams of ambitious and energetic manhood to stay at home and comfort these two delicate women. Yet (strange contradiction) she had a half fancy that it betokened weakness or lack of some kind in the very content with which he seemed to go about his daily duties. Alas for consistency! We preach content from the pulpit on Sunday, and on Monday glance with quiet contempt on our plodding neighbor, who can commune with the daisies by the wayside, while there is gold lying untroubled in desert gulches.

Honest, sturdy Jack, taking up the duty of to-day cheerfully with a manful endurance, because the hands holding his fate were too weak and tender to be wrestled with, and that in his large, generous soul he could not war on a smaller antagonist, neither was it his nature to continually thrust any sacrifice he might make before the eyes of the one he was benefiting. How much silent heroism goes unpraised in the world, while we stand on the highways, and prate of our discrimination, our quick insight! Jack might be praised for his self-denial, but the higher appreciation was withheld. Even Sylvie was fretted at times, because he would get interested in all things pertaining to the mill.

Miss Barry said to herself, "It is best that Sylvie should marry in her own circle, a man of cultivation, refinement, and position. Jack is a dear good fellow, but not the person to satisfy her for a lifetime."

Jack thought nothing at all about it. He never gave up the idea of a great wide world, where he could have a hand-to-hand struggle with something as powerful as himself. He had come to no dreams of wife and children. He did like Sylvie with all his big, honest heart. If she had fallen in love with him, and betrayed it by some girlish sign, he would have been startled at first, then thought it over in his slow, careful way, asked her to marry him, and loved her devotedly all his days, leaving the dreams to the past with a tender benediction.

But Sylvie was no more in love than he.

As I said, she decided that she was not needed at Hope Terrace, and staid away four days. Then the carriage came, with a beseeching note. Had Fred gone again?

She found him there in all his elegant listlessness. It exasperated her strangely.

"What have you been about, Sylvie?" cried Mrs. Lawrence. "Is your aunt ill? It seems a full week since you were here."

"Oh, no!" with her beguiling little smile. "I cannot tell exactly what, only I thought" —

"You thought because Fred was home I would need no one else! As if a love-story would not bore him, and an invalid's whims — well, men are not women, my dear," decisively, and with a complacent expression as if she had settled the argument beyond any question, for the first time since the world began.

"Why, you never tried me on a love-story," interposed Fred. "You do not know how deeply sympathetic I might be with your favorite heroines."

"He is laughing at us, Sylvie. Ah, well! I suppose it is a man's duty to *make* love, not to listen to it second-hand. How charming and fresh you look this morning! And how lovely it is after the shower of last night! Fred, if you could leave Latin verses and Greek essays you might take us to drive. We could stop and bring your aunt with us for lunch, Sylvie."

"Thank you for her. She has gone to Coldbridge to see about a nurse for the Orphans' Home, and will not be back until four."

"Then I can keep you without a single scruple," and Mrs. Lawrence looked oddly pleased. "Fred, tell them not to put the horses out. What wonderful health your aunt has, Sylvie! I don't see how she can endure the bother of those schools and institutions : it would wear me out in no time. But I have had a family of children ; '' and she leaned back on her pillow with a satisfied air.

The carriage came around again ; and with the assistance of a maid, Sylvie, and her son, Mrs. Lawrence walked down stairs. He handed both ladies in, and seated himself opposite with the air of a prince.

Sylvie looked so bright and gay this morning, her velvety eyes full of tender light, her cheek all abloom with youth and health, the sweet scarlet lips half smiling, and her attire far enough removed from the rigor of fashion to have a kind of originality about it. She always wore something that added tone and brightness, — a bit of colored ribbon or a flower, or a bow that flashed out unexpectedly, as if greeting you with laughing surprise.

"What do you do to mother, Sylvie?" Fred asked, with a touch of complimentary curiosity in his voice. "Yesterday she was dull and moping. I could not persuade her to drive."

"It was so warm, no wonder. I felt dull and drowsy myself. But to-day is the perfection of loveliness."

"And you have a charm, Sylvie. I do not know but it is your perfect, buoyant health. You seem to lift one up. I only wish I could keep you all the time," remarked Mrs. Lawrence with a touch of longing.

Sylvie colored, and averted her eyes : then she gave herself a kind of mental shaking, and resolutely glanced back, uttering some rather trite remark. She would not suspect or understand.

They came home again, and had lunch : then, while Mrs. Lawrence was taking her siesta, Fred carried off Sylvie to his study. It was luxuriously beautiful. Several gems of pictures adorned the wall, which had been newly frescoed to suit his fancy. Easy-chairs lured one to test their capacious depth, some exquisitely-bound books were arranged in a carved and polished case, and the table was daintily littered with papers. He had an idea that a man's surroundings were a very fair index to his character and tastes, quite forgetting that it implied length of purse as well.

He made spasmodic attempts at literary work. Abstruse essays were begun under the impression that he had something brilliant and original to say, but before they were finished a new train of thought led him captive. He dreamed delicately sensuous dreams, lapped in luxurious idleness, the rooms stifling with odorous hot-house flowers. He went clothed in soft raiment, he sunned himself in languid seas of imagination, and was too indifferent to concentrate his powers upon any great faith or belief, or even emotion. He had a contempt for cheap and plain belongings, as leaning insensibly to vitiation of taste. Nothing modern met his approbation. The old-time philosophies won him with their subtile flavor. He could propound his theories eloquently, but they did not touch him deeply enough to rouse him into action of any kind. All that his education and culture had done for him so far was to develop an incapacity for any regular, wholesome work that would be of the slightest use to any human being.

Something of this passed through Sylvie's mind as she sat there. This handsome and stalwart lily of the valley, with no desire for toiling, and no ability for spinning, would be content to drift and dawdle through life on his father's money. At that moment he was more contemptible to her than Irene, winning lovers by the score, and casting them aside with no more compunction than if they were the litter of faded flowers.

After all, why should she care if he did not reach her standard of moral and intellectual excellence, of that knightly chivalry whose rallying-cry was, "God and my fellow-men!" Why should she desire to rouse him from that complacent ease and fastidiousness, brought about by

wealth, and the certainty of no need of effort on his part?
Surely she was no modern apostle carrying around the
watchword of work.

Yet somehow — if all the subtile forces running to
waste in both him and Jack could be galvanized into earnest, active life; if the sturdy, wholesome thought of the
one could be mated with the clear, crisp training of the
other; if both could have the wide outlook beyond material wants and comforts!   It fretted her.

Yet these two, sitting here on this peerless summer
day, skimmed over wide fields like gay butterflies. She
could not be in earnest with him. Just when she was
roused and warm, he seemed to lift her by some flight of
eloquence, and waft her to his realm of fancy. It annoyed
her to find he had that much power over her.

It must be admitted that when Fred Lawrence willed, he
could be extremely fascinating. Women yielded grace-
fully, nay, eagerly, to his sway; and much delicate flattery
had their eyes and lips fed him upon. Sylvie piqued him
a trifle by her utter unconcern — or was it the fine instinct
of coquetry inherent in feminine nature?

There was no telling what this queer, bright, unconventional little thing might do if left to herself. A good
marriage would prove her salvation. She had many womanly possibilities: yet, with all due deference to Miss
Barry and her old blue blood, Sylvie might overstep the
bounds, and take up some of the reforming projects so
dear to elderly spinsters. As Mrs. Fred Lawrence she
would be held regally above them, and could depute her
charitable work to her aunt.

In justice to the man, it must be confessed that Sylvie's
dainty, piquant loveliness stirred his soul; and, if self had
not been so intense a centre, he might have been ardently
in love, or clearer-sighted. Much of the time her demeanor toward him was coldly indifferent: yet the misfortune was, her interest in all things kindled so easily that

she could not, at a moment, change to him. Her moods of reticence and shy evasion added a flavor to the cup. With a man's egregious vanity, he jumped at the conclusion that these little intangible things signified love.

One day Sylvie stumbled over Irene. She came flying up stairs with some choice nectarines for Mrs. Lawrence, a kind that seemed only to reach perfection in Miss Barry's old-fashioned garden. There sat Irene, superb, nonchalant.

"Oh, you little darling!" clasping her, and pinching the peach-bloom cheek. "I am so glad to have a glimpse of you; for mamma has sung your praises until I ought to be jealous, but out of my boundless generosity I still smile upon you. No need to ask how *you* are, but one may inquire after your aunt?"

"Miss Barry is quite well," Sylvie said with some constraint, remembering their last parting.

Irene had honestly forgotten it. She laughed now, a low, ringing, melodious laugh.

"Why, it is quite a treat to see you open wide your sunrise eyes. I have taken everybody by surprise, and enjoy it immensely. Gerty and I are off to fresh fields and pastures new, and home came right in my way. Sylvie, you are a good little creature to come and amuse mamma when her own lovely and amiable daughter is racing after the pomps and vanities of this naughty world. Sit down;" and she made room on the sofa beside herself. "Don't let such a frivolous creature as I turn you from the post of duty."

"I did not come to stay," Sylvie answered rather stiffly.

"As if the intention were cast in adamant! Oh! why is not Fred here to use his persuasive tongue?"

There was a peculiar laughing light in Irene's eye that annoyed Sylvie, for it seemed to indicate a secret knowledge.

"I can stay just half an hour," was the reply in a

decisive tone. "At eleven I take my lesson in painting.
—Aunt wanted you to have these, Mrs. Lawrence, in their
first bloom of ripeness."

"They are delightful. A thousand thanks to both of
you, my dear."

"And you really manage to exist in this dull place,
Sylvie! You are a miracle of content," interposed Irene.

"I have not come near dying yet," was the rather dry
rejoinder.

"You need not be so curt and sharply sweet, my dear.
Here I have been listening to marvellous accounts of your
amiability and devotion "—

"Don't, Rene!" implored her mother. "Sylvie *is*
good to me."

"And it might make the sweetness weak if she stretched
it out to me! Keep it intact for those who so delight in
it. I am fond of spice and high flavoring."

"These nectarines are perfect," declared Mrs. Lawrence. "One can taste the sunshine in them."

"How poetic, mother mine! Does Fred come and read
Latin verses to you and Sylvie? I may have one "—
stretching out her jewelled hand. "Oh, they are delicious! worth coming home for, even if I had not wanted
mamma's pearls."

"And money and every thing," added her mother.
"Rene, you ought not to be so extravagant. Papa is
quite depressed with the state of business."

"Yes, I have heard *that* ever since I left my cradle;"
and Rene laughed gayly.

It suddenly crossed Sylvie's mind: what if this proud,
imperious girl should be reduced to poverty some day?

"Don't plan a conspiracy against me, Sylvie Barry! I
saw it in your eyes!"

A vivid flush overspread Sylvie's face, as if she had
been caught in the commission of some crime. Irene's
laugh rang again with a peculiar irritating sound. .

"I could not form a conspiracy against you — even if I so desired. And I must go."

Sylvie rose with a haughty air.

"Wish me worlds to conquer at least, or scalps to hang at my belt. No? You ungracious little thing! There is a good-by kiss to show you that I always hold out the right hand of peace."

"Have the carriage, Sylvie: it will not take a moment" —

"No, thank you," in a crisp tone. She would have nothing of these Lawrences just now.

"Fred will get a spicy wife," commented Irene, with a peculiar smile.

"She is never so with him. They get along beautifully," said the mother.

"Fred is too lazy to rouse Sylvie. Women have quite spoiled him. And Sylvie is ever so much prettier when a trifle vexed. Don't tell me about her angelic qualities, though I suppose she does keep super-amiable before you and Fred just now. I wonder if I could if I were in love!"

"Irene, I am sorry I hinted it. If you begin to tease Fred" —

"I shall not: set your heart at rest. I give full and free consent, and approve heartily. Beside, the little thing might throw herself away if she was not looked after. There will always be some one to stay at home with you."

Mrs. Lawrence turned to her book and her nectarines; and Irene tumbled over jewel-cases, — a proud, imperious beauty, whose heart had never been touched, who cared only for pleasure and triumphs. Over yonder, men and women were toiling, that she might have gold to squander. They lived scantily, that she might feast. And the brave old world, seeing it all, uttered a silent groan. One day it would speak out.

CHAPTER VI.

Sylvie Barry meanwhile walked along rather rapidly for a warm morning. She felt irritated. Her sweet lips were set in defiant curves, the red heats of annoyance burned and faded on her cheek with each passing thought, and there was something out of harmony: a fateful discordance that swept over her, as if the parts of music had been wrongly put together.

Did they think — did Fred imagine —

She had never faced the idea before. Now she thrust it out in the garish sunlight. Her eyes sparkled, but there was no triumph in the girl's fine, resolute face. This man might lay his father's wealth at her feet, borrowed plumes in which he was quite content to shine; his heart — and a smile of withering scorn crossed her red lips. She would be a little dearer than his horse: dogs the fastidious man could not endure. Practically his wooing would be, —

> "I will love thee—half a year,
> As a man is able."

Not because of a fresher, fairer face: he would give her all he had, all that he could rouse his languid pulses to experience. She would be lifted out of her present occupations and interests; for Sylvie was too clear-eyed to blind herself with the specious reasoning that as the wife of a rich man's son, she would be a greater power in the world for good. They would fit her into *their* sphere. She fancied herself coming to an aimless middle-life like

66

that of Mrs. Lawrence, taking no interest in any thing, but reading novels, and complaining, to pass away the time.

Did she really care for any one else? More than one young man in Yerbury had paid her the peculiar deferential attention that asks encouragement if there is any to give, but is too truly delicate to proceed without. Then there was Jack, who understood her soul better than any one else; but had he touched her heart in a lover-like way?

She turned her clear, honest eyes to the blue overhead, as if taking Heaven for a witness. Her heart and fancy were quite free. Much as she cared for him, there was no thrill of that high sentiment in it.

In some fascinating ideal life she had seen a lover with whom she could walk down through the years, whose life would touch hers at all points, who could fathom the depths of the nature that so puzzled herself, who could measure and supply the yearning reaches of intellect; who could awake in her soul a love, strong, deep, and unquestioning, so fervent, indeed, that she would turn from all other dreams and desires to him. A young girl's ideal — perhaps it is well for the world that some women have ideals, and keep faith with them.

As for Fred, his vanity led him straight on. She tried honestly to place herself right in his estimation; but he misunderstood her, and liked her the better for the variety. She saw too, with dismay, that her aunt favored him. Her natural kindness of heart shrank from the pain of rejecting him, and to her the triumph had no pleasure. But in her anxiety and desperation she saw only this one course.

He dropped in nearly every day, he took her and Miss Barry to drive. He haunted croquet-parties, which he hated, because she accepted invitations to them. He never met Jack. Some fine sense warned the latter that

an encounter in Sylvie's parlor would be uncomfortable.
Yet, strange to say, sometimes when he saw the handsome fellow sauntering by, a peculiar tenderness came
over him, remembering the little boy who had clung
fondly to him.

An old-fashioned courtship would prove no end of a
bore, Fred decided. So one day he marched over to
Larch Avenue when he knew Miss Barry was alone, and
laid his case before her. She received him with graceful
kindliness, listened to his offer, and assented with evident
pleasure. There was not a happier woman that night in
all Yerbury than Miss Barry. The care and desire of
her life had been justly crowned. Her good-night kiss
to Sylvie was inexpressibly sweet.

Fred did not see Sylvie for the next two days, but
meanwhile wrought himself into a state that he was quite
sure was proper and well-bred love. Then she came to
Hope Terrace, and they kept her to tea. The late, heavy
dinners were dispensed with at present.

"Will you walk home to-night, Sylvie?" asked Fred.
"I feel in a walking mood."

"The slightest symptom of industry ought to be encouraged," she made answer gayly. She had been of
some real service this afternoon, charmed away a fretful
headache, and restored Mrs. Lawrence to a comfortable
state of feeling, and was correspondingly light-hearted.
Then, too, Fred had kept out of the way, and been gravely
polite to her at the tea-table. She liked him in such
moods.

It was a late August evening, with a small crescent
moon shining softly as if its forces were well-nigh spent.
The heat of the day was over, and the falling dew evolved
a kind of autumnal sweetness, the flavor of ripening
fruits rather than flowers. Yerbury was very quiet in the
part they were to traverse. They walked under great
maples where a shadowy light sifted through, and the

houses looked like fragments of dreams, with here and there a lamp in a distant window. The slow wind wandered through pines and hemlocks, as if some fairy Puck had laid his finger to his lips, saying to crooning insects, "Hush, hush!" A night to dream as one went down "Lovers' Lane."

Sylvie was radiantly beautiful. Her face always changed so with her moods. Every feature had a perfect sculptured look, but intensely human, — the straight nose with the flexible, sensitive nostrils, quivering at any sudden breath, the dainty chin and white throat, the red curved lips that seem to smile at some inward, richly satisfying thought, the large lustrous eyes serious as those of a nun, and the calm, clear brow that seemed to index the strength and fineness of the nature. He did not take in any of the occult meanings: to him she was simply a pretty girl whom he could dress in silk instead of lawn.

The small hand had lain on his arm without the faintest movement. Now he took it in his, and pressed it softly. She frowned, and made a slight, repellant gesture.

"Sylvie?" with a lingering intonation that was hardly inquiry.

"Well!" roused out of her quiet into a momentary petulance.

"Sylvie, I love you. Will you be my wife?"

In his most commonplace dreams he had never made love so briefly. He startled himself.

"Don't!" in a short, decisive tone, as if he were merely teasing.

"Sylvie, I am in earnest;" and in his tone the man spoke.

"Then I think you are mistaken." She seemed to look at him in the cool light of invincible candor and honesty.

"No, Sylvie, I am not mistaken," gaining courage that it was to be argument instead of sentiment. "I have had

this purpose in my mind for some time, and have solicited
your aunt's consent.   You have only to say "—

"I have many things to say, but assent is not one of
them ; " in a voice that, though low, seemed to cleave the
air with a steely ring.   "You think you love me.   Perhaps you do — as far as you are capable of loving any
thing beside yourself.   You have seen a good deal of me
this summer, and have made up your mind to marry.   I
possess some of the necessary requirements, and doubtless suit you better than any mere fashionable woman.
But you have none of that intense desire that makes a
matter of life and death of love, that elects one woman,
or forever keeps a vacant niche in the soul."

"Sylvie.! "

Her passionate words stunned him.   He turned to her
with a puzzled look, a certain helplessness, as if he were
stranded on some far, foreign shore.   And then he met
her lustrous eyes, so clear that they were almost pitiless
in the glow of undimmed truth.

"Can you not trust me?" with the gentle reproachful-
ness so winning to most women, so confident of a victory
over a heart that loves.

"I could trust you to care for no other woman when
your word was passed, but it seems to me," and her heart
swelled with something like contempt, "that you are but
playing at love.   Marriage in your estimation is a fit and
proper step : your mother likes me, you prefer me to any
one else "—

"Good heavens, Sylvie! what more do you want?"
and a flood of scarlet mounted his calm, handsome brow.
"When a man chooses a woman out of the whole circle
of his friends and acquaintances, what higher compliment
can he pay her?   I have seen women beside those in
Yerbury ; and, though it may savor of vanity, I believe
there *are* those who would appreciate "—

"I wonder you did not go to them ; " with a fine irony,
cutting short his sentence.

"Because I liked you, chose you."

"I do not so desire to be chosen," she answered quickly. "The man I marry must win my respect, my highest
faith ; must have an aim, an ambition, and not dawdle
through life as some silly woman might."

The decisive voice seemed to cut a path between him
and her as it went. It struck home uncomfortably.

"Then I suppose you call all men not engaged in manual labor, dawdlers, — scholars, poets, men of leisure, who
can devote their lives to work that requires patience and
fineness of detail, rather than the heavy swing of a black-
smith's hammer. When a man has no need of work " —
and Fred paused, a trifle out of temper.

"I do not believe God ever made an idler," she said,
with high gravity that widened the gulf between them.
"To whom much is given, much will be required."

How unreasonable she was! He hated women who
flung texts or proverbs at you ; and yet he did not hate
her. She had a girl's flighty notions, born of crude contact with inferior minds, and perhaps over-much novel-
reading.

"I do not exactly understand what a man must do to
win your love," he said in one of those calm, intensely
irritating tones. "I have chosen what suited me best, —
culture, refinement, and the education that fits me for the
sphere in which I am likely to move all my days," im-
pressively. "It is true, much of the wisdom of the world
is little to my taste. I do not know why a man should
wade through a slough of evil for the sake of repenting
afterward, for looking white in contrast to that foul
blackness. The ninety and nine just ones seem to me
the better example."

"I am afraid I shall not be able to make you understand," she went on, with a little hesitation. "Perhaps
I have not the power or patience to shape a man's soul
to a noble purpose or ambition. I want him strong and

earnest, full of energy and that high sense of duty to all around him, not satisfied to drift down the stream in frivolous content, but to make the way better for his having gone over it. I want him true as steel to his friends, generous, yet uncompromising to his foes, to all evil; the kind of man who, if crushed down by fate to-day, could see some ray above his head to-morrow, who has sufficient moral fibre not to be rigidly bound by class feelings and narrow prejudices.''

Sylvie paused, startled at herself. She had never framed her hero in words before, and that she should do it for this man !

" These are the heroes of our youth, Miss Sylvie, and you are very young,'' in that insufferably patronizing tone.

" I am old enough to know what I want,'' she retorted, all the fiery blood in her pulses leaping to the charge. " I think, too, I can discern between the true worker, and him who is content with the frivolous outside show.''

" Perhaps not. You have been advising me, now allow me a like privilege. Do not imagine me actuated by jealousy, — that vice of the Moor is not in my nature. I have seen with some surprise that your fancies were for those beneath you in the social scale. A woman always loses in this dangerous experiment. She seldom raises her commonplace hero to a level with the gods, and is much more likely to be dragged down.''

She turned suddenly, her face flaming scarlet. The indignation misled him. He took it as a sign of personal anger, and wondered if she could, if she *dared*, throw him over for that coarse, stupid, blundering fellow.

" Yes,'' he continued, glad to stab her in a vulnerable point; " you certainly have made a mistake, if you think this soul an aspiring one. A boy who excels in brute strength and force merely, a man who makes a deliberate choice between the nobler results of education and the common purposes of rude daily labor, will hardly rank with a knight of Arthur's time, even if some self-deceived woman chooses to lavish her affection upon him."

"If you mean Mr. Darcy"— And she stood quite still, tremulous with passion.

"I mean Mr. Darcy." She had not shown such delicate consideration for his feelings that he should hesitate. "I do not see how you, with your artistic tastes and refinement, can find companionship in such a nature. I understand it very thoroughly. Beware, for you cannot plead even daffodil blindness, my fair Persephone."

Sylvie Barry could have struck the man beside her. All the passion of her nature surged up in contempt, great waves of white heat. If a look could have annihilated, hers might. Even in the shady gloom, he saw the flashing eye and quivering lip of scorn.

"Do not distress yourself about me," she answered, with suave bitterness. "Jack Darcy may be a mill-hand; but he has the honor, the white soul, of a gentleman! And you — you dare to trample on what was once a friendship!"

"I believe he was once my admiration because he used to show fight so easily. He was for marching West then, and doing some grand thing; but you see his hero days are gone by. Ten years from this he may be a demagogue, a rank socialist, whining about equality. Still, if I must congratulate you"—

She made a haughty gesture, and her first impulse was to let it go; but her truthful nature could not brook the implied deception.

"You may congratulate me upon the friendship alone," with a clear, sharp emphasis.

His shattered self-confidence returned suddenly, shaped to arrogance. If she was not entangled with Jack Darcy, there certainly was no one else.

"Sylvie," he began loftily, "this has been child's

play, and I am heartily ashamed of my share of it. Let us go back, and forget it. You have had your tilt at windmills; so suppose we return to common sense. You are still heart-free, it seems; and I beg pardon for repeating foolish gossip. Your aunt has accepted me as your suitor; my mother is waiting to receive you as a daughter; and I think," with some pride in his tone, "that few men can offer you a cleaner hand, or a better record. You will have a life of ease and leisure, and— Why, Sylvie, you can teach *me*,—you can help me up these glowing heights."

"I have answered you!"

She seemed to grow tall and regal as she stood there by the gate, the long, arrowy ray of lamp-light from within illumining her proud, cold face, that could flush with such bewildering warmth. He discerned in some dim way that she had access to a life far above his; an atmosphere like hoar-frost surrounded her, raying off fine points, that thrust him farther away into darkness and coldness. Had something been taken out of his life?

The man's well-nigh imperturbable complacency had received a shock.

"Good-night," in a softer tone. One cannot break a pleasant friendship without a pang.

As one in a dream he heard the gate close, the soft footfall on the brick walk, and a waft of voices from within. Then it occurred to him that he, Frederic De Woolfe Lawrence, had been rejected by this little girl upon whose head he had meant to shower the blessing of marital protection, the regard of a soul that was not quite indifferent, after all. What was this dull pang somewhere in his symmetrical, well-kept body? Was it the night that made his pulses heavy and turgid?

Then he turned. "By Jove!" he muttered, "there's not another girl in the country that could have kept her fingers out of the governor's money-bags! Poor mother!

What a disappointment for her!   Of course Sylvie will marry Jack Darcy, — Pluto and Persephone again.''

Then he softly whistled a stave of opera-music, and sauntered about leisurely.   He had no fancy for facing his mother that night.

As for Sylvie, she knew her face was very white when she entered the door; but she bustled about with womanly evasion, and began to ask if her aunt had been lonesome, if any one had called, and declared she was tired from walking home, and her head ached a little, which was true; and presently the two women barred their doors, and went to bed.

Was she glad to have it over?   Was she sorry she had left no loop-hole for future hope?   Strange to say, she could not tell.

" But I could never live, like a pauper, on some other person's money! '' she thought decisively.   " And he did not care.   It was for his mother's sake chiefly.''

Again there was a breach between the Montagues and the Capulets, this time crossed by no lovers' hands.   Mrs. Lawrence was highly indignant, Miss Barry vexed and sore disappointed.   They went the even tenor of their way, however, while the poor self-made invalid at Hope ·Terrace grew more querulous and exacting.   Fred took a week at Saratoga to restore his wounded vanity, and then settled himself at a hotel in New York, wondering if he had not better read a little law to pass away the winter. Mrs. Minor was a queen of fashion, and she was glad to have the attendance of her handsome brother.   Irene and Mrs. Eastman flitted about like gay butterflies, with trains of admirers.   The faint mutterings in the financial world made little difference to them.   It was their province to spend, to enjoy; and what the strata beneath them did or suffered or hoped, was of no more account than the far-off ocean-froth beating up on the hard white sand, — picturesque in a drama or a story.

CHAPTER VII.

It was a dull, gray day, the first of December. Autumn had set in early this year. There had been a week of cold rain that had quite destroyed the magnificent foliage, one of Yerbury's greatest charms; and it became a sodden mass, trodden under foot by pedestrians. The ground was baked by sharp frosts at night, making the unpaved streets a mass of ruts early and late, and quagmires in the middle of the day.

Yerbury had changed much from the pretty, clean, thriving country-town, to something that aped a grand city; unfinished streets, small farms laid waste, rows of pretentious houses or florid cottages that had never been thoroughly completed, nearly every one adorned with the ominous placard, "For Sale." They needed painting and tidying: vines were left about, dahlia-stalks hung to poles, steps were awry, and gates swinging on one hinge; heaps of ashes and garbage lay here and there.

This day Yerbury wore a particularly listless air. The leafless trees hung out long and drooping arms, that swayed to and fro in the biting wind. The sullen sky overhead added its tone of dreariness to the picture. There was no cheerful whir of factories and shops, no brisk steps of men going to and fro, though there were enough standing around in groups with scowling faces and compressed lips, or flushed with angry gesticulation.

The only places that evinced any air of business were the beer-shops. Here a man harangued his fellows; there he did not deign to argue, but openly cursed. "Let's treat on that!" said one. "I'll stand to that sentiment," declared another. Sometimes voices rose so high that a proprietor was forced to command order. .

Yerbury was on a strike. There had been a new scale of prices with the opening of autumn, submitted to by most of the men with a sympathetic good-nature. Trade was getting dull. Fancy prices no longer ruled. An ominous feeling pervaded all classes. Building fell off. One tenant gave up his house, and took part with another. Housewives looked about for the cheapest market, and talked of making last year's coat or cloak do for the winter.

Hope Mills had been among the first to propose this second reduction. David Lawrence had returned from his business tour much depressed. There was an undercurrent of distrust, a disinclination to lay in stock, a wordless questioning from eye to eye, with no hopeful response.

Horace Eastman had worked himself into the charge of the inside business. He had no real interest, but a liberal salary; and Mr. Lawrence felt that he lifted a weight of care from his shoulders. If only Fred— But with college training and elegant tastes he could hardly be expected to take to the dull routine of business cares. So matters had been left more and more to Eastman, who was shrewd and sharp, who always managed to get the most for his money.

Now Mr. Lawrence was appalled by the amount of stock on hand. They had been running the mills at full capacity all summer.

"We must offer goods at a lower figure," said Mr. Eastman promptly. "We must get command of trade again. Prices *will* come down,—that is a foregone conclusion. The abundant harvests have glutted the market, and living will be cheaper. The laborer can live on less; and, if we can manufacture at less cost, we shall be all right again."

"But there seems no demand for goods," said Mr. Lawrence faintly. "Store-shelves are full. People are carrying last year's stock with no call for it. It has always seemed to me, Eastman, that a liberal policy to workmen brought its own reward. They are large consumers. Cut them down to mere food and shelter, and clothes are the first to go. In decent times your workman is ashamed of a ragged coat."

"All very true, Mr. Lawrence; but, if there is no market, we must create one. Sell cheaper stock to new men. That will make a demand at once."

"Undersell! We used to call that a cut-throat business, Mr. Eastman;" and a flush stained the fine face, now rather worn and thin.

"It is what we must come to. There is next to no premium on gold, and the first man who touches bottom will be the lucky one, to my thinking. Cheap goods, cheap every thing, will be the next cry. The farmers must dispose of their wool, and labor must come down. Why, ordinary workmen have been living like princes."

The delicate brows were drawn thoughtfully.

"I always hated to grind workmen down to a bare subsistence," spoke the honest, loyal gentleman, as God made him. Trade had not warped body and soul. He was an aristocrat, if you please, and his home was as sacred to refinement and elegance as a ducal palace. A common person would have stood in his hall until his errand was done, and he would never even have asked a workman to take a seat in his office; but his soul was honorable, if haughty.

"Let me manage it," with a confident nod. "We'll keep the topmost wave, as you will see."

So to New York Horace Eastman went, and arranged for a large auction-sale of goods, which was a remarkable success, and created quite a ripple in the sea of stagnation. Then he contracted to deliver another lot by the first of January, at certain prices. And now either manufacturer must give up profits, or workman yield his margin, and be contented with daily bread alone.

"There really was no need of workmen owning houses, having Brussels carpets and pianos," argued Eastman. "They were in some degree answerable for the hard times. Every one wanted to out-do his neighbor. They were not content to live as their fathers had lived; and, where the mothers wore print dresses, the daughters must have silk. They had gone on altogether too fast."

Yet only a few years ago workingmen had been urged to put their money into homes. Rows of houses had been built for them, and sold on such ridiculously easy terms, only a trifle down. The interest would not be as much as rent. Then the fascinating shopkeeper had flaunted his wares in the faces of the thrifty housewives. "A good article is cheapest in the end. This Brussels will outwear two ingrain carpets, at a very little advance on the first cost. No moths will trouble it, once down it is there for years, saving worry and hard work;" and the buyer was persuaded. Then there must be new furniture, and so on to the end. Was it altogether their fault? The old things were passing away. The world was awaking from its Rip-Van-Winkle nap. There was to be a wider outlook, a liberal cultivation, a general rising of every one.

So there had been years of plenty, and men had pulled down the old storehouses to build new ones.

Such people as the Eastmans and the Lawrences could not economize at a moment's warning. The screws must be put on elsewhere.

At first the workmen looked at each other in blank dismay. Winter was coming on — a hard one it bid fair to be. Coal had risen, and in spite of the abundant harvest the absolute staples of life had not much decreased by the time they reached the consumer. Coffees were high: pease, beans, and chiccory were sold at a reduction, to be sure, and you could get lumpy heavy flour that spoiled your bread, and poor butter, and teas that were colored and doctored; and this was cheap living.

There was a stormy wrangle. Meetings were held, and speakers figured out the actual cost of living. Less than the present rates meant loss, privation, and want in the end. So a strike was determined upon.

Jack Darcy, being foreman of one department, stood, as it were, between the upper and nether millstone, at present just escaping both. He thought it hard that the men should have this second reduction so soon, and it did seem to him reasonable that profits ought to yield a little, that there ought to be a sympathy between them. Personally, he should be comfortable enough; but if he had a wife and three or four children, a helpless, bedridden mother, or a drunken father, or a do-nothing brother, hanging upon him, what then?

He advised a little moderation and patience. It might be better to take the wages now, and wait until spring —

"They doant give up any thing, as we sees," broke in an elderly English weaver. "The great house is full of every thing, and coal eno' burning in the greenhouses to ripen a few bunches of grapes out of God's own season, as would keep many of us warm. Who puts our coal down a dollar in the ton, or takes it off of house-rent when wages come down? I'll work as cheap as the next one if ye'll gi' me a cheap house to live in and cheap beef and bread. I doant care for money in the savin's bank, or a house that they tax all out o' sight. When I'm old I'll go to the poorhouse, I will; but I'm danged if I like starvin' before then, and they a-ridin' over us in their carriages. I left 'em over yonder" — with a nod of the head — "for that."

"What do you think of it?" asked a thin, hungry-looking man, fingering his Cardigan nervously. "See here! If I could have one more prosperous year, I'd be through the woods, have the house I've worked so hard for settled upon my old woman, and would be out of the reach of misfortune. But this thing hits me hard, it does."

"I don't believe striking will succeed just now," said Jack candidly. "And it's a bad time. Two or three weeks lost time will more than cover the odds in wages."

"I don't want to lose time. I'd rather keep straight on."

"It's the principle of the thing," broke in another. "I'd lose six months before I'd give in an inch. I'd have struck the other time."

There was a call for the overseers, and Jack left the group. Eastman was talking to several of the men in his office. A fine, portly figure he had, indicating rich living and good wines; a man still on the sunny side of forty, stout, rather florid, a full dark beard and hair, but with eyes that were light and furtive; eyes that could stare you out of countenance, and yet not meet yours ordinarily, with a frank, outward look. He always went handsomely dressed, and wore diamond shirt-studs, an expensive seal-ring, a substantial watch-chain with two or three costly charms. He had not a flashy look, but the sign and seal of gentlemanliness was wanting in that intensely selfish face.

He had heard of the disaffection. There was not much to say except that the new scale of prices would go into effect next Monday morning. He never asked a man to work for any less wages than he, the workman, considered his services worth. Here was the work, and the wages Hope Mills could afford to pay. They could take it, or leave it. There were plenty of men at Coldbridge, thrown out by the failure of Kendrick & Co., who would be glad to come. He could fill any vacant place.

But the ball grew and grew by handling. There were union-meetings and violent harangues, much of them

truth, too, but badly and unwisely used.   And the result
was that the men demanded the old wages, were peremp-
torily refused, and struck.   The great engine subsided,
and a Sunday stillness reigned.   Down at Hull's Iron
Works the same proceedings were going on, but the
saloons seemed to profit by it.

Jack hung around the mill for a while, then went down
stairs.   The chilliness in the air made him draw his
coat together by one button, and slip his hands into his
pockets.   He sauntered through several streets, nodding
to one and another, or exchanging a few words.   Once
again his advice was asked.

"I think you had better come to work to-morrow," he
said.   "Don't muddle your brains with beer or bad whiskey : that will not make the way any clearer."

"A good enough lad!" was the surly comment, "but
why grudge a man a sup of beer when he can't have
wine like the big folks?"

Jack had hardly planned for the enforced idleness.   He
did not want to go home and read, he could not call on
Sylvie thus early in the morning, neither did he feel in
the humor for argument with any of the men.   So he
stopped at the door of a small office, and turned the knob
rather hesitatingly.

"Hillo, Darcy, is that you?   Come in, come in!   Sullen gray day, isn't it?   Off on a strike, eh?"

Jack laughed, — the sound with no real music in it, the
sort of lip-service merely.

"Come in, old fellow; don't be afraid.   I've neither
pistol nor bludgeon, and I'll promise to treat you civilly."

The man's accents were clear and curt, with a certain
ring of out-door freshness, — a capital voice to travel
with up mountain-sides and through forests.   The face,
too, indicated a kind of joyous strength; for the blue
eyes were merry and baffling, the laughing lips a brilliant
scarlet, the nose neither Grecian nor aquiline, but slightly

retroussé; a bronze moustache with long curling ends that were undeniably red, and hair a little darker, slightly curling as well. A broad-shouldered man with the deep breathing of intense vitality; healthy nerves that could enjoy laziness to the full, as well as a brisk walk across the country.

A glance at the interior showed the place to be a doctor's office. On one side a long case with glass doors above and drawers underneath, filled with bottles and books and papers, perhaps in not the most systematic order; at the farther end a fire in an open-front stove; a luxurious Turkish lounge covered with russet leather, and a bright wool blanket thrown carelessly over it; several capacious armchairs; and in one, with his legs stretched out on another, sat Dr. Philip Maverick, eight and twenty or thirty years old, perhaps.

"How nice and cosey you are! I really did not know what to do with myself. Yes, we are all on a strike, I am sorry to say."

"Bad time," and Maverick shook his head. "What's the prospect? Have a cigar."

"The prospect is that the weakest goes to the wall, of course," answered Jack. "Maverick, I am dreadfully muddled on this point. I have thought of it all the week. It *is* hard on the men. I know the general advice is to economize more closely, but how can you do it just at the beginning of winter? One cannot move to a cheaper tenement, fire and lights cost more, and provision is a little dearer. Low living in winter does not conduce to a healthy state in the spring. Then, on the other hand, if they are going to make such sales as they did last month, they cannot pay the wages, and realize what they consider a fair profit. But why shouldn't the Lawrences and the Eastmans and many others give up something, as well?"

Jack turned an anxious face to his listener.

"All you manufacturers have been crazy the last few years," he said, delicately shaking the ashes from his cigar. "The country was such an extensive purchaser through the war, that your dreams became Utopian. Then everybody came home with some money and no clothes, and the people were large consumers. Now everybody has been clothed, and the stores are full, and here is a glutted market. Over-production, my dear fellow."

"Then I do believe it would be better to leave off for a while. Still that would not suit as well. Half a loaf is better than no bread, to a hungry man. But, after all," said Jack, knitting his brows, "I don't altogether believe in the cry of over-production. The boys of war times are men now. They are pushing in everywhere for work. They want food, shelter, raiment. There are a great many more people in this town than there were five years ago. Even if we only depended on the natural increase of population " —

"But, you see, people are forever crowding into cities," interposed Dr. Maverick.

"I have a fancy they do not come much faster than they are called," returned Jack dryly. "See what we have been doing around here. The small outlying farms have been bought up by speculators, cut up, destroyed for farming purposes. Their owners with families of children had to go somewhere. ' Come to the mills and factories,' was shouted in their ears, and they came. Now they are here, depending on their labor for bread, and Eastman will bring fifty or a hundred more from Coldbridge; and in the spring, if there is any difficulty, some more will come. The old ones cannot go back to their farms if they would. Their fertile gardens lie cut up into waste squares, their fruit-trees have been despoiled : they must starve here, or tramp to some other crowded town, and perhaps starve there. Will your farmer take in half a dozen hands at a moment's notice? Can they put themselves down in any country place, and go to work?"

Maverick studied Jack intently, and then gave a low whistle.

"Upon my word, Darcy, you *have* been going over the subject. Take the stump. And of course you go against capital?"

"No, I don't," returned Jack shortly. "Only it does seem to me that there ought to be some place where capital and labor could strike hands. It appears to me, both have been to blame. We cannot condemn men for crowding into cities, when there has been a steady call for them. We do blame them for not laying up a little money against a rainy day; but many of them have. Look at the cottages that have been sold to workingmen. Look at the bank savings. To-day, perhaps, as many poor men could pay their whole indebtedness, according to the ratio, as the rich. But we fly at the laboring classes, when it is only human nature cropping out. Your millionnaire puts his money into whatever he thinks will bring him the greatest return; your poor man puts his capital, his capacity, health, and strength, where it will earn him the most money."

"Well, I don't see but they are both right enough," said Maverick. "And unless you are running over into communistic ideas" —

"I am not," was the decisive reply. "Some one much wiser than I said, ages ago, ' He among you that will not work, let him not eat: ' yet," with a humorous laugh, "if the rule were strictly enforced, there would more than one go hungry, I'm thinking. The great consolation would be that the right man would suffer, not the innocent and guiltless."

"I really do not see what you are driving at, Darcy," and the other studied him curiously.

"Well, I told you in the beginning I was muddled. I don't pretend to see my way clear, only I think we have just begun the fight. It is as much of an irrepressible

conflict as that other, for which so many brave men gave
their lives. And one point in it no one seems to take
note of. We are proud of the increase of population in
our country. Every city, town, and hamlet boasts of it,
and the depopulated places run to slow decay. We welcome these people ; and yet they must eat to live, and the
majority of them must work, or they will have nothing to
eat. I think the most of them labor cheerfully, and my
experience is that idleness is the worst foe of man. But,
on the other hand, every year invention so protects and
fortifies capital, that one must do a larger business or employ fewer men. In five years the condition of labor has
greatly changed at Hope Mills, and in five years more it
will change again. This is the inexorable law of nature,
or, I ought to say, growing intelligence.''

"Then I should say we wanted wider markets and a
better classification of labor.''

A quick light came into Jack's eyes.

"I think you have hit it, Maverick,'' he answered.
"But what is everybody's business is nobody's; and we
are so apt to forget that the world does move, and the
condition of things changes all the time,'' and Jack's eyes
dropped thoughtfully.

"See here, Darcy, take Brock's Hall, and talk to the
men to-morrow night,'' began the doctor eagerly. "They
will listen to you because to a certain extent you are in
sympathy with them, one of their number ; and you do
seem to have some clear ideas on the subject. No: we'll
say Wednesday night, and I will get out some posters.''

Jack laughed. "What shall I tell them? I can't see
how to get about the remedy clearly myself. The trade-
unions have not hit it either. When they say to a man,
'Because I will not work for a certain sum, you shall not,'
they lean on a reed that will surely break, and pierce themselves. Hunger is stronger than theory. No: I shall
have to give the point a more thorough study before I
become a blatant apostle.''

Philip Maverick blew out a curling whiff of smoke, and looked at his visitor through it.   Darcy gave him a curious feeling, as if a good deal of excellent material were running to waste, that if shaped and trained, and brought up to higher purposes, might be of much good service to the world.   Did he realize it himself ?   He was twenty-four, and had a good position as things went ; and Dr. Maverick had heard the women of the house were prudent and thrifty, and had a nice home.   Was Darcy bounded in by conservatism, or afraid of losing? or was he honest when he said he did not know just what to do? Yet he did not look like the kind of man to go plodding all his days.

"Darcy, you puzzle me!" he began abruptly.   "With that great body of yours, those strong arms and hands that look as if they could wrest Nature's secrets from her mighty soul, with that brow, and the resolute mouth, it seems as if you ought to be in better business than making cloth : pardon me.   You don't use up half your energy.   You ought to be planning a ship-canal across Darien, or tunnelling mountains.   You're the square man ; and how upon earth did you ever get fitted so smoothly to a round hole?"

Jack laughed, and told his story very simply.   To him there was neither romance nor heroism in it, just a plain every-day sort of compulsion.   The tunnelling would have been much more to his mind.

"Go on with the problem," said Dr. Maverick abruptly.   "In the next five years I think we will all have use for our wits.   We are going to see another change in matters, that will require more wisdom than is needed in mere money-making.   See here, I'm interested in the thing. Let us go out, and hear what the men say about it."

Maverick rose, and put on his great-coat, and lighted another cigar.   Then the two started together.

Maverick had been in the town just six months.   He

had studied medicine in Philadelphia and Paris, taken a
three-years ramble over Europe, when a college friend
begged him to come to Yerbury, and step into a vacant
place.   And he had what he fancied an excellent reason
for it.

CHAPTER VIII.

The men were, for the most part, in sullen earnest. From their narrower outlook they could not see that capital was on the eve of a great revulsion; that credit had been stretched to its utmost. They had their own pet plans, their own indolences and careless habits; and, as was natural, their own desires were the sweetest to them.

There were labor-meetings and harangues. There was a good deal of talk about the rights of labor and the tyranny of capital; of the rich mill and factory owners living in palaces, and the men in hovels; of what England had done, and of what we surely were coming to, — the rich growing richer, and the poor poorer. But Jack remarked that of the speakers there was not one who owned a little plot of ground, or had a bank-account. Two of them were disaffected English weavers, a third an Irishman, and the only Yerbury man was a quick-tongued, but shiftless fellow who had started in business for himself, and failed; a kind of handy Jack-at-all-trades, and correspondingly good for nothing.

Before the close of the week the men in Watkins's shoe-shop had struck. There was quite an army of them now. The saloons were filled daily and nightly. Jack thought, with a little grimness, that they might better save their money for next week's bread.

Several of the men in his room dropped in to see what he thought; and the result was, that on the following Monday morning ten of them presented themselves with a tolerably cheerful demeanor, and accepted the situation. By

Tuesday night every vacant place was filled with hungry, haggard-looking men from Coldbridge. They were jeered at, and annoyed in various ways: the Yerbury men were called rats and turncoats and cowards. The mills were driven. There was another great and successful sale; in fact, amid the failures and difficulties about, Hope Mills loomed up like a star of the first magnitude.

In the spring Mrs. Eastman and Miss Lawrence went to Europe; and Fred joined a party of young men on a pleasure-tour through California. Even Mrs. Lawrence was persuaded to try Saratoga in the summer. The great house was muffled, and left in the charge of servants; but greenhouses, graperies, and all the elegant adjuncts were cared for as assiduously as ever. David Lawrence used to think it over. Sometimes he was tempted to sell out his palatial residence, but who was there to buy? Other men had been caught with just such elephants on their hands. The papers were full of offers " at an immense sacrifice."

Business grew duller and duller. There was a very great overplus of every thing, it seemed, in the world. Harvests were so abundant, and prices so low, they were not worth the moving. Fruit lay and rotted on the ground: you could get nothing for it. And yet there were wan-eyed and hungry women and children who would have feasted regally on this waste. Mothers of families turned and patched and darned, and said there could be no new garments this winter, while store-shelves groaned under the accumulation of goods. Men were failing on this side and that; the Alton & West Line Railway stock came down with a crash, and banks were shaky. Hope Mills were closed for a month to make some repairs, as business was rather slow just now.

There was a great quaking in real estate as well. The large property-owners held on stiffly: times would improve; land was worth more to-day than ever, because every year there were more people, and they required more houses, and the thing would somehow right itself.

Jack had taken his two feminines off to a great roomy farmhouse, where they had a horse at their command. Sylvie and Miss Barry were summering at the White Mountains. Dr. Maverick found a good deal of sickness among the poorer classes, low fevers and various troubles, that he knew well enough came from insufficient diet. But what was to be done? There was so little work, so much lost time, the inexorable rent, and the importunate grocer's bill. Up on Hope Terrace the luscious grapes fell to the ground, and were swept up as so much litter; the fresh, lovely vegetables passed their prime unheeded, and were tossed in the garbage-pit.

September came in hot and sultry. Hope Mills started, but many another place did not open. There was a strange, deathly-quiet undercurrent, like the awful calm before a thunder-shower. Wages took another tumble, and now no one had the courage to make much of a fight.

The second week in October there came an appalling crash. Yerbury Bank closed its doors one morning, — the old bank that had weathered many a gale; that was considered as safe and stanch as the rock of Gibraltar itself; that held in trust the savings of widows and orphans, the balance of smaller business-men who would be ruined: indeed, it would almost ruin Yerbury itself.

There was the greatest consternation. People flew up the street, bank-book in hand; but the dumb doors seemed only to give back a pitiless glance to entreaties. What was it? What had happened? "Every penny I had in the world was in it," groaned one; and the saddening refrain was repeated over and over, sometimes with tears, at others with curses.

The old officers of Yerbury Bank had been men of the highest integrity. Some were dead; some had been pushed aside by the new fast men who laughed at past methods, as if honor, honesty, and truth were virtues easily outgrown. Among these were the Eastmans. George was considered shrewd and far-sighted, and for two years had been one of the directors, as well as Horace. They paid the highest rate of interest, which attracted small savings from all around. There had been no whisper or fear about it, so solid was its olden reputation. There were people who would as soon have doubted the Bible.

Two days after this, George Eastman sailed for Europe, on a sudden summons, — his wife's illness. There had been a meeting called, and a short statement made. Owing to sudden and unexpected depreciation in railway-bonds and improvement-bonds, and what not, it was deemed best to suspend payment for the present. In a few weeks all would be straight again, with perhaps a trifling loss to depositors. Already the directors had been very magnanimous. Mr. Eastman and several others had turned over to the bank a large stock of mortgages: in fact, the virtue of these men was so lauded that the losses seemed to be quite thrown into the background.

But the examination revealed a sickening mass of selfishness and cupidity; transactions that were culpably careless, others dishonorable to the last degree. If the larger depositors had not been warned, there was certainly a remarkable unanimity of thought, as, for the past fortnight, they had been steadily drawing out their thousands. Wild railroad-speculations, immense mortgages on real estate that now lay flat and dead: scanty available assets that would hardly pay twenty cents on a dollar.

This was what David Lawrence heard when he returned from St. Louis, a heavy-hearted, dispirited man. Two recent failures had borne heavily upon him. If last winter had been dull, there was no adjective to apply to this. His first step was to mortgage Hope Terrace. He had deeded it to his wife, unincumbered; but now it appeared his only chance of salvation. Mrs. Lawrence made a feeble protest at first, and demanded that Fred should be sent for, but there was no time. He met his pressing notes, and was tided over; but, oh! what was to be the end of it all?

An indignation-meeting was called; and so high ran popular feeling, that new directors were appointed for the bank. Mr. Lawrence would have fain declined, but the community insisted. In this time of general distrust, they came back to the loyal gentleman, who, whatever his pride might be, had never deceived one of them.

Alas! had he not enough perplexity of his own, that this new sorrow and shame should stare him in the face, bow him to the earth?

Not his own son, thank God! not any blood kin; and yet his daughter's husband, his fair Gertrude, of whom he had been so proud years ago! He went back suddenly to that old time, and seemed to see them all again as little children, a merry household; and his pale, delicate Fred, for whom his heart beat so anxiously. How they had welcomed his coming! — a son to hand down the name, a son to lean upon in his old age. Nay, those were the extremes of life: why should not men count on their sons through the burden and heat of middle life? Why wait until the evening for comfort?

Where was he now? Did he think of the one who had toiled that he might spend? for, now that he looked at it with awesome calmness, like a thing standing apart, it was one long, dreary pilgrimage of toil. To what end? Was gathering together riches the noblest use of a man made in God's image? Ah, how poor and paltry an aim!

Surely he had done something beside that! A pleasant home of culture and artistic beauty, a circle of refined people gathered about him, the evil and want and woe of the world shut carefully out by silken curtains and plate-glass. His daughters he had been proud of. No

mésalliance, no common tastes, as he had sometimes fancied that he had detected in that pretty little Sylvie Barry.
And his son?

There had been no positive evil in his life. A young
man's follies perhaps, but few vices, if any, thank God!
He would never be a libertine, a drunkard, a gambler, a
thief. But was negative goodness all? These twenty-
four years spent in shaping and culturing, but to what
end? Could he call him back from his pleasure now, and
have him take up this struggle grown too heavy to fight
single-handed? and would he be manful, brave, clear-
sighted, and unrepining? No. He felt the change would
be too great. The soul so used to ease and luxury, fine
linen and soft couches, delicate appetites, indolent habits,
intellectual pursuits and graces, to be put in rough harness
of business at once, would be cruel, nay, worse, like
chaining humming-birds to a dray-wagon. And Irene,
flitting like a butterfly through elegant *salons*, how would
she be content with poverty and a cottage?

And was this all the work of his own hands? Had he
laid up no treasure against the time of adversity, made
no homes into which he might be received in his trial hour?
For two years he had struggled manfully, earnestly; and
all this time at his very gate there had been a traitor,
turning aside the stream until there was nothing but a
barren desert left.

The crown of his life was poverty and ruin! For himself he could give up luxuries, and come to plain fare; but
what of the others? This last news had swept away all
hope.

He sought Horace Eastman, and confronted him with
his deceit and wrong: somehow he could not bring himself to call it by its true name, crime, and fasten it on
the man there and then. There was a high-bred delicacy
about David Lawrence, a little of the old knightly chivalry that in past times held a man back from striking a

fallen foe.   And then he was not quite sure.   The dishonorable work lay between the two men, and he forbore to blame this one wrongly.

He need not have wasted his pity on this man, or have so nicely worded his charges. Horace Eastman stood there, surprised to be sure, for he had counted upon getting away before this turn in the wheel of fortune. For the last year, though he had been outwardly triumphant, and had carried business matters with a hopefully high hand, he had known what the end must be, and made ready for it with a kind of exultant elation at the sense of difficulties surmounted and deceptions carried on successfully. He really despised the man before him, that he had sufficient faith in human nature to be deceived. Starting from the principle that all men are rogues when opportunity offers, he felt no more guilty now, than if he had followed any other well-known law of nature. He stood before Mr. Lawrence bland and composed: there was no vulnerable point to strike, so he need put on no armor. Many a time he had reasoned the matter out to his own satisfaction, that the failure of Hope Mills was inevitable. What with losses, dull times, and extravagant living, it would surely come. That he owed his employer any thing in integrity and sharp fighting with adverse circumstances, would never enter the mind of such a man, so inwrapped in self.

"There were some irregularities for your son-in-law's benefit," with an insolent half smile, half sneer. "He was to explain them to you. There have been accommodations for the mills occasionally. You were away : what else could I have done?"

A cold shiver ran over David Lawrence. That part of courage allied to hope seemed crushed out of him as if by torture. Could he drag his daughter's name through the mire? for it would be that in any attempt to bring Eastman to the point of responsibility.

"Do you know how much this — this defalcation will amount to?" He would call the monstrous thing by its right name now, though he shuddered in every limb, and a cold perspiration stood in great beads about his thin temples. A third person witnessing his hesitation might fancy him faltering and shrinking in the path of dishonor, rather than the other.

"I really have no idea," bracing up his broad, full shoulders with portentous dignity: "George managed that matter. No doubt there are some memoranda," pausing with an indifferent air as if it were a matter of a few dollars.

"The bank must be made good, Mr. Eastman."

"Well; as you think best, as you think best;" nodding confidently, as if the repayment were the easiest thing in the world. "Let me see, — would it not be better to write to George?"

What impression could he make upon this man? To appeal to conscience, justice, or any latent sense of right, would be a waste of words. With him success was right, and failure the blunder or sin. He was to "do well unto himself," to gain the world's verdict of approval. That solid flesh made by good eating and drinking, not debauchery or intemperance, — the man had few of these gross vices, — that complacent strength, that keen, concentrating force than could bend all energies in the one direction, never looking back when he had once set his mind to a thing, experiencing no remorse for those he crushed under his feet so long as he went to success over them, knowing · no disinterestedness, trading simply upon the credulity, honor, and honesty of others: he had chosen him for some of these very qualities. Do men gather grapes of thistles?

"Bring the books to my office. I shall go over them to-night," was the haughty command.

Eastman bowed and withdrew. The books were sent by the errand-boy. Then he threw himself into his lux-

urious Russia-leather chair, rested his feet upon the edge
of the desk, settled his hands comfortably in his pockets,
and began to consider. A man would be foolish to stay
and be caught in the ruin of a falling house. He might
not be crushed, to be sure ; but there would be the *débris*,
and he had no fancy for clearing that away. Not only
the mills, but Yerbury, would fall flat. He did not care to
retire to a garden, and raise strawberries and corn : the
clink of gold was more melodious to his ear than the
voices of nature. There was a place for talent like his :
the quick sight and keen discrimination were still able to
give the rusty old world a lift out of ruts it had stopped
in, and send it on with a rush. He had money in some
silver-mines : he might go West, and attend to that, then
take a run over to England, and see George. After all,
was George really to blame for getting hold of his wife's
portion? He had married Miss Lawrence, believing in
good faith that she was the daughter of a millionnaire ;
and, if he had been sharp enough to save something from
the general ruin, lucky for him !

On the whole, Mr. Eastman thought it would be well
to go to New York for a few days until the storm blew
over. Jeffries the book-keeper could attend to all that
was needed. Mr. Lawrence would find Hope Mills in a
bad plight, to be sure ; but he would not be the first man
who had come to ruin. Mr. Eastman put his desk in
order, — he never kept any tell-tale papers, — walked leisurely out of Hope Mills with that serene, impassable
face and high heart no misfortune could daunt.

David Lawrence spread the books open before him.
It would be an endless task. One fact kept burning into
his brain like fire. The Eastmans, or Hope Mills, owed
Yerbury Bank seventy thousand dollars, the hard earn-
ings and self-denials of poor and middle-class people.
How it stung his haughty pride, unused even to dishonorable thoughts ! If he had been an exact master, he

had also been a just and honest one. Shame and disgrace stared him square in the face, where they would have but looked askance at Horace Eastman.

It had been quite impossible to take cognizance of every thing after the business grew so unwieldy. Then he thought of his son again with passionate longing. Never had he so wanted some of his own kin to lean upon, to take counsel with, to consider what must be done toward saving honor: that was no social figment with him, but a deep, heaven-abiding truth.

Heaven! By some strange turn of thought it entered his mind. He was so tired, he had been so tired for months and months, so engrossed with cares and business, that he had hardly stepped inside a church. How they used to go in the old days; how proud he had been of his four pretty children, of his tall handsome girls, and his manly son! Respectability, and setting a good example,—these had been his motives for church-going. Bits of sermons came back to him: how strange that he could remember them! There was a rest from labor, a refreshing of soul. Oh, how dark and arid, how confused and chaotic, his felt! Was there a something he had never known?

Then he pulled himself together mentally, roused his dreaming brain, and said something must be done. Fred must come back, and face the terrible truth. As well send for him now.

He wrote out a message, and rang the bell. A tall, slim youth answered it.

"I want this telegram sent immediately," he said in his quiet tone of command. "Is Farrell anywhere about?"

"I can take it, sir, if you please: I often do."

"Very well."

Back to the books again with their long lines of figures. Did he think he would find the shame and ruin here in bold black and white? He studied them until they all ran together, and his brain seemed to become a mass of luminous light with black motes floating about in it. The tense agony abated. Strange visions haunted him, frivolous fancies, and wonders that had puzzled him in boyhood; heroic fragments of bygone declamation; the incidents of a week ago; a picture of some bold scenery, and he in the cars, whirling by.

"Am I going crazy?" he asked with a ghastly expression. Then he took several turns about the room, listened to the noise of the great engine, and assured himself that he was sane.

Had he better go home? He was so tired! In all his life he had never been so utterly exhausted. Then in a sudden, fretful mood of contradiction he wondered he should think of fatigue when his limbs felt strong, and his body knew no physical pain.

"I must shake it off!" he declared resolutely. Of what avail would be going home to a wife's peevish complaints, and sit by himself to study out this tangle? As well stay here, and master it. And that palace yonder was home, and these were the comforts for which he had spent his years and his energies! This was what he had laid up. An inheritance incorruptible — why would these things come back to him?

The mill-bell began its clang. He listened to the tramp through the passage-ways, the confusion of voices. He went to the window. The great gates for the work-hands were around on the other side; but he could see the motley procession filing down the street. Not gay and cheerful as in bygone days: they seemed to drag along, these girls and women in shabby clothes, their shawls drawn around their shoulders. Old men and boys — why, where had vigorous middle life disappeared? So many faces had a hard, discontented look, that pierced him like the sharp point of ingratitude. Had he not brought himself to ruin to give the people employment? If he had shut down the mill three years ago, he would have been a rich man.

Well, why had he not? Was it thought for them? Had the prospect of their starving lain heavily on his soul?

Ah, the love of money-getting, the fiend of covetousness! But what would these people have done? Some one had once said, "What is that to thee? Follow thou me." Was it in a sermon?

He lighted the gas, and went on wearily with his books. Some one opened the door softly, and peered in. It was Farrell, the day-man. When he saw Mr. Lawrence he touched his cap respectfully.

"Pardon me, sir: I saw a light" —

"Yes, I am going to stay — all night, I think: I shall be busy. When does the night-man come?"

"At seven, sir."

"I will send a note up to Hope Terrace, Farrell. Could you take it?"

The man thought of his long day's work and his waiting supper. "Yes," he answered rather reluctantly.

"Stop in, then, when you go."

Farrell went off grumbling. He would go home to supper first, that he would. These men had no souls. That long walk — Some people always rode in chaises, were born with silver spoons in their mouths, and looked on the rest of the world as mere lackeys!

There was some wine in the closet, and Mr. Lawrence took a glass to clear his brain. He rarely used it save at dinner. Then back to the tormenting books, — columns of business that appeared incredible now. How had all this money slipped away?

Farrell tapped, and came in.

"Jackson's here now, sir. Is the note ready?"

"Yes. There is some change. Get a hack, Farrell: it is too far to walk. Did Mr. Eastman" —

There was so long a pause that Farrell said, —

"Mr. Eastman went to New York. He said he might not be back to-morrow."

Mr. Lawrence nodded, as if that were sufficient. He would not peer into the man's business.

"If you should want any thing, sir, Jackson will be at hand," said the man kindly; for the thin, pale face, and strange, nervous light in the eyes startled him.

"Jackson," he began, when outside, "Mr. Lawrence is going to stay a bit, maybe all night. He has a great pile of books before him; but I'm afraid he's queer some way. His eyes look wild and strange. Keep a lookout, will you" —

"You don't mean that he's likely to shuffle? Are things as bad as that? Has he got a pistol?"

"I don't know, I'm sure. Maybe I'm wrong;" and Farrell counted over the money in his hand. "Anyhow, I would walk up and down this hall, and listen."

Jackson nodded, and Farrell went his way; yet now he thought the brisk walk would not hurt him. Jackson heeded his bidding, but all was quiet. Once he went in the next room, and climbed up to a high sliding window, used for ventilation. Mr. Lawrence sat there poring over the books. At twelve it was the same. Jackson tolled off the hour of midnight. Every thing was safe in the great building. Then he settled himself in an easy-chair, and presently fell into a doze.

Meanwhile Mr. Lawrence studied the books in a dazed, bewildered way. Here and there a balance had been struck, and it all looked fair. But there was a terrible wrong somewhere !

The figures danced before his eyes in lurid lights and grotesque shapes, with grinning faces, flying, whirling, in a wild, demoniac waltz. The room was full. The procession he had watched to-night winding out from the mill, stopped and jeered, and pointed skinny fingers at him.   Then he was at the bank, and they came in troops, wringing their hands, and cursing him. Strange tales that he had read mixed with them in inextricable confusion. Pictures of the past hurried by with panoramic distinctness; and hark! what was that? The grand trump of the Judgment Day? It tolled and tolled again, like a thunder-peal. Was any one dead?

He was so tired! He put his arms down on the desk, and leaned his face on them. If he could sleep off this intolerable weariness!

He was a boy again, wading through the limpid brook, stepping from stone to stone, and sometimes plashing over. Was that the dried sweetness of balsam, — the pungent odor of pennyroyal and water-mint, — the clean, resinous fragrance of the pines? Out there were lily-pads, — great golden-hearted chalices, with long, sinuous greenish-pink stems under the shady, transparent water. How cool and peaceful! The sky overhead was of. palest blue with white flecks, and somewhere a bird was singing. If he could go to it; if he could stay amid all this sweet quiet, and forget — What was it he wanted to forget? Not his little Fred, surely! How proud he should be of him in his manhood. What a help and comfort!

There was a strange, sudden darkness. The head drooped a little one side, and the visions had come to an end.

CHAPTER IX.

When Farrell returned to his post in the morning, Jackson reported Mr. Lawrence asleep in the office. No one thought of him again until about ten o'clock, when some protested notes came in. Jeffries knocked at the door, opened it softly, spoke, but received no answer; then stepped nearer, and peered curiously at the face. It was ghastly white, the eyes wide open and staring, and with a shriek Jeffries alarmed the whole establishment.

Old Dr. Lecounte came, pronounced him dead, and then sent for Dr. Maverick, to whom he had taken a great liking. Between them both they found a faint sign of life ; and he was removed to his elegant mansion on Hope Terrace, where his wife went into immediate and violent hysterics. They remained several hours, and decided it to be that terrible death in life, entire paralysis of brain, nerve, and muscle. He might linger some days ; he might drop away any moment.

Horace Eastman, looking over the news items the next morning, saw this account, and returned at once to Yerbury. Certainly fortune had favored him. Affairs were in wild confusion. He learned that a telegram had been sent to young Mr. Lawrence, and an answer received. He would be back next Monday. Mrs. Minor came up, and brought an experienced nurse.

The mill kept open until Saturday. Then Mr. Eastman called the men together.

He was very much puzzled to know what to do, he said. He had resigned his position as superintendent

of the mills, nearly a month ago ; but Mr. Lawrence had
begged him to stay on until he could come to some
decision.   The affairs were in a very embarrassed condition, and now suspension was imperative.   What Mr.
Lawrence would have done, he could not tell ; but he did
not feel justified in taking the responsibility.   He was
most truly sorry — he could say it from his heart — for
those whose cheerful faces and light steps he had watched
year after year, until he came to have a friendly feeling
for them all ; and he was shocked at the result of all this
trouble to his dear friend, to whom he was bound by a
deeper tie than that of mere business.   But there had
been two years of unparalleled depression, and Mr. Lawrence had made a brave fight.   No one beside himself
knew all the difficulties that had beset his old friend's
path.   It was not only here in Yerbury that trade was
dull : it was from the Atlantic to the Pacific.   England,
Germany, and France were suffering as deeply as ourselves.   Production had been overdone by most of the
employers using their best efforts to keep their hands
at work in the face of a falling market, or no market at
all.   Shelves were packed with goods everywhere.   We
were on the eve of a great change, and it would be some
time before values would become stable again.   If the
balance of trade (high-sounding, but imperfectly understood term) could once more turn in our favor ; if we
could export our surplus goods, and find new markets, —
as no doubt we would, — every shop and factory would
soon be ringing with the cheerful sound of labor.   It
would be a hard winter ; but he, for one, believed the
spring would open auspiciously, that business would revive, homes be prosperous, and every heavy heart light.
Let them all take courage for their own future and that
of Hope Mills in the hands of its young master.   He
regretted deeply that there was no money to pay them
with to-night ; but that would doubtless be attended to

soon. He wanted to bid them a cordial good-by, and beg them to stand by young Mr. Lawrence.

There was some rather faint cheering. Troubled eyes questioned despondent eyes; what were they to do with winter coming on? First it was the bank, now the mills, and what next God only could tell.

Fred Lawrence reached Yerbury Monday evening; and at midnight the faint, fluttering soul of his father passed over that mighty river. There had been no return to consciousness. Mrs. Lawrence still lay in her darkened room, unable to bear any sound beyond that of the trained nurse.

To say that Fred was shocked, would feebly express his emotion. He had never dreamed of his father's dying, — never dreamed of any thing like misfortune happening to him, of any keener suffering than some temporary annoyance. He felt quite helpless. His old philosophies did not inspire him with courage, or open a way out of this dark present. There was to be a funeral; there were business complications; some one had to think of the future; the mill was shut up, the fortune swept away, and he had been stranded on a strange shore, knowing not which way to turn.

Eastman was still in Yerbury. He was intensely sympathetic with the bereaved family. In fact, now that he would never have to meet the eye of the man he had so deeply wronged, his spirits rose, his pity overflowed. Fred was quite touched by it. Hamilton Minor, with his rather brusque business ways, jarred against his sorrow.

He was rather testy with Mr. Eastman. "For the life of me, I can't see how things have come to this pass," he said sharply. "Hope Mills has been considered as sound as a nut, — one of the surest places in the country. Mr. Lawrence has made thousands and thousands. I have known a good deal about his affairs."

"It is the result of a large-hearted philanthropy, — of

keeping poor devils at work when there was no demand
for goods, so that they should not starve. I should have
closed out the concern two years ago. When you begin
to lose, it is time to get out, —,not wait until every stiver
is gone. But, if ever there was a noble man, it is our
dead friend David Lawrence.''

His chest swelled as he pronounced this eulogy, and he
laid his white hand sympathetically on his waistcoat.

" What is all this bank muddle about? ''

" I really don't know. Heavy real-estate business '' —

" And you a director ! '' interrupted Minor, with an un-
pleasant quickness.

" I have had so much on my hands that I did not pay
strict attention to it, I must confess. You know, Minor,
what a tremendous shrinkage there has been in values :
it seems to me as if the bottom had fallen out of every
thing. I have an interest out in Nevada that I am
anxious to look after, and should have gone a year
ago, but Lawrence begged me to hold over until matters
brightened a little. He was so sure times would improve.
By Jove ! I think they grow worse and worse ! ''

" And Fred knows no more than a baby ! '' said Minor,
in a tone of contempt. " You'd be a help to him, Eastman, if you would stay and go over accounts.''

" I don't know about that,'' shaking his head slowly.
" The books are all on the square, as you will see. If
one could only make money as easily as one can add up
that which has been made and spent ! '' and Eastman gave
a little laugh.

" But it cannot be a total loss. The house, I know, is
settled upon Mrs. Lawrence. And the mill-property '' —

" Mortgaged for all it is worth in such times as these.
Perhaps I ought not to speak of it, but George was in a
little difficulty which the old gentleman tided over. Too
much real estate, Minor ! ''

Hamilton Minor had no great amount of confidence in

the man before him; but then, he did not have in any one. He was on a little of the paper, and just now he felt exceedingly dubious about it. Some arrangement ought to be made whereby members of the family who had stood by Mr. Lawrence ought not to be losers.

The funeral was strangely quiet and solemn; I was about to add, select. The mill overseers and officers were formally invited. Fred had a feeling about the men, — it seemed as if they ought to form a procession; but the walk to the cemetery was a long one, and Mrs. Minor decisively negatived any plan that took in the "rabble." The coffin lay in the spacious drawing-room, where friends and acquaintances, in the same set, nodded solemnly, and uttered a few words of well-bred condolence. The mourners were up-stairs. The few coaches were filled with men, a little group stood around the open grave, and David Lawrence passed out of mortal sight, — his life-work all done. Had the toil been worth the reward?

The next day Eastman left for New York, and his stay there was brief. He knew what would be surmised after much trouble and searching, but it could not be positively laid at his door. And with a cheerful heart he set out to seek a new fortune.

To the great surprise of Mr. and Mrs. Minor, they found Hope Terrace mortgaged. Mrs. Lawrence could talk of nothing, could not endure the confusion of voices in her room. Some trustees were appointed to investigate the whole affair, for Fred was as ignorant as a child of all pertaining to the mill.

The examination disclosed a pitiable state of affairs. George Eastman had built up Yerbury on borrowed capital, lived on it in luxury, speculated, lost and won like any other gaming. He had persuaded each individual that he was on the high road to wealth. There had been a peculiar fascination about the man; or is it that the appeal to greed and covetousness is so much more convincing than that to honor and truth, that the baser impulses are quicker with their response? It was a great bubble upon credit, and carried with it the seeds of self-destruction. True, the bank held mortgages on rows of flimsy-built houses where walls were cracking apart, foundations settling, plumbing in such a condition that it was a hot-bed of disease. They would not cover the indebtedness. The available cash had been drawn out by large depositors, the best bonds and stocks surreptitiously sold. And with all this there was a defalcation traceable to Hope Mills or the Eastmans. The money had gone in that direction. On the other hand, it was proven by the income of Hope Mills, and the amount paid out for labor, that there was no reason why they should not be solvent to-day.

Lavishly as the Lawrences had spent money, they had not taken it all. No one could or did accuse David Lawrence of private speculation. Minor had once tried his best to induce him to join in some enterprises, but failed. It was an easy matter to blame the Eastmans for every thing: they were away, and could not deny the charge. But had all these bank-officials clean hands? They had been given a sacred trust, the savings of the poor, the estates of widows and orphans; they had winked at investments of the most precarious kind; they had paid a high rate of interest, exacting a higher, which had been gladly given for a brief while. Safe principles of finance had been quite ignored: the new era was different from any thing that had ever happened to the world before, and required new men, and now they would have to go back to the old way. Surely there is not much that is new under the sun!

To bring back the Eastmans, and try them for their crimes, seemed hardly worth while. More than one man in Yerbury felt that it was safer to berate them at a distance, than meet their damaging retorts face to face.

They could not get back any money. Hope Mills was ruined beyond a peradventure, and the affairs of the bank were best wound up as speedily as possible. There could be no large stealings for a receiver, consequently no occasion for delay. The sooner the wrecks and *débris* were cleared away, the quicker the moral atmosphere would be purified. There are wounds for which the instant cautery means life, the careful hesitation death.

And now every one looked at the exploded bubble in surprise, and cried angrily, "What has become of the money? Yesterday we were rich: where has it gone to? Six months ago we had twenty per cent dividend: why are these stocks worthless now? Why have railroads and shops and mills ceased to pay? What sudden blight has fallen over the world?"

Alas! There had been no money. Sanguine credit had traded on the honor and faith and nobleness of man toward man, and, behold, it had all been selfishness and falsehood and dishonor. Truth and virtue had been scorned and flouted in the highway, because forsooth there was a more brilliant semblance. Like a garment had men wrapped themselves in it, and now it was but rags and tatters.

There could be nothing extracted from the wreck of Hope Mills. Indeed, Fred would have given up a rich inheritance to save his father's honor, had it been his. To go on at Hope Terrace was madness. The fires and the servants would cost enough to maintain a family. Mrs. Minor and Fred quarrelled because Mrs. Lawrence had been persuaded to mortgage the place: she simply groaned and moaned, and wondered why they must worry her about every thing!

"I hope Irene will have the good sense to marry abroad," said Mrs. Minor. "And, Fred, what a pity you haven't a profession! What can you do?"

Last winter it had been, "my brother, De Woolfe,"

whom all the young ladies in Mrs. Minor's set were wild over.

Fred gave a sigh.

"I suppose I *can* do something to earn my bread," he replied bitterly.

"Fred," began Agatha suddenly, "there is that Miss Tillon. You know how absolutely wild she was over you last winter! Her fortune is all in her own right, and it is a solid one too. Hamilton has had occasion to know about it. You cannot do a better thing than marry her."

Fred glanced up. His sister was in sober earnest. To be bargained off like a woman, for a bare existence! Miss Tillon was at least thirty, of a suspicious, jealous turn of mind, well-enough looking perhaps, but narrow, with no intellectual culture, no approval of any thing beside her money. He had been amused at her preference. Possibly she might marry him, and rescue him from the pains of poverty. And he?

He might be vain and trifling, but he was not sunk so low in cowardice. His face flushed a vivid scarlet.

"I am not quite prepared to become chargeable to a woman yet," he said in a cold, calm voice.

"What nonsense! Some man will marry her, and get the money," Agatha retorted decisively.

"Not much of hers;" in a dry, contemptuous tone.

"You know what I mean. She will live in style, and travel; and her husband" —

"Will be the laughing-stock of his friends," interrupted Fred angrily. "No, Agatha, I will be dependent upon no one for my bread: if I cannot earn it I will starve."

"Oh, very well!" with a scornful smile. "I only hope Rene will be wiser. They are in Paris — I heard from Gertrude last week. She was very much shocked, of course. I hope George has not been foolish enough to let every thing slip through his fingers. Who could have believed that Horace Eastman would turn out such a swindler ! Papa trusted him altogether too far. It does not answer to be too noble and disinterested in this world.''

Fred made no reply to this charming bit of worldly wisdom. His delicate and high opinion of self had received a crushing blow. Married off, out of hand, to save him from poverty !

Why should his thoughts turn to Sylvie at that moment? Something stirred within him, an insane desire to win her — oh, mad enough, surely ! He could, he *would*, do something ! There was all his education and talent ; yes, he really had talent. He would make himself famous. She should see that he had the right kind of stuff in him. He would climb up the hard hill in his lonely, sorrowful, proud way, until she, looking on, would come to repent her unjust verdict !

He shut himself up in his study, and made some very fair translations from his beloved poets. There were better ones, doubtless ; and, after all, fame might not lie in that direction. There was physical science, much in vogue, and entertaining : no doubt he could do something in that line. There were theories and speculations, there were old philosophies — surely the ground was rich everywhere.

It was very poor at Yerbury, though there were theories enough. But, when you took them for temporal meat and drink, they were not a fattening diet. Men lounged in the streets and on the corners, or, worst of all, in saloons, talking themselves angry and hoarse over the bad luck, and blaming every one right and left. Women sat at home, and cried over losses and crosses, cooked their scanty dinners, and retired to bed early to save fuel. The poorer ones went out to a day's washing, glad to get that. Boys played cards, read dime-novels, and dreamed of wonderful fortunes at the West : some few stout-hearted chaps set out to seek them.

There were panaceas. Mr. Rantley preached the rankest communism and broadest free-thinking. Capital, i.e., money, was the tyrant of the world, and always would be until the laborers of the world rose up and claimed their rights. Why should this man starve when the man over yonder had his store-house full of flour that he was holding for higher prices? What right had he, except the might? So long as men were allowed to hoard up these monstrous fortunes, they could control the market, and would! What were the starving thousands to them? What if half the provision in the country rotted on the owner's hands? he could get as much or more money for the other half. What if the miners were at work only a small portion of time? could not the amount of coal be managed more easily, and prices kept up? Capital desired to keep production at the lowest ebb, because it could be more conveniently mastered. The only remedy was to give every man a chance, to break up these colossal fortunes, to have no great mills and mines; to have smaller capitalists, fewer hours of labor, to divide the immense hoards among the poor and needy until there should be no more want or suffering!

The Rev. Mr. Bristow shook his head at this modern anti-Christ. Every thing was anti-Christ, with Mr. Bristow, that went outside of his own narrow creed. He preached some stirring sermons. It was God's judgment upon them for their sins. They had forgotten him, they had been led away by false gods; they had made golden calves, and worshipped them; their sons had strayed into infidelity; their daughters had flaunted in gay attire, with plaiting of the hair, and dancing away their immortal souls; and now they must return to their God, to the meat that perisheth not, to the bread of life, and to the well of living water. There must be such a returning to God, such a revival of religion, that the world would be swept clear and clean out of its old sins!

"Splendid sermon! splendid sermon!" said Deacon Boyd, rubbing his hands together unctuously. "Parson's hit the nail just on the head. We've all strayed out of the way. I think a good old-fashioned revival'll set us straight sooner'n any thing. Nothing like coming to the Lord on the spot! This very week we ought to begin."

"I think you're right, Deacon Boyd," said grave Mr. Rising. "I, for one, will take hold of the work."

They called the church together, and began. I will not disparage the work. There were hungry souls that seemed fed with spiritual food, aching hearts that were bound up, reckless minds that paused on the verge of desperation. But there were others who wondered, even in the midst of the deacon's prayer, how it was that the Lord warned him to draw his twenty thousand dollars out of Yerbury Bank a week before the failure, when there were only he and his wife to keep, and let poor Mrs. Wharton with her five helpless children lose her husband's life-insurance, her little all, by putting it in the bank just a fortnight before the failure. Special providences, whereof Deacon Boyd discoursed so eloquently, happened oftener to the rich than to the poor.

However, they prayed and fasted and repented. To many, any strong emotion that took them out of the wearing round of thought was a blessing.

Jack Darcy, with a curious disbelief in every thing, went the rounds, and dropped into Maverick's office to talk it over. Sylvie was not home this winter: she and her aunt spent it in Philadelphia. Then Jack grew dull and restless. If the end of all things had come in Yerbury, he ought to try some other place in the great world.

It was settled presently quite by accident. A cousin of Mrs. Darcy's, one of your strong, thorough, energetic women, came to spend the winter with them; and Jack's mother, watching the throes of her son's soul, a little afraid of socialism, materialism, and all the other isms, proposed that Jack should take a journey West or South, and have a glimpse of the men and things beyond this narrow boundary.

"Grandmother grows feebler all the time now; and, being past ninety, we can't expect to keep her much longer. Of course, Jack, when she is gone, I shall have no tie but you; and, if it suited you to settle elsewhere, I should not object. You are young and ambitious, and I ought to think of your advancement. There never has been a time since your poor father's death that you could be so well spared;" yet the mother sighed. "And you have been a good son, Jack: you have given up many a wish cheerfully to two poor old women."

"Don't call yourself an old woman," said Jack almost gruffly, then he stooped to kiss her.

His heart gave a great boyish bound.

"Good-by, old Yerbury!" he cried exultantly one morning, quite sure of a new, glad life elsewhere.

"Though I shall be sorry to leave Sylvie and Maverick," he thought. "These old towns do grind the very soul out of a fellow who has any desire or energy in him. The world isn't all alike, I know," giving his chestnut mane a toss like a young, mettlesome colt.

CHAPTER X.

IF Jack Darcy had taken his tour for pure pleasure and enjoyment, the time was ill chosen in every respect. Winter was bad enough ; but an unprosperous one, full of financial clouds and storms, and scurrying drifts of distrust, was not calculated to make the way brilliant.

But he had one glorious enjoyment to begin with. He went straight to Niagara, and took his first glimpse of it in its awesome majesty of frost and ice. From that high exaltation we call worship, through every intermediate degree and sense of beauty, to that of a delicate and minute fairy dream. The winter sun radiating glowing tints, with skies of sapphire and opal, the great stretches of wordless wonder, bound hand and foot like some old Norse god amid his ice-fields ; the one night when a full moon silvered it with prismatic grandeur, and made of the glittering ice-crystals entrances to diamond-mines of fabled genii, touching him weirdly with this unearthly splendor ; and the next solemn day, when the very sky seemed chilled to unfallen snow, and the ice-caverns turned a dull blue, reminding him of descriptions of polar scenery, and filling his soul with a sense of boundless solitude.

Then he began his tour of the cities. He had taken some books along, whether to perplex or make clear his brains, he hardly knew. He pored over pages of Adam Smith, he turned to Ruskin for comfort, he picked up Brassey's figures and experience, and Stuart Mill's strong, kindly reasoning, and digested them in his own slow, practical, much-befogged way, trying to solve the problems.

It was a great and wonderful world. Little Yerbury had hardly any true idea what a mite she was, when one looked at the immense labor-fields of the West and apparently endless resources. Yet there was the same depression out here. Shops and mills closed, for sale, and to let; some running on three-quarter time, with half the number of workmen, others going on at ruinous competition; anxious, moody-eyed men walking the streets, or grouped on corners, their coats and hats shabby, their beards untrimmed, old boots and shoes with the heels tramped over at one side, or a bit of stocking showing through the leather. "No man hath hired us," said their despondent faces plainer than any words. Young men and boys offering to do any kind of work for any kind of pay, sleeping in station-houses; relief-stores, church charities and soup-houses, homes for the friendless, and all such places, filled to overflowing, and new hordes crowding in every day.

Yet there seemed to be no lack of money. It lay in banks, it went begging for good security. Where was there any good security? Every inch of ground, every building, stocks and furniture, were covered by mortgages. Stock companies trembled in the balance, and went down like card-houses. Everybody wanted to sell every thing, but there were no buyers. Everybody wanted to work, but there was nothing to do. Everybody was in a chronic state of grumbling; there was no profit to be made in farming, in manufacturing, in any thing. There had been too much over-production, for which every one blamed his neighbor. The great warehouses were full of grain, the mills loaded up with iron, the factories full of cloth and flannels and cottons; and yet people were going hungry and in rags. It was puzzling and painful. We had bought too much abroad, and sent the money out of the country, the balance of trade would make it all right again; there had been over-production, and now there must be a vigorous repression; there had been too much speculation in real estate; there had been too 'great an accumulation of capital in the business centres; we were fast verging to the state of older countries, where there were the few rich and the many poor: there was a surplus of labor, and was there not also a surplus of people?

There was another sad side to it all, that made Jack's heart ache. These young men and boys tramping through the country, begging or worse, swearing, telling foul stories, herding together anywhere, corrupting one another's morals, smoking, drinking, — somehow they managed to obtain these indulgences, — looking furtively out of languid, sodden eyes, their faces hard and worn, their voices coarse and gruff; and they were to be the next generation of what?' — loyal and honest citizens, or jail-birds?

It was not all so sombre. At five and twenty a healthy, unwarped nature is many-sided. There were countless marvels to see and to study. He stumbled over people who had known Mr. Lawrence, and who had a kindly feeling for a Hope Mills man. And he had done something more in the last eight years than merely learn how to make cloth. He had dipped into chemistry, and knew a little about dyes; he had studied up in grades and kinds of wool, and was interested in labor processes. With fresh opportunities he looked into it more closely, observed new methods of decreasing waste, or saving labor. He was a well-informed, well-mannered, sensible fellow; and occasionally some one would say of him, "A smart, long-headed chap, that! The world will hear of him some day, or I am mistaken."

He kept looking about for some place where, if the world did not hear of him, he might get a chance in some enterprise where he could take a few steps upward. There certainly were more men than places. The world was a bee-hive, surely; but alas for those who swarmed out in such times as these!

After he had gone as far West as Minnesota, he went

down the Mississippi to a different kind of civilization in the quaint old cities. It was none the less heart-sickening. He found traces of the war, that we had almost forgotten, fresh at every step; still it seemed as if the hand of Nature was much more bounteous than at the bleak North. Yet Bishop Heber's old missionary hymn rang continually through his mind. Even amid the Florida orange-groves, and the great cotton-fields, some cause brought about baleful results, in the unwisdom of man.

Then to the cities of luxury and thrift, where wealth was strong enough to crowd poverty out one side, where art and music and cultivation made a subtile atmosphere that somehow recalled the Lawrences. He lingered and quaffed delightsome draughts, and at last tore himself away from seductive sights and sounds. In a dim, half-defined way the delights came to him. Would he ever be stoic enough to spurn them?

Last of all, home with its sweet welcomes, its cleanliness and order, its familiar furniture and cheerful fires, its easy-chairs and quaint fragrant air, as if every thing had lain in dried rose-leaves; the mother love and tears, the smiles out of dimmer eyes, and cousin Jane Morgan's hearty greeting; to say nothing of his delicious supper and his own bed, where sleep seemed awaiting him with open arms.

His mother had written a good deal of Yerbury gossip to him, but it had been mostly of the pleasant order. When he dropped into Maverick's office the next day, and was welcomed so heartily that it was like a brother's greeting, he listened to the other side. Affairs were worse than ever. The bank had gone into liquidation, and would pay about forty per cent. Property mortgages had been foreclosed right and left; there was nothing, scarcely, doing; there had been want and misery and sickness, and now diphtheria was raging.

"So you see the revival didn't do every thing," said Maverick grimly. "I'm of the opinion, if some of them had preached less, and distributed bread and broth with a freer hand, it would have been more of a good work. The praying would be well enough in its place, and, for those old fellows who pray on a full stomach, very enjoyable, I dare say. But I'd like them to look after their drains and their wells and their cisterns before they ask the Almighty to sanctify these afflictions to the poor wretches who suffer from them. And now, Jack Darcy, what are you going to do? Have you found better pastures?" and Maverick glanced up with curious inquiry.

"No," replied Jack, rather reluctantly it must be confessed. It seemed to him now that he had been spending his time for nought, unless pleasure counted, and he felt a trifle ashamed of it.

Maverick gave an odd little laugh that puzzled the other.

"See here, Maverick," began Jack in such earnest that he blushed like a great boy, "I haven't found any new place for myself. The world seems just full and running over. The great cities have their own men out of employment, and hordes from every other place. I'd be almost ashamed to ask for a job. I declare, I'd rather raise as much of my living as I could in our back garden, or take Perley's farm, and put it together, and set men raising strawberries, than tramp round, asking for work, with a feeling that it was taken from some one who had a better right, who was a native of the soil."

"Then you have not lost your conscience?"

"I hope not. It is the same old story everywhere. What is to be done about it?" and Jack knit his brows. "I have been going over the books that I thought would help or let in a little light on the matter, but it is a wisdom hard to get at. How to make more work in the world, how to cheapen living, how to" —

"Bring about the millennium! What dead earnest you are in, Darcy!"

"Weren't you in earnest a moment ago, Maverick, when you talked about the praying and the bread and broth?" said Jack with a great knot drawn in his brow.

"Yes, Heaven knows. And some one must take hold of the thing who has eyes to see, and brains, and — and money. You see, people have crowded into cities and towns, and if they could be sent out somewhere! Why don't we organize colonies or something of the sort? Now, there's Florida. Living is cheap, and in such a climate there are fewer needs of clothing and fuel. I have been wondering why the big dons in cities did not gather up the poor they have been feeding at soup-houses and everywhere, and send them out with some one to manage until they could stand alone. There would be less diphtherias and fevers and starvation; for that's its right name, Darcy. What can you do when one's system is all run out with meal-mush, and weak tea that is half willow-leaves, and such trash? There's Kilburn — he has had the name of being good to the poor this winter because he has given them trust at his store. Such stuff! I have looked into a few samples," and the expressive nostrils curled in disgust. "He makes an enormous profit, for he sells the poorest kind of goods to these people at the highest prices. Then he manages to get hold of something, house or furniture, or maybe clothes, — I don't know. He and Deacon Boyd — Darcy, how can a man honor religion when these two men are its exponents? So good to the poor! Pah! It makes me sick. Isn't there a cleaner air somewhere on God's earth? Can't they be taken out of this?"

"If they could be! There must be one way out, Maverick: better, perhaps, than going West where thousands are tramping about. And Heaven knows they need a new factor in civilization down there!"

The young eyes met in sudden hopeful animation. Had they solved even one strand of the great tangle, that worse than Gordian knot which could not be cut?

The door opened slowly; and there entered a middle-aged, rather grizzled man, with shaggy eyebrows, sparse beard, and bent shoulders. He glanced in hesitatingly, his eyes wandering down to Darcy.

"I declare to man!" and he stared hard, with the door-knob still in his hand. "Jack Darcy! I heard you were home. How d'y do? How d'y do?" and he wrung the hand warmly. "I'm powerful glad to see you," and he looked him slowly over, from head to foot. "Why, you've grown, or something! What a great giant you are! — Morning, doctor," nodding rather incidentally to Maverick. "So you've had a long tramp, Jack? Your mother brought some of the letters over to my old lady, who has been rather poorly the last two months. Why, you could set up book-writing! Well, what's the good word? Can't be like Yerbury all over."

"There are too many towns full of idle people, if that is what you mean. But it was splendid, Cameron! I have one more dream, — to go up and down the Western coast, and over the Rocky Mountains; but I want to digest this first. I have no fancy for mental dyspepsia," and he gave a good, wholesome laugh.

"The right way, Jack," nodded Maverick, with a shrewd twinkle in his eye.

"Well, you've come back to a dull place, — a dull place," and Cameron shook his head despondingly. "We used to be main proud of old Yerbury; but — is the whole world to go on and starve to death, with such crops, and such an abundance of every thing?"

"We are going to weather it through, Cameron," Jack answered with a stubborn hopefulness. "There have been hard times before that have ended in renewed prosperity."

"Yes. There was '57; hard enough, Heaven knows, with the banks going to smash everywhere. It ruined my father. And way back in '37, when there was such a wild-fire about real estate, and it came out just as this has. Do people ever learn by experience, Maverick?" and the man gave a short, unmirthful chuckle. "You could buy up half Yerbury to-day, for taxes and mortgages. I can't, for the life of me, see how it all came about. And that it has gone all over the world,—well, human nature in England or Germany can't well laugh at human nature in this country.—Are these things like cholera and fevers, doctor, taking a clean sweep once in a while?" and Cameron gave a twist to the end of his faded beard, as if he might wring the secret out of it.

"We have learned to manage the cholera, and see in it, not a dispensation of Providence, but the natural result of filth and greed and carelessness. Darcy and I are getting up a panacea now," with a bright little laugh. "But how is Mrs. Cameron? Is her medicine out?"

"Yes;" and Cameron drew a phial from his pocket. "You don't think it would do to stop here? She's pretty well, I should say;" and he fingered the bottle as if he were debating whether to have it filled or not.

"No. She must go on. She is getting her strength back nicely; but it's bad policy to stop at three-quarters of the race,—eh, Cameron? The first warm day I'll take her out driving."

While he was talking, he reached out for the bottle, and began compounding. Cameron nodded an acknowledgment of the last sentence, then turning to Jack, said abruptly,—

"What was the scheme, Darcy?"

Jack flushed, and glanced at Maverick.

"Emigration, the old remedy," answered the doctor. "England has tried her hand at it pretty successfully; so why shouldn't we? Only we need not go out of our own country. There are thousands of acres of productive land lying idle, and thousands of people starving, or worse. Too many here, — not enough there."

"Where to?" Cameron asked laconically, his face unmoved by any ripple of enthusiasm.

Jack seemed to be put on his mettle by it. Lack of faith in him always roused his belligerent qualities, back in the old school days.

"Yes, Cameron," in an incisive tone, looking steadily out of his determined eyes. "The cities are crowded over and over, and full of tramps, and the West swarms with them. We need not imagine we have all the idle people here at the East. But farming there has come to be a business of great things, almost as bad as manufacturing. You must have money, or the big fellows will swallow you up. But we were talking of Florida. No winter, as one may say ; and your house a simple matter, your fuel, your clothes, a mere nothing. You could hardly starve if you tried."

Cameron came back to his chair, pushed it out from the wall, planted himself deliberately in it, and tilted back, pushing up his old felt hat, as if he did not mean to have his vision obstructed. Then he gave his beard another twist.

"Can you tell me why this is, Jack Darcy? Here are countries with fine and lovely climates, where every thing grows to your hand ; yet they always seem to lie idle : Italy and Spain and Turkey and South America, and our own Gardens of Eden," with a bit of sarcastic smile. "The very ease of living seems to take the ambition out of one. Well, why shouldn't it? Even the bees, you know, were demoralized when they found they did not have to lay up for winter. Wouldn't those people come to be worse tramps and idlers? I'm sure the poor white trash of the South has helped itself very little."

"We were talking of concerted effort," interposed

Maverick, — "purchasing a large tract of land, forming
a community, taking different kinds of workmen, and
making a success of it. Why should we not have flour-
ishing towns in Florida, as well as in Kansas?"

"To be sure, to be sure!" nodding his head and tugging at his beard in a manner that showed he was not a
whit convinced. "Then you give up," he said, "that
any thing can be done at home?"

"Any thing done at home?" Jack lifted his level
brows, and stared a little.

"Yes. The going away may all be very well. I tried
it in '57; went out to Indiana with a little money, and
tried farming that I didn't know any thing about, had the
ague six months, and then came back poorer certainly.
Now, the thing is just here with a good many of us, — we
have our little homes, and in such times as these, in any
hard times, we couldn't sell for any thing worth while.
Then there's many a thing, to a man or a woman past middle life, that can't be reckoned in dollars and cents: the
home you've made for yourself, the old friends, the church,
even the familiar street you've walked over so often that
every flagstone comes to have a near look."

"But those who have no homes, no strong interests" —

"If I was going to found a colony, I should want a
little better stock," with a short, dry laugh.

"May be you have a plan?" suggested Maverick good-
naturedly.

"Well, I've thought it over a good deal this winter,
sitting in the house with the old lady;" and there came a
peculiar far-off look in Cameron's eye as he studied a
figure in the carpet. "If God worked miracles nowadays,
and was to make a dozen or so honest men with a good,
stout share of brains, there might be a little lifting-up
of the dull skies. Take this town, leaving out politics
and all that sort. Five years ago we were prosperous,
and there wasn't a prettier town anywhere about. Good

wages were paid, people were thrifty; and I will say it
for David Lawrence, if he was one of your high kind,
he was a gentleman. I've worked for him fifteen years
steady. Then the Eastmans came in, and there was
nothing but hurry and drive, grumbling about high wages,
buying cheap wools, and if cloth was poor, blaming the
men. Then wages went down and down, and, when the
men stood out, the scum of all the places around was
brought in. Yerbury improved, and beer-saloons multi-
plied. Houses were thrown together and sold; and now
they're all falling apart, and standing empty, and half a
dozen families are crowding into one miserable tenement.
Who made the money? Was it high wages that ruined
Hope Mills, and wrecked Yerbury Bank?"

"You have hit the truth somewhere, Cameron."

"Those men were thieves and swindlers; and I suppose to-day they're living on the fat of the land, milk and
honey thrown in. See here, I'm not an educated man,
but I have a little common sense. Suppose we'd been let
to go our ways quiet like, — the farmers holding on to
their farms, and making two blades of grass grow where
one grew before. Wasn't that some old philosopher's
advice? Suppose David Lawrence hadn't built that great
palace out on Hope Terrace (he was a plainish man himself), and there had been five or six beside him making a
moderate share of money. He's lost all his great fortune, there's seventy thousand or so gone somewhere, the
bank has smashed with thousands more of everybody's
money, with nothing much to show but trumpery mortgages; there's no work and no money, and a howl goes
up that there has been over-production. Not over-production of honesty, I take it."

Maverick looked at the little earnest man, and laughed
a hearty, cheering sort of laugh that was like pouring oil
into a wound. Jack stared with wide-open eyes.

"I've been to hear Rantley two or three times, — he's

going about lecturing, you know, — but I don't see as he has any very good plan for getting work on its legs again. Then I've listened to the parson this winter, to please the old lady; and he is sure all this is a judgment for our sins. Seems to me, judgment went a little askew : why doesn't it touch Eastman and such fellows?"

"Has nothing been done?" asked Jack. "I have heard no business gossip for the last three months. Can't it be proved that he was a defaulter?"

"Perhaps it could. The old lady was reading the other morning about the scapegoat being sent into the wilderness with everybody's sins on his head; and I guess they'd rather have *him* off somewhere, and pack the trouble on him. He might tell too much if he was here. They couldn't get the money back, even if he has it; but no one ever will believe that David Lawrence profited by it. That money belongs to the people of Yerbury, who have earned it, and saved it; and I say thieving and roguery have more to do with hard times than ' surplus of labor.' The big men have taken the money that belonged to the little ones."

" None of the Lawrence estate has been settled, I suppose?" asked Jack.

" Every thing is for sale. The mortgage on the big house is to be foreclosed, also on the mill I believe. I declare to you, Darcy, it makes my heart ache to see those dumb spindles, and the great silent engine standing like a mourner at a funeral. Come now, why should Hope Mills go to ruin, and Yerbury fall to pieces, while you and Maverick go and build up Florida? Wouldn't the money and the energy do something here?"

Cameron's eyes looked out of their overhanging thatch with a puzzled, thoughtful expression, as if there must be a solution to the mystery.

Jack was startled. Building up Florida looked feasible, but building up Yerbury —

" Then you will not go with us? " said Maverick with a half-laugh.

" I've my little home clear of debt, and a trifle at interest ; and over in Yerbury churchyard there are two graves dear to me and my old lady.   It would break her heart to leave them.   And sometimes, Maverick, I thank God, that I've no sons to grow up tramps or worse.   No, I'll stay here, and fight through somehow."

They were silent for several minutes, each one tugging at the knotty problem.   Then Cameron rose, reached out for the phial of medicine, drove his slouch-hat down over his forehead, and walked toward the door.

" Drop in and see us, Jack, after you have thought it over a bit.   Mother's always had a warm corner in her heart for you. — Morning, doctor ; " and, nodding, he closed the door behind him.

CHAPTER XI.

Jack and Maverick glanced at each other, a long, searching, questioning glance.

"Given twenty or forty moderate fortunes, instead of the one great one," said Jack slowly.

"And you have a greater amount of general prosperity and happiness."

"Co-operation," continued Jack.

"And now, if you don't mind, you may take a walk with me," said Maverick. "Office-hours are over, and I have some rather serious cases on hand. Jerry's gone lame, stuck a nail in his foot, so I console myself with pedestrian theories."

"All right. I may need a pilot."

It was a mid-April day; but spring was late, and every thing looked bleak to Jack after his Southern sojourn. Certainly it was quite different from the trim little town of Jack's boyhood. The blight of poverty and thriftlessness had fallen upon it. There were piles of refuse in the streets, still half frozen; there were muddy stoops and shabby hall-doors, and broken area-palings, and now and then a window patched up with paper or rags. For though there may be much high theorizing and preaching on the two or three exceptional men who have lifted themselves out of dens of poverty, and come through great tribulation, there are thousands who work out nothing but blind-destruction and utter shipwreck, and who in frantic efforts for salvation drag down those nearest and dearest, as a drowning man may clutch at his own brother.

"Not very inviting," apologized Maverick; "but I have two calls to make here in Boyd's Row,—old rookeries that ought to have been pulled down long ago, but I suppose they still bring in Boyd considerable. I have made a complaint about the drains: they are enough to breed a pestilence. Tom Byrne has three children down with scarlet-fever. Two of them will be carried out presently, but I hope to save the little girl. No—I won't take you in."

"Tom Byrne—he was a mill-hand. And I know his wife well. Yes, Maverick." And Jack followed him.

It was a two-story cottage with three rooms on a floor, and two families occupying it. The Byrnes were up-stairs.

The two beds were in the front room, for the middle one was dark. There was a well-worn carpet on the floor, and the furniture very poor. Jenny Byrne had sold her best to pay the quarter's rent in the last place which they had left the first of January, the landlord preferring it should stand empty. Her little savings had been swept away by the bank disaster: there was no work, and three children to feed, except that Deacou Boyd found Tom sufficient employment to pay his rent.

On one bed close by the window lay the little girl, heavy-eyed and crimson. The elder boy had come to the stupor that precedes death, the other was restless with a half delirium. Jenny Byrne's round rosy cheeks had vanished, and her eyes had a distraught look, the lurking fear of coming woe. She stared at Jack a moment, then stretched out her hand, but as quickly withdrew it.

"Did you tell him, doctor? O Mr. Darcy!"

"Yes. He *would* come."

She wiped away some tears with the corner of her faded apron, then answered a question of Jack's. What could he say to the poor thing?' Surely she had done her duty with truest endeavor; and Tom Byrne was a very fair average man, liking his daily glass of beer, but rarely going farther.

"Can you fix a bed in the other room, and put Kitty in it?" the doctor asked. "She is better, but I would rather have her out of here."

"And Jamie is better too?" she questioned, with tremulous eagerness. "His fever is nearly gone, and he's having such a nice sleep" —

"Sleep is the best thing for him," returned the doctor briefly. "About Kitty" —

The mother's wan face flushed. She came close to Dr. Maverick, her eyes downcast.

"The coal gave out this morning, and I've no fire there," she said just above a whisper. "The relief-store is closed" —

"Yes, yes; I'll see to it;" with a nod. "I will be in again " — looking at the sleeping child — "say about four." Then he changed the medicine for Kitty, and gave one or two orders.

Jack thrust a bank-note in Jenny's hand, with his good-by. "Tom will be so glad to see you, Mr. Darcy," she said, with an effort at calmness.

"Can nothing be done for them?" asked Jack, as they regained the street.

"No. Jamie had gone too far when I was called in. Larger rooms, fresher air, nourishing food: that's the secret of a physician's success in many cases. Poor little ones! He will not go through the night. Now, Jack, you are not to come in here, positively. Stand in this breeze, and blow the scarlet-fever out of your clothes."

He did as he was bid, and, getting tired, tramped up and down. How much of man's selfishness and dishonesty there was in this! If the time could ever come when the mists and fogs of complacency would be swept off, and we could see that it was the innocent suffering for the guilty, not that these poor souls were sinners above all men, as the self-righteous Pharisee preaches!

Maverick rejoined him with a grave face, then the two went down Main Street. Houses to let, stores and shops closed, and those open but half-stocked, and wearing a listless air. If three hard years so told on the place, and there was no prospect of better things, what would it be in five or ten? Was it some such misfortune that had overtaken those grand and luxurious cities of Oriental lands?

"Where are the Lawrences?" Jack asked presently.

"Well, I really do not know. I think I did hear that Mrs. Lawrence had gone to New York. The young man " —

Jack held his breath, and there was a strange flutter at his heart. After all these years he saw again the pale, handsome child who had given him a boy's ardent love.

"I have a fancy that he will not amount to much. Queer idea that of Cameron's, wasn't it, Darcy? Who was it that first preached or wrote of the ' duty nearest one'? Of course things cannot stay this way forever, they must mend; and maybe if some one took hold to help mend them — Cameron's idea is not a bad one. Maybe the same amount of money and energy expended here would be productive of good results: still I hold on to Florida for my poor and wretched suffering ones. But it is worth thinking of. Here, let us turn round by Hope Mills."

Jack was silent. "Hope Mills!" It rang through his brain like a chime of bells. Of course he knew that Mr. Hope had given them his name; but had he builded better than he knew? Was it indicative of something greater than the power of one man, — of many men? of strong, earnest endeavor; of truth, honor, and honesty; of thrift, and happy, jocund industry, once more?

But now it was very silent. The great yard had an untidy look, with some piles of weather-beaten lumber, and old *débris*. The windows were covered with dust; the broad stone steps showed where the winter snows had fallen and melted, leaving streaks of dirt, and more had blown in the corners. No cheerful creak of the great engine; no vapory puffs of smoke circling skyward from the chimney; no whir of looms. It saddened one inexpressibly.

"It is a big subject," said Jack slowly. "I've been puzzling my brains half the winter with what wiser heads than mine have said about capital and labor, — Mill and Brassey and Howell, and our own men, with soft, sweet bits of Ruskin, and savage bits of Carlyle. I don't know but Carlyle was right when he said, 'The beginning and the end of what is the matter with us, in these days, is, that we have forgotten God.' Cameron said it another way, — honor and honesty. Because, certainly, honor appeals to all that is noblest in human nature, — to chivalry, and tenderness and thought for others; and nothing ever prospered, in the long-run, that did not have a substratum of truth."

"Well, according to Bristow, we came back to him this winter — not I, Darcy, I don't make any pretence," — and he shook his head with slow gravity. "But I was interested in the revival on psychological grounds. I had never been so inside of one before. Bristow is a good man, no doubt; but it is just the one chosen way with him, — strong crying and praying, and believing yourself a sinner above all men, and then a sudden peace and happiness, and a courage to endure, — a blind, unreasoning courage to take the present as it is, because God sent it, and it must be for the best. Boyd and Whitlow and Kenny were the great lights. They went about from house

to house ; they exhorted and prayed.   Whitlow was one
of the old bank-directors.   Strange to say, he did not
lose a penny.   His money was in government-bonds ; and
now he has persuaded Yerbury that if his advice had been
taken there would have been no trouble.   Whitlow discharged his man this winter, and took in his place a half-
grown boy.   Mrs. Whitlow sets a good example to her
class by discharging one handmaid and making the other
do double duty.   Yet, so far as I can find, Whitlow is a
richer man than he was three years ago.   Kenny keeps
his factory open, and gives the men three days' work in
the week, and pays them in poor shoes, as much as possible ; and takes out a good deal in high rent.   Boyd, who
has the name of being the greatest saint of all, — does
what?   Opens that miserable row of houses, that he
couldn't let on any terms, and takes in tenants who are
willing to work out the rent.   He gets good prices, too.
Is he losing on them?   Faugh! the very term of charity
makes me sick.   And this winter he purchased a good deal
of the stock of the relief-store.   Wretched flour ; miserable, adulterated stuff of tea ; pork, some of it that wasn't
fit to eat ; and cheap butter, that every one would have
been ten times better without.   I went to him one day,
red-hot, in a sanitary view of the business ; and he
preached religion to me, — his kind.   'Boyd,' said I,
'there's Keppler's saloon, your own property, paying you
a good income, no doubt, in these hard times, adding to
the want and misery of Yerbury faster than your whole
church can save.   If you are in earnest, go break up that
den of iniquity!'"

Jack laughed.   "What did he say to that?"

"Meekly, that Keppler had a lease for five years, and
was going on the second.   The man is so honorable, he
cannot break faith with his fellow-man, forsooth ; but he
breaks faith with God, in a serene, untroubled manner."
And Maverick's lip curled scornfully under the fringe of
moustache.

"But there must be some gold, or the counterfeit would not be so successfully received. We have had so much false money everywhere, that, since we can make that pass, we do not trouble ourselves. And yet, Maverick, there *is* something in it that you and I don't see clearly yet; but we cannot teach it acceptably until we can show better fruit. And, when leaders of all kinds, in high places, show that self only is at the bottom of every thing they do, it seems hopeless to demand that the class below, watching them, and suffering from their wrong-doing, shall attain a higher moral status. How can they help following coarsely in the footsteps of their betters?"

"Darcy, suppose you turn parson!" and Maverick laughed half quizzically. "See here: the world wants a very old sermon preached again to it, hammered into every fibre, put up over every doorway, — the essence of all knowledge, all religion, briefly comprehended in this, ' Love thy neighbor *as* thyself.' You won't need gown or bands for that work. Not to have one code of morals for the rich, and one for the poor; one creed for Sunday, and quite another belief for Monday; to have no lofty, impossible theories and exalted moods, but truthful, honest living; not to push away the miserable, ignorant souls, but take them by the hand in hearty co-opération. Maybe Cameron has the right clew. Why should we let human love be shamed by such things as an Oneida community or a Mormon city?"

The strong, earnest voice stirred Jack like martial music. All these years he had been struggling with a great, blind, confused something, — perhaps it was not a silver-mine or a railroad, but a work just here in the town of his boyhood, where he was known, where he had played and worked.

"Seventeenthly, and lastly," and Maverick looked at his watch, "I cannot idle any more time upon you, and must cut short with a ' To be continued.' We will talk it over again and again ; and, if we cannot get it into shape, there is still Florida left. So, while you are dreaming it out by this great silent mill, whose prisoned spirits should prate of prosperity instead of desolation, I'll run my course around Yerbury, and we'll compare notes over our cigars. *Addio*,'' waving his hand.

Jack watched the compact figure as it moved briskly away ; then he sauntered round the mill, down one street and up another, strolled out to Lovers' Lane, and returned by Larch Avenue. The Barry house began to show signs of life, for old Mat was clearing up the grounds. This was the one oasis that had not been bitten by speculation. He thought of winsome little Sylvie, and one summer evening when Irene Lawrence stepped into that pretty, cosey room with the grace and beauty of a Juno. Where was she now? And what was Fred doing? Making a great leap into name and fame, doubtless, now that he was put upon his mettle. The old boyish freaks came back to his mind, the enthusiastic unreasoning adoration, the last tender parting. An intense and subtile sympathy filled his soul ; and, though he smiled a little, the memory was very sacred.

The texture of Jack's mind was not of the quick, brilliant, or sanguine order. He went over his books again ; he ruminated as he cleaned the garden-paths, spaded the beds, trimmed the trees and shrubbery, and attended to the odds and ends known only to a careful householder. Cousin Jane was in her element out here ; and they two discoursed of farming and gardening, and industry, she in a sharp, trenchant way.

She had remarked incidentally that her visit was near its end. Now that Jack was home, cousin Ellen would not need her.

'' I don't see why you should not make your home here, cousin Jane,'' replied Mrs. Darcy. '' Grandmother grows feebler all the time, and you have quite spoiled me by your strength and cheeriness. You have no nearer tie ; and if you *could* content yourself with us — Jack was speaking about it a few evenings since. We should like so to keep you, cousin Jane.''

Jane Morgan studied the beseeching eyes a while, then dropped her own, and thought.

'' Very well,'' she answered, '' if you like to have it so. While I am well and strong I think I ought to do enough somewhere to earn my living, and not use up the little laid by for a rainy day. If you and Jack are agreed, we'll consider it a bargain for a year. I like to be settled about what I'm going to do : there's nothing so uncomfortable as hanging on tenterhooks. When my visit's through I like to go, if I'm going ; not stand an hour or two with the door-knob in my hand.''

Jack was delighted. They could spare him now and then of an evening to stroll down to Maverick's office, where they discussed pretty nearly every thing under the sun. It was so in the beginning, — '' the earth was without form, and void.'' Then the Barrys returned ; Sylvie changed in some indescribable way as to a kind of delicate outside manner, but the same fresh, earnest girl in heart and soul, taking up her friendship with Jack just where she had laid it down. Yet they had both grown broader and richer in nature and experience, and there was something of the subtile flavor of new acquaintance-ship.

Yerbury cleaned house, even to the tidying-up of streets and carting-away of rubbish. It was pitiful to see the attempts of some of the poor women, who washed their worn white curtains, scrubbed the shutters and hall-door, and set out a few ragged geraniums in the front yard, or made a little bed of lettuce and onions.

Yerbury Savings Bank was in the hands of a receiver. Some sold out their small accounts for a trifle : it was agreed there could not be much in the way of dividends.

Here was a great mortgage on the Downer farm, that the Eastmans had partly cut into city lots. And, though Downer had received a large price, he was a poor man to-day, with no business, and several sons tramping the highways for work. Farms had not been profitable, but had the wealth and extravagance produced any better result? These places around would be sold presently for any sum they would bring.

"Speculation did look so tempting, though," said Jack with a humorous smile. "But for grandmother I might have been in the midst of it."

"There's just one thing that makes a man or a country rich," said Jane Morgan incisively; "and that's industry, good, honest labor. Marking up one's goods before breakfast, as the Frenchman did, realizes no absolute money. The speculators jingle their dollars from hand to hand, until some poor fool, attracted by the noise, gives them a hundred for their twenty. When a man makes money simply by another person's loss, he has not created any thing, or made any more of it; and the world's no better, that I can see."

"Cousin Jane, you are dipping into political economy;" and Jack nodded gayly. "I shall have to ask Maverick and some of the others up here; and maybe you can put in a straw, or a head of wheat, toward the regeneration of Yerbury."

"I dip into a little common sense now and then, and it seems to me that's what the world needs. There is no lack of the uncommon kind, and it's not to be altogether despised, since at times uncommon things are given to people to do. But, if all the bees in the hive thought they had a call to be queens, it runs in my mind there'd be a lack of honey presently."

"You are on the right foundation, cousin Jane. We must not only make the honey an honorable thing, but honor the bees, put labor on a better, truer foundation."

"I should just say, 'See here, my friends, it is not possible for us all to be rich, whether it is some fixed immutable law of fate, or the lack of necessary elements in one's character, or the meeting of the right person with the right circumstances; but the fact is there, true as judgment. You can be comfortable and clean if you have the energy; and it is better to scrub your own kitchen-floor, or raise a bushel of potatoes, than to sit and whine about luck or respectability. Now and then a ready-made fortune drops down upon one, and I don't know but it often brings a curse: anyhow, what you work for, you are pretty sure to enjoy.' It makes me mad when I see healthy, hearty young women sighing for servants and pianos and what not; when their grandmothers, who had as good blood, and as good sense, didn't despise honest work."

Sylvie Barry came in while Miss Morgan was in the midst of her "speech," as Jack declared it to be; and now she clapped her small white hands, with a "Bravo!"

"A new disciple, Jack," and she smiled. "Miss Morgan, we shall set you to reading our favorite authors, and solving the tremendous question, Where can we get work for these to do? For a great many stand idle in the market-place, because they have not been hired. What can we set them at?"

"Well, Miss Barry, I don't know much about the big, outside questions; but, going around Yerbury a little this winter, I shouldn't say the work was all done up; or, done in such a poor, thrown-together way, that it tumbles right to pieces again. There's skewy, ill-made beds with ragged counterpanes; there's shreds of old ingrain-carpets, that you fall over; there's broken chairs, and shabby clothes, and dirty corners, — work enough, I should say, to last some woman an hour or two. She might get out her pieces of calico, and, with the children's help, make a new spread, maybe a tidy apron, and she might braid a rag mat out of bits, and a hundred things that go toward comfort. No: all the work isn't done up yet, Miss Sylvie," and Jane Morgan stopped just then, to knit the seam-stitch in a stocking for a poor body.

Sylvie threw herself on the footstool, and leaned her arms on Miss Morgan's knee.

"I wasn't thinking so much of that when I spoke," she began earnestly; "but I do wonder if some of us couldn't take it up. There are art-schools, and music-schools, and cooking-schools, in the great cities; and why couldn't we start something of the kind here? Poor people — the real poor, I mean — are often wasteful and idle because they do not just know how to be any thing else. They buy cheap garments in stores, and they soon come apart. I had a sewing-school last summer, and I found some mothers didn't seem to care whether their children learned or not, — since there was so much sewing done by machines. But if the mothers could be taught a little " —

"That's about the upshot of what I said. You see, Miss Barry, people have been earning so much money of late years, that sewing has gone out of fashion. It didn't pay to do this or that, so they earned and spent. Now they sit listless in their dirt and rags, bemoaning hard times. It is good to know how to do more than one thing," and Miss Morgan nodded her head confidently, her strong face full of earnestness.

"Why can't you and Sylvie start a school — what shall we call it? — of useful and homely arts? You see, the girls do work in the mills and shops until they get married, and then they do not know how to make the best of their husbands' money. But don't crowd out all the beauty and the pleasure; there must be something to enlist the heart. Give a man an interest in a thing, and you awake a new feeling, an enthusiasm that makes every thing go as smoothly as oiling up machinery."

"I have often thought," said Mrs. Darcy in her soft,

gentle voice, "that the poor did not get as much good of
their money as the better classes, because they never have
enough to buy advantageously, and store-keepers so often
take the advantage of them. Now, yesterday I was over
to Mrs. Hall's, and the poor thing was trying to make
some bread, and she was not fit to stand up and knead it;
so I thought I'd try. The flour was heavy and sticky
and lumpy, and what I should call very unprofitable.
No one could make good bread out of it. She said they
traded at Kilburn's, because he would wait if they did
not have the money. The flour was seven and a half a
barrel; the eighth, ninety-five cents; and I do not believe the bread was fit to eat. So you must remember,
when you blame people for poor cooking, that they may
not always have decent materials to work with."

"Maverick was growling about Kilburn the other evening. It is a shame that he should sell such poor goods,
when prices have come down a good deal."

"Can you not reform him a little?" and Mrs. Darcy
smiled.

"Cousin Jane and Sylvie might go into business, as
did the poor weavers of Toad Lane, with their sack of
oatmeal, firkin of butter, a little sugar and flour," said
Jack laughingly. "A fair division of labor. The men
of Yerbury shall provide work, and the women shall train
the inefficient how and where to spend money."

Sylvie glanced up with bright, inquiring eyes.

"Was it some more co-operation?" she asked.

Jack brought out his book, and read the story of the
"Equitable Pioneers of Rochdale" and their wonderful success from a small beginning. The girl listened with wide-
open eyes, and even Jane Morgan laid down her knitting.

"The queen-bee and the workers again," said she, as
Jack closed the book. "It is not every man for himself,
but every man for each other. And it comes back,
always."

CHAPTER XII.

"WHERE is grandmother?" Jack asked one morning late in May, as he came in from the garden, and found her place at the table vacant.

"She does not feel very well this morning, and I told her there was no need of rising with the lark," answered cousin Jane; but, though her voice was cheerful, there was a new gravity in her face.

"It is something unusual"—

"She is getting to be an old lady, Jack. There, sit down to your breakfast while it is nice and hot. No fear but what I will attend to grandmother."

She had risen; but in the midst of her dressing her hands had lost their cunning, her limbs their strength. Jane came to look at her in alarm.

"It's a warning," she said, with her grand old smile. "But I have no pain, and so you can leave me here for a while. My strength may come back."

Mrs. Darcy was much frightened.

"Remember that ninety-four is a good old age, and she has hardly had a sick day in her life. After breakfast Jack might go over for Dr. Maverick. He is sensible, and will not torment her with experiments."

Jack rather hurried through his meal, and then ran up to grandmother's room. She put out her wrinkled hand, thin to be sure, but still slender and smooth, with no knobby joints. A proud sort of beauty illumined the old face, though the eyes were a little dull.

"Dear boy," and there was a curious quaver in her

voice, "I've had to give in at last. The Lord knows best. He has given me many a happy year with you; yet I have never forgotten the folks over yonder. I shall be glad to see them again, — your father, Jack, and the rest. 'Then they came to the land of Beulah, where the sun shineth day and night, and betook themselves to rest' — you know. We used to read it together."

A sharp pang went to Jack's heart. He pressed the limp hand to his lips, and gazed into the face that had changed in some indescribable way. Then Jane came with a tempting breakfast, and fed her with wonderful gentleness, it seemed to him.

He went out, and brought Maverick back with him.

"It is a general breaking-up of nature," said the doctor with a tender gravity. "Nothing can be done, unless she should suffer; but I do not think she will. It is the way lives ought to end oftener. Give her whatever she will take; and keep cheerful, all of you. After all, it is only a little journey."

"Where?" the young eyes asked as they met each other in solemn mood.

Jack scarcely left her. She liked to open her eyes, and find him sitting there, when she would smile faintly, and murmur a few words. Sylvie and Miss Barry were the only visitors admitted to her room. They used to read out of "Pilgrim's Progress," the book she had loved so well, and occasionally they sang some sweet old hymn.

"Jack," she said once, "you will find every thing in my old box there in the bureau. It was my mother's, and came across the sea with me. You have been a good lad. You took your father's place with me, and you must never regret that you staid here to make an old woman happy. You have been a good lad — a good — little lad" — And her mind wandered to other years.

Just growing gradually weaker, and falling asleep peacefully. A long, well-spent life, and a death to remember and desire.

They buried her in Yerbury churchyard, and the towns-people turned out to do her honor. Jack thought of another death, and the almost solitary state of the funeral.

How good it was that they had Jane Morgan now! She carried them right along.

Jack opened the brass-bound box, still fragrant with its sandal-wood lining. Some old letters, the trinkets she had saved from her poverty, and a will bequeathing her all, in government bonds, to Jack.

There was nearly seven thousand dollars. With his own little savings he felt quite rich.

"Jack," said his mother, "all these years you have waited patiently, and put by your own dreams. Do not think that I did not notice the struggle. It was very generous and kindly; and I am glad, for grandmother's sake, that you staid. But now if you like we will go somewhere else, and make a new home"—did her voice tremble a little then? "I am still young enough to take root elsewhere, and cousin Jane is so energetic she helps one to new life. There may be prettier and more prosperous places, and you have years before you in which to realize a fortune."

He glanced up at the face bending over him, instinct with the honorable grace of middle life; the hair with a few threads of silver; the soft, fine skin showing some wrinkles about the eyes and two or three light creases across the forehead; the cheeks out of which roundness had vanished, and the lips the scarlet of girlhood, but though both were pale the mouth was still tender and sweet. A womanly woman,—that seemed to him a perfect description of his mother, a woman who had loved three generations, and held by them. Now for his sake she would give up the old ties, and try a new world,—this shy, shrinking, loving woman.

What would she leave? She had never known any other home in her married life, though this had been changed and improved since her wedding-day. Everywhere some trace of his father. The porch with the roses climbing over it, the great maples in the street, planted by him; the odorous old balm of Gilead, that he had hunted up because she had cared for it, and they had one in her old home ; the trailing clematis with its shining smilax-like green, and its heliotrope fragrance ; the white rose that had been planted on the morning of Jack's birth, and had sent up many generations from the old root ; the latticed summer-house with its wealth of grapes ; and almost like a vision Jack could fancy he saw the tall figure and deliberate step, — the sweet ghost of memory that could never walk in any other place. Did his mother have such dreams?

Yes, there were better things to life than mere money-getting.

"I believe those were the wild dreams of boyhood," — smiling a little, — " the ' long, long thoughts of youth.' I used to want something that would occupy my whole soul and every energy, that was stirring, earnest, absorbing, and held a grand outlook. But I think " — very deliberately, as if he were weighing every word — " that my work has come to me, instead of my going out to seek it. At all events, I shall not go away for the present."

"Well," she returned, but she could not keep the great gladness out of her voice.

Having thus made his election, Jack Darcy looked sturdily about to see what was to be done, and the best way to do it. He asked two of the old over-lookers, Hurd and Bradley, to meet him at Maverick's office ; and there they discussed co-operation until long past midnight. They looked into the cotton-mill connected with the Rochdale experiment ; they read up the workings of those at Oldham and Lancashire, of the industries in France, and banking in Germany.

"Here we are," said Jack, "with so much of our lives·

spent in learning to manage looms and turn out different kinds of cloth. People must wear clothes until the millennium, and cloth will be made. It seems to me that it must be a good thing to identify the workmen, and get their real interest. We should avoid strikes on the one hand, the continual disputes about wages, and be much less at the mercy of all outside influence. The men will understand thoroughly that industry, economy, thrift, and perseverance is good for each individually; that he is using these qualities not only for the master, but for himself. There will be better work, and more of it.''

Hurd seemed to be taking the measure of Darcy through this speech. Now he said, —

'' Darcy, any man who knows enough to head such a business as Hope Mills, knows enough to carve out a fortune for himself; and my opinion is that he would be a fool to let the chance slip.''

'' A man may have the knowledge, but not the requisite capital,'' was the patient answer. '' Then he might think '' —

'' Well, you've a sight of faith, that's all! Your men will go on with the tramp of soldiers in good times; and when the pinch comes, then look out! If they were educated, reasonable, sensible; but you and I both know the mass are not. It will do better in the old countries, for there children expect to follow in the footsteps of their parents; but here, where every boy looks upon himself as a possible president, it cannot be done. It has been tried, and has failed. It will again.''

'' Then you will not join?''

'' I don't say that, Darcy. I can't very well get away from Yerbury: if I could, the Lord knows I'd go. But there — it is just as bad everywhere else. Don't be too sanguine though: you young chaps build air-castles easily.''

Bradley wrung his hand warmly at parting. '' I want

to look into this thing a little more closely,'' he said. ''I believe you have struck the keynote. Whatever raises the workman raises the whole world. If you get him to be self-supporting, there is one less pauper or tramp for the State to take in charge, and tax all other workingmen for his support.''

'' I rather like the scheme of the co-operative store,'' Hurd began presently. ''There's a sight of money somehow between the producer and the consumer. Farmers are grumbling all the time. I wrote to my brother-in-law last spring about trading for a small farm, and going into poultry-business perhaps ; and he sent back a list of prices he had obtained for his produce. Butter twenty-five cents, and we paid forty this winter. Milk two and a half cents a quart, while ours is from eight to ten.''

'' Transportation to be counted in,'' suggested Maverick.

'' The thing discouraged me, so I thought I'd hold on a bit, since I did not know the first rule for farming. As Darcy says, we have spent all these years perfecting ourselves in our business, and it hardly looks reasonable that we should succeed at once in something altogether different. If you don't mind, Darcy, I'd like to look over that Rochdale experiment a little at my leisure.''

Jack handed him the book, and the small party dispersed. In a week they met again, with two more, one a stubborn old Englishman who had been in the business. They had done very well for a while, then the market flattened. They could not hold their stock, so the big fish swallowed them up. That was always the end where you had no credit and no reserve capital. Truth to tell, Jack began to realize how hard it would be to convert some of the very men he would like to have.

Meanwhile Hamilton Minor came up with some capitalists, and Hope Mills was put up at auction. They looked around the town, examined the building and machinery, which was the best of its kind; but nobody could tell whether we had reached bottom prices or not, and, though the place was to be offered at an immense sacrifice, they were wary. Empty mills and rusting machinery were not profitable investments. Mr. Minor's eloquence went for nothing. These long-headed dons would rather hold· on to their money, though they expressed a good deal of sympathy for the Lawrence estate.

"I do believe it will go for the face of the mortgage," said Jack to Maverick that evening. "Twenty thousand dollars, and a year's interest and taxes. Twenty-two thousand would cover the whole thing; and three years ago Mr. Lawrence wouldn't have looked at fifty thousand. Maverick, I can get together ten thousand of my own, and if there was one other person" —

"We will hunt him up," returned Maverick hopefully. "There is the reputation of the cloth already made, which is one great step in your favor. Yes, it must be done."

Yerbury was looking a little brighter and better at midsummer. Scarlet-fever had pretty well disappeared; but malaria had come in its stead, convenient name for want of nourishment, stagnation, and despondency. The haggard-looking wives and mothers went out to a day's washing or scrubbing; but the children, better off, roamed over the fields in search of berries or a stray ownerless fruit-tree, laughing and happy in their rags and bare feet.

Darcy tried two or three pretty well-to-do men, that he fancied had the good of the town at heart; but the project looked wild to them. If David Lawrence couldn't stand up against hard times, no new men could. He, Darcy, had better put his money in government-bonds, and live on the interest. Nothing could be made in such times as these.

"It seems as if one half of the world has decided that the other half should starve," Jack declared in a discouraged tone. "No one is willing to start the ball again. If it wasn't for mother I would risk every dollar of my own. And then to think of the land lying idle about here, — enough to feed half the town! I do not wonder that we are fast coming to beggary and ruin."

Maverick was pretty sober for several days, then he went off to Narragansett Pier; "tired of my everlasting badgering," said Jack to Sylvie, who, poor child, had her hands and heart full of projects that she talked over with Miss Morgan and her aunt, and did not make much more progress than Jack.

So it happened one July evening that Jack sat smoking on the porch in a rather despondent frame of mind. Miss Morgan and his mother had gone to make some neighborly calls.

A quick step came down the street. "If Maverick wasn't in Rhode Island!" thought Jack; then it came nearer, with a little halt, and Jack sprang down the steps in the moonlight.

"Hillo, old fellow!" said the rich, laughing voice. "Have you looked after my patients, and entertained my office-callers, in my absence? That would only be fair play, for I have been about your business; and, by Jove! succeeded too!"

"Maverick!" There was an odd little tremble in Jack's voice.

"Ask me to sit down, and stay me with — well, a pipe, for I have finished my last cigar. I came in the train just fifteen minutes ago, and skulked — that's the very word — under the trees and through by-ways, lest some one, seeing, should lay violent hands on me. Yes, get out your best armchair, old chap, and treat me like a prince."

The two seated themselves again, and stretched out their legs to the porch-railing. The soft light fell around, outlining here and there a bit of vine as if it were held against a silver background. A few early insects were chirping, and somewhere down the street there was a waft of distant music.

" Succeeded ! " Jack drew a long breath.

" Yes : with a woman too. Nay, you need not look at me so wonderingly. I have not sold myself for base gold to the Evil One," laughing lightly. " I have never told you much about myself; for, like the needy knife-grinder, ' story, God bless you ! there was none to tell ; ' but there is a chapter now, and you must hear it first. My mother was left an orphan in her infancy, and her aunt adopted her. She was a canny Scotswoman, by name Jean Mc-Leod. She was very good to my mother, who married quite to her liking, although my father was not rich, but we always lived in a certain style, and my father had a fine reputation as a lawyer. My mother's death, the result of an accident, so prostrated him, that he never recovered from the shock. Aunt McLeod came to stay with us through that weary time. Then she took us both to her heart and home : it was a large warm heart and a beautiful home. My father left a little : it was made over to me ; and my sister, five years younger than I, was brought up properly, and married properly, and lives in Chicago in elegant style. Then Aunt Jean tried her hand on me, chose a suitable young woman, and insisted that the fates had decided it. The upshot was a quarrel. Not but what the girl was nice enough, and all that, but I did not care to marry ; and so I walked off to Europe, and was there three years. Some rather cool letters passed between us at first, but they grew warmer ; and when I returned it was winter, and she was in New York. I went straight up to her house. She was very glad to see me ; and there in her lovely library, all glow and softness and perfume, by the side of the grate, with a screen in her hand, sat Anastasia Lothrop. She is Aunt Jean's pet *protégée*, though she has home and lands and people of her own. A handsome woman too, by Jove! However, we have gone our separate ways. I think she (Aunt Jean) was rather annoyed at my settling at Yerbury.

"Well, I went to Narragansett, and found her alone this time; and she has promised to buy Hope Mills. I do believe there's no end to the woman's money. She talked it over as a mere bagatelle. I am to meet her in New York, and you are to go down, Jack; and we are to see the holder of the mortgage, and do no end of business. I think she is rather interested in the scheme, and I do believe she is delighted to do me a favor. Now you can keep your money for a kind of reserve fund. The mere savings of labor will not answer at first, you know."

Maverick drew a long breath then, and puffed lustily at his cigar.

"I don't know how ever to thank you."

"Don't thank me, Darcy. You see, I am interested in this experiment. I want to see if there is enough faith and honesty and industry and trustfulness left in the world to make such a general partnership a success. You know it has been said that since the war our character as a whole has degenerated fearfully. Politically there is no doubt of it. Commercially and industrially are still open questions. If we could succeed in making one hundred people comfortable, instead of one rich, nine comfortable, and the other ninety next door to pauperism, we shall have done something. If we can so educate ninety men that they are able to understand the difficulties and embarrassments of carrying on business and its numerous fluctuations, we shall have raised them higher in the social scale. And it is most sadly true of all the large failures of late, some one has been dishonest, some one or two or three have taken other people's money to speculate with. It should be called stealing as much as when a poor man takes it, even if he spends it for rum. And, Darcy, we will keep our eye single upon one thing: we shall not move the world, or convert it, but haply one little corner of Yerbury; while all the wit and wisdom the world has been saving up for ages will be hurled against us in different shapes, from puffy snowballs to the grim old fellows soaked in water and frozen hard. And sometimes I think, with all the energy you are going to bring to bear upon this, you could carve out a fortune somewhere else."

"I don't know as to that, Maverick," said Darcy in a half-funny, half-sad tone. "From New York to St. Louis, from thence to New Orleans, to Florida, and back here again, I never found an opening. Two or three people did promise to write to me, but they have not. I felt the world could go on quite as well without me and hundreds of others. So, then, the only thing is to create a place; and Heaven knows I shall try hard enough to make a success of this."

"And you will do it too: I'm not afraid. Give us your hand, old chap! I never swore friendship with but just one fellow: that was in my college days, and I have his note for one hundred dollars as a memento. I might have been keener, I dare say; but one of the transcendentally lovely things of youth is its perfect faith. These preternaturally wise and prudent young people come into the world mentally gray-headed. But I do it now with my eyes wide open; and, when you are a rich man, I have another scheme I want to take through, a sort of home or hospital of my own planning: so don't fancy I shall let you off easy."

They held each other's hands in a long, lingering clasp. Beside the warmth and magnetism that was a component part of Dr. Maverick's nature when he chose to use it, which was not nearly always, there was a steadfast kindliness, the vigor of a true and pure manhood, that made a clear atmosphere about him, in which insincerity, weakness, and selfishness seemed to flicker into pale shadows, and shrink away from the intense mental light he turned upon them.

And just here the vision of the boy face came back to Jack, the strangling arms about his neck, the fluttering breath and quivering lips, and the sound of the rather thin, childish voice, — " You are *my* King Arthur, and I shall love you my whole life long."

The sadness in the smile was for the old ideal.

CHAPTER XIII.

"THE telegram!" exclaimed Maverick ten days later, striding down the garden where Jack was at work in the strawberry-bed.

Jack Darcy flushed like a girl, through the other fine coloring of labor. He had hardly dared to believe in and hold to Maverick's promise. Manlike, neither had spoken of it since that night.

"'Thursday, at four, at the Westminster.' That is to-morrow. We must be on time, or she would never have any faith in us; and, though my credit may be *nil*, yours must be " —

"As I hope to keep it through my life," was the grave reply. "You will take the morning train?"

"Yes. It will give us a trifle of spare time, which won't be bad for a couple of overworked fellows like us. But I must look after a lot of people this afternoon, and if I can I will drop in this evening."

Jack went back to his strawberries. He had been making a mental calculation about an acre, and the profits thereon, moved to it by something Jane Morgan had said. Twenty miles below them, on Swanston Bay, which was quite a summer-resort, the hotel-keepers had paid twenty-five cents per quart for nice large berries. On their little patch they had raised a hundred and twenty quarts. There was another side to the labor-question, — diversity of industry. Jane's idea of a great fruit-garden, or call it a farm, was not bad. You could crowd ten such patches in an acre of ground. If nothing better came to hand, he might hire some of the ground lying waste around Yerbury, and set the idle at work.

Sylvie came through with some flowers in her hand. Jack looked up again, and laughed, and threw himself on the grass under a tree, chatting gayly. He felt so light at heart! She wondered a little, and then, without knowing the cause, rejoiced with him in the depths of her soul.

The two men started the next morning, and at the appointed time were ushered into Miss McLeod's private parlor. Maverick had said, "She's a little queer in some ways; but in the main you will like her, I think." Meanwhile Jack had formed a dozen ideals of her, based mostly on the personal appearance of Miss Barry and his grandmother.

The door of the adjoining room opened, and Miss McLeod entered. An old woman, of course, and a fashionable woman, but with a young-old face and fig- ure. Not the graceful airiness of youth, so often painful in its desire to impress the beholder with what it is not, but an old age to which all the good things of life, rightly used, have contributed, and brought about a delightful result. She was of medium height, and possibly had not been handsome in her palmy days; but she challenged one's respect for a true and honorable womanhood, and an old age neither inane, querulous, nor servile.

A rather plump figure, with deep chest, full shoulders, and erect carriage. The face was wrinkled; but the skin had a peachy softness, the lips were still full and finely curved, and, though the mouth was rather wide, it indi- cated resolution and decision. The whole contour of the face was slightly aquiline, the forehead high and broad, but the curling hair falling over it in the requirements of fashion softened it; shining silvery white, curling natu- rally, and very abundant, the coil at the back partly cov- ered with a diamond-shaped bit of elegant black thread lace that matched the barb at her throat. Her rich, soft, steel-colored silk made no rustle as she crossed the floor, but the diamonds in her ears and on her breast flashed a glitter of sunlight about her.

Maverick greeted her with pleasant but not effusive warmth, and introduced his friend. They skirmished on the boundary-line of small talk for a while, Jack feeling that he was being measured and gauged at every possible. indication of the real man, but his honesty of purpose kept him steadfast.

Presently Maverick plunged into the business part, much to Darcy's satisfaction.

"I wrote to my lawyer, Mr. Hildreth, about it," Miss McLeod replied. "He has seen the parties holding the mortgage; and, on account of business embarrassments, they are extremely anxious to realize upon it. Mr. Minor is naturally desirous of having it sold at an advantage; but he is on the bond, and has been making continuous efforts with no success. No one can tell how low property will sink, business property especially, that depreciates so rapidly if neglected. The mortgage is considered one-third of what the property was valued at seven years ago; but we have all shrunk a trifle since that," with a shrug, and a curious little bend of the head, as if the decapitation was not altogether a pleasant process. "This is the 4th of August, and on the 19th it is advertised for sale. There may be one chance in a thousand of a better purchaser; though Mr. Hildreth thinks no one but a lunatic, or a woman, would put money in such an adventure," her lips curving in their bitter-sweet smile. Indeed, there was nothing she was so much like as a cluster of bright bitter-sweet berries, on a sharp but sunshiny autumn day, with the leaves and tendrils brown and faded, but the brilliant life and soul still shining from the ripe centre. She impressed you with the same defiant glow of exultation.

"I have money lying idle, it is true," she continued;

"but I want to hear your plans before I decide, Mr. Darcy. Philip," nodding to her nephew, "has interested me in this scheme; but I must know what it promises before I take the risk."

Jack was confused a little by the bright, penetrating glance; and he had not quite overcome his boyish trick of blushing. Often as he had gone over the plan with Howell, Fawcett, and other political economists at his tongue's end, all his troupe of fine ideas seemed to desert him. He laughed at his own embarrassment: she smiled and nodded, and that made them friends.

"I don't know that I can put it any better," he began earnestly, "than to say that I want to take up the lever of work, and put the wheels of labor in motion, to bring the starving workmen and the halting capital together again. It is all very well for us to rush every dollar into government-bonds; but if there is no business, what is to augment our revenue, and where then shall we be finally, with our mills and workshops shut up, and our people begging? If I had enough of my own to bridge over the chasm, I would ask no one's help," he went on a little proudly. "The mills at Yerbury stand in sad silence, with ruin before them; our men are idle and dispirited, turning into tramps and vagabonds, because they hate to sit still and starve. And here am I, of no real use to the world, and the eight years back of me that I have spent in perfecting myself of no account either, unless I find something upon which to employ my ability and training. If I purchase the mills, we must hire capital to work them with, and everybody would be shy of us. We can get together the capital if we could be sure of the place for five years, at a moderate rental."

"But would not a joint-stock company answer the purpose better, and carry more weight?" she asked, listening with a sort of intent wariness.

"I want to enlist the workmen, so that we shall be reasonably sure of co-operation in other things beside money, industry, thrift, faithfulness, and a common interest in success. If times are hard, we shall all make sacrifices: if they improve, we shall benefit by the earnestness of our endeavors. Maverick and I have made a little draft, based on the workings of the best French and English societies. If you will look it over"—and he took it out of his memorandum.

She studied it with a keen, rapid glance.

"It is what I should call an industrial partnership," Darcy continued. "We *should* own the mill; but, as we cannot, that must go in the working expenses. As the men choose, and are able, they can hold shares; but at present this will be obtained—say from a dozen perhaps. Nothing now will bring in twenty or even ten per cent, and we must be satisfied with whatever we can make. We have had our good times, and now we must take the evil; but if there is any better way than sitting down resignedly, and folding both hands, I, for one, want to find it."

She was taking in the combinations of emotion and purpose that flitted over his face. A man who would do something if he could get that hardest of all things, a foothold to stand upon.

"I think you might make more money," she said with pointed brevity.

"Which would not be co-operation," with his frank, genial laugh that went to her heart. "I want to try the experiment. Not that I expect to solve all the difficulties between labor and capital; but I shall try to make them better friends, so that, when you have weathered a hard gale, pinching yourselves to keep on the workmen, they will not strike for higher wages on the first stir of improvement, as they will be certain of their share."

"You are a philanthropist, Mr. Darcy. Can you depend upon the temper of your men? They may do very well just now when they are starving; but, when times improve, are they going to wait one year or five years for the sum they consider part of their wages?   And if there should be no surplus, but losses, as has often happened in manufacturing?   Your workman will

> ' Fork out his penny, and pocket your shilling,'

fast enough; but when the tables are turned, what then?''

"There *must* be a different feeling when men are banded together in a mutual business interest.   The very spirit of association appeals to what is best and noblest in human nature.   As it has been in Yerbury, for example, the workmen contributed of their ability and strength to support one family in princely luxury, pay one extravagant salary, and several others that were out of all proportion to the wages earned, and an extensive defalcation.   No one is at all the gainer now, unless it be the thief,'' his face scarlet with indignation at the remembrance of Eastman.   ''The men have been hit the hardest of all.   No wonder they feel bitter and discouraged.   We make many an Ishmael by sending him out with his jug of water, while there are feasting and revelry within.''

" But you cannot make all human nature noble or sensible or grateful.   There is the grand co-operation of the forty years in the wilderness, when food was provided, and clothing lasted miraculously; yet under these favorable circumstances, and with the sure promise at the end, there was not a heavenly unity.''

Jack laughed heartily.

" We must keep from golden calves and such folly,'' he said.   "We are likely enough to have our waters of Marah.   But it seems to me the best way to ennoble labor, give it its true dignity, and show the possibilities for the workmen, is concerted action.   As matters stand now, few poor men can ever acquire sufficient capital to start any business; and perhaps this is not best when we consider the cost of machinery, and the ever-appearing new inventions. The small capitalist could *not* compete with the large one. Yet capital often takes as its right the best strength of the workman, the years of maturity and ability, and throws him off in his old age. I know labor retorts by carelessness, wastefulness, and utter indifference to the employer's welfare. One is a machine to grind labor into money; the other, to grind all he can out of capital. Perhaps my design is Utopian, but it seems as if something ought to be done before we train a whole generation of men to be paupers and thieves. Better that we should spend our money in labor experiments than supporting poorhouses and prisons.''

Jack had lost his embarrassment now. There was a glow on his cheek, and a steady fire in his eye, the lines about the mouth sharply drawn, and indicating not only masterly strength, but a kind of pitying patience, that would never degenerate into sentimentality. It was a very manly, trusty face; and his sterling honesty impressed Miss McLeod, long trained to reading faces, while his sturdy good sense promised much.

'' I should like Mr. Hildreth to see this paper,'' turning it in her still supple fingers. '' What if some of your men insist upon going out after a year or two, Mr. Darcy?''

'' There will be some kind of forfeiture, of course. The true business capital must remain intact the whole five years: the direct proceeds of labor may be subject to some changes, but in any event the business interests must not be jeopardized.''

There was a moment's interruption of a servant; then dinner was brought in, and arranged for three. The bright-eyed old lady made a charming hostess. She poured their tea with a quaint dignity, and made them feel quite as if she were dispensing hospitality in her own house.

She was the kind of woman whom young people, past the lunacies of sixteen, invariably like. The feminine portion told her their love troubles, the young wives came to her with tangles and little jealousies; and, if she could not always straighten them out, she had a marvellous way of comforting. Young men drifted toward her by some species of magnetism, though she had none of the fussy motherliness of some old ladies. With faculties still keen and bright, a great fund of good-humor that had the sparkle of champagne rather than any insipid sweetness, she never wearied or palled on any one. She kept herself well informed of the world's progress, she knew of the principal stars in the literary, dramatic, and artistic world, and to be asked to her house was a compliment.

The conversation was more general now; and, though Maverick had told every thing of note about Yerbury, she was not indisposed to listen to it again. They discussed the panic and its causes, and ventured upon guesses as to its duration. They all agreed that there had been too much haste to be rich, too much greed of speculation, too much personal greatness, and not enough national greatness. No generous striving together to build up what the war had pulled down, but every man for himself and for gold. If women had been frivolous and vain, and dazzled by the glare of newly acquired wealth, men had not been quite free from faults. The terrible lowering of morals, the dishonesty and fraud easily condoned, and laughed over as a kind of shrewdness, were sad examples to set before the next generation.

In her way Miss McLeod was quite a politician, having been so much in that circle. Her views of men and measures were keen and discriminating; and her bits of trenchant wisdom quite dazzled Jack, who at the last, proposed laughingly, as his panacea, that every man should undertake the mending of himself, when the world would soon be righted.

Afterward a coupé came, and they drove to the Park. There evening and the bonny new moon overtook them; but the streets and country roads were so inviting, they did not return until quite late.

"Consider yourselves my guests for the night," she said as they drove back to the hotel, and Maverick was too wise to demur.

"I have been thinking this matter over," she said as they were separating. "My part will be purchasing the mills, and I shall take so much in the shape of rent. I want you to consider what per cent you can pay, and not straiten yourselves too much. I frankly confess that I am greatly interested in you, Mr. Darcy; and as this young man," touching Maverick's shoulder, "prefers to ' gang his ain gait,' he leaves me quite free to waste my money as I like. Be fair to yourself. Good-night."

"It's all right with you, Jack," began Maverick after they had been shown to their room. "Aunt Jean is a trump! I almost forgive her Miss Lothrop. But I suppose women would be less than women, if they did not want to dip their fingers into destiny. It is their mental chessboard."

"But you do love her? your aunt, I mean."

"Why, of course. Still, I should never dangle in any woman's train;" with a curl of the lip.

Miss M'Leod was going back to Narragansett the next morning. They discussed their last item of agreement; and Jack said, with modest decision, "that such real estate could not possibly pay more than three per cent to any owner in the course of the next few years. He would rather offer her that, and a share contingent on the amount of business done at the end of five years, than assume any greater risk just now."

"Thank you for your honesty and your good sense," she replied. " If you had offered higher, I should have had some doubts of your financial clear-headedness. It

will be an equitable bargain. And will you be kind
enough to make some arrangements for me in Yerbury?
I shall come on the 18th, with a companion and a maid;
and Mr. Hildreth will follow the next morning. Get your
plans in shape by that time. I am glad to have met you,
Mr. Darcy, and I wish you success in your undertaking.''

They shook hands cordially, and went their ways. Jack
could hardly believe his good fortune, and now he was
afraid some other parties might step in and take the mills.

'' Much likelihood,'' laughed Maverick.

Jack took Cameron in hand first, as he had been the
real suggester of the plan. He, Darcy, could use his ten
thousand; and, if ten more could be subscribed, they would
not need to hire outside. As time went on, this capital
might be equalized and increased. Hurd offered two thousand and himself; and just then one of the old hands who
had succeeded in getting rid of a good bit of property that
had weighted him heavily, and picked up a little money
here and there, subscribed five thousand. Yardley had
none of his own, but persuaded his wife's sister to invest a
thousand. The other, Miss Barry offered, if no workman
came to hand. Winston was a handy Jack-of-all-trades.
He could repair machinery, or do any kind of wood-work:
he had sold cloth on commission, bartered and traded,
and had a good deal of shrewdness and good sense, and
pluck. He and Darcy would do the buying and selling;
Cameron would take charge of supplies, deal them out,
and see that nothing went to waste; Hurd and Yardley
would be overlookers as before. Every man could weave
his yard of cloth with the best. They would constitute
the managing force.

The days passed rapidly; and to Jack's great satisfaction no purchaser appeared, no curious soul even sauntered about the mills. Miss McLeod came at the appointed time, accompanied by Miss Lothrop, who was as

distant to Maverick as if this were their first meeting.
The ladies were to stay with Mrs. Darcy, and the best in
the house was placed at their disposal with simple courte-
sy. They were taken to the mills, where they made a tour
of inspection ; Jack explaining machinery, looms, shuttles,
and spindles, with an enthusiasm that amazed even himself. There was a new interest in the thought of having
a voice in the direction of that great engine now so silent,
and the work it was to do.

"We shall not use half our looms in the beginning,"
he said ; "but I hope, before the five years are ended, we
shall be doing our utmost."

They all hoped so for his sake. "If any man can make
the plan work, he will," thought Miss McLeod, who liked
him better every hour.

Miss Barry and Sylvie came to call on the ladies in the
evening.

"I suppose that is Mr. Darcy's sweetheart," Miss
Lothrop remarked afterward. "She is a pretty, enthusiastic little thing, and she takes so much interest in his
affairs. I can just fancy how they will work together,
and the earnest, useful lives they will lead. What butterflies we are !" looking down at her white helpless hands.
"Not you, but the young women of the day in general.
You are a busy bee, and still keep storing up your
honey."

"And sting occasionally," laughed the sharp, bright
old lady.

The sale took place the next morning at ten, at the
Court House. There was quite a number of spectators,
though the ladies, with Maverick and Darcy, were in a
private office. Hamilton Minor had come up, resolved
that it should not go for less than the mortgage, but desirous of ending his responsibility. There were but two
bids. The auctioneer lingered a long while on Mr. Hildreth's bid, commenting on the enormous sacrifice, but he

could move no one's interest. It was reluctantly knocked down, the purchase-money paid, and the deed made out to Miss McLeod.

Then the company's agreement was put in lawful, legal shape. The managing board of five men were to have sole charge of buying, selling, and manufacturing. They were to give all their time and ability, to watch the state of the market, and conduct every thing for the benefit of the whole corporation. Darcy was to prepare a balance-sheet semi-annually, showing profit and loss; and this was to be open to the inspection of the firm.

The parties to the second part, the workmen, were to work ten hours a day, six days in the week, under the supervision of Hurd and Yardley. The wages of the men and the salaries of the managers were to be put at the minimum rate, and both parties were to draw two-thirds of this sum weekly. At the end of the year, the profits on labor and capital were to be evenly divided; one half apportioned to the capital, the other half divided *pro rata;* but only half of this sum to be drawn out yearly, the other turned over to the capital stock, and placed to each man's credit. If any operative should become dissatisfied, and leave, his share of the profits was to be forfeited to a fund for sick or disabled workmen. Any member of the association guilty of misconduct was to be twice reprimanded, and for a third offence expelled. A standing committee of the workmen, with one chairman, was to investigate and settle such matters. Shares of capital as low as fifty dollars would be within reach of the workmen. A clause was inserted, that no ale, beer, or spirituous liquors were to be brought into the mill during working hours. It had been one of the old-time rules, but often transgressed. Each man was to use his best endeavors to promote the interests of the firm.

At the end of five years, the agreement was to cease, and the profits to be divided.

Then the five-years' lease of Hope Mills and all its appurtenances was made out to "Hope Mills Co-operative Association," and duly signed. The rental was to be six hundred and sixty dollars per annum, the company to pay the taxes, and keep the mills in ordinary repair.

Then the managers and a number of the workmen marched over to Hope Mills in a body, opened the doors and barred shutters, and entered with an exultant step. They were to try their hand at good-fellowship in labor, and see if it would solve the vexations of the old system, or prove any stronger bond. Maverick had spread a little feast in what had been Eastman's office; and they sat down together, the ladies, joined by Sylvie Barry, Mrs. Darcy, and Miss Morgan, taking the head of the table. Some speeches were made, and some toasts drank, and everybody wished success to Hope Mills. Had John Hope unconsciously foretold their future when he christened them for his own glory? Darcy thought so. The name had a higher significance now, and was to be the earnest of many souls, the watchword to inspire them.

Miss McLeod bade them a hearty farewell. "There may arise some emergency, Mr. Darcy," said she, "when indorsing a note, or a similar matter, will be of great importance to you. I shall not promise to do much of it; but I am strongly interested in this experiment, and want it to have a fair trial. Let me hear from you occasionally; and, if you are in any great strait, apply to me."

Jack thanked her warmly, and she and Miss Lothrop went their way.

"She is a regular fairy godmother," he said enthusiastically to Maverick. "I wonder that you do not adore her!" and he studied his friend in astonishment.

"Have you never heard of people being so much alike they could not agree?" he asked with a light laugh. "What ever possessed her to bring Miss Lothrop? It

was in bad taste, to say the least; and, whatever faults
aunt Jean may have, she seldom makes a blunder of that
kind."

"Why, Sylvie was — well, a good deal pleased with
her. The acquaintance was so short" —

"Miss Barry is the most generous and least exacting
woman that I ever saw. She judges people by her own
noble soul. Jack Darcy" — Maverick shut his lips
with a sudden resolution, and turned his face partly aside,
then said in a curiously changed tone, "We are two fools
to be talking about women, when there are more important
matters on hand."

"But I shall always feel grateful to Miss McLeod.
There are several moneyed men here in Yerbury whose
capital is lying idle, who would not have done this thing
for me if they knew it would keep half Yerbury from
starving. Yet, if I had offered them ten per cent, they
would hardly have hesitated. It does seem to me sometimes, that these old dons tempt one into lying first, and
swindling afterward. If you make them all straight, they
do not care how much crooked work you do elsewhere."

"Natural depravity and innate selfishness."

And now began the real work. The mills were cleaned
of the year's accumulation of dust and cobwebs and
general untidiness. Winston went at the machinery with
hearty good-will, and put it in order. Circulars were
sent out to the old patrons and to new houses, and workmen, workwomen, and children straggled in to see what
was going on. Were Hope Mills to be really opened?
and was Mr. Darcy to be master? True, a good many
of the best men had gone off to try their luck elsewhere,
but there were plenty left for a start. Only, there was
a mystery these people could not understand. Something
about wages, and something about money; and Jack
patiently explained the matter, until, as he told Maverick,
he felt like a cheap-John auctioneer, dispensing wares.

"The best thing will be to have a meeting," declared Maverick. "See here, Darcy: I'll hire Brock's Hall myself; and we will have a lecture, or a conference-meeting. Subject, 'Work and Wages.' I'll have some posters out too. Every one will know what we mean, that we are honest men and true; and you will be spared this everlasting palaver. Then we will have some rules, or by-laws, or something, for the workmen. Talk to Mr. Winston about it. He would make a capital speaker, with his glib tongue."

Darcy thought it an excellent plan, and they set about it immediately.

"But you'll have to post me," confessed Winston. "The only co-operation I ever was in was a building-association, and our treasurer ran off with our funds."

Maverick promised to "coach" him. Indeed, it was the doctor who gathered up statistics, and put them in a compact and telling form.

They had a large audience, — men and women. "Robert Winston, Esq.," was the orator of the evening. He was a fluent speaker, and had a good deal of humor. He began about the early Anglo-Saxon guilds, and the banding together of craftsmen when towns grew large and prosperous, and labor was performed in the workshops, instead of at home; of the importance of the woollen-manufacture in the days of Elizabeth, not only in England, but on the Continent, when kings did not disdain to borrow money of these corporations; of their final overthrow, and the causes leading to it; of the growth of trades-unions, and the views of conflicting writers on the subject. The workman's necessities so often compelled him to accept what he felt to be inadequate returns, because he could not wait, — it was work or starvation with him, — so that in dull times he was not only at the mercy of the employer, but every other starving workman. On the other hand, so few workmen ever informed themselves concerning the employer's perplexities and dangers, they had no broad and vital interest in the business until they all became leagued together, as in co-operation.   Then they shared one another's burdens and prosperity.   It was not the one great fortune, but the many comfortable incomes.   It was the fruit of the noblest thought and the truest philanthropy.   As a producer it had done its best work in France ; and he went briefly over the work of the masons at Paris, and the Association Remquet, which, after carrying on printing business for ten years, divided among its members an average of over ten thousand francs ; the cloth-factory at Vienna, with its flour-mill, bakery, grocery, coal-yard, and farm ; the different societies in England, that were promising, to say the least.   All this had been done by the thrift and economy of individual members, who educated themselves by doing business, and so were enabled to dispense with the profits of middle-men, and the greedy clutch of speculators.

After Winston had finished, Dr. Maverick went briefly over their plans for Hope Mills in a very simple and direct manner.

"Winston was capital!" said Jack afterward.   "When we are hard up we can send him off on a lecturing-tour. But wasn't it rather over the heads of our people?"

"It was for others beside the workmen.   You know, Darcy, some men are so used to swindling and misrepresentation, that they invariably accuse every plan of another, of the same motive.   You will have a good deal of this back talk before your five years are ended ; and I want Yerbury to know that this is an old, old scheme. I might have quoted the children of Israel, as aunt Jean did, and shocked the religious portion of the community. But, after all, isn't the greatest truth, the Golden Rule, co-operation in *all* forms?" and he glanced up triumphantly.

Jack did not gainsay him.

He had hit the truth in regard to Yerbury. Some of those who had managed to hold on to their money through all the stress of hard times raised their eyebrows and shook their heads in amused derision. "A fool and his money," said they, and "Set a beggar on horseback," besides numerous wise saws people love to fling at their neighbors. A mortifying collapse was predicted. There wasn't a woollen-mill in the country paying. The smaller people who had been easily induced to invest their money in building-lots, under the supposition that in a few years there would hardly be standing-room in Yerbury, looked askance at this project, so much more easily does speculation appeal to human nature, than the slower but more honorable results of industry.

CHAPTER XIV

Iᴛ was easy enough now to get hands who would consent to the three-quarter wages. With one winter of semi-starvation the poor of Yerbury were glad to take any thing that promised bread. The masters were going to share with the men ; but they were made distinctly to understand, that, unless the mills earned something over and above this, there could be no surplus, no dividends. Another thousand of the capital had been made up by some of the hands, who thought this promised as well as railroad-stocks, lots out on country barrens, or even savings banks.

To be sure, some burly fellows, whose wives could hardly keep soul and body together over their washing-tubs, swore great oaths that Jack Darcy was a fool to think he could find men to play into his hands that way ! Bob Winston was a blower, and never kept at any one thing ; and some of the rest were old screws, and in six months time everybody would see !

However, Hope Mills rang out its great bell cheerfully on Monday morning, the middle of September. A small procession wended their way in at the side gate. The engine, with Robert Winston at its helm, as they had not suited themselves with an engineer, puffed and groaned ; but, if it was not a merry music, it was good to hear, for all that. The faces were pinched and thin with a year's care and want and the horrible fear of the future, but they tried to smile cheerfully. More than one poor woman had tears in her eyes, and spoke in that hysterical, half-laughing, half-crying tone, that told how deeply her feelings were moved.

By night they were quite settled in the old places, or adapted to new ones. Perhaps the year's experience had done these people some good : they had learned to manage closer. Cameron and Darcy had discussed thrifty French ways of management, and now meant to profit by them if possible. The American spirit of wastefulness should not run riot as it had in times past. Dyes and oils and chemicals were to be sharply looked after, and Cameron was the man to do it.

Before the first week was out, an engineer came to hand. There had been several applications, but some men raised their noses and laughed loudly at the rate of wages. A young chap just out of his time when the panic came on, and who had tried every thing, even to rail-roading, took the place with hearty thanks ; a quick, bright fellow too, who had a love for his business, and said in ten minutes time, " She's a pretty engine, Mr. Winston ! " with the enthusiasm of a true artist.

" That chap'll blow up Hope Mills in less than a month," said Jem Stixon, who had been refused. " You mark my words ! I wouldn't have wife or child of mine working there."

Darcy watched the temper of the employees, and reported every few days to Maverick. The little social " we " and " ours " was working wonders, he thought.

" And we do nothing ! " said Sylvie one evening, in a discontented tone, as she sat crocheting by Mrs. Darcy's pretty round table in the old library, that had become a kind of general business-room. " I thought you were going to set us women at work about something. Miss Morgan and I have been waiting patiently."

" There was the cooking-school " —

" But we have nothing to cook. And how are we to get any thing? unless we set up as those poor weavers in

Toad Lane, on our pocket-money. I believe I beg from
those who have a little, nearly half my time, to give to
those who have nothing. And, would you believe it, some
of the women begin to think they *must* be provided for
Mrs. Cairns asked me to-day when the relief-store was
going to open. She didn't see why there shouldn't al
ways be something here like the parish relief in England
And when Mrs. Ray offered to take Josie this winter, and
keep her in shoes for what she could do, and teach her a
little, Mrs. Cairns said, ' if she was worth any thing, she
was worth more than that. She might have her for a
dollar a week.' "

"Such people ought to go hungry," declared Jane
Morgan sharply.

"I've been thinking," said Jack, who now raised his
eyes slowly, "there is one thing you might help do ; and
indirectly, it would be very serviceable to me. Sylvie
you know Kit Connelly's corner, as they always call it?"

"Well, so it is : Mrs. Connelly earned the money tha
bought it, and I am glad she didn't let Dennis go on in
business until he spent every cent of it. And oh, Jack
all we women of Yerbury ought to be doubly proud tha
she wouldn't let Den keep a beer-shop there, nor hire i
to any one else."

"I hope you are. I think Kit was pretty plucky to
take the black eyes and the grumbling. It was a good
job for her when Den went over to the Bowman House fo
hostler. So, of course, it has been shut up a year and a
half. You know, two blocks down below, Keppler's doo
stands open for everybody, and so many of the mill-hands
pass that way. It is so easy to run in and get a glass, and
the men who bring their lunches go down for a mug of ale
It is a terrible temptation, and I wonder if they are no
more easily tempted on an empty stomach? Well, I've
been considering for some days if we could not start a
coffee-house there, — set Kit up in business. I'm no

going to fling a temperance-pledge right in every man's face, — for that makes them spiteful.   I do not even want to exhort.   But if we put it there, — right in their way, — and there was a nice fire in the evening, and maybe a book or two " —

" Splendid, Jack !   There's no such thing in Yerbury. Let's get about it right away ! " and Sylvie sprang up, as if she would start at once.

They all laughed.

" There must be a little planning first.   Mrs. Connelly is a bright, good-hearted creature, and can make good coffee ; and Rose and Kathleen would make nice little maids.   She stopped me to-night to inquire if there was any chance of their being taken in the mill.   There must be some diversity of employment, or presently we shall all be doing the one thing again," — and Jack smiled humorously.   " Dennis gets low wages, Bernard is in the mill, and there are two younger boys.   She takes in gentlemen's laundering, as you know.   She was wishing she could rent out the store, but no one wants it.   Now, if it could be altered into an attractive coffee-room, kept neat and bright, and — you will laugh at me, no doubt — but given a kind of style, — the cups clean and shining, the spoons decent, and some nice bread and butter for noon lunches.   All this at a moderate price.   The men pay five cents for their pint of ale, and it is often shared by two : they must not give more than three cents for their cup of coffee."

" I suppose you mean that we are to plan it all out for her," said Sylvie, and she looked across at Miss Morgan.

" It will not do to buy a pound of sugar and a pound of coffee at a time," said Jane concisely.

" Then I will be the capitalist," promised Sylvie.

" Exactly.   Kit had better do this on some money that she must give an account of, and it will make her more careful. She owns a cow, so there is the milk. I should like this started quietly, not with a great blare of opposition to the dram-shops.''

"Well, what must we do first?" asked Sylvie.

"I wish you and Jane would go down and call on her, and suggest the business. See how she takes it, and look around at the capabilities of the place. I will see to the fitting-up."

They went, as desired. Mrs. Connelly—a round, rosy, buxom Irishwoman, with a mellow voice, laughing eye, and artist-red hair—was very much taken with their plan. "To turn an honest penny in these hard times, and not be wronging any one, would just suit the likes of her. And there was the store standing empty,—but it might stand till the crack o' doom.afore she'd have a drop of rum sold in it. There never was a better man than Den when he was sober, and sure she'd had sorrow enough along wid drinking. And there was Barney growin' úp, and the two smaller ones, and she'd never, never put a bit of temptation in their way."

The store had been used for a meat-shop and green-grocery. Kit had sold the fixtures when she had been in sore need of money, so now it was a great bare room, with one large window and two small ones.

"Sure I can scrub an' whitewash it myself, an' put clean curtains to the windows. And you're very good to think of such a thing, Miss Barry,—may the saints bless you! An' if Mr. Darcy will see to getting what is wanted, I'll do my very best to please you all."

Sylvie blushed a little at taking the credit, but it was Jack's wish. Jack had a small portico built over the door-way, to keep out the cold in winter, and a neat sign put up, with but two words,—"Coffee-House." Sylvie and Miss Morgan ordered some cheap, small tables, some plain wooden chairs, and found two comfortable, old-fashioned, wooden settles. Then she collected old magazines and illustrated papers, and a rack was put up at one side for them.   All the tables were covered with light marbled rubber-cloth, so that they would be kept fresh and sweet.   The sugar and coffee were forthcoming.   Kit could roast coffee to a turn.   One Thursday evening the place was lighted up, and a few guests asked in ; and the next day the fame of Kit Connelly's coffee-house began. Half the folks in Yerbury knew her and Dennis.

Rose Connelly, who was just seventeen, a nice fresh-looking girl, was to keep the books, and take the money-as she was quite a scholar.   Several of the mill-hands went over immediately for their lunches.   Such splendid wheat, rye, and Graham bread, spread already, and brought on a clean plate !   A nice bite for three cents, and a solid meal for six.   Sylvie was to go down now and then, of a morning, to keep matters straight.

" There is one entering-wedge in the cause of temper-ance," she remarked, in her piquant way.   " Only, Jack, it does not seem quite right for us women to take the credit of it.   I confess, among all my plans, there has been nothing like this."

" I would rather not be openly connected with it," and Jack made a queer little grimace.   " By and by I may have to do some real fighting on my own account, and I don't want too many vulnerable points.   Human nature is rather queer and cranky, as you have, no doubt, observed by this time."

" But I do not see why any one should want to fight against your good work, Jack," said Sylvie, with an indignant flush.   " I am sure it is no light undertaking to provide all these people with work ; and everybody ought to strengthen your hands, instead of putting ob-stacles in the way."

" I must be prepared for all things."

Maverick was very enthusiastic over the coffee-house. It was a new institution in Yerbury.   There had been in good times several so-called cheap lunch-rooms, but the fare was invariably poor.

"Keppler will be your first enemy, and your worst one," said the doctor with a shrewd smile.

"Very well.   He must fight Miss Barry and Miss Morgan.   I did send a man to do some work, but Miss Barry paid the bills.   I keep my hands out of it altogether."

"Good for you, Jack.   And how does business progress?"

"I am dubious," and Jack shook his head in a mock-serious way.   "There is too much rose-color.   Every thing works to a charm.   Whether people really have learned something by the hard times, remains to be seen; but it looks so now.   And we couldn't have a better working firm.   Owen Cameron is the same kind of a man that Miss Morgan is for a woman, not stingy here and wasteful there, but a thorough-going economist.   Every week he makes a little saving somewhere.   It is what we needed to learn, badly enough.   He manages to make the men understand that every penny saved is for the benefit of all, that a yard of cloth or a pound of wool spoiled is to the loss of all.   And that is the only way to settle this business, this everlasting wrangle between labor and capital."

Amos Hurd and Peter Yardley used to talk over the other scheme of a co-operative store.   It would not do to have too many irons in the fire in such times as these, when no one had any great deal of money.   But it did seem as if poor people were paying at the dearest rate for every thing, partly because they asked for trust, and the only man willing to trust them to any extent kept a very full line of second or third rate articles, but the prices did not always correspond.

"Now, there's coal," said Yardley one evening.   "At the trade-sale it went up ten cents a ton on the average. Our dealers here, who had their yards full, put up their prices from twenty to thirty cents. I know, on the other hand, if coal takes a sudden tumble, they may lose ; but, after watching this thing for years, I find the prices go up five times with full yards, where they fall once. Now, I was thinking, when coal was bought for the mill, some extra car-loads might be ordered for the men."

"Yes," and Hurd opened his eyes widely. "Let us talk to Darcy about it."

Jack listened to their proposal with a sudden interest.

"It will be some trouble to you," he answered. "It is not as thoroughly screened, and there is the delivering. The men cannot carry it home in market-baskets."

"I don't know about the screening," said Yardley rather grimly. "When you clean up your bin, and find several bushels of sand and refuse out of five or six tons, you think half of it, at least, ought to have been good burning-coal. And in wholesale buying you get long tons."

"I can do it as well as not," replied Jack. "In fact," — laughingly, — "it will rather redound to my credit to order largely, and we have a somewhat extensive coal-shed. But you must look up one or two men who will cart it, and a man to screen ; and, when you have counted up your labor, decide upon what price you can offer your coal. Perhaps it would be as well to canvass, and learn how many tons you can dispose of."

The workmen had their own board of managers, of which Yardley had been elected president. They generally met every week, and now Yardley laid this matter before them. There would be an average saving, he thought, of two dollars on every ton, but the coal must be paid for in thirty days. If the men chose to leave one or two dollars every Monday night (for Darcy had wisely made Monday instead of Saturday pay-day) they might give in an order for one or two or even three tons.

Meanwhile Peter Yardley found some thorns even in his

path. A good, stout Irish lad was willing to do the screening at a dollar per day; but when he spoke to several carters, who were not busy half the time, to a man they stuck to their regular price, fifty cents per ton. Not one of them would work by the day.

"I can fix that just right," declared one of the men. "My wife's brother has a heavy wagon and two mules. He used to do carting for the iron-mills, and since then he has had mostly catch-jobs. He owns a little place over on the creek-road; and I know he will be glad enough to do it, and maybe take part of his pay in coal."

Seth Williams was hunted up. He would come, and bring his son who would help about loading, for two dollars and a half a day. There were seventy-odd tons subscribed for, but they decided to make their order one hundred tons. Coal was selling at six dollars and a half per ton at Yerbury. After due calculation, they offered theirs to the men at four.

It came duly to hand. After the first day, Williams hired another team on his own account, and his son drove one to its destination, making thereby extra time. Before the seventy tons had been delivered, the remainder was bespoken. They found when it had all been disposed of, and their workmen paid, that they had counted very closely, but there was a small balance on hand. This was deposited in the bank as a nucleus for a co-operative store as soon as there might be sufficient capital to warrant it. This, at least, had been a success. So many of the poorer class of Yerbury were not able to pay for the last ton of coal until they ordered again, being always that much behind.

Yardley was quite jubilant over his scheme.

"You forget that in this you and Hurd have received nothing for your trouble," said Darcy. "Then," smilingly, "you have no bad debts to count out. Still only a philanthropist can do business this way. If you were the proprietor of a coal-yard, you could not afford it.''

"I think I have something for my trouble, Mr. Darcy," the man answered proudly. "I have saved ten dollars on my four tons of coal, and that surely pays me.''

They were doing moderately well at the mill. Several orders had come in from old buyers; and now Winston started out on a travelling tour, being admirably fitted for that part of the business. At the West he managed to talk two large wool-dealers into a trade; they taking cloth of various grades in exchange, and disposing of it to the best of their ability.

"A regular old-fashioned barter," he wrote to Maverick. "It took a good deal of talking, to be sure, but I'm never the worse for that. They were pleased to get a fair price for their wool, and I lost nothing on my cloth. It clears out the stock, and keeps the men busy.''

Indeed, Hope Mills was doing a great thing for Yerbury. There was a brisker air on the streets, a kind of inspiring music in the whir and clatter, that spoke of food and warmth and raiment. Good feeling and sympathy had been touched; and though some of the workmen, who were harassed by back debts, looked rather ruefully at their small weekly pittance, still it was so much better than no money and no employment.

At the Darcys they held what Sylvie laughingly called "symposiums." The churches were organizing their winter work, for there would be need enough. The few who had found employment merely made a ripple on the surface. Some who had stretched out their scanty means the past year now found themselves penniless. Others had tramped about the neighboring towns and cities, getting a few weeks' work here and there, but had no fancy for facing winter in this precarious manner. The hopeful feeling animating so many in the early autumn died out again. It was feared that we had not seen the worst of the panic.

To Sylvie, who the preceding winter had been engrossed in art-studies and delightful social life, the want and misery were appalling. She and Miss Morgan did organize a visiting-society according to an idea of Dr. Maverick's; and though they alleviated many cases of distress, and were the better able to distinguish who were worthy, still they increased upon their hands.

"I begin to realize that poor people do not make the best of their money," she said. "They do not know how to prepare dishes that shall be cheap and palatable. And, worst of all, many of them cannot cook a potato so that it shall be fit to eat."

"The weak point of this world, Miss Sylvie," said Dr. Maverick. "When women learn to make good bread and cook potatoes, there will be a decrease of one-half in dyspepsia. Now, what is the secret of the potatoes? Come, air your ideas! Give me a recipe, and I will take it around among my patients. I advise them pretty generally to bake them, but I find some soggy and watery even then."

"Overdone," said Miss Morgan briefly.

"Well, state the exact time."

The women looked at each other, and laughed.

"From twenty minutes to half an hour," said Mrs. Darcy. "Some kinds boil easier than others. For baking, three-quarters to an hour."

"But the infallible test?"

"Watchfulness," said Jane.

"I must admit that you seem to understand it thoroughly, judging from the specimens I have seen and eaten. But are you not a little chary in your information?" and he glanced from one to another.

"Miss Morgan shall be first spokeswoman," declared Sylvie gayly.

"If it is a boiled potato," began Jane sententiously, as if she were a child speaking a piece, "I put mine in the saucepan, and pour hot water over them, as they come to a boil sooner, taking care that they shall be as nearly of a size as possible. In about twenty minutes I try an average potato. If I can stick a fork through it nicely, it is done. Then I pour off the water, letting it drain until every drop is gone, when I shake up the lot two or three times rather hard and quick, stand them on the back of the stove with the cover partly off, so that the steam may escape; and you have a dry, light, flaky potato, unless it was irremediably bad to begin with. I have sometimes boiled new and rather small potatoes in twelve minutes over a good fire. But cooking, like liberty, has the same high price, eternal vigilance."

Maverick laughed. "I shall remember this," he exclaimed. "You will yet hear of me teaching some of my poor patients to cook potatoes. Heaven knows there is enough need of it. Wasn't there some talk of a school for useful arts?"

"Yes," answered Sylvie, "only there was no money to start with, and we have all been so busy."

"What would be needed?"

"*Imprimis :* a room, a cooking-stove, a fire, a cook, and some materials," replied Sylvie with merry audacity.

How pretty and bright she was! He liked to watch her in these changeful moods. One great charm of this place was finding her here so frequently.

"And Mr. Darcy has been so much engrossed with weightier matters," she continued in a half apology.

"I really think I ought to be more interested in this question than Mr. Darcy. It supplements my work. While cheap living is an imperative necessity in times of depression and low wages, I cannot see why we do not make it more of a study. While we are so ready to copy

the vices of our French neighbors, perhaps .their virtues
would do us no harm.   A doctor often finds himself quite
nonplussed by something in the preparation of the patient's diet.   The old doctrine preached years ago, on St.
Paul's text of ' keeping the body under,' has worked as
much damage as the asceticism of the middle ages.   A
good healthy body is the first requisite everywhere ; and
to keep it so, every one's first duty.   When men began
to consider the body a poor, vile thing, to be treated with
contumely, and fed with what would just sustain life, they
offered an outrage to the highest work of God.   When
people think it is no matter what they eat, and that no
pains need be taken in the preparation, they have made a
big lapse toward heathenism.   Confusion of the physical
senses leads to confusion of the moral sense ; and weak,
miserable bodies with hysterical nerves, though they may
dream dreams, and see visions, cannot do good healthy
work in this world.   And your poor people need a good
deal of training on this subject.   It must be made an honorable, not a despised, business.   If I were to build houses,
I should make the kitchens large, light, and pretty ; and,
if any room had to be small and uninviting, it should be
that for the storage of the best furniture,'' laughing
humorously.

"Yes,'' responded Jane Morgan, '' I like to go into an
old-fashioned country kitchen, with a nice painted floor,
and braided rag rugs laid down here and there ; with a
grandmother's corner by a sunny window, and a father's
chair by the wide, cheerful chimney-piece, and a place for
the children to play, with plenty of room to get about.
Apples and nuts always taste so good in such a place !
Instead, we have a stuffy little kitchen and a cheerless
dining-room, that no one wants to sit in, and every member of the family goes to his or her room, and sociability
is at an end.   Then we must go to theatres, lectures, and

concerts, just to catch a glimpse of the members of our own family."

" There is a good deal of truth in that," and the doctor nodded sagaciously. " And now I shall take steps for that school.   I may count on you, Miss Morgan, may I not, and Miss Barry? "

They both promised.

CHAPTER XV.

MEANWHILE what had befallen Fred Lawrence?

He had been greatly shocked at his father's death.
True, the tender, intense affection that had so sweetened
childhood seemed to have died out; when they might
have attained to an enduring friendship, they had gone
separate ways, missing the exquisite sympathy that should
have existed between them. Whether the distance was
any disappointment to his father, he had never thought.
He was the only son of the house, and his slightest wish
had always been gratified. There had been no wretched
vices that sap body and soul, nothing to bring dishonor
on the old pure, family name; and, if David Lawrence
missed something that he had hardly longed for, he still
felt proud of his son.

But his son, bending over the coffined face, was
stunned, paralyzed. Of this death he had never thought.
Was it not rather a frightful dream?

The sharp reality followed fast enough. He listened,
still bewildered by the horrible visions that crowded upon
him. Hope Mills closed, notes going to protest, workmen
clamoring for pay, Mr. Eastman quite out of reach, indeed, no one knew just where.

Mr. Minor did not spare his father-in-law. How could
he trust every thing to Horace Eastman! How could he
allow George to go on unchecked in such a career of wild
speculation! forgetting that he had speculated quite as
wildly. And now all the property was covered with mort
gages, and not a dollar to be squeezed out of any thing
184

As for the bank business, that he sneered at. Let them look to the Eastmans. They might have known that a small manufacturing town like Yerbury could not stand such galloping progress. In his heart of hearts he thought George and Horace rather clever fellows to get away before the crash began. And if David Lawrence had only managed to provide well for his family, — his manifest duty, — the rest might have gone without a sigh, such trifles as notes and wages.

Fred Lawrence he looked upon as a baby. Indeed, Fred was of but little use in settling the business, much more plague than profit, since he stood up stoutly for his father's honor and integrity. He had that much of a son's love. And he characterized Horace Eastman's villany as it deserved: his education had not quite done away with his moral sense in such matters.

"Here for five years your father has given him a clean sweep with every thing! If you thrust temptation right in a man's way, what can you expect?"

"His honesty would not be of a very high order if it could withstand no temptation," Fred answered rather scornfully. "It was necessary for father to travel in the interests of the business. He surely could not stay here to watch him. And you thought well of Eastman."

"No man would play *me* such rascally tricks! There is no telling what he has done! Books can be doctored to look very fair."

But they found enough. Pay-rolls for men kept up long after they had been discharged, and many who had never been at all; systematic falsifications that could not be brought to light without a rigid inspection and comparison by an expert. But Hamilton Minor felt, with the world's wisdom, that bringing the Eastmans back as criminals would not be likely to lead to any restoration; while it would prove a family disgrace, and perhaps add Gertrude to the list of dependent ones.

"It makes me heart-sick!" declared Fred. "There is nothing but selfishness and hollowness and greed. Are truth and honor quite dead?"

"Very fine talk, my young friend," said Minor in a sneering tone; "but the question that more nearly concerns you is how you are all going to live, granting even that there may be enough to pay the debts. Of course this great house cannot be kept afloat. You had better discharge some of the servants, and retrench while you do remain in it."

Then had followed the talk with Agatha, when matrimony was proposed as a certain and sure remedy for these present ills: a cure the young man disdained with anger.

Mrs. Lawrence kept to her room, and was too ill to listen to business details, even if she could have helped in any way, which she could not. She fancied now, like many another woman, that her husband had been her only delight in life, and that there was nothing left. When Agatha suggested that she had been very short-sighted to consent to mortgaging Hope Terrace, she cried, and said "she would have given up every thing for him, and now that he was gone she wanted no fortune, — she should never leave her room again until she was carried."

If there had been any bright little Sylvie to run in and comfort her! any strong-hearted, tender woman, to whom he could turn! He seemed now to realize more keenly what he had lost, than on the night Sylvie rejected him. And that other strong, manly soul — no, bitterly as he might regret, he could no more go back to him than to Sylvie.

He roused himself, and began his work, utterly astounded at the extravagance that met him on every side. No doubt it looked right enough when there was plenty of money; but it seemed now as if the servants had been masters and mistresses, that all these luxuries existed for their sake, — the gardens and graperies, the greenhouses with their wealth of costly flowers; the horses standing idle in the stable, with only servants to use them; his father a plain man, his mother confined mostly to two or three rooms, and occasional visitors; supplies ordered lavishly, and wasted in a manner that seemed wicked even to him. He wondered in a vague way if the system was not radically wrong that brought such waste and carelessness in vogue, when hundreds had not the necessities of life. He remembered one talk his father had with Horace Eastman over in the library yonder, with champagne and cigars between them, in the height of one of the strikes, and how Eastman had figured to a penny the exact percentage of wages the mill could afford to pay. What if *they* had given up a little of their luxury, and *he* his ill-gotten gains!

He had the pictures packed under his supervision, and sent to New York. Not without a pang; for many of them he had selected, and each one had some pleasant reminder. The choice collection of the greenhouse was offered for sale, the elegant furniture, and all the most valuable of the personal property. Times were hard, and sales were slow; but there would be sufficient realized, it was thought, to pay the floating indebtedness. Hope Terrace and the mills would probably go for the mortgages. There was a small life-insurance settled upon Mrs. Lawrence, and the children would be fortuneless.

By spring the estate was in a fair way of settlement. Fred had vibrated between the city and Yerbury all winter, but his mother had been taken to Mrs. Minor's. A gardener and his wife were placed in charge of the house, while efforts were being made to rent it. A few rooms had not been disturbed.

And now Frederic De Woolfe Lawrence looked about him to see what could be done. Up to this time he had never given himself an anxious thought about money or his future. Now it stared him unpleasantly in the face. What could *he* do?

Many things, he said at first, with the buoyant certainty of youth and inexperience. Here was his education, his talents, his fine mental training. Surely he had the magical open-sesame of some door.

So he set to work industriously, and wrote several articles on the history and the philosophy of the pure sciences. Very fine-drawn indeed, very intellectual and analytical, as he went through the different schools of thought, being able, it seemed to him, to argue as well for the one side as for the other. Then he tried Neo-Platonism with its profoundly mystical aspects and its brilliant array of philosophers, its fascinating aspects of Pantheism. The new world and to-day had nothing for him ; the dead and gone past, every thing.

Alas ! From every side he heard the cry, Literature had been overdone. No one would buy, no one would read, in this great turmoil. Everybody wrote now, school-girls, college-fledglings : even small farmers and mechanics, with the training of the present and a smattering of knowledge, set up for geniuses.

One advised him to try the realistic school : the old-time philosophies had lost the high place they once held, and to gain the attention of to-day writers must have snap and vim. Another recommended popular science made easy and attractive to general readers, something that caught at the first glance. Life was too short to be devoting years to any one branch of study. Still another was fain to persuade him to attack the pernicious systems and monstrous abuses of the present day. Then he stumbled over Crosby, one of his college-chums and a member of the L—— Club, where he had been a frequent and welcome visitor the winter before.

"My dear fellow," said he, with patronizing good-nature, "take my advice, and let literature alone. It is one of the most uncertain things. To-day you may suit, to-morrow a chap comes along with some new fandango or summersault of high art, and the world leaves everybody to run after him, and you are thrown over. A man cannot earn his salt unless he has the *entrée* of the initiated ring. As for journalism, you may hammer at that for twenty years before you get a position."

Poor Fred went back to his room sorely depressed. It was a quiet, clean room in a second-rate hotel, for which he paid twelve dollars a week. There he sat and brooded, until taking up the paper one morning he saw the arrival of one of his old professors at the " Grand Union." Perhaps he might put him in the way of something. So he plucked up heart, and went to call.

Professor Dennison received him very cordially, and expressed the warmest sympathy for the loss of his father and his fortune. He listened attentively to the young man's desires, and answered in suavest of tones.

There were so many applications : every avenue seemed full. Young lawyers and doctors, finding no opening, had gone back to teaching, and the college-graduates of every year swelled this number. He would bear it in mind, and see what he could do ; but he advised his young friend not to build too high hopes. " If I could make a place I should put you in it at once," he said kindly, just as he said it to a dozen others.

It was so everywhere. There were no copyists, translators, or writers needed. The clerkships were overcrowded. It was not that there were too many doing one thing, but every thing, — too many people in the world. Could the Malthusian doctrine be right, after all?

He dropped into his brother-in-law's office one morning, and, though he hated to ask a favor of him, discussed in a rather fragmentary and abashed way the possibility of getting any thing to do ; and a fortnight after, Mr. Minor sent him word of a broker who wanted a clerk, salary fifty dollars per month.

It was better than nothing. Then, too, it was a begin-

ning, although he could imagine more congenial employ-
ments. It did not look much like hard times, to note the
immense amount of stocks and bonds that passed through
the hands of this great house.

Just at this period Irene returned. A fine, stately girl,
with the indescribable air that foreign society gives. Yet
she seemed haughty, bitter, and satirical ; and it came out
presently that she and Gertrude had quarrelled over a
possible husband, and the amiable Gertrude had taunted
her with dependence in the future. Irene had sold some
diamonds, and travelled on the proceeds.

" I think you were very short-sighted, Irene," said
Mrs. Minor when she had drawn this story out of her
sister. "A handsome American girl does stand a better
chance for matrimony abroad than here. So many fortunes have been lost in the panic, and certainly I cannot
blame these men for choosing heiresses. You have been
in society a great deal here, and you will find fresh young
girls beginning to crowd you out. Fred has nothing, and
from present indications will hardly be able to take care
of himself. It was such a misfortune that papa had every
thing mortgaged ! So Gertrude was right," in a bitterly
suave tone : " you must be dependent upon some one until
you do marry."

" Oh, no ! I might set up millinery, — with my taste
and aptitude for arrangement. I think I have read of
reduced young women who made fortunes in that line,"
retorted Irene the queenly, in her unmoved way. She
was not one to cry out at a dagger-thrust.

" Don't be a fool ! " advised Mrs. Minor, in a short,
incisive tone.

She, like most other people, had meant to economize
this summer ; but now she made a sudden start for Newport. Irene certainly was peerless in her half-mourning,
with her statuesque figure. But there was not an eligible
at Newport, so they turned their steps Saratoga-ward.

And here they found an old admirer of Mrs. Minor's, Gordon Barringer, a widower for the second time, the owner of a silver-mine and a railroad, and Heaven alone knew the length and breadth of his possessions.

Miss Agatha Lawrence had turned up her aristocratic nose at him, as a rather coarse and self-assured person, as proud of his want of education as other men were of its acquirement. Now he was about forty, stout, high-colored, loud of voice, and with an important swagger. But money had given " our enterprising citizen " power, and he both understood and wielded it skilfully.

His wife had been dead barely six months, but when he met Irene Lawrence he decided at once that the penniless beauty would be only too glad to marry him. He was proud to think he could afford to be so magnanimous. Mrs. Minor settled herself to the fact that there must be no foolish dallying. Of course Irene *would* see. She could not be so idiotically, so fatally blind!

I do not know that at this period of her life Irene Lawrence had any ideal. She had made conquests so easily, she had found men so much alike, and in her secret heart she despised them for being so ready to kneel and bow at beauty's shrine. It seemed to her as if youth and fortune were alike boundless; and she literally took no thought for the morrow, until the tidings of her father's death was followed by the subsequent news of loss of fortune.

If George Eastman had a self-conviction that he and his cousin had contributed to this downfall, he tried to make it up to Irene in brotherly kindness and generous expenditure where money was concerned. He solaced himself with the thought that, after all, he had no more than his own, or what should have been his own right-fully, though he fancied he could not have gone on to the end quite as Horace had.

When Sir Christopher Frodsham came across the two

ladies in Paris, Gertrude exulted at the easy conquest. A man of fifty, whose young years and health had been spent in sowing a plentiful crop of wild oats, but to whom had come now, quite unexpectedly, a fortune and a title; and prosperity, after years of rather bitter economy, made him miserly, as it not unfrequently does such men. That he would have been glad to marry this young, beautiful girl, for himself alone, was most true. And Irene, in the bewilderment of the losses, inclined to his proposal, and begged time for consideration.

He was not a man she could admire, respect, or love. He was narrow, egotistical, selfish, and with the pitiful vanity of a worn-out *roué*. Frodsham Park was in a lonely, mountainous part of England, bordering on Wales; and this man would look upon his wife as a nurse and companion, and the mother of an heir.

There must have been a little strain of heroism in the girl. Suddenly, in one of those quick, vivid flashes, like mental lightning, she saw that she could not do this thing. She was not at all given to analysis; she had never dissected her own soul, or that of her neighbors; but she arrived at one of those swift, clear verdicts, — she could not marry Sir Christopher; and she told him so, with a frankness a trifle tenderer, perhaps, than she had used with her lovers heretofore, as if some way she had wronged him in thought.

Over this, as I said, she and Gertrude had bitter words and a parting. Now the same thing stared her in the face again. This lover was too obtuse to be stung by the fine arts of coquetry that lengthened practice had brought to perfection. In all the bravery of self-assertion, he did not know when he was beaten; and so he fought against the intangible spear-points with which Miss Lawrence could surround herself.

Mr. Barringer was called to New York on important business law-suits; and two days after, Mrs. Minor declared herself wearied out with Saratoga. Irene felt the walls of fate closing remorselessly about her. Why should she struggle? she asked herself. After all, what could she do but marry?

Meanwhile, Hope Mills had been sold. Fred made some inquiries about it.

"A woman — a rich old maid, I believe, by name McLeod, who knows enough to drive a sharp bargain — has taken it. Some one is to set up the business, I heard; an impecunious nephew, no doubt. No one but a fool would make a venture when the market is overstocked with goods. It is a shame that the estate had to lose such a valuable piece of property; but there was no income to pay taxes and interest, and, standing empty, it would soon have eaten itself up."

Fred sighed. For the first time, he wondered how it would have ended if he had been brought up to some useful business, and perhaps have taken Eastman's place with his father. As for stock and share jobbing, he was heartily sick of it. To him it appeared an immense system of swindling the ignorant and unsuspecting.

However, he was not destined to nurse his disgust very long in brooding silence. The last of September the great house of Bristol, Stokes, & Co., collapsed. The wreck was unexpected, the ruin wide-spread. The house of Minor & Morgan was hard hit, which did not improve Mr. Minor's temper, though, Spartan-like, he wore a cheerful face, and kept his losses to himself. Even if it should be his turn next, the world must not know it.

"There's a letter that concerns you, though it was sent to me as administrator," said Minor to Fred, as he sauntered in one morning, tossing the missive over to him.

Fred opened it with languid indifference, and his eye wandered over the following lines: —

HAMILTON MINOR, ESQ.

Dear Sir,—On taking possession of Hope Mills, for business purposes, I find some personal property belonging to the late Mr. Lawrence. It may have a value for the family, and shall be at your disposal whenever you desire it.   Respectfully yours,

JOHN DARCY.

"As soon as Hope Terrace is dispose.. of, the accounts can be audited and settled," said Minor in a sharp, business-like way. "The debts have all come in, and been paid dollar for dollar; though, if your father had been a prudent man, he would have made sure of something for his family. No one expects estates to pay more than fifty per cent nowadays."

Fred rose, and crushed Jack Darcy's note in his pocket, holding himself proudly, while his cheek flushed.

"I am very thankful," in a clear, cold tone. "My father's life was pure and honorable, and no man can fling a stone at his grave. I would rather be penniless, as I am, than have it otherwise."

"Oh! very well, very well," sneeringly.

Fred walked out of the office, and turned into Broadway. The same curious, restless, hurrying throng. Where were they all going? Did they find room and work? How clearly the sun shone! The sky was so blue, with great drifts of white floating about, — strange barques on a mystical sea. In spite of the outside roar and rush, there was a solemn and awesome stillness within him. He began to feel how entirely alone he stood. A twelvemonth ago there were hosts of friends pulling him hither and yon, proposing this and that, laughing and chatting gayly. Where were they now? Not all weak and false, but the shadow of circumstances had drifted them apart. We do not always cease to love or like when separation ensues; and in this shifting, changing life, people drop out, yet are not quite forgotten. Some of the young fellows whom fortune had buffeted had found a place in active, stirring life : he, with his education, refinement, accomplishments, and talent, was merely a piece of driftwood. Sylvie Barry had been right, — he was a useless appendage to the world. Ah, no wonder she despised him! Sturdy, honest Jack Darcy could find a place. His self-complacency was more than touched, — it was shattered, completely broken up. The present was blank and colorless, the future like a thick mist in which there penetrated not one ray of light. What did all his elaborate philosophies for him now? — art, that was to regenerate the world ; science, that explained and refined, and found a place and a reason for every thing in the universe ; man, the most important of all. And here he was, tossed aside like a weed. Who cared whether his nature was foul or kinglike? He was, in truth, one of the atoms floating about in space, and finding no use or purpose. The world could go on just as well without him. Why, if he should drop himself over into the river, there would be only a ripple. He laughed, as if his personality was something that did not really belong to him, that could be put off at will, that was, in truth, answerable to no power. All of life, then, had been a lie !

He stumbled onward blindly. A sense of dreary mystery crept over him, — an utter hopelessness. He essayed to stretch out his hand to some passer-by, but the careless faces mocked him. There was no strength or stay. He could not even cry out with his anguish, — it was a dumb, inarticulate voice. All his idols had been destroyed, and there was no God to cry to !

His last three weeks' salary had gone down in Bristol & Co.'s ruin. There were some jewels to sell, a few more pictures, several sets of rare books, and — what then?

Starvation had appeared so utterly improbable in this great, thriving world, and here he was, almost face to face with it, — he who had never taken an anxious thought

about any thing, who had felt as if he really honored
money by the spending of it.   A beggar!   An object
of charity to Hamilton Minor!

No, that should never be.   He tried to rouse himself
from his lethargy.   He went around to stores and offices
where he was not known, and asked for something to do,
as if in a curious masquerade.   The same answer everywhere.   Nothing!   The sun went slowly down, the street-
lamps were lighted.   Every inch of his body ached with
the long tramp and nervous exhaustion.   He had eaten
nothing since breakfast, but he was not hungry.   What
if he did steal quietly over to the river, and end it all?

The desperation was hardly black enough for that.
Somewhere near midnight he strolled home: how much
longer would there be a home, he wondered?

He thrust his hand in his pocket, and the bit of folded
paper struck sharp against his fingers, so he drew it out.
Hardly the familiar school-boy scrawl: Jack used to hate
writing, he remembered.   This had a decisive force
about it.   How odd that business-like " John " looked!
" Jack! "   He uttered the name aloud, and a thrill
seemed to warm his frozen heart, — to stir emotions
most contradictory.   A sense of shame predominated,
tingling his very finger-ends, crimsoning his pale cheeks,
and stinging his soul with a sense of utter humiliation.
He had prided himself so much upon the immaculate
honor of his life, and lo! here he stood, self-convicted
of one of the basest of sins, — broken faith.   Not from
any sudden, hot dispute, not from a knowledge of deception or any small meanness, but deliberate, well-considered
treachery.   It would have been manlier had he said to
Jack, " Our ways lie apart, and in the future we shall
meet so seldom, it is hardly worth while to keep up a pretence of friendship."   He had skulked away instead, kept
out of sight, — basely shunned the strong, tender soul
that had helped to make a peevish boyhood sunny and
bright.

Black as this ingratitude looked to him now, he experienced a strange and intense desire to see his olden friend once more. What was he doing at Hope Mills? Had he found a place?

The next morning's mail brought him a check for sixty dollars, for an article he had thought little of himself, and sent merely because he had happened to finish it, and was despatching his ventures out on the sea of chance. Then he went over to Mrs. Minor's: he had not seen his mother for several days.

He was quite in the habit of going directly up to her room; but, as he neared it, he heard voices raised in no gentle discussion. Agatha stood in the middle of the room, flushed, angry, an open note in her hand; Mrs. Lawrence was weeping hysterically, while Irene sat pale and sullen, but her eyes gleaming with a dangerous fire.

"Very well: if you deliberately decide to take a beggar's portion, then, do not look to me for any further help," said Mrs. Minor. "This marriage would have afforded you every luxury; and you have thrown aside the chance, like a silly school-girl. Perhaps you *have* some secret, favored lover!" and the glittering eyes might have annihilated a weaker woman than Irene Lawrence.

"If I had, I should go to him. I would live on crusts and a cup of cold water with him, rather than luxury," with a bitter, stinging emphasis, "and my own humiliation. The man would drive me mad, Agatha! Some day, yielding to an irresistible impulse, I should murder him;" and she gave a shrill, unnatural laugh.

Fred went over to her, and took her hand. His business in life was to be her champion, her defender, her support, —not only against this monstrous marriage, at which her soul revolted, but Agatha's sneers and flings, and the dependence a proud soul must naturally feel when the very bread turns to ashes in one's mouth. How it was to be done, he could not tell at that moment; but he drew one long breath of honest, hopeful manliness, and resolved to leave no stone unturned.

His mother wept in his comforting arms. She was very much shattered, — quite an old woman long before her time, made so by the follies of an indolent, enervating life. Like a pang the thought pierced his brain, that for these paltry results his father had given the strength and labor of manhood.

CHAPTER XVI.

THERE were a few faint hints of autumn in Yerbury. The air was warm, and freighted with the peculiar sweetness of over-ripe grapes and apples, of dried balsam and faded golden-rod by the wayside. The very air seemed to quiver with intense contrasts of color, the yellow beeches standing out in strong relief, the bronze-red of one great oak, the bluish-green of the spruce, and the tender tints of fading, long-armed larches, drooping in regretful sadness. Lights of silvery gray and russet-brown, pale gold and hazy purple, and a sapphire sky bending over all. The artistic side of Fred Lawrence's soul was touched as he had once fancied nothing this side of Europe could touch it.

For a moment a mighty rush of regret came over him. This magnificent place had been his home. Perhaps he would have been more than human not to have experienced a pang.

He wandered about for some time. It was too lovely to go in and explore those dusty, darkened rooms: this evening would answer for that. He paced the lawn, he lingered by the gate ; he took a turn about the grapery, now used for profit by the thrifty farmer who had charge of the place. Then he turned, and went down the street. The bells were ringing for six. From his height above, he could see the laborers wending their way, the great chimney of Hope Mills. He would walk in that direction. They would all be gone by the time he reached it.

The streets were indeed nearly deserted. In the shade

here the wind blew a little chilly. Yes, it was just the same; but then, it would not be likely to alter in a year. Why, it seemed a decade almost, since the night he had come home to his dying father!

Ah, if they had been more to each other! Did he go about with a lonely spirit, Fred wondered, feeling the uselessness and insufficiency of the life he was leading? Had he been glad to lay the burthen down?

A sudden firm, manful step ran down the stone stairway with a cheerful ring, and a voice hummed a tune softly, as one sometimes does for a seeming accompaniment, when the mind is occupied with other things;—a tall, robust figure, with long arms, and a springy step, as if he might still leap a post, or jump the creek. He was rushing off, when, curiously enough, with no other motive than an impulse, he turned, and saw an almost motionless figure.

Whether he would send for the articles belonging to his father, or visit Hope Mills in person, risking a sight of Jack Darcy, or whether he would summon courage enough to ask for his old friend, were matters that Fred had put off for to-morrow's decision. Why he had wandered here at all, amazed him now; and he stood quite breathless at the unexpected apparition, without power to move or speak.

If he had still been in the high tide of prosperity, Jack would have passed him by silently, but with no rudeness. Something in the bent head, the pale face, the general melancholy attitude, came home to his heart,—his fresh, generous, magnanimous heart. He ventured a step nearer, he put out his hand.

"Fred, old fellow!"

The rich, full voice might have melted any heart. The frank, honest eyes lighted with wonderful tenderness: there was a glow and earnestness that could come only from a large, forgiving soul, capable of putting by its own sense of pain or any past discomfiture.

Fred Lawrence crimsoned to the very edge of his hair, to the farthest depths of his soul. He would have taken the hand: then he drew back with a gesture of self-reproach, as if he could tread his past sinful pride in the dust.

"Let's forget the bygones," the hearty young fellow began, "that is, if you would like to have it so," drawing back a trifle to give him his choice as a delicate woman might have done.

"Thank you, Jack," grasping the warm, firm hand in his own pale, cold one, and raising his soft dark eyes, so near to tears. Just now no other words would come.

Jack drew the hand through his arm. "I've thought of you so many times," he began, as if they had parted the best of friends. "It has been a sad year for many, doubly so for you."

"Sad indeed. O Jack!"

It was all uttered in the long tremulous swell of voice that tells the whole story.

"Yes."

With that, their friendship was renewed. Women might have fallen into each other's arms with expressions of penitence and forgiveness; but they had said their say, as was characteristic of both.

"Were you coming in?" and Darcy turned back as he asked the question.

"No: I only reached Yerbury an hour or so ago on a little business. Some remembrance of old time brought me hither."

"I am glad it did. Shall we walk down Main Street? Are you staying at Hope Terrace?"

"I shall be for a few days."

A silence fell between them. There was no one else in the street; and their steps sounded with a steady tramp, as if they might walk on to some definite end.

"Jack, dear old friend, after requiting your tender

love to my exacting and selfish boyhood with a pitiless treachery that will always shame my manhood, I wonder if I dare ask it back, if I dare come to you."

" There is nothing to give back. I do believe I have kept up a sort of girlish hankering for you. And now, if I can do any thing, if you are in any perplexity " —

" Come up to Hope Terrace, and take tea with me. I want to talk to you all the evening. You have just the same mesmeric strength that used to soothe me when a boy. What a milk-and-water cub I must have been! I wonder you did not throw me over."

Jack laughed.

" Let us turn back to Kit Connelly's, and I can send a message home, so that mother will not keep tea waiting."

That done, they strolled on together the same path by which Fred had come. The sun had dropped down behind the hill, and the glowing tints had faded to purple-black and indistinct grays. They wound around the hills, and came up to the very gate where their last good-by had been uttered. And Fred remembered then that this was the first time Jack had shared the hospitality of Hope Terrace, now when it was no longer his.

Mrs. Milroy gave them some supper in a pretty little apartment which had been the servants' parlor, and was now hers. Then they went up to Fred's room, which had been opened and aired. Some of its choicest belongings had been taken away, but another than Fred would not have remarked this. And here they renewed the remembrances of the years that had fallen between.

" It seems cowardly to come to you in trouble, and to take so large a share of your sympathy again," Fred said with his good-night. " But you always were so strong and earnest."

He went down to the mill the next day, and was much interested in the working of Jack's plans.

" You found your place," he said with a curious intonation, as if he half envied the man before him.

"Yet in all truth I should not have chosen this," Jack answered with honest gravity. "But, when I found circumstances would keep me here, I resolved to work at it persistently and faithfully; and I learned in it the larger lesson of the true dignity of labor. If I should solve my problem successfully, I can ask no more. Five years is a long while when you count the days," and he smiled.

"You will succeed, I know. You have just that mastery over every thing."

Jack finally persuaded Fred to come down to the well-remembered cottage, and see his mother. Mrs. Darcy would have welcomed her bitterest enemy if Jack had desired her to.

All this time Jack was thinking whether he could do his old friend a good turn. He hated to offer him any subordinate position in the mill. At present he could attend to the book-keeping. Then he heard there was to be a change at the paper-mills, and went over. They wanted a clerk and foreman, one with taste enough to select pretty designs, and who could keep books.

"I do not know as you would like it, Fred," he continued with some hesitation in his cheery tones.

"I have been a dawdler long enough, and I have had a bitter experience in finding *any thing* to do. I shall be glad to take it, and you may believe I will try my best. Many, many thanks for your kind interest."

There had been a sharp, short struggle in Fred's soul. He would rather have gone elsewhere, where he was not known. But if fate had resolved to bring him back to Yerbury, if she had offered him bread here, while it had been stones elsewhere, he would certainly be a fool to starve for pride's sake. Some wholesome ideas had found lodgement in his brain, along with the Greek myths and synthetic philosophies. If he could not astonish the world with brilliant reasoning, he might at least get his own living.

He went back to the city, and discussed the project with his mother and Irene. She had a tender longing for her son: to be with him would afford her greater satisfaction than the magnificence of her daughter's house. Irene consented stonily. It was burying herself alive, but then no one would torment her with hateful marriages. To stay here with Agatha was simply unendurable.

Mrs. Minor made no further comment than to say she did not think her mother could be kept as comfortable. Irene was her own mistress.

So Fred Lawrence went back to Yerbury and work. It was an altogether new undertaking. He had no business training and no experience, except his desultory two months in Bristol's office. Yet from the very first day there was something that interested him here, although for awhile the smells, the dust and disorder, half sickened him. As for any wound to his pride, he felt that less because the whole world seemed to have taken a general overturn. Half of the elegant houses in the neighborhood of Hope Terrace were for sale, and shut up. Expensive country mansions to be used for a few summer months were quite beyond present incomes. A month at the seaside cost much less. Costly scientific, or rather unscientific gardening, — since the true aim of science must be the best adjustment of power to the desired result, — graperies, green-houses, henneries standing empty, the money lavished upon them so much waste material at present, — where had the wealth gone to so suddenly? He could not understand the rapid and wide-spread ruin. Even of themselves, — how was it that for years there should be no stint, but absolute wastefulness, and then nothing at all?

He was so new to any business results, that he seemed like a child groping in the dark. And here was Jack Darcy, with his academy training merely, managing one of the great problems of the day, taking hold manfully to right the wrongs brought about by selfishness and utter disregard for one's neighbor. Had Plotinus struck the grand key-note when he said he " was striving to bring the God within us in harmony with the God of the universe " ? For might there not be false gods within?

He found he had not much time for abstruse speculations, which was all the better for his mental health. After enduring the dirt and disorder of the office for a week, he set about remedying that. He might not be able to regenerate the world, but he could make one little room decent. The office-boy and the scrub-woman were called in ; the desks and shelves were cleared of the accumulation of months, and presented quite an orderly aspect. He found his hands blistered by the rough handling, but the reward was a wholesome hunger and a good night's sleep. Not quite as entertaining, perhaps, as a scramble in the Sierras or the Alps, but productive of as beneficial results.

Then there was a home to be found. Living at Hope Terrace on a thousand a year would hardly be possible, even if it could be had rent free. So he asked Mrs. Darcy's advice about the matter, and she proposed a pretty cottage, — there were so many standing empty. It seemed very queer to be counselling this proud, sad-eyed young man, who a year or two ago had hardly deigned to look at them. Yet, like Jack, she still held a tender feeling for the pretty, enthusiastic boy she remembered.

There had been in his mind a great struggle about Sylvie. He knew now that she belonged to Jack. That thorough manliness and integrity, that earnest, unflinching soul, the rich, generous temperament that could be so tender to weakness, so forgiving to wrong, was the soul of her ideal hero. And he had dared to offer her his poor, paltry affectation of love ! Blinded by his own arrogant self-esteem, he had spurned the pure pearl, and taken the empty, glittering shell to her as the kind of treasure he was satisfied to deal in.

How thoroughly he despised himself! It was such a keen, bitter humiliation! Not only that he had aspired to her, but that he should have misrepresented and traduced Jack, not from an overwhelming passion of jealousy, — that might be pardoned, — but a shallow, overweening vanity of wealth and position.

"She shall see that I have learned to respect and honor him!" he said to himself with an intensity of regret that was very honest and real. "If I can never regain *her* esteem, I shall at least try for my old place in his regard."

They found a pretty, convenient cottage, quite on the opposite side of Yerbury, suiting Fred much better than to be near his old friends. The furniture was brought over from the great house ; and, though it had seemed but odds and ends there, it was amply sufficient. Irene's piano and some of the old family silver had been saved out of the wreck, a few of the less expensive pictures, and sufficient books to form quite a library. Fred really enjoyed arranging and planning. It was quite a matter of astonishment to him, that rules of art and harmony were needed at every step: if he could not make them remunerative in a written article, he could put them in practice here.

He kept much to himself, being busy in the office during the day, and at home in the evening. He was sick of society, of the world in general. He had met Maverick a few times, but he shrank from strangers. Mrs. Darcy's tender, unobtrusive motherliness, he enjoyed, but he did not dare to accept much of it. The duties of his life were marked out plainly before him, and he must not swerve from the path. It was to be a kind of neutral tint, twilight rather than sunshine ; and the joys he might come to long for, he must put away with a firm hand.

The first of December every thing was in readiness for his small household, even to the tidy housekeeper Mrs. Darcy had found for him among her poor. Mrs. Law-

rence and Irene came in the promised train; and he met
them with a carriage and a multiplicity of wraps, although
it was a bright, pleasant day. His mother clung to him
with tremulous hands: he realized more than ever how
much she had broken in the past year, — very little older
than Mrs. Darcy if counted by years, but whole decades
if judged by every other point.

Irene was cold and stately. She did not like coming
here, — neither did she like staying at Mrs. Minor's.
Wild thoughts had flooded her brain of going somewhere,
and under a new name making a mark in the world. She
had a fine voice, and a decided talent for histrionics, but
how to get to this place where fame and fortune would be
at her command? How to bridge across any chasm?
Nothing, she said to herself, but just stand helpless, and
see the great world go on, with no part nor lot in the
matter. If she must be buried alive, as well at Yerbury
as anywhere.

There had never been any sentiment between her and
Fred; in truth, none of the Lawrence women ever were
given to sentiment. She walked into the little parlor with
the step of a queen, and gave a cool stare around.

"I hope you will like it" — with some hesitation.
"There is your piano. And mother's room looks as it
did at the Terrace, with the exception of its being so
much smaller. And here is a library. Here is our dining-
room — some of the old engravings, you see."

"Could I go to my room? Which is it, Fred?" and
his mother looked up with a weak, pleading smile.

"Yes: let me carry you. You are so thin and light
now, and you must be fatigued after all this journey;"
and, taking her in his arms, he bore her up-stairs.

It was a pleasant room over the parlor, with an alcove
toward the south, in which the mid-day sun was shining.
A bright fire burned in the grate: there were her own
easy-chairs, a bit of the carpet she had once chosen, the

Persian rug she had admired so much when Fred first sent it home, the bed with its snowy drapery, and little ornaments with their familiar faces.

"It is delightful," she said, still clinging to her son's arm. "And I am to stay here with you? Agatha is very good, of course; but I have always had my own home, and if I did sign it away it was to save your poor dear father. I don't see how things could have ended so, only, if he had lived, it would all have been different;" and she wiped away the tears that came so easily now.

Fred put her in the chair nearest the fire, and began to unfasten her wraps. He had been quite an expert in delicate ways during his prosperity.

"Your room is next — there," nodding his head to the open doorway, and glancing up in his sister's immovable face. "I hope I made my divisions rightly: I thought you would like to be near mother."

"It is all as well as it can be, I suppose," she answered with weary indifference.

There came to Fred Lawrence just then a painful sense of want and loss, a far-reaching sympathy in something that had never been, and now, when the outside glitter was torn away, left life cold and barren. Was human love so much?

His mother went on in her weak, inconsequent way, yet her foolish praise was very sweet to him. He had been living such a lonely life for months, that even he was grateful for something that looked like home, for a woman's figure flitting about, and some voice beside his own.

The dinner-bell rang presently.

"I ordered yours brought up here," said Fred; "and I will have a little with you, then I must go back to the office."

"It is terrible, Fred! That you should have to" —

"Dignify labor," and he laughed. "Mother dear, I

was so thankful to get something to do!   And I am proud
of making a home for you.   Am I not your only son?''

"But a clerk!'' ·Some of the old Hope disdain spoke
out there.   "I cannot bear to think of it — with all your
education and talents aud genius.   I wish you had found
some business.   There is the five thousand dollars of the
life-insurance, you know·; and you could take it, though
Agatha made me promise that I would not have it fooled
away in any thing.   But I should be glad to have you use
it.''

Fred stooped suddenly, and kissed her on the forehead.
There *was* something in mother-love, after all.

Just then Martha West came in with the tray.   Fred
drew out the folding breakfast-table that his mother had
so often used, while he was introducing Martha to his
mother and sister.   She courtesied, and proceeded to lay
the cloth and the dishes, and disappeared for the viands
themselves.

"Is one woman expected to do all the work?'' asked
Irene at length.

"She thinks she can — with so small a family.   Of
course I'' —

Irene raised her hand deprecatingly.   "Spare me details,'' she said.   "It is very bitter to eat the bread of
dependence: I have learned that already.''

He made no answer.   Mrs. Lawrence looked from one
to the other in helpless bewilderment, but Martha entered
again, and changed the troubled current.

It was quite a picnic dinner.   Irene unbent a little at
the sight of the rare china and beautiful old silver.   She
supposed every thing had gone down in the whirlpool of
ruin, and that humiliation would be complete in delft and
plated ware.   Then she ventured to glance around.

Fred chatted gayly, making talk.   It had not used to
be one of his accomplishments in his magnificent days
when women vied with each other in the delight of enter-

taining him. It was pleasant to see his mother touch the bell, and sit back in her chair while Martha brought in the dessert.

"And now I must go. Do not expect me much before seven. I wonder if you will feel able to come down to tea? Ah! there are the trunks, just in time. I will send them up, and you will feel quite at home when you have your belongings in place."

Then he went back to his desk, and for the next two hours was too busy to think. After all, there is nothing like energetic employment to keep dismal forebodings out of one's mind.

But that evening after supper, when they had gathered in the library, Mrs. Lawrence began to question him concerning Hope Mills. Agatha had said some one had started the business anew.

Fred explained.

"But how could the workmen do it alone? Your father never trusted them, Fred; and I am sure *my* father had trouble enough with them in his day! They were always an ignorant, unreasonable set. Don't you remember how they struck several years ago, and workmen had to come from elsewhere? They must have some head. And who found the money? Mr. Minor says they cannot possibly succeed."

Some time Fred would have to stand Jack Darcy on his true pedestal. As well do it now, and have it over.

"The project was Mr. Darcy's. I believe he had most of the capital. It was very generous of him to risk it in such times as these."

Irene looked up from her moody contemplation of the fire. A dull flush suffused her face.

"Not Jack Darcy," she said, — "Sylvie Barry's great hero."

"Yes."

"Sylvie Barry!" re-echoed Mrs. Lawrence, and she

looked sharply at her son. "And she gave you up for him! Who is he?"

"He used to be in the mill," answered Irene, with all her olden scorn. "His father was there also. And the Darcys" —

"The Darcys can boast as good blood as we!" exclaimed Fred, his face in a sudden heat. "And Jack Darcy is a gentleman by birth, by instinct, and, best of all, the impulses of a true and noble heart."

The discussion recalled an old remembrance to Mrs. Lawrence. She looked vaguely at her son as if she were not quite certain, as she said, —

"Was there not something about him when you were boys? He was coarse and rough, wasn't he? and Agatha used to worry. I knew it was only a boy's folly; but she was glad when you went to college, and I think — there was his sister " — her maternal instincts taking alarm.

"No, he never had a sister. His father died, and he staid at home. His mother was delicate, and his grandmother old. She is dead, and he gets his small fortune from her. No, he was not coarse nor rude, but he was my champion in boyhood, my hero then ; and it is the shame of my life that I should have let him drop out of it because I was the richer of the two. I despise myself for any thing so narrow and unmanly, and yet he was generous enough to forgive. I do not wonder at Miss Barry's choice when she contrasted us, and I honor her to-day for her discrimination. She never encouraged me, blind, idiotic fool that I was! and I have only my wretched vanity to blame. He is fully worthy of her, and that is the highest compliment I can pay him."

"Very magnanimous for a rejected lover," commented Irene with a touch of sarcasm.

"But you *did* love Sylvie?" Mrs. Lawrence said, bewildered by his rapid defence.

"I blush now at the thought of having offered her such

a paltry regard.   To me she will always be a sweet and peerless woman.   I am glad she will have the strength of manhood to lean upon, the purity of its honor to trust, the exceeding tenderness of a soul that will never know a narrow or grudging thought, to confide in.   All my years look poor and barren beside his.''

"I can never forgive her '' —

"You must, you must!'' and Fred seized his mother's hand, pressing it to his lips. "There is nothing to forgive,'' he went on.   "You would not have had her throw aside the love of her life for my fancied fortune that has taken wings.   It was my blunder.   And I want to say that I have taken up my old friendship for Jack Darcy, come back to the truth that money is one of the incidental surroundings of the man, but it can never be the man himself.''

Irene's haughty lip curled, but no one openly gainsaid Fred.

CHAPTER XVII.

The winter was a rather open one, with but little snow. Matters were somewhat better in Yerbury, but bad enough, Sylvie Barry thought. The churches began their usual work, — parish aids, clothing-clubs, and sewing-societies. It was as she said: they begged from the rich to give to the poor. Women met to make or to alter over garments, and devise means to render the poor more comfortable. There were so many miserable homes, so many inefficient wives and mothers, who were ignorant of the commonest principles of economy. They could live on meal-mush, they could go in rags, but the science of thrift was utterly unknown in many instances.

Sylvie had done her share of church work as a growing maiden. Every year there had been some mission, and a sewing-school.

"And yet it doesn't seem to do much good," said she. "The girls learn to hem a handkerchief, which a sewing-machine can do in ten seconds: they sew a few patches together, and perhaps make an apron. By the next winter they have forgotten all about it. And some of their mothers do not seem to care."

"The mothers need educating," Miss Morgan began, with a decisive nod of the head. "They were married out of shops and factories, and know very little, and have brought up their children to know less. I'm not one of the kind who can see no good in the world's progress, and who want to go back to the days of spinning-wheels, wax polish for tables and chairs, and a day spent every week scouring the brass andirons and candlesticks and door-knobs, and various other matters ; but I do think we have gone to the other extreme. Women dawdle away half their lives. It is of no use to make clothes, you can buy them cheaper ; it is of no use to mend, to do this or that, and so they do nothing.''

"I was struck with a contrast I saw yesterday," returned Sylvie. "I had occasion to go to the Webbers, —you know the little cottage on Alden Street, Miss Morgan, where they always have such pretty flowers in the window. Mr. Webber works at satchel-making, and even in good times did not earn very high wages. They have a garden, in which they raise the most wonderful succession of crops ; they keep some chickens, which they manage to have laying most of the time ; and they have five children. It was quite late in the afternoon. Mrs. Webber sat by the window, making lace, on a cushion, at which she realizes about a dollar a week ; Christine, the eldest girl, who still goes to school, was crocheting a baby's hood, — she does a good deal of work for Mrs. Burnett's fancy-store, and yet is a very smart scholar ; Amelie, the next one, was darning the stockings ; the boy, who comes third, was out-doors, tidying up the chicken-house ; and the two little girls were in the corner, cutting and sewing patchwork, with a doll in the cradle between them. The house is always clean, the children are well and rosy, and play about a good deal, and Christine last year earned thirty dollars. Her mother puts half the money she earns in the bank for her marriage-portion. I was so glad it wasn't in Yerbury Bank ! You wouldn't believe, that, though she is not quite sixteen, she has almost a hundred dollars saved up. And I must tell you, also, there was a most savory smell of the supper cooking. Altogether, it was so tidy and thrifty, with the clean, bright, and not unpretty faces, that I thought it would make a charming ' interior,' if only some Dutch artist could

do justice to it in his minute, pains-taking way.   Then I
went to the Coles, who live around in the next street.
The gate was off its hinges, and the two big boys were
firing stones from the street at a post in the yard.   They
were ragged and dirty.   I went in the house, and found
the mother and the two girls in the sitting-room.   I do
not believe there was a piece of furniture whole, and every
thing was dusty and shabby, with that close smell some
people always have in their houses.   Mrs. Cole sat by the
window, in a listless manner, doing nothing.   Martha had
her baby on her lap, asleep, in a soiled and ragged dress,
while she was reading ; the little girl, who is about twelve,
was cutting up some pretty pieces of silk into nothing,
that I could see, but a general litter over the table.   The
kitchen looked dreadful.   I had some baby-dresses for
Martha, that Mrs. Kent gave me : so I unrolled my
bundle, and displayed them.   'Oh,' said she, ' they are
long, aren't they ! and I've just put my baby in short
dresses.'   If you could have heard the kind of helpless,
dissatisfied tone in which it was uttered !   I had half a
mind to bundle them up, and take them back.   ' You
can shorten them,' I answered, ' and some of them will
make two dresses.'   ' Yes,' she answered reluctantly,
' only I should want something for yokes and sleeves.'
Then her mother came to inspect them, and she was
rather more gracious.   But I could not help contrasting the
two families.   Mr. Cole is a carpenter, and has earned very
good wages.   Martha ran a machine in the shoe-shop,
bought a melodeon, and took two or three quarters' music-
lessons ; purchased a very handsome set of amethyst jew-
elry and two pretty silk dresses when she was married.
And in the two years of her married life, her husband has
done next to nothing, although he is a steady, pleasant
fellow.   Now he is at Pittsburg, earning just enough to
pay his own board.   She has her sewing-machine, but she
doesn't know how to make any kind of garment decently.

When they had money they bought every thing ready-made.   She paid Miss Gilman twenty-two dollars to make her two silk dresses.   If she had put one of them in some plain, simple garments, how much more serviceable it would have proved ! ''

" Such people are hardly worth helping,'' Miss Morgan said sharply.

" Isn't it a faulty system that makes them so ? '' asked Sylvie, drawing her brows into a little, perplexed frown. " Martha worked for two years, and earned a good deal of money.   At one time she made ten dollars a week.   It was just one thing, — fine stitching on shoes, — yet one would think she would understand a sewing-machine so completely that she could do any thing with it.   But she actually hired part of her baby's wardrobe made ; and the dresses she bought, — cheap coarse-trimmed things, I should have been ashamed of.   Christine Webber wants to study for a teacher ; and, as there is so little for girls to do, I think she will.   She will make wiser investments of her money than Martha Cole, and think of the kind of wife her husband will get ! ''

" The era of prosperity was too much for some people,'' said Mrs. Darcy, with her motherly smile.   " I used to wonder six or seven years ago, how it was that so many middle-class people could afford a servant, or fancy they needed one.   A little more time spent in household duties would not have injured the women ; and, if they had accustomed the children to take a part, it would have been much better for them.   Then so much sewing was hired ; and, although the income looked large, the expenditures swallowed it all up, and no one was any better off.   How few had any stock of underclothing, bed-linen, or useful and durable articles ! ''

" Industry must come around in the fashion again. Even the despised patchwork doubtless had its uses.   It taught children to sew, and to manage economically.   I remember that I once had three quilts on hand at one time. The larger pieces went into the first, and so on. My last one was a very pretty little thing, and I saved all the scraps for it. Yet we often hear people laugh about the folly of cutting calico into bits to sew together again. Why should it not be considered honorable and respectable to put every thing to the best use?" and Miss Morgan glanced up with a confidence no one could gainsay.

"That is the grand secret," cried Sylvie, — "making economy honorable. You never see the nice old families flaunting their best silk and their point-laces on ordinary occasions. Something is kept sacred. And I do think there is more real economy among them, than among those who absolutely have a need for it. If wastefulness could once come to be considered a sin of ostentation and low-breeding, it would not have so many followers. Some people do it because they are afraid of being thought mean; but if they could be trained to that bravery of spirit that makes a work of beauty out of the poorest and smallest things because they are well done, and fitting to the place and season" —

"Bravo!" said a laughing voice as the door opened. "Mrs. Darcy, when the committee of ways and means have worn out your carpet by their frequent meetings in your charmed temple, you must insist upon their buying you a new one. Good-morning, ladies! Miss Barry, I set out to find you; and your aunt fancied you would be here, the place of all waifs and strays. I want you and Miss Morgan to go and inspect a room, or rather two rooms, to see if they will answer our purpose. Mrs. Lane had a school there."

"Oh, I know the place!" began Sylvie eagerly, buttoning up her sack again, and looking smilingly in Dr. Maverick's face, that had a sparkling wholesomeness born of the fresh air and brisk walk. And whenever he caught her eye with this light in it, so friendly and earnest, a thrill sped through his veins.

Miss Morgan was soon ready, and the three started. The place was only a few squares away, in a block of buildings where the stores on the lower floor stood empty; indeed, some of them had never been rented. Up-stairs there was one large room with three front windows, and a smaller room at the back with a fireplace, sink and water, and a large closet.

"I have had the offer of this place rent free until spring," began the doctor. "I have also collected fifty dollars in money and provisions, — *imprimis*, one barrel of flour, one box of miscellaneous packages, rice, barley, corn-starch, &c., — and a second-hand range that will be put up as soon as you decide. In return for my arduous exertion and great benevolence, I shall call upon you now and then for meals or delicacies for my sick and famishing."

"You are just magnificent!" declared Sylvie, in breathless pleasure.

"I am desirous of getting this experiment started; and, since we shall have to help the poor and needy this winter, I shall put my gifts into this. Now you must consider what you want for furnishing. Biddy McKim is to work out a doctor's bill cleaning the place; Ward Collins will let you have ten dollars' worth of house-furnishing goods on another bill. I am going to look up all my bad debts to start you two women in business!" and he laughed gayly.

"Very good," said Miss Morgan, while Sylvie's face was still blending pleasure and astonishment.

"We are going to reform Yerbury, you see. The parsons tried their hands last winter; and, though there was need enough of spiritual food, there's something else required as well, while we are here in the body. You think the rooms will do? I want you to put a large table in that one," — indicating the larger with his head, — "and we'll get two or three long benches, and have a tea-party now and then. Well, Miss Morgan, now you may take the floor. I see a crowd of ideas in your face."

"I am going to propose that when the place is cleaned, both floors shall be painted to begin with. Then a simple mopping up will keep them bright and fresh. Some idle half-grown boys can do it, I am sure; or I can do it myself — it would not be the first time."

"I'll look over my accounts, and levy on some delinquent," said the doctor. "I like that idea."

"Can we make out a list now?"

"Why, of course. Put down about all the things you will be likely to need, and I will have them sent if they do over run the account. Biddy will come to-morrow, and clean. Now, you can hardly have the school open every day unless you get more assistance, so I think I should take it at first two days in the week."

"A very good suggestion," replied Miss Morgan.

"It might not be sufficiently attended to warrant more than that. My experience has been that nearly every housekeeper considers herself a finished cook."

Maverick laughed.

They discussed necessary articles of kitchen paraphernalia, and finally walked down to Collins's store, and made their selection. Early the next morning Bridget McKim was on the spot: the place was cleaned, the stove put in place, the floor given one good coat of paint. Two days after, the second one was added. Sylvie drew up a code of regulations. The school would be open Tuesday and Friday, all day. The dinner would be cooked and eaten; the baking, and whatever was left over, divided among the scholars to take home. Miss Morgan was elected president, Miss Barry vice-president, a secretary, a treasurer, and two in an advisory board. At each session two ladies were to be present, and give instruction.

Invitations were sent to all likely to be interested. Dr.

Maverick used his strong influence wisely. The idea amused some, others wondered how ladies like Miss Barry knew about cooking and economy.

"Let her undertake to live on the money we common folk have, and she'll see!" exclaimed Mrs. Stixon. "Our kind don't want to learn fussin' and fixin' of puddens and pies and such like! Good for us if we can get a mess of biled potatoes and bacon. My gals'll get along athout any such larnin'."

They opened one Friday morning with seven pupils; a discouraging number, Sylvie thought, when she saw the spacious room and the nice preparations. The bashful girls sat in a little huddle, looking very much as if they were afraid of being laughed at.

Miss Morgan was equal to the occasion. She made a short, sensible address, and hoped the girls who were present would interest not only their companions, but their mothers and friends. Then she questioned them a little. Had they ever boiled potatoes?

At this they all laughed a little foolishly, and looked as if the art of boiling potatoes was held in rather low esteem.

"The dinner for the day," announced Miss Morgan, "will be boiled potatoes, broiled steak, and corn-muffins. Which of you girls would like to try the muffins?"

"I never heerd of such a thing," said one girl timidly.

Sylvie pleasantly corrected the speaker.

"Well, you may try," said Miss Morgan. "First, read this recipe aloud."

Mary Moran stumbled through it, partly owing to ignorance, and the rest to feeling very much abashed.

"Please go through it again, Mary," said Sylvie, in an encouraging tone."

This time she did much better.

"Now you may prepare the table and the dishes, and one of the girls may measure the meal and the flour. Put the ingredients in this dish — so. Keep your mind on the recipe. What comes next?"

Mary was quite awkward. Miss Morgan corrected the slightest mistake. The other girls stood around in wondering amusement, and now and then a little titter broke out. But Mary went on, gaining courage. The tins had been set on the stove, now a bit of butter was put in each one, and stirred around, then the dough dropped in. This was quite entertaining.

"What did I say about the oven?" queried Miss Morgan.

The class looked aghast a moment, then one girl said quickly, "That the oven-door must be hot enough to hiss."

"Right. Try it and see."

It was in the proper condition. Mary slipped in the two trays of pans, shutting up the door. "To look at them, and turn them around in twelve minutes, and in twelve more to try them with a whisk," were the final directions.

The potatoes were brought out next. Miss Morgan asked each girl to pare one, which they did in various uncouth ways. One girl cut off the skin in square bits, leaving a figure that would have distracted a geometrician; another ran round it rapidly, leaving in all the eyes; and out of the six potatoes there was but one neat and shapely. Miss Morgan held it up.

"There is an art in so slight a thing as peeling a potato," said she. "It is very wasteful to cut it away in this manner, or this, and careless to leave in the eyes. Now each of you may pare another."

The second attempt was a great improvement. They were put on to boil; one girl was detailed to watch them, another to prepare the steak, while a third arranged the dinner-table in the kitchen, as the family was to be so small. Mary looked after her corn-muffins. They had

risen up like little pound-cakes, and a glad smile illumined her rather stolid face.

Sylvie had brought a bit of tatting along, and now took
it out.

"Oh, how beautiful, Miss Barry!" exclaimed Kitty
Miles. "I can do just the plain little scallop; but I
never could get these other jiggers!"

Sylvie laughed, "I believe they have a name beside
'jiggers,'" in an odd, half-inquiring tone.

"O Miss Barry, we girls can't talk nice like you!"
and Kitty blushed.

"I don't see why you cannot with taking a little pains.
All words that are not names, and 'what-you-may-call-it,'
and 'Mrs. Thingnmby,' and such expressions, are the result of carelessness. If any thing has a name, that is
the proper word to be used; and by being watchful one
comes presently to talk in a lady-like manner. Now I
will show you about these."

"Oh, my muffins!" cried Mary, rushing to the stove.
They were quite brown. She tried them with the whisk.

"Some stick a little bit, Miss Morgan."

"Push the pan back to the other side. Indian requires very thorough cooking or baking, or it will be
soggy, and have a moist and not agreeable taste. Try
your potatoes now."

In a few moments they were done, and Kitty Miles
undertook the steak. Mary let her muffins stand a
moment or two, then turned them out. Two or three
stuck fast, and broke: the rest were a perfect success.
She was delighted beyond measure. They had no tea or
coffee, but they gathered around the table, and enjoyed
the meal very heartily. Sylvie desired them to ask any
questions they liked; and by the time they were through,
their awe of Miss Morgan had quite vanished.

Afterward followed dish-washing. This was made
quite a science, as well. They had hardly finished when

Mrs. Miles and a neighbor came in, and through the course of the afternoon the numbers doubled. Mary begged that they might make some muffins to take home : Miss Morgan assented, and the girls had quite a gay time. But the oven was not precisely right.

" Open the draughts a little. Although not so hot, the oven is very steady now. Close the draughts in five minutes."

Mary forgot, and the result was that some at one end were a little burned.

" Why, they're elegant!" exclaimed Mrs. Miles. " And what a cheap, hearty supper they'd make, when one has three hungry boys to feed! Mrs. Stixon, now, was thinking you'd go into all the fancy branches. I didn't know ladies ever " — and Mrs. Miles paused suddenly, her face scarlet.

" Ever had occasion to practise economy!" cried Sylvie with her piquant smile. " They do a great deal of it, Mrs. Miles. My aunt would no sooner think of being wasteful in her kitchen than she would of wearing her velvet dress out on a rainy day. There is a neat, pretty, tasteful method about these things, that is as much of an art in its way as painting a picture, and in some respects a more important one, for the health of the body depends upon well-cooked food."

" Since Kitty's nothing much to do, I mean to have her come every time. I'm sure you ladies are very good to take so much pains."

The other officers dropped in. The cost of the materials used was ascertained, minutes of the session made, and a recipe for corn-muffins given to each girl. It was decided to attempt biscuit on the following Tuesday, and on the next meeting, bread. Then the fire was pretty well poked out, the stove-lids raised, and the class went home in an extremely interested spirit.

Just as Sylvie and Miss Morgan had turned the corner,

they caught sight of Dr. Maverick, who crossed the street to speak. Sylvie described their day with a few graphic touches, interspersed with much genuine mirth.

"Some people were afraid to come," said he. "Before a month you will have your hands full."

Sure enough, on Tuesday there were fifteen scholars. Miss Morgan and Sylvie had hardly a moment to spare until the dinner was through. Then the latter proposed that every scholar should bring some sewing, garments they wished cut out, any thing that perplexed them, or whatever they would like most to learn.

All days were not so fortunate. Occasionally some dish would be spoiled by haste, carelessness, or want of attention. There were burned fingers and divers cuts; but Miss Morgan patiently explained her deft, neat, labor-saving methods. There began to be a great interest; some of the mothers coming in for an hour, or bringing a special dish to cook. Sylvie discussed the relative value and nourishment of different articles, the many changes that could be made at slight expense, the saving that a little carefulness brought about. She gave brief lectures on cleanliness, order, taste, and neatness; the right way and the wrong way of doing many things, the giving out and the taking in; the art of making the best, not only in such times as these, but in all times; of being brave and true in the lowest and smallest of life's duties; of throwing out false pride and shams, and the desire to appear richer or grander than one's means would allow.

Then the last half-hour they had what Miss Morgan called an inquiry-meeting. Everybody was at liberty to ask one question, and those who knew answered it to the best of their ability. New teachers were pressed into the service. Dr. Maverick gave them a talk on health, and another on preparing food for the sick, and the special care some diseases required. And Jack Darcy proposed that Christmas Eve the cooking-school should give a supper, the tickets being at the low price of twenty-five cents. Every dish was to be cooked by the scholars.

It created a deal of excitement. Hard as times were, the tickets sold rapidly. The large room had two long tables, with benches for seats. The first table was to be served at eight o'clock, the second at nine. Sylvie made a dozen of the girls pretty Suisse aprons and dainty caps, and they waited on the guests. Dr. Maverick offered three prizes, — one for the best loaf of bread, one for the best plain cake, and a third for the nicest and cheapest invalid broth.

The room was full, and they had a very gay time. Indeed, it seemed as if half Yerbury turned out, either from honor or curiosity. At nine o'clock they ran short of provision, when they honorably decided to refund the money for all tickets offered after that, and explain to new-comers the state of affairs. But some of the young men proposed a dance; and they went on for the next two hours in hearty, healthy jollity.

Out of ten loaves of bread offered, Mary Moran took the prize. That for the cake was awarded to quite a new scholar; while Kitty Miles carried off that for broth, three doctors concurring in the decision. And the treasurer found they had cleared fifty dollars above expenses, so that it proved a success in more ways than one. There had been a great dearth of amusement for the poorer classes in Yerbury this winter.

" Sure, it was just splendid ! " said Bridget McKim. " My boy Mike had a week's wages in his pocket that night, and he was goin' off to the Ivy Leaf to raffle for a turkey ; an' ses I, ' Mike, ye niver took me out of a Christmas, so do it now along o' the cookin' school party, an' ye'll get the best bit o' turkey yes ever put in yer mouth.' An' so he did ; an' he said it was the best show he iver was to, and he wouldn't 'a' missed seein' Mary Moran get the prize fur twice the money. An' so he went home with me, ye see, as sober as an owl, and we bought our own turkey ; but if he'd gone to the tavern, not a cint would he had of his week's wages, and been drunk beside ! An' he used to be swate on Mary too, so there's no knowin' what may happen ! "

The school took a fortnight's vacation. Sylvie and Miss Morgan felt that it was no longer an experiment. It would be put to wider uses, and perhaps was the corner-stone of a great work, sorely needed in this world ; the same kind of work Jack Darcy had begun over in the mill yonder, — planting beacon-lights on the path where so many had stumbled and gone down for want of true and honest guidance.

" It will have to be remodelled somewhat," said Miss Morgan. " I can't have you working like a slave, even if it is in a good cause. There is something still higher for you."

CHAPTER XVIII.

After the first of January it came off bitterly cold. Coal went up half a dollar on a ton; and flour rose, more by the greed of speculators than any scarcity, or any demand for it abroad. There was considerable suffering, though not as much as the winter before. The men and women and boys and girls at Hope Mills were thankful enough for their seventy-five per cent, and did their very best. A spirit of economy and emulation ran through the whole brotherhood. Every month Cameron announced whatever saving had been made in different departments, and the hands were proud enough of it. Those who had taken their whole winter's coal out of the share were quite jubilant. Once a week the workmen had a meeting, and discussed matters a little. Three men had been reprimanded, but on the whole the *morale* was excellent. Winston was on the alert continually, east, west, anywhere, buying here, selling there, seeing in every thing the promise of better times.

" We've reached the last ditch as surely as they did in the war," he said to Darcy, rubbing his hands in great glee. " I tell you, old chap, it was a lucky thought of starting just as we did. You see, we shall come up with the good times; for I do honestly believe the worst is over."

Jack smiled, but was not so sanguine. They had only gone such a little way on the five-years' journey. But there were some very encouraging rays right around them. Kit Connelly's coffee-house was working to a charm

Jack began to think that drinking liquors was not so much a besetting sin, as a natural sequence of having nothing else to drink when you were cold or hot, or tired or hungry. The men fell into the habit of going to Kit's for their midday lunch, and presently some of the women went over. The room was so bright and pleasant; and, with Miss Rose there, they were on their best behavior. In the evening Mrs. Connelly brought her work, and sat by the desk. Some of the younger men, who had no homes; as one may say, dropped in, and looked over the books. Once two young chaps had come up from Keppler's to have a little fun, as they said, and were rather noisy. Mrs. Connelly rose.

"Gentlemen," she said, "you forget yourselves. This is an orderly, quiet house, not a tavern. If you cannot submit to the rules, you must leave it."

"Leave it! Come, who'll put us out!" laughed the bully. "Let's see you try," with an insolent leer at the lady.

Two men were sitting at a table just a little back of them. Their eyes met. Both rose; and, each seizing a shoulder of the bully, he was marched out before he could make the slightest resistance, his companion looking on in amazement.

"Next time you insult a lady in her own house, you will not get off so easily! Just bear that in mind."

The fellow uttered an oath, but the door was shut in his face.

"Thank you, John Kelly, and you, Ben Hay," said Mrs. Connelly, in a brave voice, though her heart fluttered a little.

The other young ruffian rose, and walked out quietly.

"If you didn't mind, Ben Hay," she said, an hour or so after, as they were shutting up for the night, "I'd like to have you drop in quite often of an evening. The boys are hardly big enough if we should ever be beset by such scamps as that, and you've always been so friendly-like."

"Yes," answered Ben, flushing, and casting a sheepish look at the desk, where Rose's curly head was bent over her accounts. "Yes, I'm at your service. It's enough sight cheerfuller here than in Mother Mitchell's boarding-house. I'll be glad to come."

"Thank you."

Miss Barry heard of this, and told it over to Jack.

"Ben Hay is a good, plucky fellow. He used to go down at noon for beer, but I do not think he has been since the coffee-house was opened. Sylvie, do you know, I believe reformers in general would be more successful if they put a good and pleasant thing in the place of the evil they assail. Too often they leave their convert to pick his way alone. Hay is very much interested in the plans of the mill. The meetings have done this much already, — a spirit of inquiry has been awakened in some of the men, and they are reading up what other people have achieved in this line. I want them to get well grounded before there comes any strain. We can't go on prospering forever. That would be too much like fairy-land."

"But every one thinks the panic nearly at an end," and Sylvie studied the grave face before her.

"I do not want to croak," and Jack gave a little laugh that sounded forced, "but we have just begun to pay off our debts. Every city and town, and nearly every indi-vidual, is in debt. If we could pay with promises to pay, we might tide over a while longer; but when interest reaches a certain point, it swallows capital. If we can meet our indebtedness everywhere, as fast as it matures, well and good: if not, then we have only nibbled at the crust of our bitter pie."

"Anyhow," cried Sylvie, with the woman's sanguine nature, "Yerbury is a great deal better off than it was

last winter. Every one admits there is much less suffering."

"There is more employment, and no broken bank,"
with a cheerful smile.

"Do you know," said the young girl presently, while a
faint color went wandering over her fair face, "that they
are doing a marvellous stroke of business at Garafield's,
even if the times are bad? Mrs. Garafield was down to
tea a few evenings since, and she was greatly encouraged.
There is such a rage about the new style of papering.
Everybody has run mad on dados and friezes, and fresco
patterns, bordering, and harmonies of color," laughingly.
"And they have some wonderful new designs."

"Fred is in just the right place. If he has courage
to fight through," and there came a curious, almost fore-
boding expression in the sympathetic eyes.

"You care a good deal for him, Jack! And yet he
did not use you nobly," with a peculiar regret in the tone.
"It is the one thing" —

"Sylvie, if I forgave it, surely you can." Then he
turned his eyes upon her, and read or rather dreamed of
something in a dim, dazed way, the story of a bygone
summer. Had it been more to her than any one thought?
Miss Barry had hinted to his mother that Sylvie's decision
in the matter was a great disappointment to her. There
had been a decision, then, and one adverse to Fred Lawrence.

"I hate a false and cowardly man!" her cheeks were
flaming now. "And when you were schoolboys together,
— when Agatha and Gertrude were so afraid he would
lower himself if he looked at any boy below his own
social position, — he used to stand up for you, — yes,
he did, — and fight; of course not in a brutal way with
fists," and she laughed at her own conceit, "but in that
higher, finer manner, with no shield or weapon save his
love for you. I used to like to see you together, — you

so sturdy and manful and true, and he delicate and handsome and adoring. And then " —

" Sylvie, I wonder if a woman can understand a man's friendship. We never had any quarrel. We just drifted apart. I don't believe we forgot each other. Circumstances took him out of my sphere, into a new one. If I had been there in college, going along with him step by step, don't you suppose he would have stood up for me in the face of his fine friends, just as he used to with his sisters? "

" I hope so: I would like to believe it."

" I am more just to him than you, Sylvie," said Jack, a little wounded. " I *know* it. I don't doubt it any more than I doubt — well, myself. He might have come — I was always sorry to see him avoid me, and I think he was weak, but he never forgot."

" He *was* weak, he was worse, Jack." There was a curious cry of anguish in her voice, and her shoulders swayed unconsciously, while her eyes looked out on the summer night he could not see.

" Don't get so excited over it, Sylvie," and the pleasant, cheery laugh seemed to bring healing on its wings. " Whatever it was, and we will let all that go, he made the *amende honorable* the night we had tea together up there in the great house. We took up our friendship just where it had dropped. Men never go over those crooked and thorny steps of the past, they have so much work to do in the present and the future. I wanted then to make a position for him in the mill; but it was not possible, and would not have been the part of wisdom under *any* circumstances. Yet it seemed as if I had stepped in his place. I was glad to hear of this other, though Fred would have been happier elsewhere. Sylvie, I do not believe you realize what it cost him to come back to Yerbury, to walk about, a working-man, where he had driven in his carriage. So down at the bottom there is the temper of the real blue steel, which *can* bend."

"How generous you are, Jack!" There was something more than admiration in her tone, and yet she was wondering if she could ever forgive her fallen hero.

" See here, Sylvie, I don't mean to question any one's religion, but I've often thought about the rejoicing up above, over the one who went astray. I do not believe we rejoice with a very full heart: maybe we are not heavenly enough. We can never be sure of our own strength until some far-reaching test is applied, and yet it may not be an entirely true test. It may quiver about the weak spot in our souls ; but, while there is any feeling, one cannot be entirely lost. That is why I say he never forgot. And you and I ought to rejoice that he *did* come back instead of going off in that gloomy, diseased, Manfred style, and upbraiding the world. ' Whatever his hand found to do '—that was one of grandmother's texts, and he went bravely at it."

"I do believe you are a better Christian than I," she answered softly, her eyes limpid with emotion.

" No.   Perhaps not even a better friend ; " and a smile played about his mouth.

" A truer friend, a more generous one " —

" What were we talking of ? " in a sudden change of tone. " Oh, the business at Garafield's ! Fred is a good deal of an artist, an intellectual artist I should say ; and, though he may not attain to fame by painting pictures, there are many other points coming to be appreciated. He is in the way for usefulness ; and, if he wins the bays for beauty as well, I am sure we shall all rejoice. I heard he had been designing."

" You hear every thing." Sylvie made a capricious little *moue*. Her nods and gestures were so much a part of her, so piquant, decisive, and full of expression, when she did not intrench herself behind a studied dignity.

" I am glad you have heard it. I was wondering how best to tell you. I thought Garafield's might be a stepping-stone, these hard times, but it may prove the veritable ladder itself.   Only " —

" Well! " with a trifle of impatience, as if she could not endure the suggestiveness of the tone.

"I wonder if you understand the courage it took for Fred Lawrence to make a home here in Yerbury, to bring his mother and sister ; for you see he must endure for them as well as himself.   Mrs. Lawrence will always be an invalid, I suppose.   He thinks her quite changed and softened : evidently she clings to him.   They see none of their old friends.   Miss Lawrence never goes anywhere."

" As if one could help that ! " almost passionately. " Auntie wrote a note to Mrs. Lawrence, and it was merely answered.   They do not desire to receive any one.   We can only let them alone, Jack."

" Even then we can hardly fail to appreciate what he is doing, possibly suffering.   I think he will come in time to win back all the regard his friends ever gave him," Jack Darcy said in a steady tone.

Was he pleading for him?   Sylvie was somewhat puzzled, the most so, perhaps, about herself.   How much had she cared for Fred in that old time?   If not at all, why did this feeling of shame over a fallen idol continually haunt her?   She compared the two men in every thing, and sometimes was vexed to admit that Jack was the nobler.

Their walk had come to an end.   They paused at the gate ; and a third person striding up Larch Avenue took in the drooping, attentive, and pliant figure, the strong, protecting, powerful personality of the other, — and wondered, as he had more than once before.   Were they friends merely?   It was not possible for a woman to see so much of Jack Darcy's noble, manly life, and not admire, not love, Dr. Maverick admitted.   She showed in many ways that she did care for him.   Oddly enough she sheltered herself under his friendly care when other admirers came too near. Could not Darcy see! What a blind, stupid mole he must be in this respect! and the doctor kicked a stone in his path with such force that the two turned in the midst of their good-bys, and waited with smiling faces for him to reach them. Not a shade of annoyance in look or tone at the interruption.

"The queerest lovers," he thought to himself. "If I stood in that man's place "—

Jack went homeward in a curiously speculative mood. He has always fancied for Sylvie some handsome, spirited knight, whose mental intuitions would be as delicate and refined as hers, whose enjoyment as intense. Little as he knew of love, he understood their friendship too thoroughly to be betrayed into any mistake. And he wondered now if he held the key to Sylvie's spiritual enfranchisement of all other men? If she had not loved Fred Lawrence, she had come too dangerously near it ever to free herself entirely from whatever thrall his soul had thrown over hers. She *had* been disappointed in him, he read that from her tone ; but surely, if he brought himself up to a finer and truer standard than any known in that enervating atmosphere of luxury, would she still be implacable? How could he best serve these two people, whom he loved so entirely?

He had many other things to busy himself about beside love and friendship. March came on apace, and the balance-sheet for the six months had to be put in shape. The accounts had been systematically kept : that he had insisted upon in the beginning. Cameron knew every gallon of oil, every pound of wool, every penny spent for repairs and stock ; Hurd and Yardley had kept account of every yard of cloth, and what quality, that had passed through their hands ; Winston, of travelling, advertising, commissions, &c. ; and Jack went over every thing. They had done wonderfully. There was actually a balance of profit to every man, woman, and child. The forms were printed, and distributed to every employee, and there was a great rejoicing time. They engaged the Cooking Club to provide them a supper, and the young people had a merry dance afterward.

"It's hardly safe to halloo until you are out of the woods," said some of the solid old men of Yerbury, who were living snugly on the interest of government-bonds. "Six months is no test at all. Wait until there is a hard pull, and you will not be so jubilant."

"No," answered Jack with a humorous twinkle in his eye: "it's right to have the rejoicing now, when we have fairly earned it. The man who croaks when Providence has smiled upon him, deserves the frown; and he who is unthankful for small successes hardly has a right to great ones. I do not expect all fair sailing, but we will weather the storms together."

"It *is* rather unfortunate," commented another wiseacre. "I have observed these wonderful beginnings seldom end well. If you should have a run of bad luck now, your men will be dissatisfied, and likely blame you for not keeping up to that mark. I shouldn't have made such a great effort, and then there would have been a chance for improvement."

"A new broom sweeps clean, but it *will* get worn out," with sundry mysterious nods.

"I declare," said Jack to his friend and comforter, Maverick, "half the town looks at me as if I must have robbed a bank, or falsified accounts, told a lie, or cheated, or maybe murdered some rich old don, and made merry on his money. Why can't people rejoice with you when there is any thing to rejoice about, — an event which does not happen so often in these evil days? I do believe Boyd, and a lot of the others, would be glad to see the scheme fail; but I'll work night and day to make a success of it. It shall not go down," and Jack set his lips together in a way that spoke volumes for his resolve.

"I have observed before that some people are fond of disparaging plans that they have no hand in," returned the doctor coolly.

"And philanthropy is a much-derided virtue. If the old Athenian had been a stock-broker or a bank-director, he might not have been sent into exile, eh?" and Darcy laughed good-humoredly. "If I have kept a few people from starvation this winter, I ought surely to have as much credit as to have dealt around alms. As for the success, we had the reputation of Hope Mills in our favor, and every man had his own fortune at stake, and brought out the best that was in him."

He sent Miss McLeod her half-yearly rent, a copy of the statement, and a very temperate letter. He was quite proud to think he had no need of accepting her proffered favor, but he thanked her again for it.

She answered promptly. She had shown the statement to Mr. Hildreth, and he thought it remarkable. Wasn't it a trifle too rose-colored to last? Count on her as a friend, if evil days came; and we none of us could tell exactly what was in store. The financial horizon was by no means clear.

A few others gave him words of heartfelt encouragement. The Rev. Mr. Marlow spoke of him in very high terms, much to Sylvie's delight, and said already there had been a great change in the mill-hands. The coffee-house he considered an especially commendable thought.

There was a quiet change going on that was destined to bear more abundant fruit in the future. Some of the men and women had begun to think a little for themselves. The pupils of the cooking-school were beginning the A B C of beauty and neatness. Their rooms were swept cleaner; their clothes took on a more tidy aspect. With the opening spring, gardens and court-yards were cleared of their rubbish, and flower-beds flourished again. Sylvie gave her girls one very instructive lecture on slips and

flower-seeds, and one Saturday they went out to the woods
for ferns and wild flowers.   It was only one little corner,
to be sure, but it was the leaven that was presently to do
a wide-spread work.

Hope Mills took up its steady march again.   Half a
dozen new hands were added, though Jack wished that he
could find employment for some of the poor souls that
besieged him daily.   If times really were coming better,
if orders only would increase, and he could with safety
enlarge his borders!   But "slow and steady" was his
motto.   He was not one to disparage the present by exaggerating the advantages of the future.

There was one home that these cordial little excitements
never entered.   The three souls in it, although they should
have been very near and dear, wrapped themselves in
their own thoughts and sorrows, and took no note of their
fellows.

Mrs. Lawrence heeded the outward change least of the
three.   She had her pretty room, her glowing fire in
winter, her fur slippers, and zephyr shawls; her late
breakfast in bed, then her luxurious dressing-gown, and
her books.   She had settled herself into the *rôle* of an
invalid for the remainder of her days.   The loss and
suffering had not taken her out of herself, or raised her
narrow, vapid nature.   She was at once patient and complaining, — even her affection for her son was combined
with great mental and moral weakness.   She was profoundly grieved that he should have been compelled to
accept so unsuitable a position; but to her it was only
a temporary event.   Something *must* happen.   In some
mysterious way they would come back to their former
grandeur, — not that she cared especially, but for the
sake of Fred and Irene.   Then for days she would lose
herself in the joys and sorrows of her heroines.   To such
people novel-reading is certainly a godsend.   A readable
book was as exhilarating to her as a splendid morning

drive or a good deed is to many others. She had society without being bored. She had wit, poetry, art, music, travels, dinners, and balls, with no worry, no late hours, or fatigue.

Irene could not so yield up her personality. She brooded over her lot in a haughty, bitter spirit. She uttered no complaint, — she was far too proud for that, — but she took no interest in any thing. Like a melancholy ghost she wandered up and down, or sat by the window for hours in a listless attitude. There were moments when she wished herself Lady Frodsham, times when the change and bustle of such a life as that of Mr. Barringer would have been heaven itself.

Fred could never persuade her to go anywhere. She took no walks, except to pace up and down the garden path when the quiet of the house drove her well-nigh crazy. Once in a great while she opened the piano, and played as if a demon had taken possession of her soul and her fingers.

Fred breakfasted early and alone. After a while he fell into the habit of taking his lunch in his office, and coming home to a late dinner. Martha was certainly the perfection of maids. The housekeeping went on with the regularity of clockwork: there were no complaints even. Fred used to sit in his mother's room until her bedtime, when he would go down to the library, and work for an hour or two.

The utter dearth of interest would have been terrible to him but for his business. At first he preserved a wide and punctilious distance between himself and Mr. Garnfield. He was the employer, to be sure ; but then Fred Lawrence had a dignity of his own to maintain. One day, however, the dignity suffered a collapse. Mr. Garnfield brought in some new designs, and they lapsed into an exceedingly entertaining art discussion. The employer had excellent taste, trained and shaped by practical experience: Fred possessed the wider mental reach and exquisite perception of harmony and color, the sentiment of genius.

"Why do you not take up the idea, Mr. Lawrence?" asked his employer. "House finishing and furnishing is fast coming to be a fine art. An intelligent, harmonious beauty is demanded. We are leaving behind the complacency of mere money in our adornments, and asking for something that evinces thought and refinement. I am sure you could succeed if you once set about the work."

The compliment touched Fred profoundly, roused him to a new venture. He practised his almost lost art of designing to some purpose: he wrote two or three art essays that happened to find much more favor than his abstruse philosophies. After all, he was young, and the whole world lay before him. Surely he could carve out some kind of fortune. The light of earnest endeavor shone in his eyes, the languid step quickened into one of courageous elasticity. He had dawdled away years enough: he would put a purpose into his manhood, that some distant eyes, seeing, might not relegate him entirely to the regions of contempt.

"There's quite a good deal in that young Lawrence," declared Phil Maverick decisively. "I was in at Garafield's the other evening, and, I must confess, listened to a fine art lecture. All about wall-papering, too!" with a genial laugh. "What an education that fellow has! Couldn't he find any thing to do, that he must drop down upon a paper-factory? I am sure I should have made a big fight out somewhere in the great world."

"'Beyond the Alps lies Italy,'" quoted Jack. "Not on the top, you observe, but perhaps in the valley. I wish you would be a little friendly with him, Maverick: you couldn't help but like him."

"There is more in him than I gave him credit for. I thought at the time of his father's death I had never seen so useless a fine gentleman, with all the stamina educated out of him. I had half a mind to turn him over to Aunt Jean and Miss Lothrop.''

Darcy laughed absently, and Maverick saw that his mind had wandered elsewhere. How odd that these two should be friends! Maverick could not discern the fine bond uniting them.

CHAPTER XIX.

Summer came on apace. The Cooking Club took a vacation, or rather turned into a gardening club, and studied the sensible part of botany and floriculture. People began to look at the waste land lying about, with envious eyes. Here and there some one started a garden, or indulged in a flock of chickens. The Webbers traded their snug cottage for a place on the outskirts of the town, with two acres of ground, which they improved rapidly. Men who had sold farms, and spent the money in vain business speculations, looked back regretfully, and in some instances hired where they had been proprietors. There was no money to be realized in farming, but if one could even make a living! No one was making money but those lucky fellows at Hope Mills. Of course that was a bubble, and would burst presently; but doubtless it was good while it lasted.

Miss Barry, Sylvie, and Mrs. Darcy went away to a pleasant, quiet seaside resort. Miss Barry appeared to be ailing a little. Mrs. Minor so far relented as to invite her mother and Irene to spend two months with her at Long Branch. Mrs. Lawrence consented, Irene refused flatly. " She had no money to spend for dress, and she would accept no one's charity," she declared in her haughty way. But she could not stay in the house forever: so she took long walks over wild country ways, angry with the world, herself, and every thing. A fierce-eyed, beautiful girl, clinging desperately to her isolation, and yet eating out her very heart in loneliness.

The time ran on rapidly. September came around. Hope Mills did not make as good a report this time. Business had been very dull. Sales were next to nothing. People did not need much in warm weather, and orders were very light. However, several other branches of industry in Yerbury improved a trifle. Railroads, stocks, and real estate were fast becoming dead speculations: so men ventured to put their money warily into business again.

But the bottom had not been reached. Early in October there was a tremendous failure of an old and well-known firm of woollen-manufacturers. The bankrupt stock was sold at auction. Then another, and various smaller houses. The market was suddenly flooded. No one could sell. No one seemed to need new garments of any kind. Men wore their old clothes, and shrugged their shoulders in a sort of contemptuous content, as if they had suddenly found a great charm in a half-worn, shabby overcoat. Robert Winston went hither and yon. Not a piece or a yard would any one take.

There was a great deal of discussion in various daily journals. The business had been overdone again. Foreign markets must be found. We could not compete with foreign manufacturers. Our wool was inferior, our looms were inferior, our men knew so little, and demanded such high wages. Then we never could do any thing under the present wretched tariff and the skinning system of taxation. It took all a man could make. Another sapient statesman declared nothing could be done without more money. The contraction had been so great that not a man could do business. Then came a long list of figures to prove what a very little money was left in the country. Newspaper war raged, first on this side, then on that. If we did this, we would surely be ruined: if we did not, then ruin was inevitable.

Jack used to try for some light, no matter how faint.

It seemed to him, if the great men at the helm of the national ship would set to work vigorously to widen and strengthen the commerce of the nation, instead of discussing such frivolous issues, prosperity might dawn once more. He went over his political economists again, and realized sadly that men had always disputed these points, and that each writer or prophet was sure his was the only creed that would ever save the world, while by following any other they would surely go to ruin.

Winston and he took counsel together : then they called in Cameron, who looked blue enough.

"Any ordinary factory would shut down for the winter," said Winston ruefully; "but that would be to confess our scheme a failure. We are piling up goods — but for what — a grand auction-sale by and by? And the men have worked so cheerfully — no, we can't give up."

"Giving up is out of the question at present," Jack answered solemnly, as if he was passing his word at the bar. "Our balance at the bank has been expended, and we have some notes out that must be cared for in a month's time. Wages are falling, and it seems to look now as if we were coming back to the era of cheap living. The bargain was the ruling rate of wages, you know. I think they will have to come down."

"I will not give up beaten," declared Winston. "I'll have one more try. Keep up heart, shipmate."

With that Winston started West again. He talked, he plead, he offered for the mere cost of production, — just to get the money back would be something. The coal-venture of this winter had been much larger, though coal was declining, and the profit somewhat less. Everybody pared the margin to the mere skin. Winston had a little luck, however. Two sales of some note were effected, and a barter, that only a man with a shrewd eye for bargains, and a glib tongue, could have managed. Flour, apples, and potatoes were the stock this time. The workmen took them gladly, at a little less than store prices. They knew how full the wareroom kept all the time.

The first of January, wages were lowered. There was a little grumbling among some of the men, but the women took it in wiser part. The half-loaf was much better than no bread at all. They remembered the dismal year when there had been no employment, and stinted food purchased on credit. One wouldn't starve with flour and potatoes, nor freeze with a full coal-bin.

Hope Mills had exhausted every source, — had even paid a horrible discount, being hard run, — when Darcy wrote to Miss McLeod a true statement of affairs. If they could hold out until spring, times might be better. They were economizing as they never had before : yet the time had come when disaster really stared them in the face, unless they could find a true friend.

Miss Barry had generously offered him her store and her credit. Though there had been a time when she with-held Sylvie, and fancied Jack Darcy not quite the equal of her pretty niece, that time had long gone by. She knew now his genuine worth, — she had tested his integrity. Of course Sylvie would drift that way ; and so, by many delicate turns, she showed Jack that she could trust him with any of her treasures.

"You are so good," said the honest fellow, with tears in his eyes, — for he was touched beyond measure. "If I can't get through I will gladly accept, unless the prospect is so bad that it would be sure to jeopardize any one's money. But I hope it will not come to that."

How breathlessly he waited for Miss McLeod's answer! The morning's mail did not bring it ; night closed in without it. A chill drizzle had set in, freezing as it fell, and the keen air fairly flayed one's skin. Yet he dreaded to go in-doors, to hear his mother's pleasant voice. Cousin Jane had been called away by the illness and possible death of a relative, so they two were alone.

When Mrs. Darcy saw her son so grave and pre-occu-
pied, his eyes sadly pathetic with trouble, mother-like, she
tried to comfort with the small talk that women often offer,
and that answers the purpose like bathing one's brow with
Florida-water in a severe headache. She never mentioned
business to him when in such moods. Now it was a
bit of newspaper-gossip, concerning some discoveries in
Greece, that he and Maverick had been quite eager
about.

The poor fellow was distraught, and could not listen.
He ate his supper, choking down the food, for her dear
sake, missing strangely Cousin Jane's pungency and
seasoning. Then he tried to interest himself in the
paper, but could not; he paced the floor softly; he
whistled a tune, for his mother's benefit also, but broke
down in the middle.

"I must go out a little while," he declared in desperation.

"Not in this storm," said his mother pleadingly.

"Yes. I'll be back by — ten," looking at the clock.
"It is too bad to leave you alone," with sudden regret,
kissing her tenderly.

"I shall not mind for a while. But this wretched
storm " —

He laughed, a little strained and forced; then he put
on his great-coat, almost wishing that every man in the
country was without, and had to buy one to-morrow. He
tramped up the street, drawing long respirations, every
one of which was nearly a sigh. Was this the way Mr.
Lawrence felt when times went bad? Was some such
trouble the cause of that fatal disaster? He bowed his
head in a sort of touching and profound respect to the
dead man. He experienced an earnest sympathy for all
struggling capitalists. What did unreasoning labor know
of such nights as these when every thing, even good name,
was at stake ! He wondered if his mop of curly hair

would turn gray, and then, in a ridiculously trivial mood, remembered he must go and have it cropped. As well now as any time; but when he reached the barber's, the place looked so uninviting, with the smoky kerosene-lamps turned low. He did not stop: he used to wonder afterward how it would have been if he had, until he came to have a sincere and reverent belief in God as the disposer of human events, the Hand back of the curtain, that guided every step, and kept sacred watch even over two sparrows.

He walked down past Maverick's; but half a dozen people were in there, so he went on and on to the very end of the street, when by the dim light he saw a figure in advance of him, a woman, tall and stately, muffled in a waterproof and hood. There was something in the bearing different from most of the Yerbury women who ran out of an evening for a neighborly gossip, or some provender for their next morning's breakfast. There were no stores in this direction; it was quite lonely; perhaps she was going home. It would annoy her to be followed, doubtless; and on such a night as this no roughs would be abroad in this vicinity.

Jack Darcy was in that nervous state when the brain seems rarefied and empowered to wrest secrets from the very elements in his path. He pursued several chains of thought at once, with lightning rapidity, and, with curious mental inconsistency, dropped them, and lapsed into others. Now a sudden interest sprang up in this wandering traveller. He listened with the wariness of an Indian to her step. It had in it the essential principle of flight, but a baffled, fruitless longing for escape, rather than a nearing to some distant haven or goal. He had not used to be so keen in this subtile discrimination, until Maverick crossed his path, and helped him out of his psychological bondage. And ordinarily his senses had not the electric keenness of to-night.

The figure paused. The face seemed to turn to the drear, blank sky — was it in appealing, or a desperate daring? an impotent resistance, or a wild, agonizing prayer? The hands were thrown up: he had come gradually nearer, and could see them, ghostly white in the long feeble ray of the distant lamp. What was she deciding or asking? A shiver ran over him as the thought of suicide entered his brain. At all events, he must not let her go to destruction.

Her hands dropped. She took a few slow, irresolute steps, then turned and came so quickly, that before he could stir or think, she confronted him. A wild face with staring eyes, a wilder shriek ringing out on the night air, making muffled echoes around, a desperate plunge, and a fall. He sprang and essayed to raise her from the half-frozen hail-bed of the sidewalk; the hood fell back, and he was more than astonished at beholding the face of Irene Lawrence.

He appeared suddenly to comprehend the whole fact, though he came to know afterward that he misjudged her. Only a desire to put an end to life and suffering, real or fancied, could have brought her out this night, in the lonely neighborhood, still, not so far from her own home. He must take her back, and then go for Maverick, who had become quite a favorite with Mrs. Lawrence, and prescribed harmless remedies for her, since she insisted she must have them.

Jack Darcy never experienced a more exultant pride in his strength than now. He lifted the helpless form, settled the swaying head on his broad shoulder, and, clasping the body tightly, picked his way through the slippery streets in a manner that would have done credit to an Alp climber. Round this corner and that, to the quiet, deserted street, where every window was closed, and perhaps half the inmates in bed. Only in one house was there a sound of life. Some one was playing an accom-

paniment for an evening hymn, and youthful voices were
singing. Two lines floated out as he passed, making a
kind of glow on the sullen night : —

> "Though long a wanderer,
>   The sun gone down " —

Unconsciously he tightened his arms around this wan-
derer. Of course all their brief acquaintance had gone
through his mind, especially the day when in her haughty
pride and beauty she had given him that cold, insolent
stare ; but he forgave her freely, just as he had forgiven
Fred's sin, unasked. How strangely he was destined to
be mixed up with these Lawrences !

He paused on the low porch, where a honeysuckle rioted
in summer, and was still full of withered leaves. His
burthen had not stirred, and was a dead weight. Resting
it against his knee, he pulled the door-bell gently, and
waited.

"Is that you, Mr. Lawrence?" asked a voice from
within.

" No. Jack Darcy," for he guessed rightly that it was
Martha.

She opened the door.

" Don't be frightened, Martha," in a re-assuring tone.
" It is Miss Lawrence."

" Oh, good heaven ! " in tones of terror.

" Hush ! do not disturb any one. Is Mr. Lawrence
home? Where shall I carry her? she is in a dead faint."

" Bring her in the parlor. Oh, Mr. Darcy ! where was
she?" with a look of wild affright. " I did not know
she had gone out. I always felt something would happen
to her ; and a long while ago I offered to go out with her,
but she is so hard and disdainful that one soon comes to
letting her alone. She made me promise not to tell her
brother, or rather she defied me to : she wouldn't put any
thing as a favor if she was dying. Talk about the pride

of Lucifer! And I knew it would worry Mr. Lawrence dreadfully."

"Was she in the habit of going out — alone — at night?" asked Jack, in amaze.

"I think it was from pride," answered Martha simply. "You see, she needed some exercise, and she seldom went out in the daytime. And I don't think she is afraid of any thing. I never saw such a cold, bitter, strong girl — for she is only a girl yet. I've sometimes felt afraid she would do something desperate. Oh, if she would only let the Lord help her bear her trouble! And Mr. Lawrence is so kind and generous! He would do any thing for her. Oh, he ought to be home! There's the clock striking ten."

"And I must run for the doctor. Heaven grant she may not be dead! Take off her cloak, and try something" — glancing about in alarm.

Then he seemed to take one devouring look at the sculptured face, with closed lids, and jetty lashes sweeping the marble cheeks. Hurrying away, as if by some great effort, he ran down the street again, despatched Maverick, and hastened to Fred's office. The building loomed up dark and silent. He might possibly be at Garafield's house: he often went there of an evening, he and Mr. Garafield were so engrossed with their plans.

It was a long walk; but Jack strode on, getting rapidly over the ground. The hall-door was open, and Mr. and Mrs. Garafield were saying good-night to Fred. Jack waited until he came down the steps, and then called to him cheerfully. They linked arm-in-arm. The hail and rain had turned now to fine, hard snow, and the wind seemed to scurry through the deserted streets like a forlorn, wailing spirit.

Jack told his story briefly, also repeating what Martha had said about Irene's habit of lonely walking. He felt the sensitive nerves in the arm he held, quiver with a shuddering pain.

"Thank God it was you!" Fred said, with a great, tremulous gasp. "She is so strange, so cold and self-contained, — so bitter against fate! Believe me, Jack, I have tried my utmost "— and the voice broke with something like a sob.

"I know it, dear old fellow," drawing him nearer as the blast whistled around them.

"We never learned to make each other happy, you know. We never supposed we had any special duties to one another, so it was a new task to me. I tried to interest her in something, to make her more cheerful; but she would wrap herself in that haughty, unconquerable coldness. Yet if I had known or guessed "—

"After all, there is very little danger down your end of the town," said Jack, in that light, comforting tone. "There's nothing to call tramps or roughs; and, I dare say, to-night all would have gone straight if she had not run against me, as one may say, and the fright made her faint."

"But if it had been some one else! Oh, my God!"

"It was not; so never give that a second thought. There is no use in bringing up an army of ' might-have-beens ' to worry you to death when you have escaped danger. And — here we are."

"You will come in, of course?"

Jack followed his friend. Maverick had succeeded in restoring Miss Lawrence to consciousness; but she was now in a burning fever and raging delirium. Outraged nature had at last asserted its sway.

"It is better so, I think," remarked Maverick, in a quiet, decisive tone. "She will have a severe run of fever, for this has been some time coming on; but she has youth and a naturally fine constitution in her favor. I believe she will pull through. But some arrangement must be settled upon. It will not do to take her up-stairs; for the effect upon your mother will be too great a risk.

If you could bring a bed down here — to-morrow I will see about getting a nurse.''

"I think it would be better to bring her bed down stairs," rejoined Martha. "The parlor is used so little. And she would be so much more comfortable " —

Martha's eyes went over the heavy, clinging dress, the disordered hair, the bracelets that were like manacles as she threw her arms about, moaning, muttering, and laughing shrilly. The eyes rolled wildly in their senseless stare, until one's blood almost curdled.

" We must get about it immediately," began Dr. Maverick. " She will be quieter presently, and I shall remain all night. Darcy, you watch her: do not let her injure herself, while we bring down the necessary articles.''

Just at this juncture Mrs. Lawrence's bell rang. The noise had startled her from her first sound sleep. Dr. Maverick explained simply, and gave her a composing draught.

"A fever! Is it any thing contagious? Yes, it is better to keep her down there : my nerves are so weak, and I think I have a very sensitive, susceptible nature. I might take any disease so easily, — do you not think so, doctor?" and Mrs. Lawrence looked up from her frills and laces and snowy pillow with the helpless air of a child.

" Much better. She may be delirious, too, and that would distress you. Now be as quiet as possible, and try to go to sleep again. I shall remain to keep you both in order," with a laugh.

" That is very kind," she answered, with a pretty wave of her delicate hand. Her daughter might be dying below, but her nerves must be settled and cared for. Still, to do her justice, even in her intense selfishness, she never considered other people's ailments dangerous, while she held that her own precious life was constantly in peril. She talked of dying with the calmness of a saint, and admitted that there was no further charm to life, but still she must have the choicest care.

Under Martha's supervision they soon dismembered the bedstead, and brought down all necessary belong-ings. Jack had watched his charge, strangely exercised by her curious, changeful moods. Once she had looked meaningly at him.

"I *might* marry you," she said, in soft, mocking tones, her scarlet lips taking on a bitter, scornful smile; "but I should come to hate you so that some night when you lay asleep I should rise and murder you! I might endure you in London, where I could be in a continual round of gayety; but at Frodsham Park, with an old man like you, — May and December! May and December!" and she laughed shrilly.

She did not mean *him*, then! Honest Jack Darcy blushed to the roots of his hair, to his very finger-ends. Some old man had wanted her: well, she was braver and truer, then, than most people would admit.

The three came in, and transformed the parlor to a hos-pital-ward, without the simplicity. Jack suddenly thought of his mother, and hurried away. What an eventful walk it had been! and Hope Mills was quite driven out of his mind.

He found his mother frightened and hysterical; and drawing her down beside him he told her the story of his wanderings, expressing with some tender kisses his sorrow for her alarm, and advised her to go to bed at once, as he meant to do. And, though it might not be romantic after such an adventure, I must admit that in ten minutes my hero was soundly asleep, oblivious of both storm and business.

At the house he had left, there was but little refreshing rest. Mrs. Lawrence drowsed away when the confusion of re-arrangement had subsided. The gentlemen retired to the library while Martha disrobed her young mistress with inward fear and trembling, hardly being able to judge what was due to delirium, and what to natural imperiousness.   Then Dr. Maverick kindly dismissed her.

"You will need your strength in the morning," said he. "Try to get at least one good nap."

He took his station at the bedside, and motioned Fred to an armchair just out of his sister's range.   The opiate was not working sucessfully, but at present he did not consider it wise to increase it. . He questioned him a little as to Miss Irene's habits and resources, and imagined the part withheld, from that rather reluctantly admitted.   He understood that here kindred blood had not produced harmony, but a horrible discord, the more wearing in that every note had been muffled.   The self-commiseration of the mother, and her weak love for her son that could only pity, but never encourage or brace to any vigorous effort ; her total inability to comprehend any such character as her youngest daughter possessed ; the wearisome platitudes enunciated in the belief that they were golden grains of worldly wisdom, the only kind she supposed existed ; the weak, vapid repining that she had not married when she might have done so well, the discouraging certainty that no marriage was possible in this second-rate town, and that to remain single was a stigma and a misfortune.   In her weak but querulous complaints, which she meant in part for sympathy, she had worn and exasperated Irene as much as Mrs. Minor : only here there were no lovers, and there Mrs. Minor looked upon every single man of means as a fish to be skilfully angled for.

If Irene had been thrown completely upon her own resources, if she had been compelled to step entirely out of her olden sphere, and earn her daily bread, there would have been a sharp, bitter fight, but the bracing mental atmosphere might have dispelled the thick darkness, the chilling vacuity, and evolved from the discordant elements a questioning and not easily satisfied soul, but one destined to develop into strength and nobler uses. But here, she said to herself, there was nothing. Friendship could not come to her aid — she would have none of it. No one should study her with curious eyes, to see how she bore her trials, her losses, the downfall of her pride. Strangers who had glanced at her with envy in her pretty pony-phaeton, or the magnificent family barouche, should not smile in triumph as they saw her walking by. As she had scorned others in her grandeur, so others would rejoice that she had been brought low. She had seen so much of the narrowness, the petty spite, the sharp stings of the world, that her sensitive flesh shrank at every pulse.

She could understand now how high-bred women, when friends and fortune had flown, had shut themselves in convents. That she would have been glad to do. Any entire renunciation would have met with her approval. But to gather up the threads of a commonplace existence, to find joy and solace in daily duties, to work for others, to even show others how trials and misfortunes could be borne to the perfect working-out of nobler aims and uses, was not for her. She had never been trained to any such purpose. A heathen of the heathens in a Christian country, the product of fashion, wealth, and so-called refinement.

In the solitude to which she condemned herself, she came to brooding over a desperate, worldly philosophy. Should she go back, and retrace her steps, and marry? There were days when she absolutely contested the ground inch by inch, and almost decided.

Her long rapid walks, generally at night when her brain was wild with the bitter warfare, had served a useful purpose, and kept her in better health. But the strain could not last forever. For days she had alternated between a chilly, stupid languor, and hours when her brain seemed on fire, when, indeed, she hated the whole world with a bitter, awful intensity. In this mood she had stolen out for her walk.

And now the outraged soul had burst its bonds, and revelled in a fearful revenge. All the ache and repression put upon it; all this silent endurance; all the solitary hours of maddening thought, the wasted riches, the spurned sympathy, the youth poisoned by false doctrines, — every secret sin committed against it, cried aloud, and would not be throttled, nor thrust back into the dreary dungeon.

Fred listened to her ravings in stunned, helpless astonishment. His trial had been so much less intense, after all. Could it be possible she had suffered this as she sat so like a statue in the little circle, disdaining every aid? His startled eyes questioned the doctor.

"Yes," was the reply: "she has been too much alone. She has brooded over these things until she has become morbid and imbittered. The curse of fashionable life is, that it provides a woman with no resources against a dark day, no wisdom, no faith in any thing outside of herself. And then we wonder at insanity! A thousand times better that the body should be racked with pain, if so be that the soul is purified in passing through these fires. It may be her salvation."

CHAPTER XX.

THE morning's mail brought to Darcy the letter he had hardly dared expect. It was brief but cordial. Would he come to New York, and the matter could be arranged to his satisfaction? "He had not been very eager to ask favors."

"We'll weather through, Winston!" he cried joyfully. "I must go to New York. Miss McLeod has sent."

Then he ran off home, and arrayed himself in spotless linen and immaculate cuffs, complained a little that Jane Morgan should be away, and begged his mother to ask in some of the pretty, friendly girls living in the next house, if he should not be home to supper. There was a late train that he would be quite sure of, if the business detained him until night. Then he kissed her tenderly: she was still a little shaken from her last night's vigil.

He went around by Maverick's office, though it took him out of his way; but he must hear some word of Miss Lawrence.

"She is very ill, and will be for some time to come; but I am wonderfully interested in the case. It's a brain-fever. The girl is a study in herself. She has the force and power, and capability of both suffering and endurance, that would answer for half a dozen souls; but it has come pretty nearly to a wreck. Did you ever know much about her?"

"No. I once spent an evening with Miss Barry when she was there," and Jack flushed. "It was before Mr.

Lawrence died.   They used to be great friends, you know."

"And it ended like most women's friendships, eh?" with a peculiar light in his eyes as he spoke.

"No: it broke off in the middle; regards have a trick of doing that when they're not ended, you know. Sylvie is very generous: she would go there to-day if she were needed."

"Would she? She may be before it is all over."

"Go down aud tell her, Maverick, when you are in that direction."

Maverick nodded.

Darcy was just in time to catch his train. There had been quite a fall of snow from midnight to dawn, and the trees were glittering with thousands of diamond-sparks and patches of fleecy ermine. The winding roads were white; the cottages and the fence-posts were hooded; and the snow caught all the tints of sun and shadowy lights, reflecting them back like a mirror. His heart was so light as they whirled along, he smiled, and could hardly forbear shouting at a group of boys who were snow-balling by the roadside.

He met Miss McLeod at Mr. Hildreth's. They had the private office to themselves; and he related the mishaps of the past three months, showed her the actual figures, and admitted that times seemed really harder than last year. There was such a horrible shrinkage everywhere! Still there must be some trade presently, — it always had been so in the history of the world.

"I think you deserve a great deal of credit for having pulled through so far on your limited capital," said she. "Some of the business-men I meet, think this will prove the hardest year in our history. It will winnow the chaff from the wheat pretty well."

"If it does not winnow us all into chaff," returned the young fellow, with a touch of grim humor.

"We shall come back to smaller profits and greater industry. The world will not be able to play at being ladies and gentlemen, and perhaps a little wholesome work will not be a bad discipline."

Then she wanted to know what amount would be likely to tide him over for the next six months. He said he did not desire to exceed ten thousand dollars. She would make it twelve, however. After the notes were duly signed, she took him to her bank, and introduced him. As he had some other parties to see, she drove him about in her carriage, and insisted upon taking him home with her presently.

What an elegant old lady she was in her sables and velvets, and her royal air! her eyes bright with spirit and energy, her cheeks a little pink with the crisp air, glad sunshine, and perhaps her own hearty, wholesome mood. Occasionally she leaned out and nodded to some friend; and once her carriage drew up to the sidewalk as she summoned a fine, portly-looking gentleman to her.

"Mr. Throckmorton," she said, with gracious dignity, "I want to introduce my young friend Mr. Darcy, of Hope Mills, Yerbury, to you. If you can serve him in any business-way, I shall be glad to have you."

The gentleman bowed, and held out his hand, with cordial fine breeding.

"Hope Mills! It belonged to my friend Lawrence, did it not, — David Lawrence?"

"Until his death, yes."

"Sad misfortune, that. He ought to have retired years before. There was some villany in his manager, was there not? It is difficult to find a purely honest man nowadays; but I do believe Lawrence was one. We dealt with him a great many years, but toward the last there was some dissatisfaction, — goods not coming quite up to samples."

"We try to do our business on the square, Mr. Throckmorton," returned Jack, with a proud curve of the lips that was almost a smile, and illumined his face. "If any thing is not exactly as represented, we shall make it good; but we try never to have occasion to do that. We should be glad to have you test our honesty and skill."

"Thank you, — I will, I will;" and, touching his hat to Miss McLeod, they parted.

"If men were as generous as you!" cried Jack, with enthusiastic candor, "how splendid a place this world would be for business! Did you ever have a jealous .thought in all your life?"

She laughed brightly. "I have had nearly all the things I wanted," she answered, with tender solemnity. "There would have been little excuse. Mr. Darcy, we do not always realize how hard life is to some; and, where every man's hand is against one, it is natural for him to be against every man."

Their four-o'clock meal was an elegant little dinner. They were quite alone, which pleased Jack. She questioned him about Maverick, his practice, his friends, and wondered if he ever meant to marry. Jack said laughingly no one in Yerbury dared to make fascinating eyes at him.

Did she care so much for Maverick? Surely these two ought to be together, yet what would *he* do without his trusty comrade?

They veered round to the mills presently, and discussed honesty. Jack admitted that Mr. Throckmorton and other customers had a right to complain. There had been a deal of cheap wool used, and many poor workmen employed, during Eastman's last year or two.

"Mr. Darcy," she began energetically, "why do you not think up something new? We import pretty material for ladies' wear, that could as well be made here, for we women are growing sensible enough to believe something beside silk admissible. And though men may cling to superannuated coats, with an affection most commendable

in hard times, I never heard of a woman being attached
to an old gown."

" I never thought of it," he admitted frankly.

" That is what you were put in the world for, — to
think," and she smiled with quaint humor. "Invent
something. I'll take a sample to every store to match,
and lift my brows in surprise when clerks confess they
have not seen it. Give it a pretty name, of course."

" That is worth considering, surely ; " and his eyes
sparkled. " Hope Mills ought presently to be the grand-
est place in the country, you take so much interest in it,"
and his whole face expressed his admiration.

" I do hope to see you a successful manufacturer, Mr.
Darcy ; and, woman-like, I want the scheme to succeed.
I should like to see even a small party of men trained to
honesty and fair play. And, if I lose my money, it is no
worse than a downfall in stocks."

" I shall do my best now and ever," he answered
heartily.

They parted with much warm gratitude on the honest
fellow's side. He took the evening train for home ; and
his mother had a good cup of tea awaiting him, along
with her smile. He related his grand good luck, and
there were not two happier people in all Yerbury. When
the bank found he had an account at New York, and a
good backer, they were extremely affable again.

Jack broached the new idea to Winston and Cameron.

" To be sure," admitted Winston. " Some one will do
it presently, and we might get the lead. Darcy, your old
lady is a trump, and always carries the honors. There
will have to be some new processes : see here, talk to Ben
Hay about it ; he's made two or three improvements, and
has some brains. Gad ! It'll be quite jolly to have a new
line of goods. Get the ladies on your side, and you're
all right ! "

He had not a spare moment until after his late supper,

when he told his mother he must run over to the Lawrences, and stop a moment at the doctor's, though he had despatched the good news to him in the morning.

He found matters worse than he had feared. There had been an alarming change in Miss Lawrence. Martha ushered him through the hall to the library, where Fred was sitting. The two clasped hands, and then sat down together. A hard, dry sob seemed to tear its way up from Fred's very soul.

"Jack," he cried in a strained, despairing tone, "could I have done any thing to save her? I have been engrossed with my own affairs, my own dreams of advancement. I wanted to have money again, but it was for her sake and my mother's," with a lingering tremulous intonation. "She has been too solitary, she has brooded over every thing. But she would not go out, or see any company; and somehow it was our misfortune to grow up without any warm, vital interest in each other. When I was a boy I used to like it at your house, because your father and mother took such a real delight in you. It is the pith of life. Poor father — he was very proud of me, he gave his life for our pleasure and grandeur and reckless extravagance, yet all the later years we were well-nigh strangers. Why can't people get nearer to each other, Jack, or is it only given to the very few? Does the greedy world swallow up every sentiment, every bit of tenderness, and make a mock of it?"

"No, no! Nothing can quite kill it, thank God! You and I have proved that. It may be smothered under dust and rubbish, and frozen with neglect, but the germ will revive, — just as the brown woolly ball evolves the fine delicate fern-leaf that it has held in its heart through winter storms, you know. Don't blame yourself. Every soul has to fight its own battle somewhere, with no day's-man between but God. We get back to the old truth in spite of the new philosophies, and own in our vanquished moments that we cannot *make* strength, that ours is only a broken reed, and the true upholding force must come from some knowledge higher than our own.''

Jack paused, strangely stirred in every fibre. He seldom essayed sentiment: with him the deeds of life had to answer, rather than any eloquence of words. He laid his strong, warm arm over Fred's shoulder, the old boyish caress with which he had often comforted unknowingly.

'' I think you have been doing nobly,'' he went on presently. '' I did not look to find you so brave and persevering, so earnest in thinking of others ; for, after all, a man's training does throw a great many shackles about him.''

Dr. Maverick entered at that moment. He had hurried off his office-patients to come and spend an hour watching this case, which held a fascinating interest for him. Some most unfavorable symptoms had supervened, but he did not despair. The nurse had been regularly trained, he had kept her busy in Yerbury the last year. He could trust her to note the slightest variations.

Just now Miss Lawrence lay in a heavy stupor, so like death that one could not detect it from any motion. Her eyes were half open, her face had a dull purplish tint. The abundant hair had been confined in a thick plait, and brushed straight across her forehead. How distinct and finely clear the brows were pencilled, how haughtily sweet the curve of the pallid, fever-burned lips, how exquisitely round and perfect the chin, the slope of the throat and neck ! Jack stole one glance, — they had both gone in with the doctor, — but it seemed almost sacrilegious, now when she was powerless to frown the intruder out of her presence. And he had carried her in his arms !

'' O Darcy,'' Maverick exclaimed presently, '' I did not go to Miss Barry's, after all. I have been so desperately busy to-day.''

Fred glanced up, and his eye met that of his friend. Both flushed, and both mistook the cause.

It was a curiously auspicious moment. Jack went over to him. "I wonder," he began, with a marked persuasiveness in his tone, "if you would like to have Sylvie Barry come over? She and your sister used to be such friends. And, in times like these, animosities and foolish prejudices ought to die out."

Fred gave him a startled look, and half turned, his lids drooping to veil the secret in his eyes. Jack waited with breath that half strangled him. He had marvelled how these two souls were to be brought into friendly contact again ; how Sylvie was to have an opportunity of knowing that Fred was redeeming the manliness of manhood, instead of grounding among its trivial shoals, and, if she ever had cared for him, to understand that he was not utterly unworthy. He had spoken — what if the chance should fail !

Fred very naturally misinterpreted the emotion. Jack offered this out of the boundless tenderness of his heart, so confident was he of Sylvie's regard.

"You think — she would come ? "

His own voice, under the great stress, sounded miles away to him, quite as if some other person had spoken.

How often the tense strain of feeling is relieved by a tone or an incident quite out of the magnetic current !

"Some one ought to drop in occasionally, for your mother's sake," said Dr. Maverick. "We shall have her in a fever from sympathy," putting the fact more delicately in words than it was in his thought.

"She would be glad to come, I know. She would feel hurt if— You empower me to ask her?" with an abrupt transition of tone.

Fred Lawrence bowed his head. He could not trust his voice.

The sick girl started, opened wide her eyes, threw up her arms, and began in weird, passionate tones, as if it were a stage declamation. Oh the lurid thought that seemed to travel from regions of bliss to the nethermost hell; to display a boundless capacity for enjoyment, for pleasure or pain, for tenderness and bitter, brilliant satire, a keen knowledge of the world to the very dregs, — the dust and ashes! She implored her lost idols to come near, and in the next breath she tossed them from her with a mocking laugh. She had no faith in God or man, and before her was a blank wall of despair.

Jack led him away. He took him out in the keen air of the starry winter night, and began to talk of Hope Mills and the new projects. It was too late afterward to call on Sylvie, so he waited until the next morning.

She was inexpressibly shocked. "Of course she would go," she made answer; and she went that very afternoon, with her aunt for companion.

They found Mrs. Lawrence in a dreadfully disturbed and apprehensive state. She was so weary of solitude that she welcomed them gladly, quite forgetting this girl had insulted her by rejecting her son. In a weak, shuffling manner she excused herself for not having accepted their overtures before. She had been so utterly overwhelmed by the death of Mr. Lawrence, that, in her state of nervous prostration, it had been impossible to see any one. And now she was positive she should take the fever. Her health was so delicate, her nerves so susceptible, and to hear the raving of delirium, — the laughs that were quite like a maniac, — would be sure to shatter her beyond any help. If it were not in the dead of winter, she should go to New York at once, and stay with Mrs. Minor until all danger of infection was over. She did not seem to comprehend the gravity of Irene's case, though she wept over her suffering in a soft self-pity.

"If you could be removed to our house," suggested Miss Barry, in her gentle way, "we would take the best of care of you; and it must be extremely wearing for you here."

" Ah, you have no idea! I never slept last night. I have heard of people in these dreadful fevers who have left their beds when the nurse was absent, and committed some horrible crime. I locked my door last night; then I was afraid I might faint away alone, and Fred had to come and stay with me. It was terrible!" and the washed-out eyes dilated with real fear.

Martha was despatched for the doctor, who not only came himself, but brought a close coach, thankful to dispose of one patient so comfortably. Before dusk Mrs. Lawrence was snugly settled in Miss Barry's best room, where a cheerful open-front stove made amends for a grate, and the new surroundings served to take her mind from her late apprehensions. Indeed, she felt so much better for the change, that she insisted upon coming down to tea.

It was beneficial in many ways. They removed Irene again to her own room, and used her mother's for various convenient purposes. Sylvie went back and forth, and shared the day-watching, beside entertaining Mrs. Lawrence. The two dropped insensibly into their olden positions. Sylvie listened patiently to the death, the loss of fortune, the changes, which Mrs. Lawrence dwelt upon with the exaggerating vividness of a nature completely engrossed with its own sorrows.

Dr. Maverick had to come every day. Mrs. Lawrence had arrived at that stage when a woman depends upon the doctor as a sort of bulletin for her own health. Fred, too, must visit his mother frequently; but at first he chose the hours he knew Sylvie would be with Irene.

Dr. Maverick used to watch Sylvie Barry with an interest and admiration that grew upon him. Her tact was something marvellous, born of a certain exquisite harmony and almost divine unselfishness. But of this last she appeared serenely unconscious. I think, indeed, that she was. A higher love and faith had interpenetrated her soul, her very being. Instead of agonizing introspections and lightning flashes to the inward depths of her nature, she seemed to live continually on the outside of herself, radiating warmth and light as the sun. Her patience was of a rare, fine quality, born of health, and spirits not easily wearied.

It would have been quite impossible for any two people to go through such a strain of feeling, and not be drawn together in love and sympathy, or friendship. With Fred and Sylvie it was unconsciously a little of all. If he had gone back with the old love, even exalted and refined, he would surely have blundered again. But now she was another's, sacred in his eyes. And though in his blind pride he had once thought the greatest favor he could do her would be to save her from any such *mésalliance*, he recognized now that Jack Darcy was immeasurably above him in all the qualities that went to make up pure manhood. Even in his work : Jack's ambition was not for himself, but a cause ; and his — ah, how poor and paltry it seemed ! So he accepted his place with outward bravery, and a great wrench of all a man holds most dear. For now he loved her.

The days passed slowly on. It seemed at the last as if the fever would prove the victor. A consultation was held, and new remedies employed. Irene's beautiful hair was cut off and laid away, the clear skin seemed to grow brown and shrivelled, the hands lost their plump whiteness, and the rosy nails were dull and gray. There came a time when human skill had done all, and they could only wait for that Higher power to whose eternal force death and love alike submit.

There followed upon that awful night of suspense, days when she was but just alive, when a turn of her head on the pillow caused a lapse into unconsciousness. But the spring came on ; and she did rally, at first, it appeared, at the entire sacrifice of her regal beauty. Would she care to take life on such terms ?

They brought Mrs. Lawrence home.   Mrs. Minor came up, and insisted that both mother and sister should be removed to the city at once.   She had her horses and carriage, her servants, her luxuries, and she could make them so much more comfortable.

Dr. Maverick interposed a decided negative.   The body had not yet resumed its normal state; but the brain was to be ministered to, as only those of experience and study could minister.   It was to be brought out of the hell of its own despairing self-torture, and enfranchised, set free from the demons that, standing in the present abeyance of weakness, had lost neither strength nor desire, and were only waiting the auspicious moment to seize their prey again.   And he was too much fascinated to relinquish the study.

Sylvie persuaded her aunt to indulge in a pony-carriage. Miss Barry was breaking a little; but she still kept her interest in good works, and found she was much more useful with this aid.   Winsome little Sylvie looked more piquant than ever with the reins in her hands, flashing hither and thither through the streets of Yerbury, gathering a harvest of smiles and nods.   She fairly compelled Mrs. Lawrence to trust her precious self to what she laughingly declared was superior horsewomanship.

Dr. Maverick used to stop her often, just to catch a delicious ripple of laughter, or a bit of trenchant talk.   If it were not for Jack Darcy — did Jack love her?   At all events, she loved him: any one could see that by her frank, fearless manner.   Oh, sapient Dr. Maverick, with all your knowledge of brains and nerves, of occult causes and mysterious effects!   So it happens that sometimes a simple, direct truth is the greatest puzzle of all.

The schools and clubs had not been neglected with all this excitement.   But this winter Mary Moran had been teacher at a small salary; and a bakery and refreshment or dining room had been opened down stairs, which really made quite a little money. Wholesomely cooked food was offered for sale, with bread, rolls, and biscuit. The club had also given two successful suppers. When Jane Morgan was home, Sylvie was relieved of the actual care: she would have it. She had come back to Yerbury a thousand dollars richer for her relative's death, and she and Jack were drawing plans for a co-operative store.

CHAPTER XXI.

"I'D rather lose five thousand dollars than do it."

Jack Darcy leaned back in his office-chair. He had just made up the third half-yearly account. It was bad enough. They had known this all along, and had not concealed it from the men. Now it was to be confronted in black and white, with searching eyes.

It was not that they had not made any thing: that would have been endurable, considering the kind of winter. But they had gone back, and eaten up the profits of last year.

"You see, there co-operation comes in," said Bob Winston. "It isn't *your* loss alone. It's mine and every man's. That's what we agreed to when we went in. Labor and capital should share in the ups and downs. See here, Jack, I've learned a good deal myself. I have more sympathy with employers. Gad! what a pull we've had this winter! If it hadn't been for your fairy godmother" —

"Well, it must be done!" and Jack pulled a long face. "There, it is all ready to print. Now old fellow, we must brace ourselves up for the shot and shell. We'll have to do the fighting all over again. If every man had as easy, philosophical a mind as you, or as sensible, reasonable a one as Cameron, I should not have so many misgivings."

The statement was printed and distributed. The men looked blue and cross. Had they really lost nearly all of last year's balance?

Winston asked them to stop one evening while he went into a slight explanation. He was well armed. Without having a logical mind or parliamentary training, he had a woman's quick intuitions, and often jumped at very decent conclusions with hardly a glance at the premises. He had a way of massing his forces, too, that was very telling.

Now, after what he called a little skirmishing, he read that the Barnable Mills had been running on three-quarter time all winter. Wages had been a trifle lower than with them. Middleham Mills had been closed for two months. He gave the figures of loss to the workmen. Crowley and Dawson had gone into bankruptcy, owing their men in the aggregate more than all Hope Mills had used of last year's profits. Then he read a statement from an eminent manufacturer, that he had used fifty-four thousand dollars of accrued capital rather than turn off his workmen to starve. There had been strikes in several other places, in which the workmen had lost much more than at Yerbury.

"So that our showing, bad as it is, is not the worst," said he. "In the very dullest of times we cast in our lots together, and we must take the good and bad. If you had been living this winter on the private capital of any one man or corporation, you would never have given the matter a thought. You know now, by experience, that capital does not always float on a serene and indolent sea, and gather in treasures for which it has cast out no net. You can appreciate the struggle we have gone through; though, while you have been going along placidly, with the larger weight of care lifted off your shoulders, a man with less energy and pluck than our intrepid pilot, John Darcy, might have let us founder. We help him now with the readiness and good-humor with which we relinquish the profits which were dear to us, and the product of our industry; but he has taken us through a very narrow channel, on a dark night, without striking rock or snag. He and I thank you heartily for your fidelity to our keystone, — co-operation.''

''Three cheers for Darcy!'' sang out some one in the crowd, ''and three cheers for Bob Winston!''

It was given heartily.

''And three cheers for the men of Hope Mills,'' responded Winston.

They shook hands, and dispersed with a little better feeling. Several of the men seemed to breathe a clearer mental atmosphere immediately.

'' You may be sure it's right, whichever way it is,'' said one man sturdily. '' I've known Jack Darcy, boy and man, and his father afore him. He comes of good, clean stock, and, if he says a thing can't be bettered, it can't; and, if it can, he's just the man to do it. Give him a long tether, say I.''

Then Winston procured a list of weekly wages ruling in this country, and in many places abroad, the hours of work, and the average cost of living, with the articles in most general use. The mill-men had their flour and coal cheaper, and altogether their winter was proved as satisfactory. This was pasted up in the hall.

The matter was discussed through the town, of course. Some people saw in it a speedy dissolution of the plan, — a plan that never had worked, and never would. Others did not see that this method of getting back part of the men's wages was any better than any other swindling scheme. They never had any faith in Bob Winston, — Darcy might be honest, but he wasn't very bright, — and in five years Winston would own every thing there was in the mill!

Winston laughed over the gossip. Jack could not take it so light-heartedly. He was an earnest, honest reformer, and hated to have things go awry. Winston, not believing there was very much capacity for reform in human nature, did not distress himself.

Ben Hay, and a dozen or so others, did their best with the new cloth, and succeeded in producing a really creditable article. The heads discussed the feasibility of having an auction-sale to clear out some of the piles of goods; then concluded that it might be misconstrued at this present juncture. They could hold on until fall.

But the delightful *esprit du corps* had vanished. The men did not seem to work with a will. There were moody faces and discourteous greetings, half-insolent nods, and more than one wrangle at the workmen's meeting. Hurd felt anxious and discouraged. Yardley took a low fever, not severe enough to confine him to the house, but it made him irritable, and every sneer or innuendo cut him to the quick. Cameron was a great comfort to Jack, with his queer, wrinkled, grizzled face, and an expression that always puzzled you as to whether nature meant him to laugh or cry.

"I am not surprised," said he, one day, in the office. "I knew we would have to come to just this time. A wife shares your joys and sorrows, gen'ally speaking; but you see there it's a force put, she can't well get away. Other partners like your joys, but they make a wry face over the sorrows, and like to squirm out of them if they can. But it is the only way to train men to the real responsibilities of business. Now, I'm sorry enough to lose, but it stands to reason that times will come better. We're getting through the panic; but after the battle there's some dead to bury, and some wounded to care for, and you see that's tedjus. You can't march straight home, covered with glory. Here's our money in the hospital, first up, then down, and all the doctors in the land. tinkering with allopathic doses and homœopathic doses, and blisters and poultices and remedies, when all it wants is a little honest letting-alone. It doesn't occur to these long-headed doctors that the best way out is to show everybody that we're willing to go to work and pay our debts just as fast as we can. And any fool might know that when you are paying up back debts you can't have much money to sport around on. Never you mind, Jack : we're coming out straight in five years time, — I'll bet my old hat on that ! ''

Jack wrung his hand warmly.

In May there was quite a jollification over the marriage of two mill-hands. Ben Hay took to wife pretty Rose Connelly ; and the coffee-house parlor was denuded of tables and benches, trimmed with evergreens and flowers, and such a merry-making as did one's heart good. There was a bountiful supper, plenty of tea, coffee, and lemonade, dancing, and ice-cream, and the utmost good-humor and good wishes. Connelly *père* had gone back to his cups, thrown up his situation, come home and stirred up a general "ruction," and had now gone off on a tramp. Ben Hay was to cast his lot with the Connelly household for the present.

"But I tell you what it is, Mr. Darcy," said he, "if any luck comes to Hope Mills, in five years' time I'll have my own little house and garden. I tramped around a bit in the dull times, but I didn't see many prettier places than Yerbury. And, the more I study this business of co-operation, the more I think it will succeed in the end."

Jack experienced a great throb of comfort when he heard such words as these.

Another mill-hand had married Mary Moran. She was not the beauty of Yerbury, by any means, but everybody declared she had improved wonderfully, and that she was the smartest girl in town. Their wedding-party was given at the club-room. It was a larger and rather more boisterous affair ; and some of the Morans' warm-hearted Irish friends brought a "dhrop of the craythur" in their pockets, to drink the bride's health. Everybody admitted that there wasn't such another bread-maker in town, unless it was Miss Morgan.

In fact, it was quite astonishing to see what a revolution had been worked in this most important article of diet. The women had learned to distinguish between poor and good flour, and Kilburn's trade in the former had fallen off largely. Of the bread that in Samantha Allen's view "required cast-iron principle to back it up," very little was seen. It had been rather hard work to convince some of the mothers that bread wasn't naturally born into the world heavy and sour, but it had been done.

If Hope Mills failed, the impetus to general knowledge that had been diffused throughout Yerbury would remain and bear fruit. An evening-school had been opened for boys too large to stay at home evenings, and just the right age to fall into temptations. It began with the mill-boys, but it soon drew in others. There was a short session of study, then a talk about some useful art or science. Maverick had treated them to sundry experiments, and explained many general rules of health. Mr. Winston had described Western cities in a vivid and picturesque manner. There had been some astronomy within the reach of all, some philosophy of common every-day things ; and it had given the boys ideas above "high, low, Jack."

Darcy tried to find comfort in this when other matters looked dark to him. A little good seed had been sown. The generation growing up would not be quite so dull and brutish. One thing was remarked, — the saloons were not as full. This was laid to dull times, and ascribed to the "revival" of two years ago ; but that had not touched the poorer class of Irish and English, who, even during the hardest winter, had managed to find drink-money, when their families were being supported by the relief-store.

Business did "pick up" a little. Prices went lower and lower, however. They looked at their great store of goods with dismay. If the currency question could ever be settled, if we could export more and import less, — though there were people who argued that, the more money we spent abroad, the more it really strengthened us, and money lying idle in our treasury at home was no evidence of prosperity : partly true and partly false reasoning ; and, to our astonishment, while we were brilliantly theorizing how to do it, our vain and superficial neighbors across the water, crushed and beaten down by a useless and costly war, and a government of gigantic selfishness, went to work with intrepid courage and industry, and did it.

Meanwhile it must be confessed that Jack's interests were very much divided. The practical part of him never lost sight of the mill. He had the dogged tenacity that holds on with a 'deathless grip until it conquers, or is wholly beaten. It seemed to him this summer that he had several distinct individualities. He was so deeply interested in Fred and Sylvie ! They had slipped into an easy friendship, — a friendship in which neither crossed a certain line, but from widely different motives   Fred's strongest and highest one was honor toward his friend. He began dimly to realize that high culture and refinement of the intellectual senses, a perfect state of outward finish and polish, did not always strengthen the soul's morality and purity. Patience, self-sacrifice, obedience to a creed simpler in words, and yet more comprehensive, than any of his grand philosophies, were needed to form a strong and manful soul. His had been so long bound about with swaddling-clothes, airy, sensuous, fine as a gossamer web, yet strong in beliefs and prejudices. There were times when he felt, through that instinctive knowledge we can never wholly define or explain, that Sylvie Barry belonged to him, that they two could reach a point in mental and artistic life, that she and Jack would never attain. His whole soul cried out for her. With the charm of self-satisfying and blinding theories swept away, he clung passionately to the love that had been only a complacent fancy three years ago. The mere touch of her hand, or glance of her eye, quickened and kindled his entire soul, and made him acutely and agonizingly conscious of the wealth of adoration he had hardly dreamed of possessing. There were moments when her presence filled him with a heavenly satisfaction, when he understood that divine fusion of spirit with spirit in its entirety, when love overcame pride, and he was humble enough to go to her in his poverty.

He tried honestly to crush out the passion, but found that neither will nor duty could destroy love. It rose up and swept imperiously through every pulse of his being, it flooded his heart like a mighty current, it would-fain have drowned out his sense of honor to his friend ; and he learned presently that it was of no avail to fight battles with this unconquerable foe. He must always love her, therefore he could only bury the passion out of the sight of all other eyes. To him it would be the root of higher resolves and purer motives. When he had made this great sacrifice for his friend, he had offered silently the highest atonement in his power.

But his temptation was not to end so soon. He was to be led through the fire, that he might be purified and ennobled in other virtues beside that of abnegation. He was to learn how sacred a thing strength might become ; he was to hold the soft hand on his arm, and never clasp it, to feel the pressure of the dainty fingers, and make no sign ; to meet her bewildering smiles with the calmness of a strong spirit held in thrall ; to listen to words that seemed cruelly pregnant with the dangerous glamour of hope, and yet to steel his heart against it all. In such times as these we come to believe in a living, loving God, who gathers up these great drops of agony as he " makes up his jewels," and that to him this pearl of inward anguish is above price. Then, of all times, we need to know that he cares for us, that we are not mere atoms floating in unregarded space.

Dr. Maverick decided that his patient must have a change. She had attained a certain amount of physical strength while her brain still lay dormant, utterly exhausted after the great drain upon it. Now it began to act again, and, not being in sympathy with the body, consequently re-acted upon it. She walked about her room a little; she viewed herself in the mirror, a horrid shadow, a mere caricature of her former beauty. Dr. Maverick had tried his best to save her hair; but the fever had burned out its vital essence, making it dry and harsh, so he had uttered his reluctant edict. It was cropped short, and had lost its gloss; her brilliant complexion was a ghostly, sallow, opaque white, her eyes large and melancholy, every feature sharpened into that thin, worn, hungry appearance. "A perfect fright," she said to herself. Why had they not let her die? Of what avail was life to her?

Before her illness, in her desperate impatience with circumstances, she had fancied herself a martyr, with the fagot and stake of a conventional marriage on one hand, and the dreary desert of neglect and enforced seclusion on the other. She had tried to make her own wretched and passionate imaginings consume her very soul. She could rule no longer. She could not exact homage and admiration from society; and, though in her secret soul she despised it, yet what was there to life beside it? No one wanted or needed her. No human being cared for her above all others. She had gone on in ruthless pride, trampling, crushing, and now the great world would be only too glad to pay her back; but it never should. Even in this extreme bitterness of spirit an acknowledgment of that divine rule of love was wrested from her. She had never offered love and tenderness and sympathy to others, and it would not come back to her: it was just and right that it should not.

Why then vegetate through a narrow, dreary existence?

She was only a drag on Fred. Even if she were willing to make an essay of work, he would not consent, partly from pride, but still more from that innate sense of chivalry, a part of some men, who would be more cruelly wounded to see a woman dear to them, struggling with distasteful toil, than to make any sacrifice on their own part. If she were a man she would starve in secret before it should be done. David Lawrence had in him some of this pure, nobly generous blood ; and many of his finer virtues seemed to have been transmitted to these two children. The mother's individuality had been absorbed by the two elder ones. Gertrude would be just such a woman when she came to her mother's time of life.

Mr. Eastman had floated into another channel of prosperity. He was to go to Russia as a railroad-director at a large salary, and ample chance for speculation. Gertrude was all elation. She wrote to Irene, generously forgiving her for not having submitted to be buried alive at Frodsham Park, and proposed that she should rejoin her as soon as she was able to travel. They would go to Vienna and Berlin, and spend the winter in St. Petersburg. " I hope your beauty has not gone off," she wrote very kindly. " One needs it to compare with some of the Russian women I have seen."

Mrs. Minor had taken a summer cottage at Long Branch. Servants, children, horses and carriages, were to go thither. Irene and her mother must spend the season with them.

" You do look dreadfully," she said to Irene ; " but moping here will not mend you. It was a most absurd step for Fred to come back to Yerbury, and take that paltry position ! He has no real Lawrence pride, and I don't see that his elegant education has done much for him. Why didn't he study law, and go into politics? With his style and Mr. Minor's connection, he might have filled some high position."

"Really," returned Irene, with a touch of the old sarcasm, "I suppose he thought starving hardly a pleasant process while he was waiting for this high position. I have sometimes wondered why Mr. Minor did not take him into *his* office, and induct him into the mysteries of stock-broking."

Agatha bit her lip.

"Because he did not know enough," she flung out. "And he will potter away his best days there at Garafield's, never amounting to any thing! Father had better have put him in the business."

"Jack Darcy is master at Hope Mills. He was once quite a *bête noir* of yours, I believe. He and Fred have floated together again, an exemplification of the power of early attraction."

"He will not be master of Hope Mills long, if what I hear is true," said Agatha in a vengeful tone, as if she would be glad to bring about such a greatly-to-be-desired downfall. "Fred always did have low tastes. But about yourself: you had better come to Long Branch, and recruit for two months, or so, and then go out to join Gertrude. Of course, Irene, you know your best time has gone by here. I intend that *my* daughters shall be married before they are twenty. I will not have them wasting their best years."

There was a long pause. Agatha studied Irene's apathetical face, and wondered how she could have changed into such a fright.

"Irene!" in a commanding tone.

"Agatha, I may as well tell you,"—the voice was slow and incisive, as if every word was measured,—"that I shall *not* go to Long Branch nor abroad. No one shall be troubled by my failing looks and possibly poor health. I will live my own secluded life, asking nothing of the world but to be let alone."

"You are a fool, Irene!" Mrs. Minor scanned her

with her pitiless black eyes, and raised her own tall figure to its most impressive height. "You are a deliberate, wilful fool!   You will maunder and groan and sigh through the. next few years, and become one of those wretched bundles of nerves and whims and conceits, a miserable old maid, whom the world holds up to ridicule, and rightly too; a faded, insipid, querulous, worn-out belle, whose past triumphs are remembered only to her disfavor.   We can forgive a woman of mother's age, who has had her day; but the other shallow creatures are fit only to be bundled into a convent, out of sight."

A dull scarlet had slowly mounted Irene's face.   She did not raise her eyes.   In an emotionless tone she merely said, "Thank you.   I wish there were convents without the fuss of religion.   I should go into one now."

"The best place for you certainly."

Then Mrs. Minor gave Fred a piece of her mind, and washed her hands of Yerbury.

The result of sundry after-discussions was that Dr. Maverick found a pretty seaside place not many miles distant, with just enough interest to keep one entertained, and no fashionable, exhausting life.   He managed to persuade Miss Barry and Sylvie and Mrs. Lawrence to go, and insisted upon Irene having the variety of air and scene.   There was a roomy furnished cottage at their disposal: they could cook their meals, or have them sent in. Fred should come down once or twice a week, and he and Darcy would enliven them with flying visits.   Miss Barry must take her pony and carriage.

Jack approved of the plan at once.   It would bring the two beings in whom he was so warmly interested more closely in contact with each other, give them those bits and fragments of leisurely indolence so conducive to sentiment.   Sylvie would judge more truly and tenderly than it was possible to do at present; and he could not see her alone, could not be her companion in walks and drives, without betraying his regard.

While the plan was still under consideration, Dame Fortune resolved to smile upon Fred Lawrence. Late in the winter he had sent a paper on household art, with several exquisite designs, to a magazine, and for once happened to hit the prevailing fancy. He was asked for a series of such articles, with the offer of having them collected in book form afterward. It more than encouraged him: it gave him a feeling of certainty that he had struck the right vein, that here was a fair and appreciative field for his talent, his fine taste, and high culture. A little utilitarian, perhaps; and he smiled, thinking of some past dreams. And was true art so ethereal that it must exist only in the exalted states of the mind? Was it not to embellish and beautify all lives, rather than crowd out the thousands that the few might feast on some exquisite vision? Was any art higher than that which boldly thrust aside shams, and went to the shaping of true, strong, faithful aims in the work placed before one? Were those wonderful Greek fragments, wrought in times of social depravity such as the world now shrank from mentioning, to be one's guide and inspirer, to the despising of purer if less sensuous forms of beauty? If one enlightened and sweetened the life of to-day with the work of to-day, would it not be as worthy as hugging to the soul some useless theory?

He mentioned his new offer to Mr. Garafield. It would not be honest to take the time that was another's; and surely Fred Lawrence's mental capacity had largely cleared when he came to put into every-day work the fine sense of honor that he had hitherto supposed belonged only to a liberal education.

Mr. Garafield was a shrewd business-man, although fanciful in taste. He should be the gainer by associating this true artist with him. Decorative art was coming to be a truly recognized branch; and its leaders and apostles would reap not only credit, but financial success.

Fred was amazed. Only yesterday, it seemed, he had well-nigh been refused the privilége of earning his bread. To-day, in an unexpected quarter, prosperity opened upon him.

" I have no capital, as you well know," he said stammeringly to Mr. Garafield.

Garafield smiled and nodded in a satisfied manner.

" The brain-work and the ideas are sufficient capital, Mr. Lawrence. By this partnership you will be free of drudgery: some other clerk can keep books' and take orders for us. You will gain time for your literary labors, and those in turn will carry weight in the business. Neither do I think you will regret taking my offer."

Fred went down to Jack Darcy's that evening, and told over his plans, as in other years he had confessed his college ambitions and the laurels he was to win. And Jack's face lighted up with honest enthusiasm, while his voice took on a curious little tremble. He was so glad ! for Sylvie's sake and love's sake.

CHAPTER XXII.

When Fred Lawrence came next day into Sylvie Barry's presence, there was a certain proud humility shining in his handsome face, that was now quite worn and thin; a dignity born of honor in having achieved at least a standing-place in the world. He was not her hero, never had been indeed; and his pale face flushed at the remembrance of his once complacent claim to her regard.

She was sitting in the room with his mother, but she sprang up from the low ottoman.

"I am so glad! your mother has been telling me the news. Why, it is" —

She had held out her hands as she began her sentence, but as he took them she made a sudden pause. His were icy cold.

"More than I could have expected in such a brief while, hardly at all. Both offers have surprised me greatly."

He strove so hard to render his tone calm, that it was absolutely cold.

She turned with a petulant but charming gesture, while her peachy cheek took on a riper tint.

"You are not a bit enthusiastic," in that pretty, imperious, chiding tone. "I suppose you think good fortune ought to fall down upon ·you, be thrust on you, like greatness."

"No. I am very thankful for it. I can give my mother and sister some needed indulgences that it would have pained me very much to see them go without. How is Irene?"

"I don't know," said Mrs. Lawrence fretfully. "She does mope so. I shall be so glad to get away."

"I have just come from the doctor's. We are to start on Thursday. Sylvie, are you all ready?"

"Yes," with a positive little nod.

He stepped into the next room. Irene had been worse after Mrs. Minor's visit, but was the same again now, quiet, cold, impassible. It made no difference to her whether they remained here, or went to Depford Beach. She evinced neither pain, pleasure, nor interest; but she liked best to be alone. She endured Sylvie with rather more equanimity than she did her mother, but even the fault-finding energy would have been welcome to the doctor. Nothing mattered: that was the trouble.

She heard now they were to go in two days. The cottage was all ready. Martha and Miss Barry's trusty handmaiden were to do the housekeeping. The place was so arranged, with the spacious hall through the middle, that each family could be by itself.

"I have ordered a carriage to come every day for you and mother," Fred said quietly. "I thought you would like it better than being dependent on Miss Barry."

Irene gave a slow, acquiescent nod.

"Good-by," cried Sylvie, looking in. "I will run over again to-morrow."

"I wanted her to stay to tea," said Mrs. Lawrence complainingly. "It is so dull!"

"I will come up and take tea with you. I will order it at once." And he ran down.

There was a subtle perfume in the hall. She had a bunch of violets in her belt, he remembered. He said over softly Ben Jonson's quaint lines, —

> "Here she was wont to go, and here, and here,
>   Just where the daisies, pinks, and violets grow:
>   The world may find the spring by following her."

But he could not follow. Had fate smiled on him to

make the renunciation more bitter ? For now he could work his way up to something worthy of her acceptance. And had he not learned the past winter, had he not been slowly learning ever since the death and loss, that the manhood of a gentleman was his thoughtfulness for others, his courteous delicacy, his consideration, often his denial of self, rather than the exquisite polish of cultivation, and the veneer of society's affectations? How blind he must have been, ever to have offered these last to a woman so true and pure of soul!

But a still larger sacrifice had been demanded of him. He must see her in seductive solitudes, in still more intimate association. If he could stay away from Depford Beach! but that was not possible. He was to spend Sundays with them. But surely Jack would be there then. An almost careless lover he thought his friend. Was every smile so dear to him ?

The doctor and Fred went down with them. Darcy had decided to take a business trip, so presently Mrs. Darcy joined the seaside household. In the bygone years Mrs. Lawrence would not have deigned to notice her; but she found this delicate, mild-mannered, middle-aged woman very companionable. Circumstances had rendered Mrs. Darcy exclusive, rather than any inherent trait of birth or breeding. She had lived with a few people always, and two or three strong attachments had given to her character the kind of concentration that passes for strength. Yet all of these had been more positive people than herself; and while this had softened the tendency to that querulous exactingness that weak, sweet natures are apt to possess, it had also shaped to certain generous instincts that were quite free from vanity. Her natural kindliness gave her the charm of good-breeding, and this settled her in the estimation of Mrs. Lawrence. She might have possessed all the virtues in the calendar, but an inharmonious, unpolished

turn or act would have tabooed her. We generally
ascribe this grace to life-long culture, or a certain inheritance of blood, but it occasionally springs from other
causes.

The three women, with natures and aims widely different, fraternized in the most amiable manner. Sylvie
glanced in and out between them as a gleam of sunshine
penetrates the interstices of a wood, and brings out all
lights and tints, itself untouched by any. Their greatest
diversion was driving. Back of the little settlement—
it was hardly large enough for a village, and had a powerful rival some seven miles farther on — there were country
lanes and by-ways, sleepy-looking farms, and picturesquely
careless houses. Below them there was a great fish *entre-
pôt*, with fishing-boats plying up and down, brawny fish-
ermen trilling their musical half-chant, half-song, as they
floated over the bay

It was curious how, presently, Sylvie came to watch
for Fred. Truth to tell, she found Depford Beach a trifle
monotonous. No interest of schools or clubs or young
people's affairs, no strong energetic talks with Jack about
mill business, few people coming and going that she
cared about; the three ladies purring through the drowsy
hours on topics that she fancied she had exhausted years
ago; and Irene, between whom and her there had never
been any real electric sympathy, and who was now coldly
indifferent to all matters. For hours she would sit with
her hands dropped nerveless in her lap, glancing over the
wide sea out to the farther horizon. What thoughts were
in her mind, Sylvie wondered? She could not even pro-
voke her to the wordy combats of old. The flashes of
temper and imperiousness had alike died out. She was
courteously polite, and acknowledged all favors with a
punctiliousness that built the wall around her still more
firmly. "If one could only rouse her," Dr. Maverick
said; but that seemed just the thing no one *could* do.

Yet she certainly was improving in health. Her step became more assured, her eye less languid, and her complexion cleared up to the hopeful tints of renewed bodily vigor. Her slender hands filled out a trifle; and sometimes she would take a book, as if she needed an interest beside her own sombre thoughts to while away the hours.

So Sylvie established her easel, and had recourse to painting. Oddly enough she began to ask herself what it was all for? Filling her own rooms, and bestowing gifts upon friends, was very well for a season; but was there not a higher purpose in all art, or at least a wider purpose? It surely did not tend to isolation. She thought of her winter in Philadelphia, — of the friends she had made, of the desires that had been awakened. She longed for some purpose, some sympathy and aim. The enthusiasms of girlhood could no longer inspire her: there must be a reality and definite end, or work lost its great charm. How was she to get to this? Her aunt was coming to depend upon her in a peculiar way, that at times startled Sylvie. She would say, with her quiet, tender smile, " Will you do this or that, Sylvie? I believe I am growing indolent: I never thought to so like being waited upon."

The secret in Miss Barry's soul was well kept. In how many lives there comes a demand for heroism greater than that which led the martyrs of old to the stake, or the brave women in the reign of terror to the guillotine! Their inspiration to bravery was patent to all around: their cause was a lofty one, and they were apostles of that high creed of self-abnegation which leaves behind a memory in the hearts of all noble men and women. But there are other pangs quite noiseless: there are other martyrs who suffer without the sign, who cannot even confess the reason for the high faith that upholds them.

It was quite natural that she should desire to see Sylvie married. She could never get over her distaste of having

women taking bold strides for the world's fame and favor.
If left alone, this was what Sylvie would surely do. The
delicate womanly charities and kindnesses that had filled
up so much of her life would not satisfy her niece. And,
now that she had brought herself to the point of satisfaction with Jack Darcy, either she had mistaken their regard,
or he was proving himself an indifferent lover. By a
subtile intuition, she understood that Fred still cared for
her, nay, that he held now a reverent admiration that he
had never thought of in the past. His melancholy eyes
followed her about, now and then scintillating sparks of
passion that seemed almost to rend his soul. She experienced an intense and exquisite sympathy for him that drew
them together in a manner that he felt, and was grateful
for, but did not clearly understand.

As for Sylvie, curiously enough, she was at war with
herself, though she wore such a calm, light-hearted exte-
rior. When she rejected Fred Lawrence, she was quite
sure she despised the present man, and his narrow, futile
purposes of life. Truly, to have been the wife of such a
man would have proved irksome to the last degree. But·
his misfortunes had brought out the fine gold, the solemn
strain of strength and endurance, that had come from his
father's blood. I think even Sylvie had been a little
mortified first, that he should have come back to Yerbury,
and taken such a very inferior position. She wanted him
to do something noteworthy with his pen and his high
cultivation. It seemed so much choice material quite
thrown away. Designing patterns was surely no high test
of genius. Women with a purely technical art education
had done it.

But out of it had come this other opportunity that he
had grasped with the pure instinct of genius. Employment for pen and pencil both, for the embodiment of the
exquisite outward forms of beauty, and the rare, delicate,
inward graces of imagination, for the true standards of

taste and art in which he had been informing himself all these years ; in the spirit of dilettanteism, it was true, but now when the intellectual impetus was added, and the positive need of daily bread, these complicated motives worked together as a strong stimulant. Perhaps, too, he had a not unworthy desire to show Sylvie Barry that the man who had loved her was not utterly unworthy or incapable.

They had drifted together again in the ordinary purposes of life, which, after all, occur much more frequently than any grand or overwhelming shock. She took up the friendly, half-sisterly way, pleased with the instinctive deference he paid her. He understood that it would be quite useless to aspire to any regard of hers : that was all done with in the past. She could afford to evince an interest in his plans, since Irene cared not, and to his mother they were so much Greek, a subtle flavor that she admitted was the proper thing, but could not understand, — did not care to trouble herself, in fact.

So these two young people, working in a common bond of sympathy, insensibly strengthened the regard that had grown with them from childhood. Fred gained sufficient courage to discuss some plans with Sylvie : she brought out her easel, as I have said, and accepted from him friendly criticisms. The difference between their work was soon manifest, — he had an earnest purpose, with breadth and scope : she had none. How had they so queerly changed places? she asked herself. Why were not her talents made of some avail, instead of this puerile pottering to please one's self?

She began to wonder — dangerously fascinating employment to a woman — if he had ever cared for her. There seemed an adamantine wall built up around him, and yet the fruit in the inner garden was more rarely sweet than she had ever dreamed it could be. She could not know that the passion for her he had put away with such despairing hands, was blossoming all the sweeter, and bearing more exquisite fruit in other directions. She saw the lovely tenderness toward his mother, the unwearying patience with Irene, the fearless, animating ambition that seemed to have set his æsthetic desires to a steady, comprehensive strain of music, to which he was keeping invisible step, but which thrilled and roused every fibre.

All this he had done without any assistance from her, she thought, blind little girl; as if the kinship of a true passion could not reach from the life that went before to that which was to come afterward! *She* had not inspired his genius, but stern necessity; it had been no longing or desire to win *her*, but the material support of his mother and sister. She began to feel curiously jealous of these extraneous influences. She unconsciously exerted herself to make his visits at the beach more interesting. They drove together in her pony-carriage; they studied glowing summer sunsets, where fantastic clouds piled up wealth of gold and amber and purple and opaline splendors, and shot out arrowy, dazzling rays; they paced the sands after it had all faded into tintless space, and delicate vapors of grayish green and vague violet rose from the crested waves that broke far out at sea, and trooped across like airy spirits; they listened to the slow, regular rhythm that came marching from some weird country, with a grand crash at last, a sobbing crescendo, and an interval of silence that still pulsated on the dusky, odorous air, when the moaning billow was dead.

They came so near to Nature, there were moments when they seemed empowered to wrest the shadowy secrets out of her bosom; and yet they did not come near to each other. Ever this distance between, — a man's honor, and faith to his friend, Fred Lawrence thought, never allowing his secret soul to swerve. There were midnights when he softly paced the floor, his lips com.

pressed, his brow ghostly white, and his hands clinched in the throe of a man's deathless love. Then he thought he could not endure it, that he must stay away. But circumstances were stronger than will. Did God mean that this anguish should redeem that other old treachery, that his soul should be purified by its baptism of fire, a more worthy offering for his friend? If so, then he must not abate one jot or one pang.

There were within Sylvie Barry's soul certain coquettish instincts. She was fond of admiration for herself: a purely intellectual regard, with the passion-dream flown, would soon have wearied her. A warm, bright nature, loving to please others, but to be pleased in return, cruelly hurt by surging against this rock-bound coast, piqued and almost angered, sent into moods of daring, seductive warmth and gayety, quite capable of making a foil of Dr. Maverick, who was strangely puzzled by her contradictory moods. But for one thing, he must have tried to cage the dazzling, elusive spirit: he, too, had a strong sense of honor toward his friend; and he could only imagine her playing sportively with the few who came within her radius, not setting herself to win any forbidden regard. What might have made some women sad and silent — the consciousness that an old lover had over-lived his passion — seemed to sting her into renewed effort.

Coming back to them, Jack Darcy was more than puzzled, set at sea in a bewildering way, without chart or compass. Had Fred ceased to care for Sylvie? Had she never loved him? Or was some other feeling holding him back, — a kind of family complication, a sense of duty to the others so high that he would not offer them a divided regard, any sooner than her? He believed mothers had a peculiar sense of possession in their sons; but they surely had married other women's sons with small scruple! Mrs. Lawrence was warmly attached to Sylvie. In his honest, inconsequent man-fashion, he wondered why they could not always live together, as they were doing here.

Fred was strangely worn and thin, with the kind of nervous alertness that accompanies an intent watching of one's self.

"Hillo, old fellow!" cried Jack; "what have you been doing? Working yourself to a shadow? If high art is so exhaustive, there must be a little let-up. A man has no more right to kill himself in an artistic industrial way, than in any of the ruder forms of suicide."

Fred shivered visibly.

"Don't speak of suicide," he answered in a shrinking tone. "I never thought of it but once; and that was when I fancied myself of no use to the world, or myself either. I am not overworked"—and he paused, to study Jack a moment. Why, he was positively handsome, with that superabundant strength and vitality, the clear red and white of his complexion, the bronze beard, the healthful, honest eyes. He seemed to be surcharged with a magnetic current of energy and courage.

"Yes, you are. I dare say you have carried your plans and sketches, and what not, down to Depford Beach, and pored over them until almost morning. You must take a vacation."

"I expect to when the families return;" and he gave a faint, wan smile. "I have had another streak of luck, Jack. A lady, a very wealthy widow, is building a house in one of the pretty towns up the Hudson, and it is to be finished with all the elegance art can bring. She saw one of my articles, and sent to me; and we have been corresponding. In September I am to go to New York, and make arrangements. There is to be painting and frescoing, and rooms finished in different styles, — indeed, I cannot tell the half myself, until I see her."

The pale face had kindled with a fine and proud enthusiasm. More than ever, Jack recognized the artistic refinement of his friend. What would law or medicine have been to him as a profession?

"Humph!" grunted Jack. "A great vacation that will be! But you *must* be careful, or you will not live out half your days. You've a look in your face like the little chap I first knew."

The smile that crossed it then, Jack did not understand. It seemed to Fred Lawrence that half his days would suffice, when Sylvie Barry was his friend's wife.

"Yet you see the 'little chap' lived"—with an attempt at gayety.

"Yes. And, Fred, I am more glad than I can put into words, to know that you have been so successful. It is just the career for you. It's odd that a great commonplace, blundering fellow like me should have two such artistic friends as you and Sylvie Barry."

The well-trained face did not blanch a muscle. He felt, with a flash of subtile inner consciousness, that Darcy was studying him. Thank God, he could stand before his friend free from a thought of treachery! All these weeks he had walked over burning coals, but the smell of the fire was not in his garments.

Jack thought it over long after Fred had gone. Why could not these two people see! Surely they were meant for one another. It puzzled, it almost fretted him. Sylvie was so peculiar, so changed in these few weeks! What did it all mean?

And on Saturday when he was to go down to the beach, Fred pleaded some urgent business to a neighboring city. He was not quite brave enough to see them together.

"I have been meaning to go for some time," he said with gravity, "but I did not like to think they would be alone over Sunday. Now that you will be there, I certainly can spare three or four days."

"See here," returned Jack,—"wait until Monday. Come, we'll have a nice day together down there on the sands. Sundays always seem so wonderful by the ocean, with the grand chant forever in your ears. The very waves are saying, —

"'Let every thing that hath breath praise the Lord.'"

But Fred Lawrence would not suffer himself to be persuaded.

CHAPTER XXIII.

JACK DARCY's business-tour, while it had not been productive of any great financial results, had restored his healthy mental equilibrium. He found other firms were having it just as hard, and that the country was still overrun with men willing to work for any wages. Prices were certainly falling. All kinds of raw products were offered at the very lowest figure ; and, labor being so cheap, manufactured goods must perforce be low. Men were not now counting on a speedy return to good times and high prices : they began to admit that the latter were the outcome of extravagant speculation. They bought what they wanted, and no more. They gave no extensive credits, and now really appeared to be anxious to reach a permanent basis.

"We shall have to sell most of our stock at cost," he said to Winston. "Lucky to get that, I suppose. And we shall come out about even — no profits for this six months. Still, we shall not run back, and that is something gained."

"We can count on the new goods, I'm pretty sure," returned Winston. "I've had some inquiries, and sent samples. Some of the fancy overcoatings are to be duplicated. That looks like business."

It did, indeed. Jack sat at his desk, ruminating upon it, and feeling as if at last they saw a light through the woods, when a step startled him, because it was not the kind of step usually heard through that hall, so he turned.

It was Fred Lawrence, with a face of ashen pallor. Jack sprang up, dazed with the vision.

"I was to come and tell you — Maverick has gone to Depford Beach — Miss Barry is very ill, and they have telegraphed for him. He left word — that we were to come."

The voice had a strained, unnatural sound; and the eyes looked like those that have wept out a passionate sorrow, and are dry from despair.

"Ill — Miss Barry — not Sylvie?"

Could he speak of her in that calm tone? A passion of rage swelled in Fred's heart, and flushed his face. Only a moment, for the great throb of thankfulness that it was *not* Sylvie restored him.

"It is Miss Barry.   You will go?"

The tone had that peculiar, wandering cadence, as if somehow the soul had dropped out of it.

"Certainly," and Jack sprang up, puzzled by something quite intangible in Fred's demeanor.

"There are just twenty minutes to catch this train. The eight-ten does not stop at Depford, you know."

"True: I will just speak to Winston " —

"I will meet you at the station," returned Fred hurriedly, turning away.

Much as he loved Jack, it seemed as if he could not walk to the station with him. A feeling of profound pity for Sylvie rose in his heart. This man, noble, generous, helpful, and affectionate, had not the finely responsive nature Sylvie Barry needed. There would be some distance or coldness, or, worse still, a fatal dissonance. One part of her nature must remain unmated : her soul would have a language in which he would not only be deaf, but wholly dumb. He could express no more than the possibilities of his nature. It was not the fine and essential difference between man and woman, but that more fatal gulf in which there would appear no certain glimpses of a royally endowed love in all its spontaneity, its glow of feeling, its variation of rich emotions. How would she, with her versatile, changeful soul, with its cycle of moods, ever live in the strong, steady prison of his heart!

If he had thought perfect honor to his friend the greatest trial of his life, what was this to be? He could not stay and see the slow, consuming inward fire that would burn her soul to ashes while it was still in the body. Thank God, he could go away, would go soon indeed, and never return! He would nerve himself for these few days of torture.

Jack waited on the platform until the last moment. The bell was ringing when Fred appeared, and the strong arm grasped him. They sat side by side, but were silent after one question as to the nature of Miss Barry's illness. Never had they been further divided in heart, for in the days when there had been no semblance of friendship the trivial repulsion was not to be compared to this wall of adamant. Fred would not have gone at all but for his mother's sake, although his heart was with Sylvie through every instant of her trial.

The house was very quiet when they reached it. Maverick came to meet them, and was as sorely puzzled as Fred by the certain composure of Darcy's face.

"It was not altogether unexpected by her or myself," Maverick explained in answer to their inquiries. "It is the result of a complication of disorders, some of long standing and incurable; and the present effect is partial paralysis. I hoped change of air and a quiet summer would delay what we knew must come before many years."

Darcy was astonished beyond measure. He would sooner have thought of his own mother dying. True, he remembered now that Miss Barry had been about less, and looked rather more delicate, and that through the summer she had kept extremely quiet. So amazed was he, that at first he quite forgot about Sylvie.

Fred Lawrence paced the floor in an agony. Would the man never ask the question that was torturing him, because he had no right to ask it first!

"How is my mother?" was his huskily tremulous inquiry, as he still went up and down like a caged lion.

"The shock was really terrible to her. Mrs. Darcy was invaluable," bowing to Jack. "But for her, Sylvie would have been in despair," — looking furtively at the broad, slightly bowed figure.

"Poor Sylvie!" he murmured, "poor Sylvie!"

Fred turned to the door, compressing his lips over a throb of anguish.

"Of course," began Maverick, "they must all be removed as soon as possible. I think it would be well for Mrs. Lawrence and her daughter to go to-morrow. Neither is strong enough to bear any prolonged strain."

"Yes." Fred's heart swelled within him. They were all to be thrust aside as quickly as possible. This was Sylvie's sorrow — sacred to her and Jack.

He went to his mother's room. She was lying on a couch, and was still hysterical. From her he heard the story; and though, as ever, she was selfishly alive to her own sufferings, she evinced an almost motherly tenderness in her sympathy for Sylvie.

Fred spoke of the return. If it could be to-morrow; if he could settle them in their own home, and go quite away for a while! he thought.

"And leave Sylvie here alone?" said his mother reproachfully.

"I do not know what you can do for — for Miss Barry." How studiously cold and calm the tone was! "The doctor wishes to remove her as speedily as possible. I thought we would be out of the way, at least."

"It *is* terrible here; and if you considered it quite right — the summer is so nearly ended, and the nights are growing cool, — yes, we might go."

They settled it over their quiet supper. "Miss Barry was comfortable," Martha said, "and Miss Sylvie was lying down."

Mrs. Lawrence retired early, her nerves were so shattered by the terrible incident. Irene had disappeared; and, when Fred could stand his loneliness no longer, he went to walk upon the beach.

It was a moonless night, but with an intensely blue sky that gave the Milky Way the appearance of a luminous trail across the heavens. The murmur of the waves seemed sad and softened, and they touched the heart of the man who paced beside them. Once he had held so much in his hands! Surely he could have won the love of this woman then. Oh the blind, insensate, idiotic folly! He could have thrust his own soul down here on the sand, and trampled the very life out of it!

Hark! some one was coming with hasty strides. With the wild instinct of a wounded animal he turned to flee, and yet — whither should he go?

The hand was on his shoulder. The well-known voice uttered his name, and he turned at bay.

"Sylvie" —

"Don't repeat her name to me!" he flung out, beside himself with passionate jealousy and love. And then their eyes met, the one lurid with an emotion well-nigh beyond control, the other wondering, pitiful, amazed.

"Yes, let me go my way. I had not meant you to know it; but once — yes, I will confess it to you — I scorned you to her. God knows how I have repented; for I was beside myself then, blinded with my own folly and arrogance. And now you have won the woman I love, whom I shall always love, and it will be at once my bliss and my punishment. Take your triumph — tell her that her erring knight came back, and paid her the highest homage of his soul." Then, in a sudden, changed tone, freighted with a pain that pierced the other's heart, he cried, "Jack Darcy, I have made amends for that selfish blunder of my young manhood. For weeks I have endured such pangs, that Heaven grant you may never know! I have walked by her side with polar wastes between us; I have touched her hand with fingers that have had no more passion in them than the dead; I have watched her dewy lips ripe with kisses, and remembered they were for you; I have been true, *true* in word and deed and desire, but in thought I must love her to her life's end. I will go quite away" —

Up to this point his words had come with the heat and flow of a lava-torrent. Now his impassioned voice faltered, trembled, and seemed to lose itself.

Jack Darcy stood transfixed. Was it a dream? Had Fred been so blind all this while? He essayed speech; but the lines about his mouth were constricted, and his breath came in quivering gasps, as the vision of torture, suffered for honor's sake, rose up before him. Ah! if ever he *had* sinned, — and the temporary forgetfulness appeared such a little thing to Jack's generous soul, — he had redeemed himself nobly.

"Oh! you thought — she doesn't love me, Fred, — not in that way," and his voice had the full, throbbing inflection of a great joy. "We are friends, such as a man and a woman can truly be. Do you not understand that some people are so alike they run in parallels? there are no angles to create the intense friction of love, they are so evenly balanced that there is no desire for possessorship, they have just as wholesome an influence over each other remaining apart. There is hardly Sylvie's equal in the world. Half that I am, I owe her."

Had the night changed? Was the world flooded with a serene and tender light? Was the moaning ocean filled with the wondrous music of immortal love and longing, reaching out to glad fruition? Was that sudden rare peace, creating a reverential atmosphere about him, an earnest of days to come? He experienced a vivid lightness as if he were being borne on clouds, while fragments of delicious remembrances floated through his brain. The very refinement of his nature seemed to exalt him to that high heaven of love, whose solemn mysteries it is not lawful to utter.

"I cannot quite understand" — in a curious dreamy tone, still spelled by the mastery of impassioned emotion — " how you could miss loving Sylvie ; how she, woman-like, could help adoring you for your strength and heroism. Jack, if I were a woman, your very power would compel me to worship you. I should love you, whether or no."

Jack gave a bright, cheerful laugh. " It is that kind of strength you like in Sylvie," he made answer. " She will always spur a man up to his best. Her well-trained ear is quick to detect a false note in honor, ambition, or love. She will never be any kind of dead weight, and yet she is so deliciously womanly. There was a time — don't be vexed, Fred," — in a tender, pleading tone, — " when I thought you were not going to be worthy of her. But that is past."

" She rejected me then," Fred Lawrence said simply. " I offered her my father's wealth, the home he had made, my own folly and arrogance and self-conceit ; and then, Jack, she boldly admitted that you were her hero ! When I consider the sort of man my training and surroundings made me, I am filled with disgust. And yet I was no worse than hundreds of others at the present day. When I look at my mother, Irene, and myself, I feel that we were the product of the so-called culture of the day, which substitutes shallow creeds, conventional manners, and systems, for all that is pure, strong, and noble in manhood or womanhood. It is the sort of Greek temperament on which we pride our intellectual selves. We revel in a glowing, sensuous enjoyment, that intoxicates the brain, and leads us to disdain the real work of the world. We are trained to consider what society demands of us; we are polished and refined, and in too many instances left morally weak and ignorant. No wonder so many of us have not the strength to buffet across the stormy sea of hard experience, but are lost in the great whirlpool!"

Jack peered into the pale, handsome face by the faint light. Surely this man had to make a tremendous effort for salvation, when nearly every tide had been against him! He experienced a keener sympathy than he could express; he drew the arm within his, and they paced up and down again in silence, understanding dimly the sacred mysteries of each other's hearts, that needed not to be dragged to open day for inspection. In a pure friendship, faith is the highest element: with that there is supreme content; without it, distrust gnaws like a canker-worm.

They heard the little church-clock striking ten, and turned their steps toward the house. On the porch, Fred paused a moment, while an icy fear seemed to wring every pulse. He turned cold with apprehension.

"What if I have been deluding myself!" he cried with sudden intensity. "Even if you and she could not love, she may have no such regard for me as I desire. I could not endure her pity."

A warm, hopeful, generous smile illumined Jack Darcy's face. His hand thrilled with an electric force and sympathy.

"I have no fear," he answered; "but I will not dim the grace of your exquisite joy by any prediction."

They entered the quiet room. Dr. Maverick came out to meet them.

"Miss Sylvie is asleep," he said. "Miss Barry is comparatively comfortable. Hester will stay with her through the night. I have sent your mother to bed," nodding to Jack. "I do not know what we should have done without her. I shall camp down on the sofa, to be within call; and to-morrow we had better begin the process of removal."

"I had arranged to take my family," remarked Fred Lawrence, not exactly certain now that it was best.

"Your house must be opened and aired thoroughly, before any one goes into it. So must Miss Barry's. Miss Morgan will see to this, I think. I am compelled to return in the early morning train, for I have some critical cases. One of you had better remain here."

He looked at Jack as he said this, but was amazed at the frank answer, —

"Fred will remain."

He studied Jack with almost angry intentness. Had he been so mistaken in the man? Could he so calmly leave the woman he loved to bear her terrible trial alone, or did he think his mother's sympathy sufficient for her? And, although there were many admirable qualities in Fred Lawrence, the two had never fraternized with the deep cordiality that must underlie all friendships. They had not the magnetic attraction for each other that Darcy held for both.

"What do you think of Miss Barry ?" the latter asked hesitatingly.

"It is the beginning of the end ;" and Maverick sighed, as he thought of the impotence of human skill past a certain point. "Miss Barry consulted me a year ago, and was not in ignorance ; but I hoped, nay, felt assured, with care and quiet her life might be prolonged. She may linger some months, and it may all be ended in a week. Good heavens! what a shock for Miss Sylvie!"

He took two or three turns across the floor.

"Go," he said abruptly, with an imperious wave of the hand. Then, a little scornfully, "You will both be better in bed. Lawrence looks as if I might have him for a patient to-morrow ; but, Jack, are you made out of adamant?"

The thrust hurt him, but Maverick was not in a pitying mood. Indeed, just at this moment his temper was sav-

age. He had witnessed the pain and the suffering of the
woman he had begun to love, until it had been hard to refrain from taking her in his strong arms, and sheltering
her from the keenest pangs.

The household remained the next morning as he had
ordered. He was rather sulky all the way up in the train
with Jack; but a talk with brisk, pungent Miss Morgan
quite restored him.

"Open the houses, and build fires immediately," he
commanded. "Burn up and blow out the confined air,
that there shall be no pestilential foes to greet them on
their own hearths."

He went down again that evening. If he had been
annoyed before, he was puzzled now. There had been no
word spoken between Fred and Sylvie; but the now, to
her, sweet knowledge had come in a gesture, a glance,
that could no more be described than the fine pulse of love
can be dissected. She seemed to have waited breathless
for just this strength and support. A hasty lover might
have placed himself in the foreground. It was as if he
said, "Here is my love, take it, use it, rely upon it; you
cannot wear it out, you cannot wound or hurt it by any
thing that may look like coldness; it is a blessed atmosphere to surround you until you stretch out your hand, and
draw me into your very soul. I have been trained in
patience and humility; only let me prove myself worthy in
your eyes."

Three days after, they all came up to Yerbury. The
evening before, Irene Lawrence had gone to Sylvie's room,
and found her kneeling by the open window, her face
tnrned heavenward in a wordless prayer for strength. She
knelt beside her, she took the passive hands in hers, she
even touched her own cold lips to the colder forehead of the
other.

"Sylvie," — the tone still had the awful dreariness of
that utter inward living, — "Sylvie, I have been drawn to

you in this your anguish by some power quite outside of
myself. I think we have always liked each other in a
curious way, but we were neither of us sentimental girls.
I could not cry over you now, nor kiss you with effusive
fondness ; but I wish, oh, how passionately I wish, I could
save you one pang ! I wish I could die in *her* place ! My
life is of so little value " —

" I believe God is right," Sylvie answered with a great
struggle. " She has used her life so well; she has gar-
nered ripened sheaves of mercy and kindliness and good
works. There is not only golden wheat, but the sweetness of rose and violet, the pungent purity and strength
of heliotrope, the use, the beauty, every thing. She is
ready."

" And I am not worthy to be taken even for a ran-
som ! " said the proud, cold voice, not betraying any
inward hurt.

" God does not mean that. You are to shape your life
to something better. Irene, did you ever think how easy
it might be to die for those we love, but oh, so hard to
live for *them*, not ourselves ! "

Irene rose, and stood there like a statue. Sylvie felt
for the hand, pressed it to her lips, folded it about her
chin in a softly caressing manner. How had Irene become dear to her?

" I am no heroine, Sylvie. ΄ I have been tossed up by
the breakers of fortune, and am out of joint, broken,
bruised, of no avail."

" You can comfort *me*. You can help to give me
strength and sympathy. You can become a warm, living,
active woman. There is always room for such in the
world, and a work for them to do. God never put an
idle or useless thing in the world, much more a human
soul ; and it must go sadly astray before it comes to
despair. Irene, you will not shut your heart again, you
will turn its warm side to me, you will take me in, with

my great sorrow;" and she buried her face in the other's dress, with a shivering sob.

"I will do — what you wish. I am physically strong again. Let me help you — anywhere, anyhow. You were so good and patient through my dreary time."

Then she stole softly away, astonished at herself. Within was still the coldness of Alpine glaciers. But oh, if she might be warmed!

Miss Barry's journey was performed in an easy carriage. A paralysis of the lower limbs had supervened; but otherwise she had rallied a little, and her mind was clear and cheerful. There was only to be a peaceful waiting for the end, no feverish fluctuations of hope and fear. It was curious how they settled themselves to the fact. A nurse was installed for night watching and the more onerous part; and the invalid's room took on a pleasant aspect, — Christiana waiting on this side of the river.

CHAPTER XXIV.

For the first time in his life, and for some unfathomable cause, Jack Darcy found business cares irksome. Balance-time was at hand. He was a little tired of the dreary round. The men's disaffection re-acted upon him. With his keen and intelligent faculty of making the best of every thing, he was disappointed because he had failed to inspire others with it.

"It's not so bad, after all. We have nothing that can be passed to capital, but we have held our own. Only, there is no dividend for the men."

"I'll explain that to them," exclaimed Winston with a confident nod.

He did, and he had a rather stormy venture. All the old arguments and agreements had to be gone over. Men unaccustomed to business are quick in prosperity and stupid in adversity. They only had three-quarter wages: why should they be called upon to lose beside? It was little enough, and waiting five years, — and no one knew, — the whole thing might go to smash another year! A few wished, with an oath, that they were well out of it. They would never be bamboozled into any co-operative scheme again.

The grumbling grew louder and louder. It was discussed at Keppler's over beer and bad whiskey, and quite inflammatory speeches were made. Then Winston called the mill-hands together.

"My men," said he, "you know we opened the mills in starvation-times. Every man who could raise fifty dollars was entitled to a half-share of the capital, and he who could not was to have a little capital made off of the savings of his labor. Last year you were all pleased and merry and satisfied, because we made something: this year it has been the reverse, though I declare to you, I, for one, have worked twice as hard. Now, we shall never do any thing if we are all going to row different ways. It must be the long pull, the strong pull, and the pull all together. You know that if any operative became dissatisfied, and left, his share was forfeited to the fund for the sick and disabled. Many of you *are* dissatisfied; but maybe you won't leave, thinking of last year's money. Now, I want to say, every such man who would like to *sell* his share, may do so. I have had some applications from new men, that I have been very sorry to refuse. I shall open a book, and any man who wants to go out may put down his name there, and, just as fast as the shares are resold, he can go; *but he never comes back into Hope Mills again!* Just think it over, and decide in the course of a few days."

"O Winston!" cried Jack, "I am afraid there will be a stampede!"

"You're nervous and blue, Darcy. Now, you see if this isn't the very best move. There were two men here the other day from Little Falls. They had been taking out half their wages in store-pay, and the concern burst up, owing them the other half. They knew of a dozen men, not beggarly poor either, who would be glad to come. I'll bet my old hat there don't six men go out. Come, now!"

"You can't tempt me with your old hat," returned Jack laughingly. "Make it a treat at Kit Connelly's."

"Agreed. We'll take in the household."

A dozen names were put down on the first day, two on the second, then there was a lull. Afterward four were erased; and, when it came to the actual pinch, five men went out, two of them very reluctantly.

"I felt so sorry for Davy," said Jack when they had made the transfers. "He didn't want to go, and I do not believe he would if it had not been for his brother-in-law."

"A good lesson for all parties. There will not be any grumbling for some time to come, I'll warrant. It is rather irregular business; but sometimes you can't wait for a regular surgeon, or the patient would be past help."

Events pointed the lesson pretty forcibly. By the middle of October there was a sudden rush of orders. Prices rallied a little. There were some tremendous bankruptcies, but it seemed more in speculation than legitimate industry. The new men brought a fresh infusion of spirit and energy. One of them, a small, middle-aged man, Gilman by name, who had once been manager and had a share in a mill that came to grief through a defaulting cashier who had successfully forged the name of the firm, was especially enthusiastic about the system. Jack admitted that the culmination of the discontent was the very best thing that had happened for the mill.

Davy went almost wild over his mistake, cursed his brother-in-law roundly, and forbade his wife to visit her brother's household. Nothing to do, not even three-quarter wages to live upon, with cheap coal and cheap flour. He even waylaid Darcy, and begged to be taken back without any share.

"I'm sorry, Davy, but it cannot be done. We resolved, whatever happened, we would not go back on our word. You had time enough to think it over."

"Just you wait," said Price, when he heard this. "They've three years more to wade through, and they'll never hold together all that time. It has a very queer look, too, that, just as soon as they shoved us out, they began to make money again. Bob Winston's the sort of fellow to look out for himself, and he had this thing all cut and dried."

"Look here," remarked a listener, "you signed your own selves out. Nobody made you. I haven't any faith in the scheme, but I like truth for all that."

The men worked with a will. The monthly club meetings took on a new interest; and they decided, if the prosperity continued, to open a co-operative store another year. They were growing more thoughtful and intelligent, and Gilman's influence upon them was excellent, while his experiences widened their views. A little fresh blood certainly worked no harm.

Jack was very cheery again. It seemed to him they had pulled through the worst. The larger outlook was better: goods were going abroad, and money or bonds were coming back. Here and there some new enterprise started, but still there were hundreds of men out of employment. Yerbury showed various signs of a new thriftiness. The farms about were better managed. Some idle men had ventured to hire a little ground the past summer, and raise sufficient to have something over for their trouble. The Webbers succeeded beautifully. Of course there were slurs about a Dutchman living on a cabbage a week, but every one knew the Webbers were not that kind. What Germans were able to do nicely and wisely, Americans might copy to their profit. When some of the natives were out of work, they patched up their fences, painted a bit, laid a bad place in the sidewalk, instead of hanging round a saloon.

As for those who were living through the sad sweet lesson of loving and losing, time went on with them also. If they could have stayed his hand! Sylvie recovered from the first shock: she could never suffer quite so intensely again, for there was one to share her least thought, her most trivial to her greatest pain. The explanation had come about very gently, making only a small ripple. Mrs. Lawrence was delighted: she always had liked Sylvie, and she was certain that Fred was a better match than

Jack Darcy, though she admitted he was remarkable for a young man with no better opportunities.

Miss Barry was truly satisfied. She would cling to her little dream of "orders" and "kinds" to the last, but she always did it in an unobtrusive way. She had felt all her life long, rather all *their* lives, that they were made for one another. Less practically clear-eyed than her young niece, — brought up in the active reasoning and doing of to-day, rather than the doctrine of passive suffering that had been in the old creed for women, — she would have assented when Sylvie refused. To be sure, if Jack Darcy had won her he would have had a delicate and sincere welcome; but I think her eye would never have lighted with the true mother-love at his coming, as it did at Fred's. The worth of his years of refinement and polish came out now. He never seemed at loss or awkward in the sick-room. If he was reading, he warily noted the first droop of the eyes; he could tell by the lines in her face when talking wearied her, or when she preferred being alone. Every thing between them was harmonious.

She amazed even Dr. Maverick by her improvement, though she held her life even yet on the same frail tenure. She really hoped to live until spring, when she should plan for Sylvie's marriage. Fred had made a very profitable engagement with the widow he had spoken of, and was to furnish designs for the interior of her house and furniture. There was to be one purely Grecian room, one on the old Roman model, a sunset room where every thing was to be in accord, and a "sea" room fit for Naiads· or Undines. Sylvie was intensely interested. This Mrs. Spottiswoode was young and handsome, the widow of a man nearly three times her age, and childless.

Fred Lawrence was proud to have something of his very own to offer Sylvie, and she took it as the highest of all compliments. She did like the profession, if that it could be called; for it brought them nearer together, it was something they could both share. She copied designs and art essays, she drew patterns, she painted now and then, days when Miss Barry was at her best. She would make of herself something that should enhance Fred's pride in her, — as if he was not proud enough already!

The one least contented with all this was Philip Maverick.

"I never was so thunderstruck in all my life! That's just the word to express it, for it left me dazed as the blackness does after the lightning. I would have sworn, Jack, that she loved you, and you loved her. Good heavens! if I had not believed that, if I had not been too honorable to seek to play a friend a scurvy trick, it would have gone hard with me if I had not won her for myself."

"Honestly, you would not have succeeded, Maverick. Neither would she have married me. I think she belonged to Fred from the beginning. He used to hate girls, judging from his sisters, no doubt, but he always liked Sylvie. I was afraid of girls, — their sharp eyes and sharper tongues, — but I liked her too; yet in my own mind he always had the first claim. And they will be suited in the farthest fibre of each soul."

"He is not half worthy of her!" growled Maverick.

"Who is?" There was a peculiar tender intonation in the voice. "Sylvie Barry's womanhood is unique, like some rare gem. She has the sparkle but not the hardness of a diamond; the warmth and vividness of the ruby, but not its heats; the serenity of the sapphire, and yet to me that is always cold. Rather I think she is a changeful opal with all hues and tints and surprises."

"And yet you have never loved her!" in intense surprise.

"I worship her," said Jack reverentially. "I should as soon think of wooing an angel."

"And yet this man, who is not as strong, or noble, or high in purpose, takes her with your consent. You can see her sit down at his feet, wind her own rich, pure, sustaining life-melody about him, to make his path seem like going through an enchanted land. She has genius, but it will ever linger in the shadow of his; it will help, and purify, and shape his; she will give her whole soul to the work. Is he worth the best there is in such a woman as Sylvie Barry?"

"No; and we never go by our deserts when a woman loves us," said Jack, with frank honesty.

"I am quite sure you will marry a woman I shall hate," returned Maverick testily.

Jack laughed. "Marrying has not been much in my thoughts;" and yet his fair face flushed. "I have to fight Hope Mills out to the end first."

But just now there did not seem much of a prospect for fighting, though he firmly believed he should always be on guard after this.

There was one other person in this little circle, who was of much interest to the others, even if it was for the most part unspoken. Maverick had tried to rouse Irene Lawrence from her lethargy by appeals of different kinds. She certainly was not an intellectual woman, though she had a strong and well-cultivated mind, and was accomplished in many ways, — society accomplishments, with a view to the admiration they might win. He could seem to strike no electric spark, though he succeeded in restoring her to health. Every week of her stay at Depford Beach, she had improved; but there was the old, dreary, listless life. She used to think herself, if some shock like that of an earthquake could lift her completely out of it! but none came.

For it could not be said that Miss Barry's illness was any shock to her. People were sick, and died, and their perplexity was at an end. A generous, kindly life like this of Miss Barry's would have its reward — if any life ever was rewarded. She did not doubt so much: she had never really believed.

As she said to Sylvie, something stronger than herself had sent her that night, — one of those powerful, impelling influences that few can resist. And Sylvie was wise enough not to lose her hold. She drew her in very gently, she preached no sermon, she asked favors frankly.

"I want you to take my pony-carriage," she said one day, after their return to Yerbury. "I ought to go out every day, and if you come with it I shall; but if I am left to my own fancies, there will be so much to occupy me. Then, too, companionship is always very tempting."

"I should be glad to do any thing for you," was the quiet, unemotional reply.

So the carriage was brought every morning to the door. It seemed so odd, the day she first drove around Yerbury! Unconsciously the old stateliness returned. Her heart swelled with contradictory phases of thought and feeling. She was too really proud to suffer from the stings of petty vanity. She knew there were people who stared at Miss Lawrence; and she allowed them to stare with the serenity of a queen, going her way unmoved.

She and Sylvie went through lanes and by-ways this gorgeous October day. Her heart was strangely touched by the glory, by the odorous air, the softened sounds, and brooding tenderness. Sylvie had a few errands to some old parishioners of her aunt's; and, while she went in cottages, Irene sat with the reins idly in her hands. There was much in the world she had never seen, though she had climbed Alps, and wandered in sunny vales. The ripeness and perfection of this midday was exhilarating. They talked in little snatches, and then were silent.

Coming back they drove through the town: it was nearer. Crossing over to Larch Avenue, a tall figure confronted them. Sylvie bowed, and looked straight on, remembering such a rencounter years agone. Irene Lawrence turned her head with its proudest poise, but her face flushed scarlet under her veil. She would have made the *amende honorable* then, if it had taken all the strength of her soul.

She and Jack Darcy had met occasionally through the summer. Mrs. Lawrence rather liked to talk mill affairs with him, and his name was quite a familiar one in their household. Now that it had come, she was rather glad to offer this wordless apology for a crime against good-breeding, that only a rude young girl could be guilty of, to one she considered her inferior.

She had wondered more than once, why that long-ago evening at Sylvie's should haunt her, — the talk of costumes, the bright chat, the dainty ripples of laughter, and that face with its cool, steady power. If it had been that of any other man, she would have pitted herself against it, and conquered, she fancied. Now conquests were things of the past. She was not one of your soft, maudlin women, who sigh for a little love. She looked straight into the coming years, and saw herself always alone, with no feeling of pity or regret.

As for Jack Darcy, when they had passed, he turned and looked after them, — after *her*, in her state and dignity. He held one secret of her life that she would never know. He had questioned Maverick, who learned that she had no remembrance of going out that night. He had bound Fred over to a most willing secrecy.

Ah, Jack! any remembrance that you can carry so guardedly in your soul is a dangerous thing, — a spark that may kindle a great fire " that many waters cannot quench ! "

Sylvie did not relinquish her own outside interests. The school that had had so small a beginning was now merged into a regular enterprise, and been re-christened an Industrial School. It had a permanent teacher, and occupied the whole house, the rent being paid by some benevolent gentlemen. A committee of ladies assisted in the different classes. The store was kept open, one side

being reserved for articles of clothing or fancy goods made
by the pupils, the other as a bakery on a limited scale, and
a lunch-counter. It certainly was doing a good work.
Some young girls, after being trained, had been provided
with service places, and had given excellent satisfaction.
Irene went through it one day with Sylvie, and was oddly
interested.

"I wish I had a genius of some kind," she said abruptly to Sylvie afterward. "If I could write a book, or
paint a picture, or design exquisite adornments, or if I
could hold the world spell-bound by my voice" —

"You do sing," returned Sylvie. "Auntie was speaking of it yesterday. She said, 'How I should like to hear
Miss Lawrence sing some of her pathetic old ballads!'"

"You know all the sweet and tender ones."

"I sing mine over daily," and Sylvie laughed with a
dainty inflection.

Irene went home, and opened her piano. It might have
made jarring discord, but for Fred's thoughtfulness. She
found it was in perfect tune.

Was it the music that brought a curious intensity to her
after all these long, dreary months? Her fingers seemed
a little stiff at first, and some things had gone out of her
mind. Then she dropped her face into her hands, and
thought.

"It is my only gift," she said slowly. "When they
are married I will not be a burthen on them: I can make
my way. I shall never try to think of marriage again;"
and she shuddered.

"I declare, you are quite like yourself," said her
mother that evening.

The weeks went on. Miss Barry was making plans for
her niece. She could not live here alone, even for a few
months. And she longed to see her married. Though
the others had almost forgotten how surely her days were
numbered, she had not.

Fred assented delicately to her proposal.

" It is not as if there were only your income," she said with a touch of pride. " Sylvie will have enough to keep the old house as it is kept now, and your mother and sister have some claims on you. Still, for her sake " —

Sylvie would fain have put it off, but she was gently overruled. The wedding-garments were ordered, the day appointed. A quiet marriage in the pretty parlor, with only a few friends. They brought Miss Barry down stairs, and she listened while her darling reverently repeated her vows. They kissed the new bride while the tears were shining in her eyes, and sent her on a brief wedding-journey with heartfelt blessings. Maverick was to telegraph to them every day.

Fred Lawrence could hardly believe his happiness. They were like two children out on a pleasure-excursion, not needing to realize the gravity of life in these golden days. What cared they for pale winter suns and shivering blasts !

Long ago he had planned a brilliant tour to Europe for her. He had gone over it all, and would only have been bored ; but it was the thing to do, and he might enjoy her fresh delight in it. But to both of them — to him especially — had come the higher revelations of life. It is the aggregation of individual characteristics that makes the sum-total of national character ; and though at first retrenchment and economy seemed hideous words to the pleasure-loving, easy-going, self-indulgent souls nursed in the lap of prosperity, there was coming a realization to those who had fought their way valiantly across the yawning gulf, that the hot race for show, the desire to exceed one another, was not a lofty aim for an immortal soul, hardly for a cultured nature.

They both understood that beauty and grandeur were not far-off, hardly attained ideals, and that the great pleasures were set in the world rather as incentives and rewards, than highly seasoned daily food which must inevitably produce satiety. Some time, when they had earned this glorious vacation, they would take it hungering with the healthy appetite of a well-trained soul. At present the duty was to deny one's self firmly and contentedly, to round off the sharp corners, to shape the daily living to high, pure purposes; so that the greater excellences of Art should not despise the minor forms, the steps whereby true perfection was attained, the tangled threads that often required more real genius to comprehend than the one great moment of inspiration.

They came home again fresh and bright, with the peculiar fragrance of a new life about them, just as you shall smell spring in the woods on some mild, sunny February day. Fred fluctuated between office and city, quite a prophet of household art, welcomed warmly back to the old circles which had so quietly dropped him for a while. Is there not a great deal of this unconscious proving of the fine metal of souls in the world? We cry out as we are thrust aside, or given some hard task to do; we wonder people do not hold out kindly hands, smile with sympathetic eyes; and yet their very help might weaken us. When we have beaten our way across with the roar of the distant waves still in our ears, the shadows of the black, fierce, jagged cliff hardly faded, the taste of the brackish spray still lingering on our lips, an exultant thrill speeds through every nerve as we clasp a hand that has had to buffet through the same fateful current.

Early in April Miss Barry had another seizure, a fatal stroke this time. For a few days she lay in sweet content, and then dropped peacefully out of existence.

It seems always a mystery, why such earnest, useful souls, doing that highest of all work, — a pure, unselfish charity, — should be taken away, and the slothful, dependent, ease-loving, selfish ones left. The Darcys felt that Mrs. Lawrence could have been spared much more easily, and served a higher economy in point of usefulness. But God, who sees every end from the beginning, and is all-wise, judges differently. Miss Barry had done her work, no light life-task either. Only God knew what it had been, days of toil and nights of watching and prayer, such pain as only a strong soul could have kept to itself, and smiled over. Yet she had her exceeding sweet reward in this world, — years of peace and comfort, the child-love she had missed in one way, supplied in another, the hope of her days crowned more wisely by the waiting.

They did not think it worth while to keep up the two households ; indeed, Mrs. Lawrence would not have been separated from her son : so she and Irene brought their worldly possessions over to Larch Avenue. The old house was large enough. Sylvie was a courteous and charming mistress ; though Fred realized, with the sensitiveness of true tender love, the burthen he had brought to her.

"It is not without its wise compensation," she said, tears in her sunny brown eyes. "You see, I shall miss auntie so much less ! She would not desire me to grieve despairingly for her, and here is the new claim to take her place. Beside," with a sad yet arch smile, "we shall have to strive against the temptation to selfishness that besets newly married people, when their pursuits are identical, as ours are. It will give a greater breadth, a purer tone, to our lives."

HOPE MILLS passed through a very prosperous six months. With some new processes, invented by the combined energy and ingenuity of the men, they made a new line of goods which was a perfect success. Interest and discount vanished ; and there was a snug balance in the bank, of which every man was duly proud. They were beginning, too, to take a great interest in the finances of the country, and to see that a stable currency and wise economy and honesty were the best friends to commercial and industrial prosperity. One little incident made them exceedingly jubilant.

They had been undersold, in the same line of goods, with quite a large customer. Winston was rather blue about it at first, then laughed it off as one of the fluctuations of trade. To his great surprise, six months after, he received the largest order for goods that had yet been sent.

" We have been much deceived in the quality of cloths from Yates, Collins, & Co.," ran the note. " They do not stand wear, though they resemble yours so closely. Our customers have made numerous complaints, and desire the old stock, which we are glad to order again.

" MILES, CHAMBERS, & CO."

This was put up on the bulletin-board, and discussed with much pride at the club. Every man had an interest in it, and an ambition to excel in his particular branch. It paid in the long-run to be honest ; and, though there might be a higher principle than remuneration, that was not a bad test, after all.

So the third summer opened brilliantly. Yardley, Gilman, and four others drew up an agreement for a co-operative store. They hired one man who had been a very successful buyer for a large grocery-firm, which had failed, and took with it his small invested capital. He was to keep the books, take orders, and do the buying, subject to the advisement of the managers. A certain low per cent of profits was agreed upon, just enough, they calculated, to pay expenses; and the goods were to be offered as low as possible for cash. The snperior quality and reduced price, they decided, would be more agreeable to most of the men than a small balance at the end of the year. An account was to be kept with every member, and the agreement to remain in force one year from date.

And yet there are shoals and quicksands for prosperity, as well as yawning abysses for adversity. There were people in Yerbury — not bad souls either — who were not content to allow the world to revolve on any axis but their own. They could see their neighbors' planets go to destruction with equanimity — following some law of nature or ethics that regulated supply and demand of any force, in their estimation; but when some bright particular star flashed out of the orbit they had set for it, of course it was beyond the pale of safety. There has always been a great deal of just such obstinacy in the world, just such narrow prescribing, and yet — "it does move."

One of the favorite objections of these wiseacres was, that Hope Mills was founded on a wrong basis. Who knew *just exactly* what amount of goods Winston sold? Well, there was the amount manufactured, — the amount on hand every six months. True, — with a disbelieving shake of the head, — but he was up in the ways of the world; and what would hinder him, Ananias-like, from keeping back part of the price? When this was shown to be an utter impossibility, they still were quite sure Winston harbored in his secret soul some plan for cheating the workmen at the last. Here would be all this accumulation of capital, and by some successful *coup-d'état* Winston and Darcy would swoop down upon it, and take the lion's share. They were very much afraid that the workmen were going to be wronged in some underhand way. A defaulting cashier, unprincipled managers, thieves and forgers, committed their crimes in an out-and-out way; but there was going to be a profound mystery about this — the most simple and above-board management, when every man knew, every six months, the best and the worst of the details.

Employment was becoming more general all through the country. Everybody drew a long breath, and decided that the grinding times of depression had passed. We would soon be back to the brilliant era of past prosperity.

And then there arose a new light in the labor horizon, a prophet who had discovered the magic key to the workingmen's paradise, and it had only to be turned by themselves, to gain entrance. Wherever he went, he was hailed with acclamation.

It was the old, old war upon capital, the old seductive science of equalizing things, values, money. Every poor man in the country had a better right to a cottage and garden and a few hours of leisure, than these few magnates to grasp every thing in their own hands, to roll in luxury, to feast in magnificence, to clothe their daughters in silks, velvets, and diamonds — it was to be noted that Mr. McPherson wore an immense diamond, but it was to be presumed that his wife or daughter did *not*. Everywhere one could see the rich growing richer, the poor poorer, the workman trodden down, brought to the level of slavery with his long hours and scanty wages. Where was it to end but in a nation of paupers, of thieves, of criminals of every grade? for, when you made a brute of a man, there came a time when he turned a brute's hand against you. This had been the underlying cause of all the world's great struggles: it had uncrowned kings, it had razed thrones, it had swept states. There were bits of distorted historical facts, fallacious but brilliant reasoning, and much bombast.

They heard of him in this city and that, and there was a great deal said about the cordiality with which he greeted "the horny-handed son of toil." No town was so small that he disdained it, no city so great that he feared it. There had been "demonstrations," but he seemed proud of his defiance of danger.

Men who could not altogether approve of him admitted that he was "smart," that he uttered a good many truths, half-truths they were, dressed up in specious falsehoods, all the more dangerous, since the world does pay homage to virtue and truth. They were troublesome questions: the great difficulty was the haste made in settling them. A balance will finally adjust itself, though there may be many vibrations at first.

It was a fact much to be regretted, that with returning prosperity the gin-mills and beer-shops of Yerbury had, as a general thing, increased in their business. A notable instance to the contrary, however, was Keppler's saloon. It had depended a good deal on the men from Hope Mills and the iron-works. The latter had been closed so long; and, although the coffee-house did not seem much of a rival at first, it had gone on steadily, and given the men time to think. It was not simply the one glass of beer they took to wash down their midday lunch, but the treating when a crowd gathered, the many drinks during a heated discussion of an evening. Not half a dozen of the mill-hands went there now, so occupied had their minds become with other matters. Keppler's lease was not out, and his rent was high for the times: he had lost money and customers, and felt sore over it; he had a grudge against Jack Darcy as the exponent of a system that interfered with his profits.

McPherson was discussed over pipes and ale one warm June evening, with brains cleared, of course, by frequent potations and stifling smoke. It was proposed that he should be invited to lecture at Yerbury.

"I like to see fair play!" cried Keppler. "These fellows over here" — nodding toward the mill — "have had it all their own way because they took up a lot of starving men in dull times. That was all well enough, — praise-worthy — praise-w-o-r-thy," with a long accent. "But things have changed now, — changed!" with a confident nod. "I'd like to hear what the man has to say. You see, he has come up from the ranks, he has been poor himself!"

So the ball was put in motion. McPherson's speech at Millville, a great laboring-centre, was read aloud with frequent cheering. And the laboring-men at Yerbury began to wonder why wages were not higher, when so many shops were running on full time! Somebody was making a great deal of money: *they* could barely live. Bread and meat had not fallen in the ratio of wages. It was still next door to starvation.

Finally some self-constituted labor-committee sent the letter of invitation, and received a cordial and flattering reply. Mr. McPherson had heard of Yerbury. He would be only too glad to come among them in his humble capacity, and shed what light he could upon the side of right and truth; raise his voice for the oppressed against the oppressor. And he mentioned that open-air meetings were generally more successful.

They put up a platform on the Common, the largest park in Yerbury. The day was very fine, not too hot, and a shower the evening before had laid the dust. At precisely four, a deputation awaited Mr. McPherson and his party at the station, escorted them to the Bedell House to refresh, and then to the grand hall of nature, with its waving arches of glistening green overhead.

Already a great concourse had assembled. Mr. Mc-Pherson mounted his rostrum, and, after a few preliminary flourishes, began in a clear, strong tone, that had the power of concentrating the attention of his audience. He went back centuries, and proved that from the very beginning of all industries there had been the desire to oppress, that the working-classes had to combine and fight for every advantage gained, to wrest from kings, peers, masters, even equals, the privileges they held to-day. Plainly, capital was a tyrant fattening on unpaid toil. "Were not the rich always in the ranks of capital, always against the poor man? They squeezed him to the utmost when they had need, then they flung him away. Did it matter to them if his wife and children starved? If he stole a loaf of bread to appease the pangs of hunger, he was sent to prison; but if a bank president stole half a million, he went to — Europe! [Laughter and applause.] Does the capitalist employ the laborer in order that there shall be fewer starving men in the country? It comes in the market, and buys at the lowest price, solely for its own benefit. It does not concern capital, whether this man can support wife and children on such a pittance: what business has he with wife and children! If the man drops at the work-bench, the victim of long hours, exhaustive toil, insufficient food, the town will thrust him into a pauper's grave, and another will fill his place. Even negro-slavery was more noble than this: it was to the master's interest that the slave should be well fed. Capital was shrewd, selfish, experienced, astute, strong: labor was kept in ignorance lest it might learn its worth, its rights; it was half-starved that it might be weak; it was driven from pillar to post with a more cruel than slave-driver's whip, that it might never be able to perfect a successful organization."

And so on and on. The crowd increased. The six-o'clock bells rang, and the procession from shops wended their way thither, many from curiosity, some from a hope of a new truth, and not a few filled with a secret sense of wrong and dissatisfaction. Mr. McPherson was still belaboring capital. Now he had declared it "a stupendous fraud, a hollow bubble, a reputation for wealth where no wealth existed, a fictitious claim for what was not, but which still managed to hold the workman in its iron grasp; the concentrated labor of the men, not the lawful working interest of money. Some way this system of evil was going to be uprooted by men standing firm, refusing the wages of sweat and blood; and in the general overturn by legislation of state and country, every man was to have a farm or a factory, to quit work in the middle of the afternoon, and sit with folded hands on his own doorstep, his own master, a free man!" [Great shouting and applause.]

He talked until seven, and wound up at last with a desperate but covert onslaught on Hope Mills. "No two men or six men, or company of any kind, had a right to band together to starve not only the men in their own town, but the laborers throughout the world, by so reducing wages for their own sole benefit; and every workman who submitted to have these chains forged around body and soul, no matter by what specious expedient, was a worse traitor, a more cruel oppressor of wife and children, than the red-handed capital that stood ready to make him a slave!"

There was an immense deal of cheering and applause. Mr. McPherson was invited to supper at the Bedell House by a deputation of working-men, though I think there were few horny-handed ones among them. Liquors flowed freely, and the feast was rather noisy. A purse was handed to him when he went away — he was too noble to make any charge when he spoke in behalf of a cause so near his heart.

The seed was sown, and it is too true that "foul weeds grow apace." There were club-meetings and union-meetings. The shoe-factory, which had struggled hard to get on its legs again, soon became a hotbed of discontent. The hatters held meetings, the paper-makers were aroused, and then began preparation for another grand strike. The weavers from Coldbridge and Stilford sent over a deputation to Hope Mills, warning, exhorting, and threatening. "No system," said they, "should interfere with mutual strength and protection."

And this was not all. It seemed as if Yerbury meant to make them the scape-goat of every thing. Robert Winston was broadly caricatured; and there was a bit of insulting abuse, calling them traders in their brethren's blood, pasted up on the gate-post. "The Evening Transcript" went over the system of co-operation, and showed to its own satisfaction, that it was a system full of errors and miscalculations based on the credulity of workmen. It hinted that the same mysterious cause which reduced profits last year would reduce them again next year, that at the end of the five years the bread and cheese would come out just even, although there had been a great deal more bread than cheese, as everybody knew. If the corporation were working for the best interests of the men, why had they not sold off stock when every one knew prices were going permanently down, instead of waiting to sell it below cost? Why had they paid exorbitant prices for wool when the market was flooded with it? Why had they not done this or that? until one wondered why, understanding the woollen-business so well, and being able to see just where enormous profits could be made, and losses avoided, they had not all gone into it themselves. The article wound up with a covert and insulting insinuation. Human nature was the same, the world over. Men of the highest probity and honor had succumbed to temptation: these men who had never really been in any responsible position had yet to be proved. If men like David Lawrence and Horace Eastman could not make a stand against fluctuations and difficulties, it was hardly likely success would crown any such abnormal undertaking.

Jack did not see the paper until the next day. Some one laid it surreptitiously on his desk. His face flushed darkly at the attack upon his honesty, and for a moment all the belligerency of his boyhood rose to the surface. He had half a mind to hunt up the writer of the article, and pound him to a jelly with his two fists. But presently he laughed to himself, and then made a tour of the mills in his cheeriest fashion. He saw with grief that the seed had found root. There were some sullen faces and short answers.

It certainly is a hard thing to keep on fighting an old foe that can only be beaten, never killed.

Jack stumbled over Cameron in the store-room.

"Cameron," said he with a white, rigid face, "I wish to God this was the last day of the five years! I should walk out of Hope Mills, and never set foot in it again, no, not even if they implored me on their knees. A thankless, miserable set! The lying article in last night's paper made me mad for a moment, but could not sting: yet the faces of my own men did as I came through the rooms."

"You've had a hard pull, Jack!" Cameron's voice was fatherly and soothing. "You might have put your money and your brains in something that would have proved much pleasanter. But the man who takes up the first end of a truth always gets hard knocks: it is the people who come after who find a smooth path. Don't you remember," drawing his wrinkled face into a queer smile, "the shrewd application your New York lady made about the children of Israel? Jack, if the salvation scheme of the Bible was all proved false, — which it never will be, to my mind,—there's so much wisdom in it beside, that a chap could take it just for a sort of guide-book in every-day matters, all the same. And now we're going to have a big fight."

"You think that?" cried Jack, in vague alarm. "I wish Winston was here. He can always talk so to the point!"

"Well, he isn't: we've got to go through it ourselves. But this settles it! You see, there's been Price, and Pickett, and Davy, to stir up strife and bad feeling, and all this outside influence; but my old woman's praying us through, and I set a good deal of store by her prayers, Jack! If these ruffians go on, Yerbury'll be half ruined again, but it is their own fault. I'm not much on capital punishment, but I would go to the hanging of that Mc-Pherson. If he'd staid away, we should have done well enough."

Jack drew a long, troubled breath.

"I'd let every man go out who wanted to, but I wouldn't pay him a red cent, there!"

That evening Jack went down to Larch Avenue. He found Fred and Sylvie up in arms. Indignation was a mild term.

It was a magnificent night, with a nearly full moon. The light flooded the wide lawn path, and made shadows of elves and gnomes on the porch, as the wind wandered in and out the great honeysuckle, whose ripe, rich perfume was shaken about with every waft. Within, an Argand lamp, and porcelain shade with a minute painting of Puck and his fairy host, sent a softened radiance on the old, rich-hued carpet, and antique furniture. It was but little changed, yet wore an indescribably antique look.

Over at an open window sat Irene Lawrence, dressed in white, with a single deep-red velvety rose at her throat, which Sylvie had pinned there. Her hair had grown

rapidly, and, though it did not quite curl, the ends tumbled
about loosely, framing in the face with their dusky purplish tint.   It was very clear now, and a little pale ; the
old brilliant coloring had not all returned ; the passionless
grace, the deep eyes with their steady lights, the mouth
suggesting mobility and warmth and passion, rather than
defining it, the droop of the white lids, the unruffled brow,
and the pose of the bowed head and slightly-yielding
throat, made a marvellous picture.

The three were talking earnestly, as people do in the
great crises of life ; Sylvie wondrously piquant, with some
thin, black, trailing stuff making shifting billows about her
restless feet.   She questioned Jack eagerly, she denounced
the attack as cruel and cowardly.   What did he mean to
do?   What should Fred do for him?

"There is nothing to do, but just wait for the result.
The dragon's-teeth have been sown.   The only comfort I
have is, that you never can put a lie on the face of truth,
and nail it there.   No amount of arguing or talk can
make a thing so when it is *not* so.   Higher than this little
human round, God garners every truth in his keeping, and
will make it tell somewhere ! "

Miss Lawrence raised her eyes, and glanced over to him.
Had the slow impassiveness of her soul been touched, that
this sudden peculiar grace of sympathy, or some hidden
kindred feeling, rose and asserted itself ?   And yet she
might have been in some magnetic sleep, for all actual
movement of her features ; it was the dawn of an expression that seemed to transport him to some strange world,
where he had known her long ago, — where he had
watched for her coming, listened to her voice, — rather
than any present interest or meaning.

He rose abruptly.

"You are not going ! " cried Sylvie, in her pretty wifely
imperiousness.

"I " — for a moment he had the sensation of a man

drowning. The surging waves were about him, throbbing, leaping, strangling him. There was a ringing in his ears, there was a long shuddering sensation, like being over-whelmed.

"It is very warm," he went on in a faint, strained voice, wiping the beaded drops from his broad brow.

"Come over here," pleaded Sylvie: "you will be cooler. The wind is south, and doesn't blow in those windows. You are sure you feel quite well?" scanning him anxiously. "You look pale."

"It was only momentary." He wondered now what had so moved him. "I am like good old John Bunyan's Pilgrim,"—laughing faintly,—"'tumbled up and down' with these excitements. I wish they were at an end. We were going on so nicely when that McPherson came! Don't let us think any more about it," throwing up his head with a nervous shake. "Sylvie, I wish you would sing something."

"With pleasure. Fred and I have been practising duets. When Yerbury is laid in ashes we can go off as strolling minstrels;" and she laughed gayly, as she went to the piano. That exquisite tact in changing a mood or scene was a familiar characteristic of Sylvie Barry.

As the sound of their blending voices floated out on the summer night air, there leaped up in Darcy's soul a subtle, forceful, vivifying flame, touching to a white heat the farthest pulse of his being. Resistance appeared impossible: he did not even dream what manner of influence this might be. Long afterward — it seemed ages to him — as their heads were bent together over the pages of the music, he raised his eyes, and let them wander slowly toward Irene Lawrence.

Was there something quite new in the face, — a sort of strange, wondering, troubled expression, as if some unseen, almost unknown, depth had been stirred?

He did not need to ask the question now. Wild as it

was, he loved that statue over yonder, and it seemed to him that his passion in its enduring vitality must awaken her soul to kindred life! An exultant strength and determination rose within him. What might have abashed another man, filled him with a deathless courage, as high as it was pure.

He thanked Sylvie and Fred for the song, but resisted their entreaties to remain. When he said good-night, he went over to Miss Lawrence, and took her hand. It was cold and passive, and her eyes fell beneath his.

CHAPTER XXVI

THE excitement ran very high not only in Yerbury, but all over the country. Strikes seemed the order of the day again, and for what reason, was not clearly made manifest, unless labor felt that it had capital a little by the throat, in that its services were again somewhat in demand. "Now," said the prophets. Surely, if they did not strike when there was employment, they could not when there was none.

It began in the shoe-shop. The next Monday morning the men made their demand in no gentle terms, and were refused. There was a large contract at stake, however, and by Tuesday night the matter was talked over in a better spirit. The employers were willing to accede to one-half of the demand, otherwise the order must be sent to another firm. Thursday morning they went to work with a rather ill grace, yet some elation. Then the hatters took their turn. The hands at Hope Mills were served with a notice that the mutual protectionists in all the towns around were to be out on the following Monday; and stirring appeals were made to those who had any feeling of honor in the cause.

It was exceedingly hard on the men. They gathered around in little knots on Sunday, wild with conflicting emotions. Their faith in Hope Mills and co-operation was undergoing a severe strain. The fear of secret frauds, of underhand dealing, of distrust in Winston and Darcy, had been dinned in their ears by outside influence, some of it very potent. Not one appeal had been made

by the managers: Cameron and the others decided it
was best.

Jack went over to the mill on Monday morning. The
gatekeeper and the bell-boy were there. The engineer
came in with a quiet, solemn "Good-morning." The
Brotherhood of Engineers had warned him too, and he
was a little troubled; but he had cast in his lot with the
rest, and it might be as well to wait and see what they
did. The main shaft was turned.

Jack from his office-window watched the streets filling
up with men and women, many beside the regular opera-
tives. They came to a halt.

"Ding-dong! ding-dong!" the bell rang out cheerily
on the summer morning air. "Come to work, come to
work! The birds build homes, and rear their young; the
bee skims the fragrant air in search of flowers; the rivers
run to the sea, turning wheels, driving ships: nothing
in the great economy of nature. is idle, " sang out the
clang of the bell.

The hands glanced at one another in doubt and dismay,
and there was an awful silence for a few seconds.

Some one elbowed his way through the crowd. He had
come from the bedside of his sick child, who might be
dying even now, — a small, wiry, middle-aged man, with
a set, resolute face. He glanced about, then he sprang
up on a pile of packing-boxes. It was Jesse Gilman.

"My fellow-workmen," he began, "I don't know how
you all feel about this matter; but Hope Mills took me
in when I had tramped the country half over, and found
nothing to do. I've tried the old system, and this can't
be any worse; and, if I have to lose money by an employer,
I'd rather it would be John Darcy of Yerbury, than any
man I know. No man on the face of the earth has a right
to say I shall not work in Hope Mills when I made my
own bargain long ago to do it. That is all I have to say.
I am going to work."

"Three cheers!" cried some one as Gilman jumped down.

There were cheers and groans.

Ben Hay followed him, and stood a moment in the gateway.

"Boys," said he in his rich, ringing voice, "Hope Mills was opened to receive a crowd of starving men. I'll take my oath to Jack Darcy's honesty. He's stuck by us, and we'll stick to him. That's the beauty of co-operation. You can't get away, and tramp off with the first fool that asks you! It isn't merely keeping company: it's a good, honest, up-and-down marriage. I'd as soon think of leaving my wife because some day she didn't give me two dinners instead of one!"

There was a shout of laughter. The ice was broken in good earnest. "Three cheers for Ben Hay! Three cheers and a tiger for Jack Darcy!" and amid all this hubbub the men and women, the boys and girls, rushed in pell-mell. A gladder crew one never saw. To decide when others doubt, to go forward boldly when others hesitate, to stand up for the principle of right when others have traduced and blackened it, to take the first step, is to be as heroic as the "six hundred" of deathless fame.

They went to work with a will, though some were a little sore and doubtful, but they were carried on by the enthusiasm of the others. The street below was still blocked up, and there were yells and groans. Presently there came a shower of superannuated eggs. Two landed in Darcy's office-window. After that, a stampede of the riotous crew.

Darcy sent Andrew, the bell-boy, to the police-station, and two men were detailed. The workmen were allowed to go home peaceably, except a little jeering at Keppler's. They heard then the trains had been stopped on the two roads leading out of Yerbury. The whole world seemed to be going crazy.

Darcy and Cameron remained in the mill that night until almost ten : then the latter went home, and Darcy thought he would go for Ben Hay. The streets of Yerbury had presented a very peculiar aspect that evening, something like a beleaguered town. Groups of men and boys collected on the corners, or wended their way through the streets with low, ominous mutterings. People barred their doors, and locked their windows, though it was a hot summer night. Some women were abroad; but they were of the rougher sort, and now and then their shrill voices rose on the air in derision or vituperation. Still there were no overt acts of violence, and at ten everybody began to breathe more freely.

The coffee-house had been shut up that evening : it was deemed advisable. Darcy went round to the side-door, and was admitted. Hay and three other workmen were within. They had been figuring up possible and probable profits by the end of the five years, and looked very well satisfied.

"There's a sort of hope and expectation about it," said one of the men, "that kind of stirs and warms a body. And when you come to count lost time, and fluctuation in wages, it makes a pretty even thing, after all! In '73 I worked in a shoddy-mill that *had* been making money hand over fist, — eleven hours a day, — not a man of us made more than five dollars a week. Some poor fellows with families earned only three. You've never been as hard up as that! God only knows how they lived : it's beyond my guessing!"

"And if that was co-operation, how the system would be blamed!" exclaimed Ben Hay. "I declare, it makes me madder than a hen in a fence — I've caught that of Cameron," laughingly, — "to hear the things people have said about us. They're forever blathering about fair play — I wish they'd give a little, as well as take all. Wait till we've come to the end, say I, before they tell what we can do, or what we can't or sha'n't or won't!"

There was a tramp in the street. The startled eyes studied one another. Then a shuffling and muttering, and a knock at the door.

No one stirred but Mrs. Connelly, who threw up her hands, and cried, "The saints protect us!"

"Earthly saints, Mother Connelly,—this kind," said Ben Hay with gay re-assurance, doubling his fist, and baring his brawny arm.

The pounding increased. Rose ran down stairs wild with affright, followed by her sister. The boys fortunately were asleep in the back chambers.

"Let us in, Mother Connelly: we want some bread and butter!" shouted a voice.

"Cakes and yale!"

"Pretzel and zwei lager!"

"A sup of the craythur!"

"A dhrop of whiskey to warrum us this could night! Av yees the heart av a sthone, Kit Connelly?"

A roar of laughter succeeded this.

"Go away, it will be better for you," declared Ben Hay.

"Come out here, Hay, and fight like a man! Don't skulk behind a woman's petticoats!"

There was a terrific onslaught at the door. It creaked and groaned, and was succeeded by a volley of oaths and imprecations. Rose began to cry, and the youngest girl came screaming down the stairs.

Darcy had sent a man out of the back way for policemen. Hay and the two other men mounted guard. Again the door shivered and creaked: then it flew open, bolts, locks, and hinges having given way in a mass of splinters.

Like a flash the men were on their assailants. The mob had not expected this. Right and left valorous blows were dealt, and two or three burly fellows were laid low. Some nearer sober, and more cowardly, took to their heels. Two men fought like tigers; and once Ben Hay came near

getting the worst ; but, by the time the dilatory guards of
peace arrived, there was only a pile of bruised and battered
bodies lying on the door-step.

"A pretty tough scrimmage !" was the comment.
" Weren't you a little hard on these fellows ?"

" A man has a right to defend his own life and his own
nose," said Ben Hay decisively.   " His life *may* be useful,
his nose *is* ornamental when it is a handsome one like
mine."

What with drunkenness and the drubbing, two of the
ruffians were unable to walk.   Two others were marched
off under the escort of the officers, the disabled sent for,
and a guard detached to protect Mrs. Connelly's house.
When everybody had been quieted, Jack took a tour down
to the mills.   Some poor object was huddled up in the
corner of the main stoop.

" What are you doing here?" demanded Darcy.

" Oh, Mr. Darcy, don't strike me!   I'm Bart Kane.
I've had enough of this night, and I crawled here " —

The boy began to sob and talk brokenly.   He lifted his
face in the moonlight.   It was ghastly ; one eye swollen
shut, and purple-black, and streaks of blood and dirt
over it ; the clothing torn, the throat bare.

" Were you down there at Connelly's ?"

" I warn't nowhere.   It was along o' father : he comed
home drunk."

Barton Kane was a mill-boy, about nineteen now.
Darcy's first feeling had been one of outrage and anger,
but he cooled suddenly.

" Tell me, my lad," in a kindly tone, taking the shivering fingers in his.

" You see, Mr. Darcy, father'd been out along of the
hatters all day, gettin' more and more rum in him.   He
said on Sunday, as how't I should strike ; but they went to
work here, and I worked with 'em.   When I went home,
mother, she gev me my supper, and ses she, ' Keep out o'

sight, lad, happen thy dad's powerful mad wi' thee!' So
I went to bed. But about nine he comed home, and tore
up the house wi' his tantrums, and then lathered me. He
called me a rat, and a sneak, and a turn-coat, and kicked
me out o' the house, and threw my traps to me. Then
afore I was fairly dressed he at me again, and said if
ever I darkened the door, he'd murder me! I strayed
round, afeared of everybody, and crawled up here.
'Pears like every bone in my body is broke, and my eye,
he do hurt so!'"

With that Barton Kane broke out sobbing again, and
clung to Jack Darcy's knees.

"My poor lad!" the tone was infinitely tender. "Can
you walk a little way, to Kit Connelly's? You can be
nursed up there, and go to bed peaceably. Come, Barton,
my boy, you are the hero of Hope Mills. When this is
over, we shall have to give you a medal."

He put his strong arm around the shivering body, and
led him back to a kindly shelter.

"Hay, Mrs. Connelly, and all of you: here's a lad that
has been half-killed for standing by his colors to-day.
Look here, Armstrong, would you mind going for Dr.
Maverick? this poor chap needs some patching-up. And,
Kit, give me some water and a napkin: we'll get his face
a little cool and clean."

"Let me do it, Mr. Darcy. Sure, I've boys of my own,
and am used to it. Oh, the poor, poor lad!"

Barton told his story over again. He was weak and
hysterical now, and they made him a shake-down on the
floor until the doctor came.

"Now I'll start on my inspection-tour again," said
Darcy, turning away. "We are all likely to make a night
of it."

He thought he would go around before he went in to
see the watchmen: they had placed a force on guard
quietly. He had just turned the second corner, when he

saw a man jump from the high fence, and lie for an instant as if stunned. He hastened on, but the man sprang up and ran down the dark side of the street. His first impulse was to follow; then it struck him as strange that the dog gave no alarm. He had a gate-key in his pocket, and unlocked it at once.

"Bruno!" he called, "Bruno, good fellow, come here."

There was not a sound. The ominous silence thrilled Jack.

"Bruno!"

Hark! a curious crackling or sweep of wind, and smoky smell. He ran round to the rear. Close up against the back door, quite out of the moonlight, something was piled. Forked tongues of flame were shooting out of it everywhere. He seized the chain attached to the factory-bell, and rang it rapidly. There was a window thrown up, and a voice called.

"Fire! fire!" he shouted. "Turn on the hose, — the lower back door."

The flames streamed up fiercely now. It was plain that the mound had been saturated with kerosene.

Daly hurried down, and opened a door. "Hurd and Byrnes are at the buckets and hose," he cried. "Where is it? O Mr. Darcy!"

"Quick, quick!" shouted Jack, rushing by him.

The men had the hose ready. They put it out of the window, turned on the stream, and in a few moments a column of dense smoke rose amid the arrowy flashes of lurid splendor. The watchman ran down from Connelly's.

It was subdued in a few moments. They tore away the charred boxes and *débris*, smoking and smouldering. Underneath all they found the body of princely Bruno.

"This is fiendish!" cried Jack, dragging the poor fellow away, his scorched coat smelling horribly. "Brave Bruno, you are the second hero of the night!"

"Whatever dastardly devil did this, knows as much about Hope Mills as you or I," shouted Hurd savagely. "Bruno was poisoned first; and he wouldn't have taken any thing from a strange hand. But the fellow was a fool to build the fire here."

"I don't know about that," said Darcy. "If it had burned the door down, it would have gone in the hall, and up the hatchway — if it was open."

"By thunder! so it would; and right to the stock-room. That place must never be left open again while Hope Mills stands, or co-operation waves her starry banner in the breeze."

"Loud applause!" said some one.

The fire was thoroughly extinguished; and the guardian of the night decided to remain here, being within call if another disturbance should occur at Mrs. Connelly's. The bells rang out for midnight. A few, who had gathered at the alarm, dispersed; and every thing became quiet again, — deadly, solemnly quiet.

Jack wanted to see Maverick, so he paced back to Mrs. Connelly's. He was trying to remember some distinctive mark of the man he had seen jump. He was too stout for Davy, and he could not believe such villany of the man. Then Price was a little lame from an old rheumatic affection, and would not have dared such a deed.

Barton Kane had been washed, patched, bandaged, put to bed, and given an opiate; so now he was in a sound but rather disturbed sleep. The men gathered in the lunch-room, and discussed the cowardly attempt upon the mill, the day's affairs generally.

"See how great a matter a little fire kindles," said Maverick. "But for McPherson's lecture here, I don't believe any of these things would have happened. It is a free country, of course, and a man has a right to air his ideas; but capital is not set firmly enough on its legs to stand a severe fire, and labor is in too great a superabundance. To seek to drain the ocean with a silver mug may be grand, but quite hopeless."

One! The witching hour, and a few sleepy men began to yawn.

"How odd it seems, not to hear trains in the night!" Maverick said presently. "A queer lock-out this."

One, again. One, two, three : this time the fire-alarm.

They rushed out toward the mill. Then they as suddenly wheeled around. In an instant the air seemed full of shouts and cries, and a broad sheet of flame flared up in the face of the tranquil heavens. A roar, like a mighty tramping of hosts, a crackling, snapping, sweeping sound.

"It's Keppler's. Boyd's block will surely go!"

The houses were frame, old and dry : Keppler's on the corner, the rest joined, like a row of sheds, and filled with the very poorest; a few apartments standing empty. The engines were out, but it was of little avail. The corner was just one brilliant sheet of lurid light. Shrieking women and children fled for their lives. The street swarmed again, and people trampled over one another in their wild terror. There was a crash, and the building fell in. The flames licked up the other fiery flood, and had a brave battle in the cellar. The engines played until the air was filled with smothering smoke, and there was nothing left but a long, blackened ruin.

"It may be ungenerous to rejoice in any man's misfortune," said Maverick, "but in a sanitary point of view I am thankful those old rookeries have come to an end. Boyd wouldn't do any thing to them, and they were unfit for pigs to live in. And, as for Keppler's, there will be but one verdict this end of the town."

Some one laid a hand on Jack Darcy's shoulder. He turned and saw Fred Lawrence.

"They are all worried to death about you, old chap," began Fred. "Your mother, Miss Morgan, Sylvie, — and Irene is walking the floor. I have not seen her so excited since — since she had the fever. What a horrible thing! Was any one lost, do you know?"

"They will not be able to tell that until morning, every thing is in such confusion. Pray God that the morning may dawn soon! I seem to have lived through years."

The dawn came up by and by; first in faint opaline splendors, then scarlet and gold. The moon paled, and the stars dropped out, and there was a chirp of birds to welcome the new-born day.

The shock of the fire cooled the temper of the raiders, for half the men were idle hangers-on, rather than absolute strikers. One frantic woman flew to the scene of devastation: her boy, four years old, was missing. They tried to comfort her with the thought that some neighbor had kindly taken him in, but she kept wildly imploring them to search.

There was no further molestation of the men at Hope Mills. They walked in the yard quietly at seven o'clock, their faces touched with surprise and terror when they heard the story of the night. Barton Kane lay disabled at Mrs. Connelly's, and poor Bruno was buried with honors, regretted by the whole force.

Jack called the men together, and addressed them briefly. He was very pale, and his usually bright, clear eyes were heavy.

"I want to thank you," he said, in a tone that was a little unsteady with exhaustion and emotion, "I want to thank you for standing so bravely by me, and by your principles. We are all partners together, and what is one man's interest is every man's. I feel sure that we shall never have another difficulty. We have gone through the worst, and in a little while every man will have his free choice again. Let us all keep the warmest of friends until then."

There was no cheering: they were not gay enough for that. Some of the men wrung his hand silently; then the women pressed forward, and invoked a blessing upon him.

"We know better nor any of.'em what it was to have no fire, and childers cryin' for bread," said one woman, wiping her eyes with the end of her faded shawl. "And, thank the Lord, I've had bite, and sup, and fire, ever since the day Hope Mills was opened."

The men outside were working at the ruins, — among them some of the strikers of yesterday. They found poor Mrs. Rooney's little Johnny, burned to a crisp; and in the house next to Keppler's they exhumed the body of Biddy Brady, a good-natured, efficient washerwoman, whose greatest fault was her intemperance. She and her son had gone to bed very drunk, after having a good time through the evening. The boy had been roused in season, but she had perished. It was as vivid and fervent a temperance-lecture as ever was given in Yerbury.

About ten in the morning Jack Darcy returned home dead tired, as much with the excitement as the fatigue, took a bath, and went to bed.

The Yerbury authorities looked sharply about them that day. The strikers were orderly and quiet, but they had lost ground. "The Evening Transcript" deprecated all this sort of business, and for once had no fling about the "Utopian theory of co-operation." But "The Leader" of the morning came out strongly in praise of the good order, forbearance, and *esprit de corps* of Hope Mills, and called Mr. Darcy "our young and enterprising citizen, whom, we doubt not, we shall hear of in higher positions in life, which he has proved himself eminently worthy to fill."

There was no great lament made about Boyd's Row

or Keppler's saloon, except for the sad casualty it had caused; but the dastardly attack on Mrs. Connelly, and the fiendish attempt to burn Hope Mills, met with the severest condemnation.

Maverick came around to the Darcys that evening. "I fancy I have found your man, Jack," he began. "Mrs. Stixon called me in towards night, saying Jem had been on a spree, and was dreadfully beaten. I found one side of his face scratched and bruised, and bits of gravel still adhering to the flesh. The right arm, on the same side, has one bone broken, and his shoulder is dislocated. He said he fell off of a stoop, and is dreadfully sullen. I asked him what stoop, but he would not tell. Do you remember which way the man fell?"

Jack thought a moment. "On the right side, Maverick, away from me, or I should have seen his face. Just such a size man as Jem Stixon, too," with a satisfied nod.

"What will you do about it?"

Jack took two or three turns across the floor. "See here, Maverick, we will not do any thing. You cure the poor fellow, and I think he will never try to damage Hope Mills again. I can hardly forgive him Bruno, though."

"If I were Sylvie Barry," — he never called her Mrs. Lawrence when speaking of her, — "I should say, 'Jack, you are an angel.'"

Jack flushed. "Masculine angels!" he laughed.

"Well, wasn't there Gabriel and a host of them? Why, Jack, they were *all* masculine!"

There was no need for earthly justice to meddle with Jem Stixon. His arm inflamed: he had led a hard life late years, and his system was in bad order. He would not listen to amputation until it was too late, and in less than a month he was dead. It was better for his poor hard-working wife and family.

One other death grew out of the summer riots, though this was at a distance. Dennis Connelly had been work ing with a railroad-gang, and the strikers there had a desperate struggle with the civil authority. They were worsted in the end, and Connelly was one of the victims, or perhaps more truly speaking, a victim to bad whiskey, for when sober he was very peaceable. Kit sent for his body, and had him decently buried.

CHAPTER XXVII.

The strikers at the hat-factory did not carry the day.
The employers were very indignant, and tabooed the
union men altogther. At Garafield's the men were called
in council, the points discussed, and a small advance in
wages allowed. The co-operatives went their way quietly.
Perhaps the most convincing argument was a very jubilant letter from Winston, part of which Darcy put up in
the hall. He had just succeeded in making an important
contract for two years, on very fair terms. That would
see them through safely unless the whole world came to
grief again !

Jack wrote Miss McLeod a graphic account of the
" labor troubles," and she replied with equally characteristic *verve*. " She could hardly decide," she declared,
" whether to be glad, or sorry, that her young friend had
grown so independent of her ; but in any emergency she
wished to be remembered."

There was now a certain respect paid to Hope Mills,
among the community at Yerbury. Perhaps there are no
people so exacting and difficult to satisfy as those friends
and neighbors whose advice you have not taken, and prospered without it. They indulge in a righteous self-complacency if you are unfortunate, and pity you grandly ;
but to own themselves mistaken is the one bitter flavor in
the cup. There seemed to be but one point now upon
which they were doubtful, — the honesty of the managers
at the last moment. Every workman knew or might know
exactly how affairs stood, but *they* did not have the capi-

tal. Just at the end of the five years *somebody* might ab-
scond with the money-bag under his arm. It seemed so
every way certain that human nature could not withstand
the temptation.

Yet there was growing up among the hands a curious
neighborly sympathy, as if they were in some degree relatives ; and they were made so, in fact, by some marriages
of sons and daughters. They were more intelligent ; they
kept their houses cleaner, their little gardens prettier, not
allowing them to go to weeds before the summer was half
over. Those who could go to the industrial school
learned a deal about sewing, and became seamstresses
instead of mill-girls. Some made their own family
dresses, some were very tasty milliners. It gave them a
reliance upon what they could do themselves. The two
daughters of one workman kept a little poultry-yard
" scientifically," and dressed themselves from its proceeds.
Industry became more general. Instead of dawdling away
whole evenings in gossip, they had some light employment,
and worked as they talked.

The September showing was very encouraging. There
were still a great many bankruptcies and losses, but some
of them could not be guarded against. Darcy and Winston regularly eschewed speculation, though the latter
confessed his fingers sometimes burned to be in the pie.

" But, after all," he said frankly, " if the energy, ingenuity, ambition, and strength that are expended to
make certain people buy and sell, over and over, a thing
that can be no more valuable than the money it makes
year by year, which often is not much, — if this were
turned into industrial and commercial channels, — gad!
what a country we would be! Our flag would float on
every sea, our goods be in every port. And yet they go
on, rich to-day because they have beggared their neighbor, poor to-morrow because their neighbor has beggared
them. What idiotic business! "

But I must go back a little with my hero. There were many things to occupy his mind, the summer of the "strikes;" yet through it all, like one strain of heavenly harmony in a clash of discord, he came to know the diviner needs of his being. Another man might have been dismayed at the revelation. Like a flash when the horizon is opened, he saw the light; and he knew, from the depths of the darkness the next moment, what manner of storm it would be.

He had never weakened or frittered away his sweetest emotions on the various flirtations that fill the early years of so many men. He had liked and admired Sylvie Barry above all young women he had ever met; but this emotion, though pure and lasting, never stirred the ardor of his soul. Had it really lain untouched so long, or had some vague dream slipped into it the night he and Sylvie had planned the costume for Irene Lawrence, the time he first encountered her beauty in all its vivid splendor? To him she was a glorious young goddess.

The long-ago summer day he had met the two in the phaeton, he was more keenly pained for her sake than his own. To be sure, his first emotion was that of angry indignation, sending the outraged blood through every pulse; then, as it cooled, the act appeared so utterly unwomanly. If she had passed him by carelessly — but to designedly attract his glance, and stab it thus, was as if a giant had taken a club to kill a butterfly because it breathed the fragrance of the rose. He shut out that vision. You can tell what impression she had made upon him, when he always thought of her as he saw her in the glow of Sylvie's pretty parlor, that summer night. His healthy, active temperament never brooded over disagreeable things a moment longer than necessity kept him there.

She faded from his mind by degrees. Even when he took Fred back into the old regard, he thought of her as the possible wife of some millionnaire. When she·returned to Yerbury, and shut herself up in stately despair, refusing even Sylvie's proffered sympathy, she puzzled him. How could she, so fond of admiration and gayety, live this nun's life, without the nun's spiritual exaltation? He passed her once or twice in the hall, as he was calling on Fred, but neither made any sign.

Then came that terrible night, when he had found her astray, her brain consumed by the smouldering fire of iso- lation, when you have only the black, choking smoke that never blazes up in purifying flames. There are thousands of women who have done this, weakly, sentimentally, through the period of adversity that has tried the metal of all souls; but she, being stronger, more self-reliant, could not drop into puerile whining.

At Depford Beach they had come in contact again. There was both attraction and repulsion in these two people, as there often is in strongly-marked, positive natures. She tolerated him because he was Sylvie's lover; despised him, believing that he meant to make a stepping-stone of this girl's wealth and position; and, in spite of herself, felt the current of his strength and buoy- ant energy. By slow degrees the unwilling truth was forced upon her, that God never created any human soul for its own self-destruction; that there was no absolute virtue in warping and twisting circumstances into chains and bonds, that were ordained for higher, nobler purposes. Her mental disease had run its course. Sylvie's sorrow was the final electric shock that broke the heavy soil of apathy.

Her utter surprise when she found that through all these years Jack Darcy had refrained from influencing Sylvie in his behalf, was something quite indescribable. She thought she had fathomed men's souls with her keen insight, but this man was a Saul amid his peers. Had there been some subtile, far-reaching foundation for Fred's regard in the boyhood days, — something that their eyes, being holden with golden bonds, could not see?

After the marriage there was a certain degree of association, not intimacy.   And yet she set herself to watch him.   Somewhere she would discern the print of the feet of clay this idol of Fred and Sylvie's possessed.

It was a most fascinating yet dangerous employment. She used to sit there in her impassive grace, as they talked, weighing every word, testing every sentiment, watching the expressions that flitted over Jack Darcy's countenance, until it went everywhere with her, the blue-gray eyes piercing the very depths of her soul.   They came to the one night when a glance stirred and troubled both, when the depths of both natures experienced that curious shock of repulsion and wonder.   It was not love, it was too near, too awesome, yet too spiritually pure, to be hate, still it sent them apart none the less surely.

By degrees, even amid the hard struggle of the strikes, he came to a self-knowledge.   His perceptions were not easily confused ; and by that intuitive process born pure in every soul, but too often marred and dulled by the many counterfeits put upon it, he knew this was love, a life-long passion for one woman, not because she had as yet answered any need of his nature, or promised any expansion into higher life.   He loved her just as she was ; for her beauty, her swift, proud grace, her virtues if she had any, her very faults, and of those he was not in doubt. And he set himself to win her with the same high courage that had taken Hope Mills in hand.

Occasionally we see a man wrecked by this steady, persistent, overwhelming love for an inferior object, caught perhaps by some occult fascination that flashes all laws out of sight.   We wonder how he can be so led astray ; and yet it is an integral part of the man, a quality of the soul which he would not overcome and put in bonds if he could.

He did not cringe or flatter, or adopt any of the fears or weaknesses of passion.   It was not weak, and he did not

fear. He meant to be master of her soul, and win her
through that very power, struggle as she might. He
would wait, if it were years, until she laid down her few
weak weapons, and capitulated. From that time onward,
there would be neither "mine" nor "thine."

And now the fine, tested quality of his patience stood
him in good stead. He might long to draw near, to clasp
the snowy hand, to study the fathomless dusk of the eyes,
and note the frightened droop of the fringed lids; but he
held aloof. Still he went to Larch Avenue night after
night; he dropped in of a morning when least expected,
occasionally finding her alone for a few moments; he
walked from church with them, by her side, the only
times he came near her, and she felt in every pulse of her
being the indefinable something that she was impelled to
struggle against.

A curious change came over her. The cold indifference
melted to a rose hue of interest, a pliant softness stole
over her figure, a certain buoyant tenderness diffused
itself in her tone, her dusky eyes came to have a startled
softness like a shy, frightened fawn. The old brilliant
color returned to cheek and lip, yet toned with the tremulous throbbing of a new inward life, so exquisitely attuned
that she could but listen to the harmonious melody.

She came to understand presently; the intangible power
in his demeanor roused her, I think; and her whole soul,
every fibre of her body, rose up in mutinous revolt.
Whither was this swift current carrying her? What great
wave was this that struck at the very props of her own
strength and reliance? How did this man dare to invade
the walled sanctities of her being? She would have none
of him: she would go on her solitary way, sufficient for
herself. She, who had never loved amid all the beguile-
ments the world had to offer, to be conquered by the very
man she had trained herself to despise!

Irene Lawrence found it hard fighting with this unseen

foe.   He seemed always lying in ambush, always armored with a word or sentiment to which she must assent, always before her in the place she had meant to be ; and she would not throw up the white flag of defeat.   She would not own to herself she experienced any alarm or annoyance.

One evening Fred and Sylvie had gone to a neighbor's, and were momentarily expected.   A peculiar temptation entered her soul.   If this man must needs flutter in the flame, why should she be tender and careful of him?   Others had dared her, to the burning of their very souls : if the experience was worth the pain, he should have it, and decide.

She sat down at the piano, and shook a shower of melody out of her slender finger-ends.   All the affluent grace of womanhood with the polish of society spoke in every curve of her pliant figure, in the dainty, delicate, high-bred gestures.   The eyes hung out their false lights of treacherous intent amid the half-slumberous fire ; the very lips seemed shaped and blossoming with a rare thrill of passion that could turn to a caress at a look.   All along the brow ran fine sinuosities of light that dazzled like the tracery of pale flame.   Had she blossomed into some royal midsummer flower that is seen but once in an age?

She had motioned him close beside her with an impelling wave of the hand.   He could feel her warmth, her fragrant breath ; her soft billowy dress fell against his foot in a crested wave ; her white hand and slender wrist, just toned, but not hidden, with rare lace like that of Arachne's spinning, wandered temptingly over toward him.   A sudden delirium took possession of him, an exhilaration that steeped the brain, that stirred every pulse, that awoke in him an almost maddening desire to clasp her in his arms, to drain such sweetness from her lips that the whole world might be beggared ever after, and he not care.

She knew the signs. She had seen more than one man dally on the brink, and then topple over to the blankness of despair. Even if she had pitied herself, which she did not, she could have had no mercy on him. Now she was set to her work, and she meant to do it if she brought into play every fascination art and nature had furnished her with.

His soul rose and glowed within him. The music, the most ravishing of its kind, stirred him to that intensity of pain, it seemed as if he must cry out with torture. No suffering had ever been like this: if the doctrine of sacrificial fires were true, he might have purchased paradise.

Did he mean never to stir or speak? Could that hand, lying so passively on the corner of the piano, remain unmoved, with hers just below it? Its defiant strength stung her.

"They do not come," — looking warily around, and passing him with her veiled eyes, rather than looking at him. "Are you growing weary? Shall I sing for you?"

The tone had the melody of some lotus-freighted stream. She had thrown all her sweetness into it.

"If you will."

His was tremulous and husky with repressed passion.

Her voice was not pure: it had the rich depth and pathos of contralto, and the vibrant clearness of soprano. Now it threaded a tremulous pathway among the pathetic minor notes, while the fingers seemed to drop a faint sigh of accompaniment, —

> "Oh! when ye hear me gie a loud, loud cry, —
>   The broom blooms bonnie, and says it is fair, —
>   Shoot an arrow frae thy bow, and there let me lie,
>   And we'll never gang down to the broom ony mair.
>
>   And when ye see that I'm lying cauld and dead, —
>   The broom blooms bonnie, and says it is fair, —
>   Then ye'll put me in a grave wi' a turf at my head,
>   And we'll never gang down to the broom ony mair."

The last sad note died into summer-night sweetness. A current of bland, dangerous magnetism passed between them. She turned her splendid, passion-lighted eyes to him, and the subtle, measuring, conquering forces in the man and the woman met. With a mighty effort he thrust back desire, and compressed his lips to a line under the bronzed-gold moustache, while his eyes, like points of steel, never wavered.

Irene Lawrence turned blindly, and held out her hands as if to grasp some sure stay. Just as surely as she had not won, she had lost.

" I have tired you," he said, —a murmur just under his breath. " But you can hardly know the exquisite pleasure you have given me. It is perfect. We will have no more music to-night;" and he rose, shutting the piano down.

She went to the open window like one in a trance, so stunned she could not even feel angry at his defiance of her. A long, long moment of silence: then they heard Sylvie's bright voice on the porch, and she came in with a waft of dewy, outdoor fragrance.

Miss Lawrence went to her room presently, to fight out the battle with herself. She admitted then that she had come to love Jack Darcy; but she was strong and resolute, and would not be mastered by the passion. What could she do? for go away she must! Her imperious will and knowledge of men had availed her little to ward off this one's influence. Every instinct had been baffled, every movement had been met with a counterpoise. To stay here, and struggle, would be to yield eventually.

There were dark circles under her eyes the next morning, tokens of her vigil and strife. She intrenched herself again behind that dumb apathy: she stood aloof from Sylvie. For days she escaped the watchful sight of Darcy ; but she heard his voice, and every rebellious pulse was a-tremble. She cast about for some expedients whereby to escape her prison honorably, and after several fruitless efforts found one.

In their early days there had been a girl-friend between Agatha and Gertrude, who had always held an attraction for the child Irene. Wealthy, beautiful, and accomplished, she had married a man who had already made for himself a name in statesmanship, a cultured and polished gentleman, and her bridal had been the theme of the day. But the fiend of intemperance had wrought destruction of her brilliant prospects, and made her life an open scandal. When it could no longer be borne, she gathered up the wreck of her fortune and her two little girls, and opened a boarding-school in a quiet, aristocratic old town. Irene had met her in New York after her own loss of fortune; and, though she had disdained sympathy, she was touched by Mrs. Trenholme's kindliness.

She wrote to her now; and, of half a dozen applications, this was the only one that elicited a favorable reply. Mrs. Trenholme needed a teacher of French and music, and she knew Miss Lawrence's accent was perfect. The salary was not large, being four hundred dollars a year; but the duties were not very arduous, being all confined to school-hours.

Much as Irene desired to go, there was some struggle with her pride before she could bring herself to accept. Only the prospect of that greater pride being laid in ruins before her eyes, could finally have induced her. Mrs. Trenholme expressed her delight warmly.

There were strenuous objections on Fred's part when it came to be talked over. "She had no need. He was as much her protector as her father had been: indeed, was he not paying back the kindly care to himself, honoring his father's memory by doing as he would have done?"

Sylvie came to the rescue presently.

"I would let her go, Fred," she counselled. "Beverly is a delightful place, with many cultured people, and Mrs. Trenholme is just the woman to have an influence over Irene. You see, she gets so tired of having no pursuit, no strong interest. I could not endure it myself."

"But she might have — I have dared to dream " —

"Put away dreams, my darling." Sylvie's voice was unconsciously sad. Then, with a smile, and tears, "If God kept watch over us, and brought us to our haven, can we not trust him for her, — for them?"

And so they acquiesced.

When Jack Darcy left Miss Lawrence on that fateful evening, his whole soul was full of unrest. He paced the quiet streets in that tense mood which makes thought and breath alike torture. Now that it was over, he said, with the inconsequence of love, that he had been a weak, cowardly fool to fear his fate too much; and yet the next instant he knew he would surely have lost it all, and that in time she *must* come to need him. If he *could* wait! Well, he *would* wait. He had not trained himself heretofore in these long reaches of patience for no purpose. That richly satisfying, inward sight, she could not take from him, that exultant faith which was warmed and fed from a thousand secret rills.

He understood why she shunned him, why she had resolved to leave Yerbury; and he was thankful now that he had not ruined his cause by impatience. To think of not seeing her, of not hearing her voice, was like madness! His face grew thin, there were tense lines about his mouth and a set resolve in his eyes; yet to his fine temper came no moodiness or irritability. The task he had set for himself must be accomplished. He was as absolute in his self-denial as he would be in his happiness when that came.

So she went away with the merest friendly farewell, and asked herself angrily, an hour after, what power this man had over her, and why she feared him? Surely there was not much of the lover in that calm face!

He threw himself into the business with renewed energy. As I said, the September account was inspiriting. Prospects began to look brighter, only it was admitted on all hands that the days of large profits and quick fortunes were over for a long while, if not for all time. Industry was coming to be respected, and you heard less talk about luck.

The outside world kept watch of them narrowly, jealously. If they turned out thieves and swindlers, it would not be for the lack of advice. However, they tramped on and on. Their store gained a little, and was productive of much good. Keppler went to a different part of the town. Boyd sold the ground, and a row of decent cottages were to be put up. Kit Connelly had been reimbursed by the town for her damages, and with Ben Hay's advice and counsel built an addition to her house, which he and Rose took for housekeeping purposes. The lunch and coffee room was a regular and profitable institution, and would be a business for one of the boys as he grew up to manhood.

Sylvie and Fred went to the city for a winter holiday. Fred's book was elegantly brought out, and won him much praise and a little money. Sylvie achieved her ambition, and sold two pictures at what she considered marvellous prices, but she wisely confessed it only to her husband. They were invited to clubs and soirées; and Mrs. Minor was extremely affable, though she did blame Fred for allowing Irene to take such an idiotic step.

Darcy and Maverick indulged in two or three flying trips. Miss McLeod liked nothing better than to get these young people together, and listen to the animated conversations, herself as spicy and sharp as any one. Miss Lothrop was married; and in the slim, fair, blushing girl the old lady had for companion now, he saw no danger.

So the winter wore away, and the spring came again; and the man who was counting the days wondered wearily at times what his summer harvest might be.

CHAPTER XXVIII.

THE regal woman who stepped from the car to the station-platform at Yerbury, one balmy day in early June, to be greeted by Fred and Sylvie Lawrence with the warmest of welcomes, was indescribably different from the pale, cold, haughty statue that had gone away. There was an elasticity in her step, a self-reliance in her air, and the peculiar confidence discipline wisely used inevitably imparts.

Yet there had been no romantic or highly-wrought change in her. She had not taken up teaching from any heroic motive or the possible benefit to any one, but simply to protect herself from what she considered the weakness of her own soul, to get away from a danger she could not fight. Oh, how she had hated French verbs and exercises! If hers had been a susceptible musical temperament, she would have gone quite crazy with the blunders and sentimentalisms of young girls.

After a month of it, she would have welcomed any relief, even the face-to-face conflict with Darcy. But she could not well run away from here, and her physical health was perfect: so there was nothing but to go straight on, and find that circumstances had to govern, that she could not shut herself up in sullen majesty, or fling off the daily duties for some wiser and more patient hands to pick up, and restore to beauty and harmony.

She had a friend, the best and truest that a young woman could have, perhaps; a woman so admirably adapted to the training of girls, that it was no marvel she succeeded. Out of the ruins of her life she had built up another, wise, sweet, and strong. As Irene began to comprehend what Mrs. Trenholme had suffered and achieved, for the first time she paid an honest reverence to the nobility of character. And now she despised her own petty, shallow thoughts and beliefs. Her lofty despising of the world and the vain and selfish people therein had been only a kind of scornful regret for the treasures wrested from her, the glitter of fashion, the gauds of society. Fred had made a braver stand than she. He had not sought to poise himself on the easy, graceful rounds of past promises, and to dream futile weakening dreams, nor shut himself up in morbid isolation.

After all, how little the great world really cared! It was the few friends, the small circle, the near influences, that were of importance. And when she found that here in cultured, delightful Beverly, she was sought out as an entertaining guest, that she had not lost caste because the great bubble of fortune had shivered into fragments, that dressing and shopping and flirting were not the highest of human enjoyments, she came to a very rational frame of mind, and to a certain extent enjoyed her life. But nature had not made her a teacher of children, and never does such women, until, informed by that highest of all love, they teach their own.

She came back beautiful, strong, and brave, resolute to dare any thing. She dazzled them at the little tea-table by her swift, easy animation, her brilliancy, the color that went and came, the smiles that were like rippling billows over a sea. And Sylvie's heart went down like lead, though it was such a fair picture. "For now," she thought, "Jack will never dare to love her!"

Perhaps not, if he had to begin now. But the love was in him and of him, and would be hers all his life long, whether she took it or no.

He did not come for a day or two. She wondered a

little: she even laughed lightly at her own past fear, the shadow she had conjured up, the warm blood ran so healthily through her veins now.

He sauntered in one morning to find her cutting roses with Sylvie, the two the fairest flowers in all the garden. He was in no wise abashed at this vision of loveliness: if she had a dower of beauty, he had his unstained manhood.

They chatted and laughed. Sylvie pinned a pale bud and geranium-leaf in his coat. He held out his hand to Irene with a curious little gesture. She had two or three great royal purple pansies clasped lightly in her fingers.

She meant to refuse courteously, but their eyes met. Was it the old spell working?

Surely, surely all these fine-spun barriers, all these cunning Alps that she had thrown up day after day, were overleaped at a supple bound. Master herself she might; but he stood in his man's power and pride and love, a suppliant, yet king, asking with wordless lips a little favor, taking with · calm yet passionate eyes a royal largess. Her heart sank; her breath came in one long, tremulous sweep. Whether she gave, or he took, she could not have told; but he went away with the pansies in his fingers, despite Sylvie's pleading for a longer stay.

When he was quite out of sight, he kissed them, sweet, tender, longing kisses. Then he dropped them between the white leaves of a little book, to be sacred forever. Sylvie's *boutonnière* might keep him company outwardly, but those no eye must feast upon.

He took the fine right of a lover, not declared, yet certain of his ground, not using any power that she could disdain or wound, it was so delicate, intangible, the perfume without the flower, the little thoughtfulness for her, reaching for her fan, folding her shawl about her if the evening blew up cool, seeming to know her wants the very instant they occurred to herself. And though she rebelled in secret, though she resolved heroically to put an end to it all, the golden moment never came.

It seemed as if the four were always together. Not
but what Yerbury opened spacious doors to them, and
proffered flattering welcomes; but they could not tone
themselves to the insipidities of society. There were
more complete and intense enjoyments. Sylvie and Irene
took long drives through country lanes, or of a moonlight
summer evening they all went. They sat on the porch,
and Jack came strolling by: they went within, and there
were books, music, desultory talking, and that wondrous,
unseen guest in their midst.

Sylvie rarely left her alone. They were not the women
to tease one another by flippant jests or allusions; and
Mrs. Fred, of all others, had a dread of thrusting any
vulgar face on this colorless, yet delicious, atmosphere.
Love knew his own, and was sacredly known of them.

Irene Lawrence could no more help blossoming under
the intense yet steady warmth of his temperament, the
vivid creative life in every feature, than she could have
helped being at all; and to have refused or destroyed the
love would have been as sure spiritual suicide as a poison
to the body. He understood that she came to see this
presently; and then his suit was half won, — more than
half: he had only to go on to the royal fruition of hope
and patience. She no longer shunned him: she dropped
that pointed, distant "Mr. Darcy," and, in the soul's
own language, gave him no outward name.

And, when he took her at her royal flood-tide, the words
of asking and answering mattered little. A look, a tone,
a clasp of hands, a last struggle of her pride, and she
was his.

The wide, warm summer night closed about them: the
dusk was rich with floating dewy perfumes, and golden
stars dazzled in the clear, moonless sky. Out in the trees
a little bird, startled from her nap, sang a brief, sweet
song to her little ones. He drew the proud yet yielding
figure closer: their hearts beat, their flushed cheeks

touched, their lips met in one long, heavenly caress, their hands clasped until pulse throbbed with pulse in impassioned unison.

Only a death and a great love can so change the aspect of life. As in the grave lies buried the dearest promises of love, hope, existence itself, and we learn in time to cling to every faint dream, so, like a resurrection, love sweeps away the sins and follies and weaknesses of the past, and rises from the dust and ashes transformed, renewed, nay, born again to the most sacred purposes.

A strange, swift impression rushed over her as she met the eager, intense eyes. Was it in another world these arms had closed about her with their strong, restful clasp? She started abruptly: she seemed to listen, to puzzle herself with the bewildering impression.

"What is it, my darling?" in a deep, ardent voice.

"I don't know" — with a nervous laugh and shiver. "Have we met in some other country? Did you carry me over mountains, or through valleys, or hide me from a storm? Was this why I could never get away, try as I might?"

Oh the wordless, entreating beauty of those eyes!

"My queen, my own, you will never try again."

"Never!" with a long, delicious, sobbing breath. "Why are you so irresistibly, so powerfully strong, Jack? Do you know, — you *must* know how wicked I have been! If you cast me out, it would only be a proper punishment. I don't mean that my lips or my hands are blurred with other men's kisses. I never could endure that," shuddering. "But they laid down their hearts, and I walked over them: they were weak, and I was strong! And one night I tried" — her voice sank to a beseeching, half-shamed murmur.

"Yes," he gave a pure, genial laugh, rich in his own sustaining strength. "You would have broken my heart, your own too; for I think, even then, you loved me."

"I surely have never been indifferent. It was either love or hate. Do you remember the first evening I saw you in the parlor yonder?"

She learned ere long, that he had never forgotten any thing; but the depth and perfectness of his love she could not learn in a day.

If Jack Darcy had been patient hitherto, that grand quality seemed suddenly exhausted. He absolutely hurried her into a marriage, — hurried Sylvie too, who wanted the courtship to proceed with measured, golden steps.

"As if it were not to be a courtship all one's life!" said radiant Jack. "Now the moments break in the middle, there are tangled ends, and endless beginnings, and one can hardly remember where one left off. Were you sorry to go to Fred?"

"Why, no!" with wide-open, surprised eyes.

He carried the day at last, and September was appointed. They would be married in the old church. Mrs. Minor responded to the tidings by a visit. She had treasured up a great many things to say to Irene; but for once she was quite overwhelmed, and her sneers and patronage fell to the ground. Though she did remark to her mother, —

"Of course I *am* disappointed that Irene, with her face and style, has not done any better; but you cannot expect much after one passes twenty. Mr. Darcy has improved certainly, and Irene is not as exclusive as we older girls were. It is a great pity she did not go out to Gertrude."

For George Eastman, with a cat-like propensity, always came down on his feet. He was now at the flood-tide of prosperity — on other people's money. Mrs. Eastman was regal in velvets, sables, and diamonds, queening it at St. Petersburg. Some day there might be a crash again, but they would be well out of the way.

Miss Lawrence would have no diamonds, and no show;

but she was dazzling in her radiant loveliness; and, if Jack was not handsome, his superb manliness redeemed him. Hope Mills took a holiday. All Yerbury went, it seemed; and those who could not get in remained outside for a glimpse.

Sylvie and Fred leaned over the registry in the vestry-room. In a bold hand the bridegroom had written, " John Beaumanoir Darcy."

" A compliment to Irene's pride," laughed Sylvie. " The most aristocratic name of them all ! "

The old house was brightened up a bit before the young couple returned. Gentle Mrs. Darcy wondered how it would be between the old and the new love; but she remembered with charity, that she had taken the fresh young love of another Darcy, and was content with her day.

The young people brought a new atmosphere with them, but it did not clash with the old. Jane Morgan was planning a home for herself. One of the cut-up farms had been put together again; and she had taken a five-years' lease at a low rate, to try a prudent and sensible scheme of philanthropy. Maverick had been intensely puzzled by Jack's love-affair, and could not yet account for it satisfactorily, but watched them both with a kind of amused interest, and dreamed of the deft, dainty little fairy down at his aunt's.

I suppose I ought to say that Mrs. Jack Darcy vied with her husband in all good works, — in schools and clubs, and plans for everybody's improvement; but it was *not* her *forte*. He was too well satisfied with her love for him, her music, her enchanting ways, to wish her any different; and I think he would have been jealous, with that exclusive, tender, adoring jealousy, that cannot endure its choice treasures lavished upon others. She was kindly and generous in a stately, queenly fashion; but what between Jack, who was a more importunate lover than ever, and the baby born at Larch Avenue, she had her hands quite full.

The five years of mutual copartnership drew to a close. Their young engineer had not blown up the mills; Bob Winston did not go off at the last moment with the balance at the bank; Jack Darcy had not falsified accounts: but it came out just as *everybody* had predicted that it would! " If your men were honest and honorable, co-operation could not fail of success. It was the simplest of all schemes," said " The Evening Transcript."

The two offices were thrown into one by the sliding-doors, and the workmen and women assembled in their holiday gear. Jack Darcy was really struck with the change in their faces and the general demeanor. They had a brisk, cheery, self-reliant air: there was a certain neatness and respectability about which they used not to care in the old times. The boys of five years ago were grown men, and there wasn't a sturdier one among them than Barton Kane.

And now Jack Darcy proceeded to read the statement of the whole period, to which every one listened with the most profound attention.

At the close of the first year, after rent, wages, and all other expenses were taken out, the accumulation of prof-its had been $21,642.27.   One-half of this, $10,821.13.5, had been turned directly over to capital: the other half, the profit of labor, was divided again in equal shares, one going to capital for every person, the other, amounting to $5,410.56.7, paid over to them as compensation for three-quarter wages. Of course the men had been de-lighted. They remembered their first joy even now.

Then had followed the disastrous second year, which had no such golden story to tell. The first six months, interest and discount had made horrible inroads into capi-tal, and there had not only been no surplus, but an actual deficiency. The latter half showed a poor frightened balance of $137. But this year they improved greatly in economic management and several new processes that gave larger profit with less labor and outlay, so the hard strain had not been entirely without its uses. Capital had gone down in the valley of humiliation, and had a sorry time of it; but with it had come a knowledge and sympathy they could have acquired in no other way.

The third year had proved a grand success. They had all worked so heartily together, and business had been undeniably good. Profits had been $41,854.92, with very limited discounts. After this there was none, and unused capital began to draw a little interest. This year there had been $10,963.73 to pay over to the men on the quarter share. The fourth year there had been numerous bankrupt stocks thrown on the market, and every one trying to do his utmost again: still the balance had been by no means disheartening, amounting to $34,982.67; capital's share being $17,491.33, and the wages overplus $8,745.66. The last year's profits had footed up $43,-101.56.

There was now in accrued capital stock $106,288.81.5; and this was to be divided in the *pro rata* of each man's share, the larger amounts making the most, of course. And now they saw the object of saving. They had earned full wages and something beside; and, though wages had not reached the high point of good times, on the other hand they had not fallen below a reasonable standard, even with the bad year. There had been steady work for the whole five years, and every man had been practised in thrift, economy, and self-denial.

Of those who had begun with them, seven had been discharged for drunkenness and insubordination, their share forfeited to the fund for sick and disabled workmen; three had gone out from loss of faith in the plan, accepting Winston's offer to sell; four had died, and thirteen had left from various other causes. So that there had been a much greater degree of steadiness than usually obtains among factory-workmen. This led to a decided improvement in many other respects. With a prospect of being permanent, the men were induced to buy homes, and took a greater interest in the management and welfare of their own town.

The balance was divided, each man receiving his check, and with it a detailed statement of the whole five years. They were now quite free, the industrial partnership having legally expired. Hope Mills would take a fortnight holiday for repairs and re-organization.

"What if there were to be no re-organization?" exclaimed Ben Hay suddenly.

The men stared blankly at one another. No "Hope Mills," and the foundation-stone of life would have fallen out!

Robert Winston addressed them, thanking them very heartily for their co-operation, and expressing a hope that each man would be satisfied with the result of five of the hardest years the country had ever known. There was no doubt now, judging from our exports, and the amount of money coming in from every quarter of the globe, as one might say, that we had entered upon an era of prosperity. We had been educated to the practice of prudence, of common-sense, and sound principles, we had gained fibre and stamina, and he hoped we had gained honesty and integrity. If we could not always compete with low-priced manufacturers, the solid truth was made manifest in the end. They might take for their passwords, "Honesty, industry, and fidelity."

There was a great deal of cheering, and then Darcy was called upon for a speech. He did himself infinite credit, for in these five years not a man among them had made more rapid strides than Jack Darcy. As he stood there now, noble in form, in bearing, and with his good, strong, manly face, they felt somehow that he was *their* hero, and the cheering was heartier than ever.

Then Cameron must say a few words, and Ben Hay and Jesse Gilman; and, as Jack declared afterward, it was a regular experience-meeting among brethren. They pressed around, and shook hands with Darcy and Winston, the captain and the pilot with whom they had weathered gales, and been brought safely into port. And they would not let them stir out of the building until they had appointed a meeting to form the company again, this time on a somewhat stronger basis. They were firmly convinced now that this was the only way in which it was possible for workmen to make any advancement.

At length the crowd began to disperse. Jack started homeward; but, before he had walked half the distance, Davy, one of the men who had gone out in the first trouble, confronted him suddenly, seizing his hand.

"O Mr. Darcy!" said he in a most eager tone, "are you going to form over again? Do you think there's a chance for me to be taken back? There hasn't been a day nor a night but what I've cursed myself for being such a fool as to let anybody talk me out of a good job. I see just how it is now. And, if I can get back again, I'll stand by the old ship through thick and thin. O Mr. Darcy! please speak a good word for me!"

"That I will, Davy, if it is needed."

"Thank you, thank you, a thousand times!" cried the poor fellow gratefully.

Yerbury had plenty of praise now. To be sure, times *had* improved. If every year had been like the second, it would not have been possible to make co-operation work; but then, would it have been possible to carry on any business with continual loss? The starting of Hope Mills had inspired other disheartened firms, and given an impetus to Yerbury industries that might have lain much longer in the Slough of Despond.

Fred and Sylvie came over to the Darcys to tea that evening, and Maverick dropped in of course.

"Mrs. Darcy," he exclaimed, "I do not see why you did not have a daughter for me to marry! Then we could all have been relations, you see. I think it a great mistake on your part."

Mrs. Darcy glanced at her son with a peculiar light in her eyes.

Jack laughed. "She is thinking," he explained, "that if there had been another one, I should have gone off long ago to seek my fortune. I have learned that God may have better work for one than simply following out his own will;" and his voice dropped to a reverential tone.

Maverick studied him with a peculiar interest. All these years there had been growing up in Jack Darcy a plant of nobler promise than mere worldly ambition. Not that he in any manner despised wealth: he had come to understand its true uses. The same power that had educated the workmen had been going on with silent, steady processes in him. He had come to comprehend the dignity of the soul, and that God desired his return in the deeds done for one another, in the continual progress, the greatness, nobleness, and loyalty we offered "to one of the least of these." Was this true religion, — the simple doctrine of the Cross? And Maverick bowed his head in unconscious reverence.

They started homeward presently. Sylvie and Irene had some "last words" about baby Lawrence, and the two men paced up and down the porch a few moments.

"Thank God that it all came out so well!" said Jack in his strong, reverent tone.

Fred put his arm over Jack's shoulder. The two men seemed types of all that was highest and finest in human nature.

"Jack," began the other in his full, rich tone, tremulous with emotion, "do you remember that in my romantic boyhood I used to liken you to King Arthur? You have merged into a nobler hero since that day. Who but a Sir Galahad, true, strong, unselfish, at once just yet tender, ambitious for the Holy Grail of our times, yet never swerving from the path of honor ; keeping his own soul stainless amid the many temptations of the world — who save such a soul could have gone on in your path to the end? And of the other Christ-like virtue " —

" Don't, don't, Fred ! You always did rate me too highly, you know. I am only a man."

" It is something to be a man in these days," returned the other.

The shady blue eyes smiled out of their twilight depth.

" Fred, where are you? " cried a sweet voice.

" You gave me *her*. You taught me to gain the great prize of my life as surely as you trained the men in the mill yonder. God bless you ! "

www.ingramcontent.com/pod-product-compliance
Lightning Source LLC
Chambersburg PA
CBHW021717110726
47902CB00005B/1234